Gabby & GATOR

by James Burks

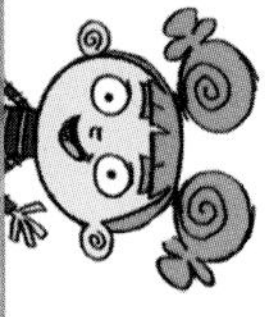

150 West 30th Street, 19th Floor
New York, NY 10001

Visit us at jyforkids.com • facebook.com/jyforkids
twitter.com/jyforkids • jyforkids.tumblr.com • instagram.com/jyforkids

First JY Edition: October 2020
Originally published by Yen Press in September 2010

JY is an imprint of Yen Press, LLC.
The JY name and logo are trademarks of Yen Press, LLC.

The publisher is not responsible for websites (or their content) that are not owned by the publisher.

Library of Congress Control Number: 2010920174

ISBN: 978-1-9753-1856-7

10 9 8 7 6 5 4 3 2 1

LSC-C

Printed in the United States of America

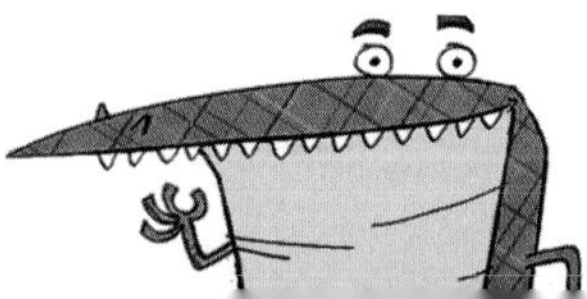

For Maddie, Max, and Suzanne

Special thanks to Bob, Frank, Allan, and Kelly
for being my second, third, fourth, and fifth pairs of eyes.

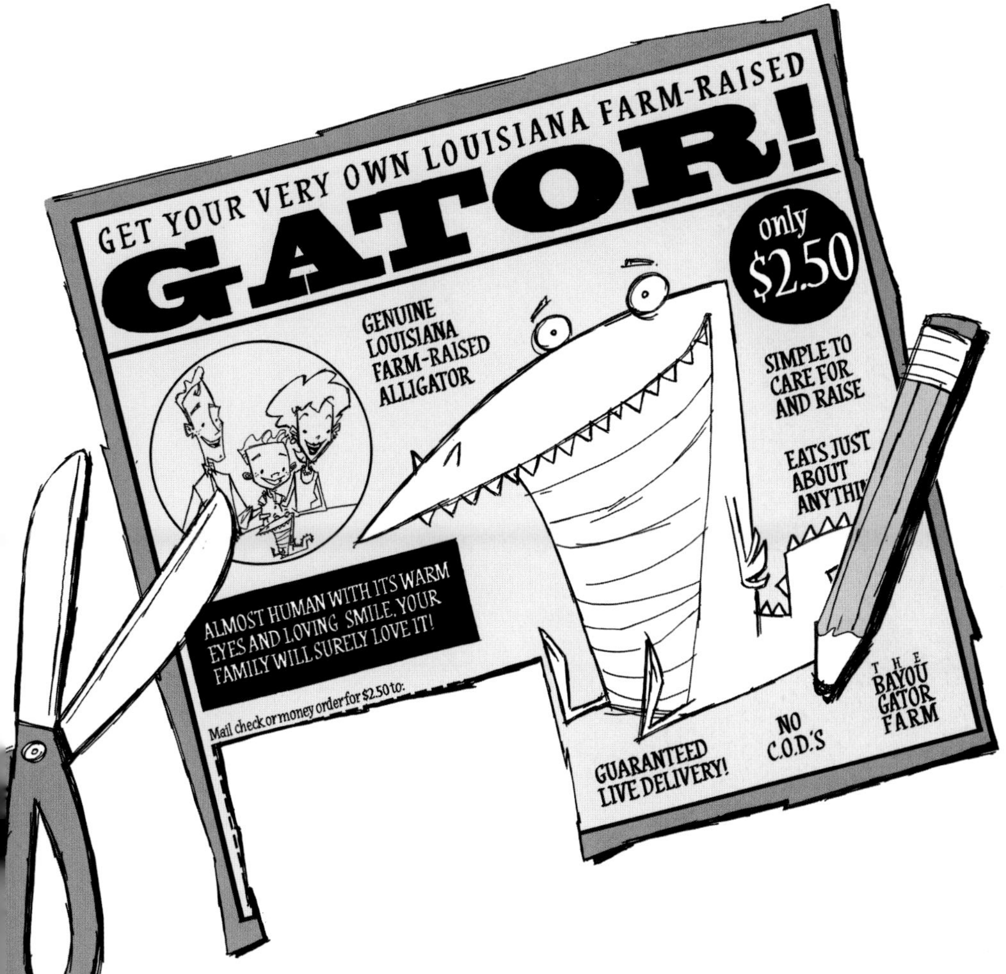
GET YOUR VERY OWN LOUISIANA FARM-RAISED
GATOR!
only $2.50
GENUINE LOUISIANA FARM-RAISED ALLIGATOR
SIMPLE TO CARE FOR AND RAISE
EATS JUST ABOUT ANYTHI
ALMOST HUMAN WITH ITS WARM EYES AND LOVING SMILE, YOUR FAMILY WILL SURELY LOVE IT!
Mail check or money order for $2.50 to:
THE BAYOU GATOR FARM
NO C.O.D.'S
GUARANTEED LIVE DELIVERY!

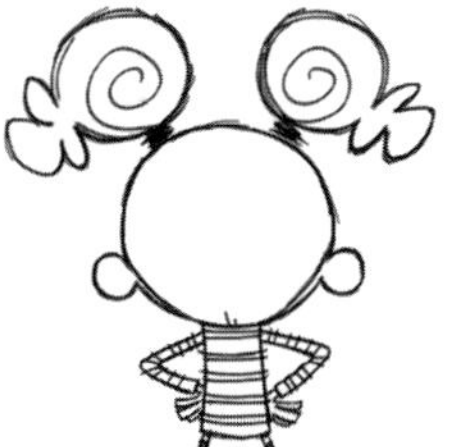

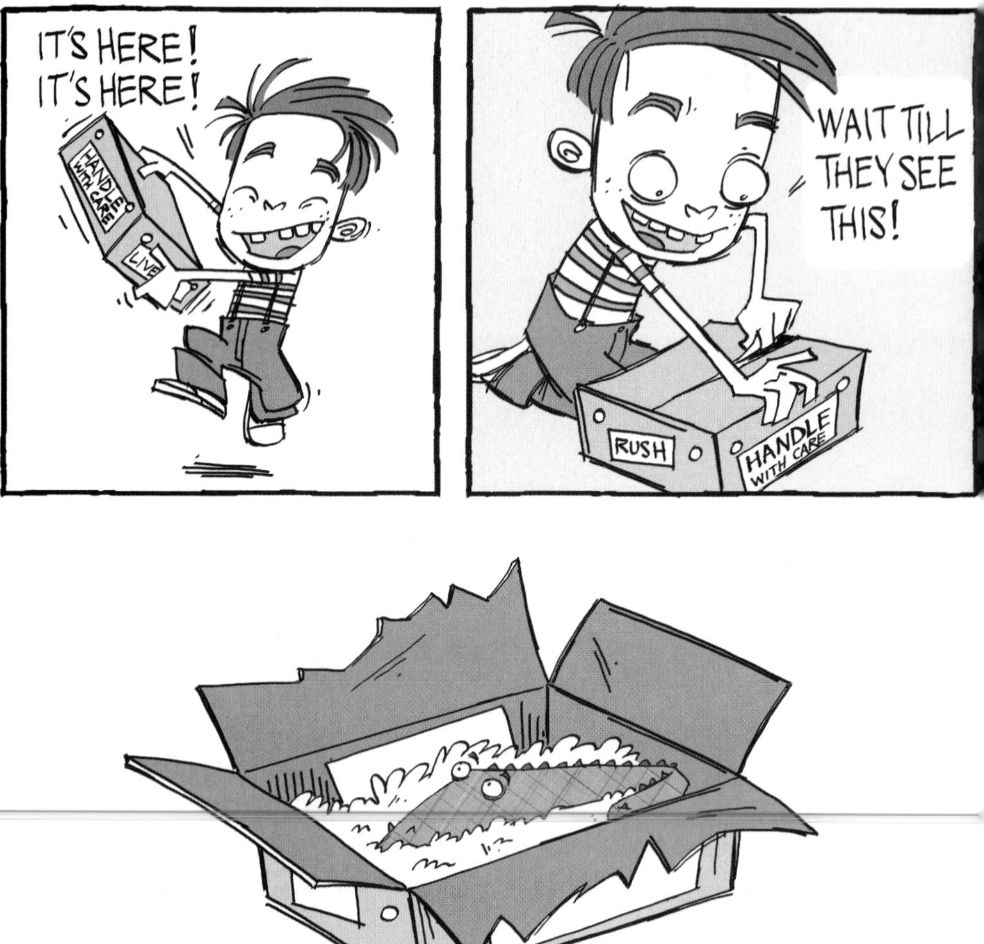
IT'S HERE! IT'S HERE!
HANDLE WITH CARE
LIVE
WAIT TILL THEY SEE THIS!
RUSH
HANDLE WITH CARE

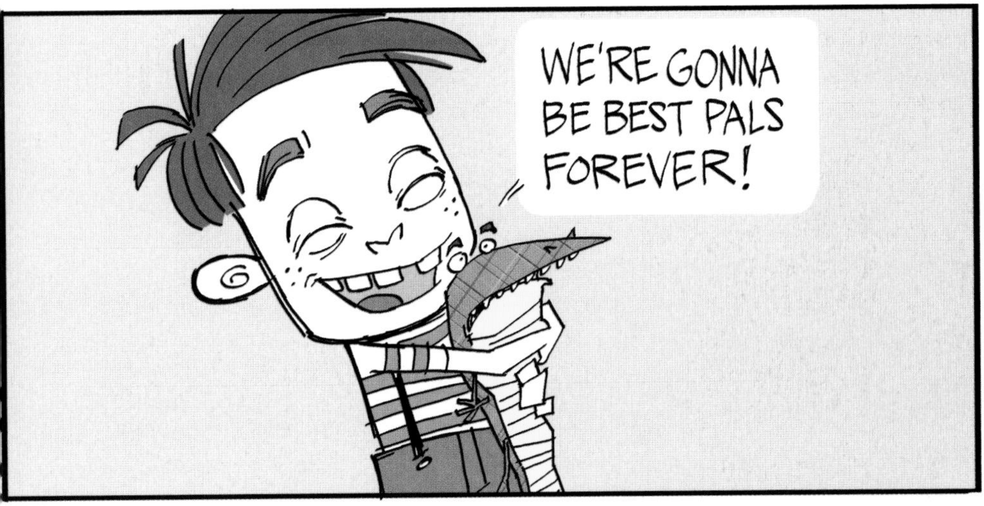
WE'RE GONNA BE BEST PALS FOREVER!

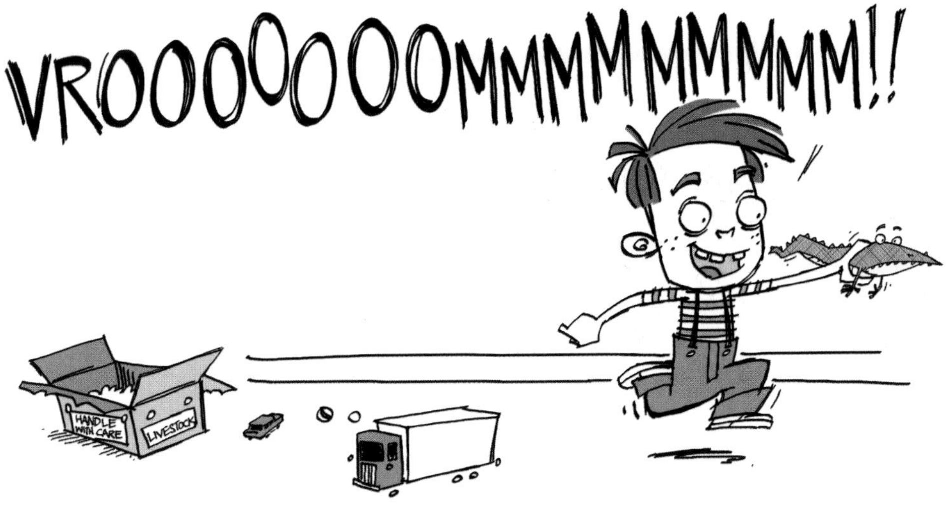
VROOOOOOOOMMMMMMMMM!!
HANDLE WITH CARE
LIVESTOCK

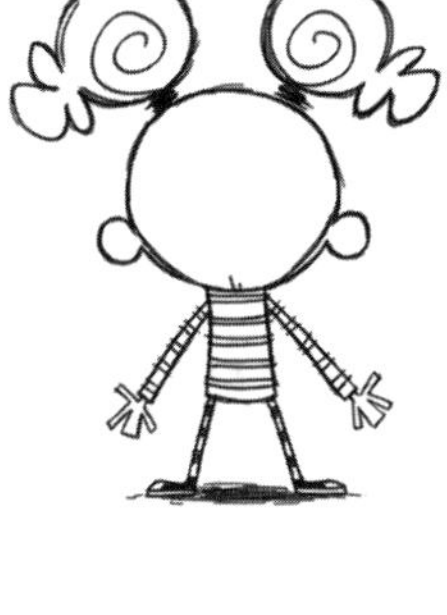

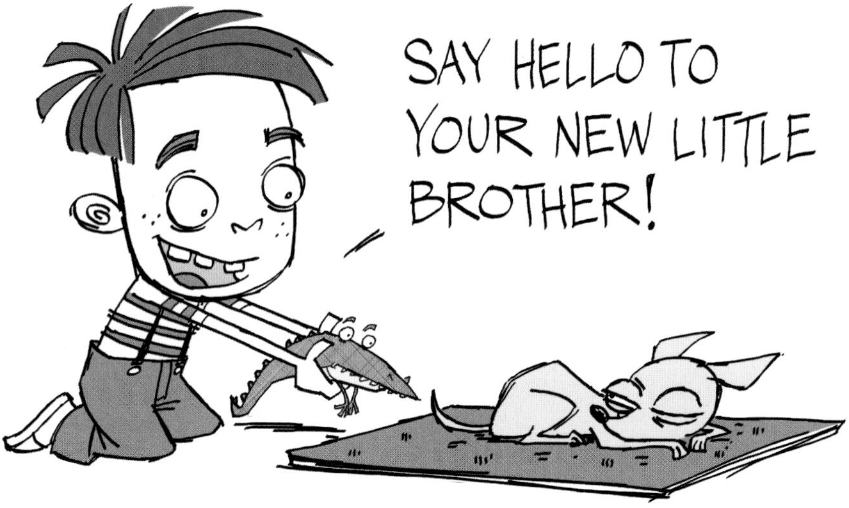
SAY HELLO TO YOUR NEW LITTLE BROTHER!

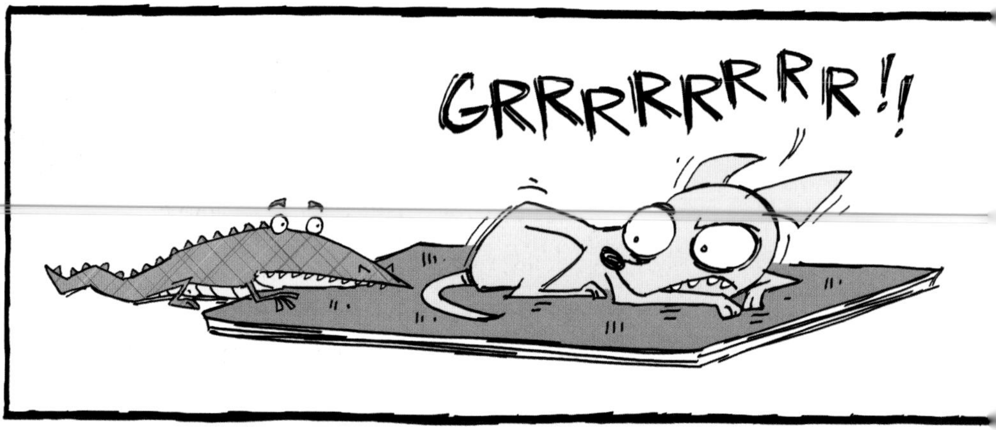
GRRRRRRRR!!

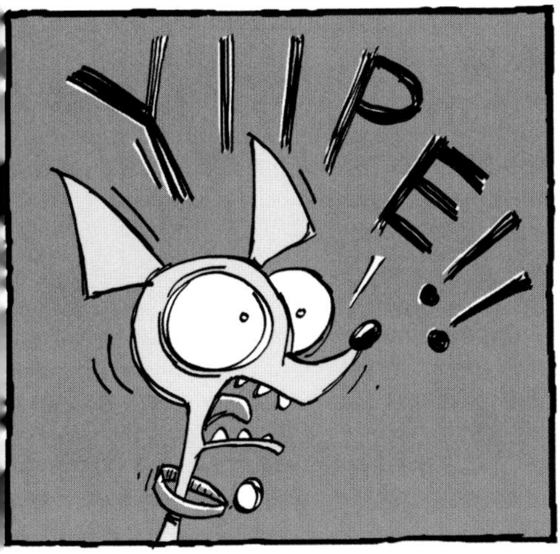
YIIPE!!

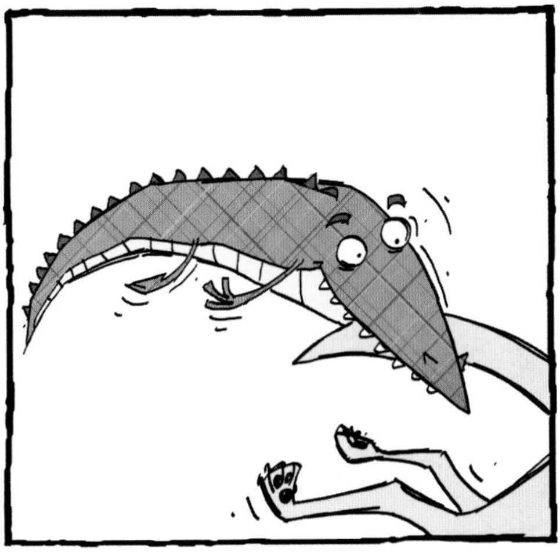

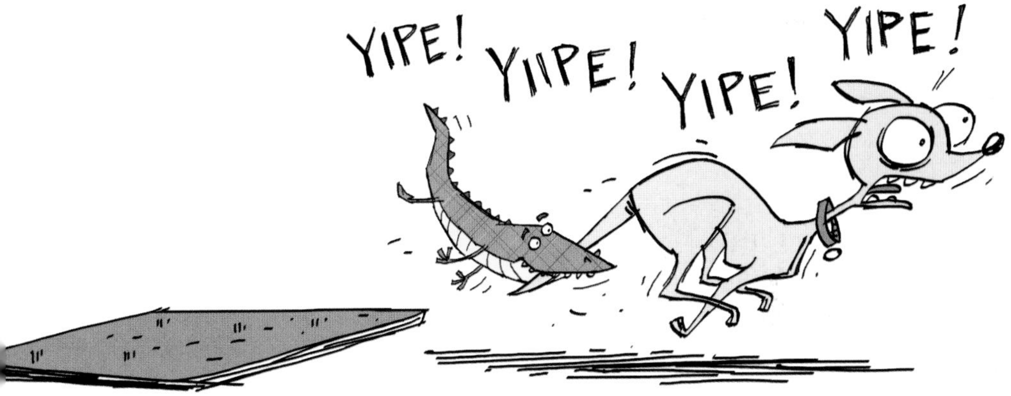
YIPE!
YIIPE!
YIPE!
YIPE!

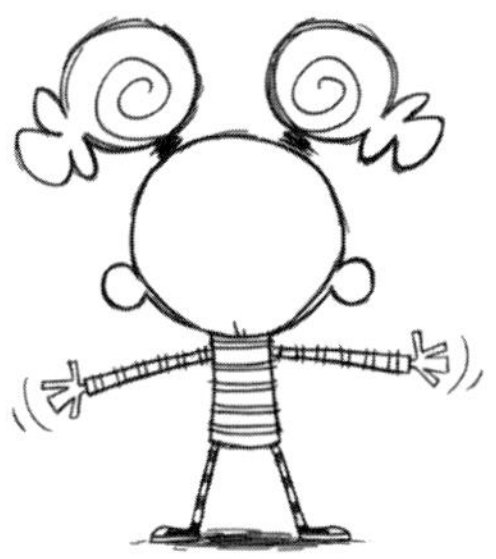

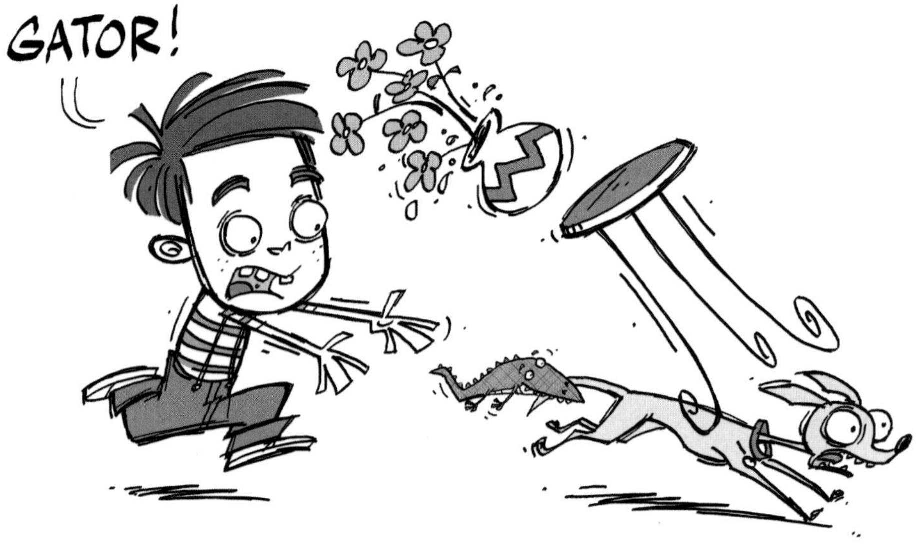
GATOR!

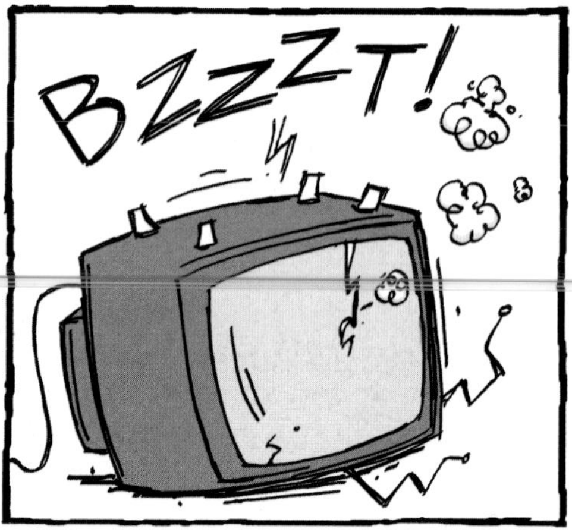
BZZZT!

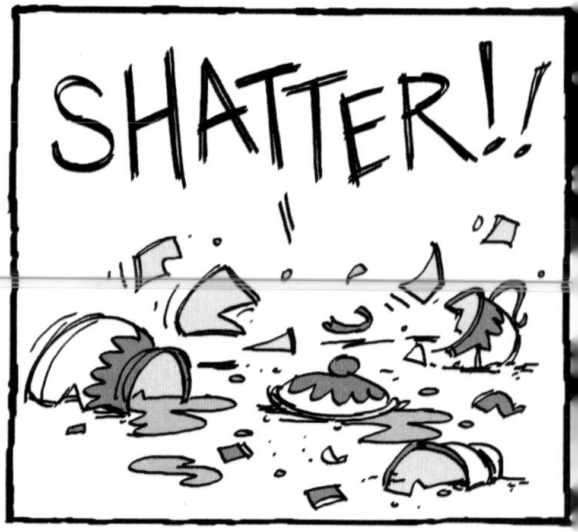
SHATTER!!

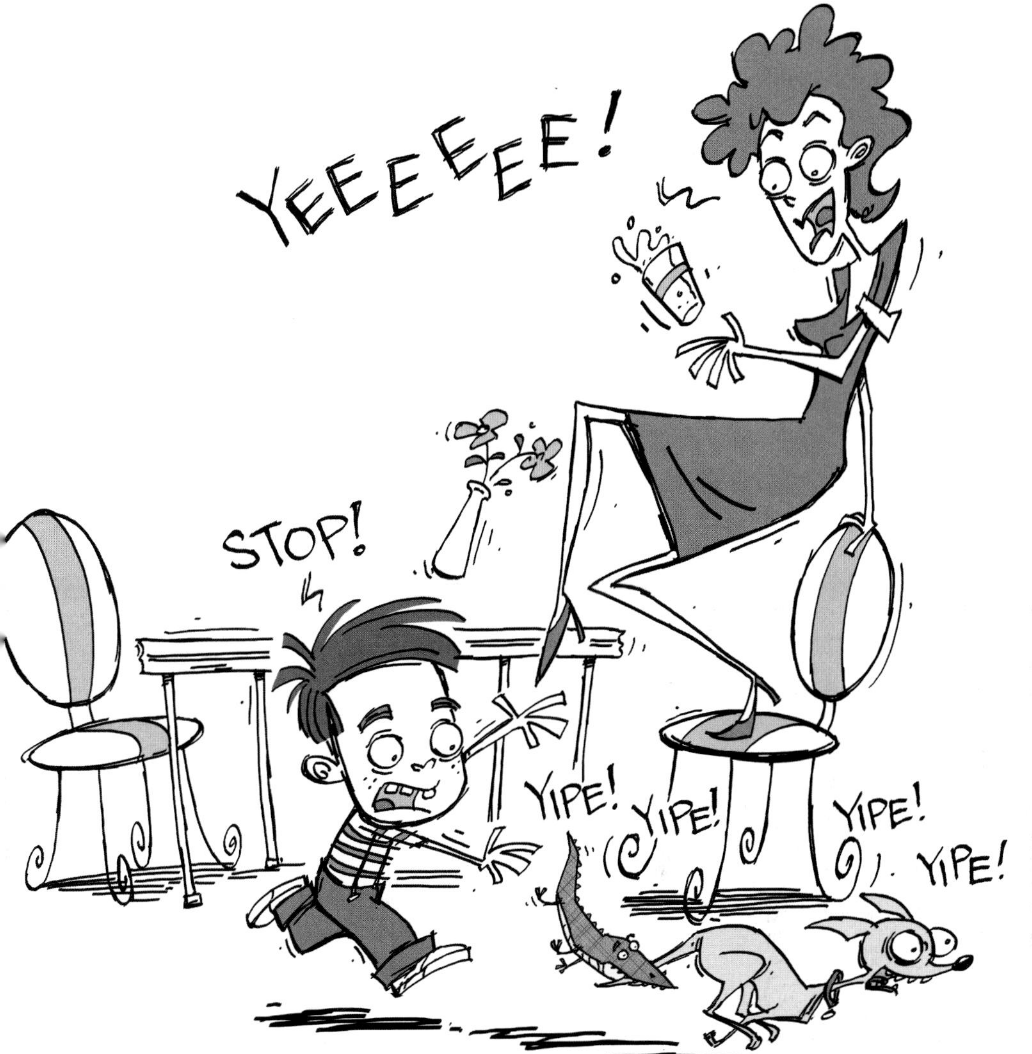
YEEEEEEE!
STOP!
YIPE!
YIPE!
YIPE!
YIPE!

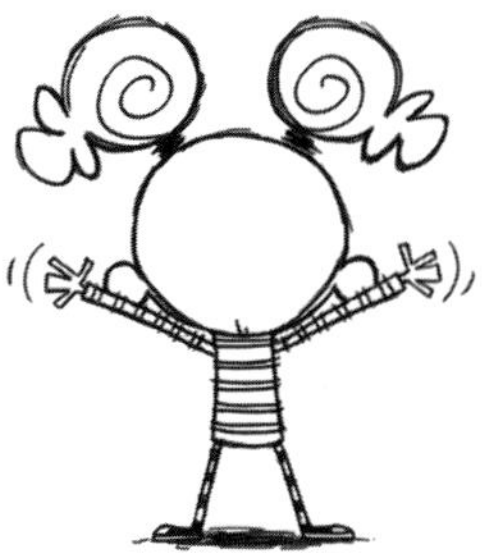

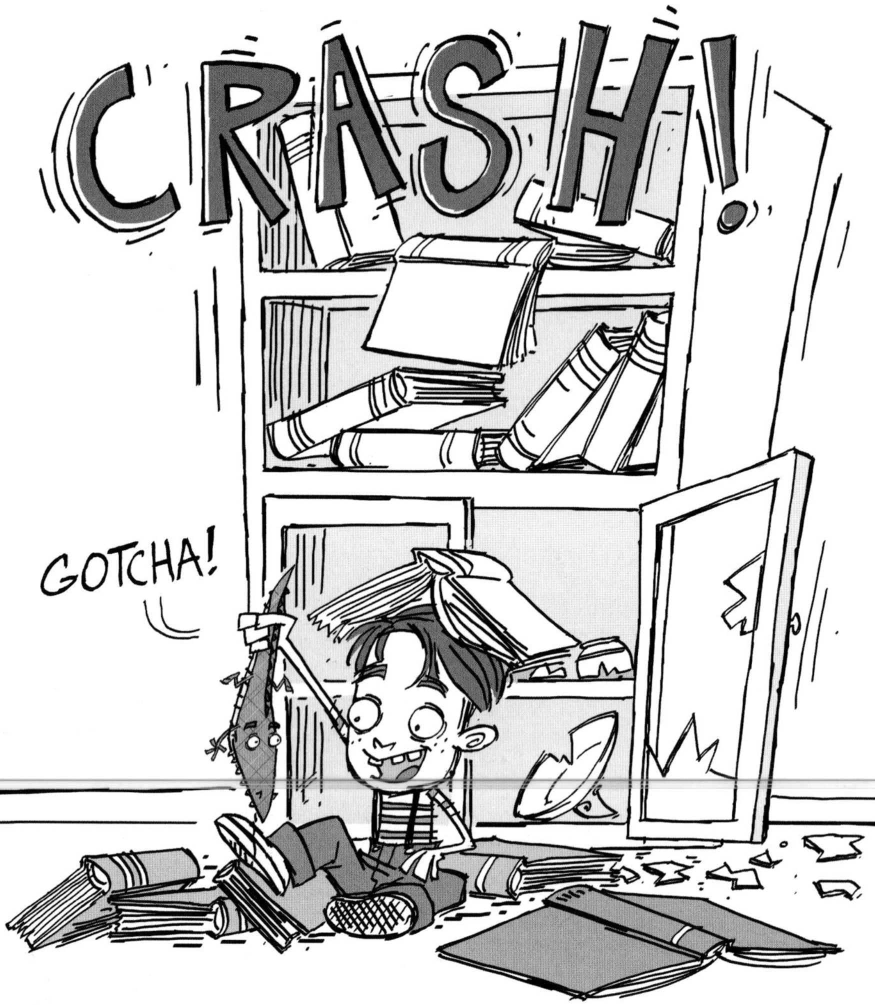
CRASH!
GOTCHA!

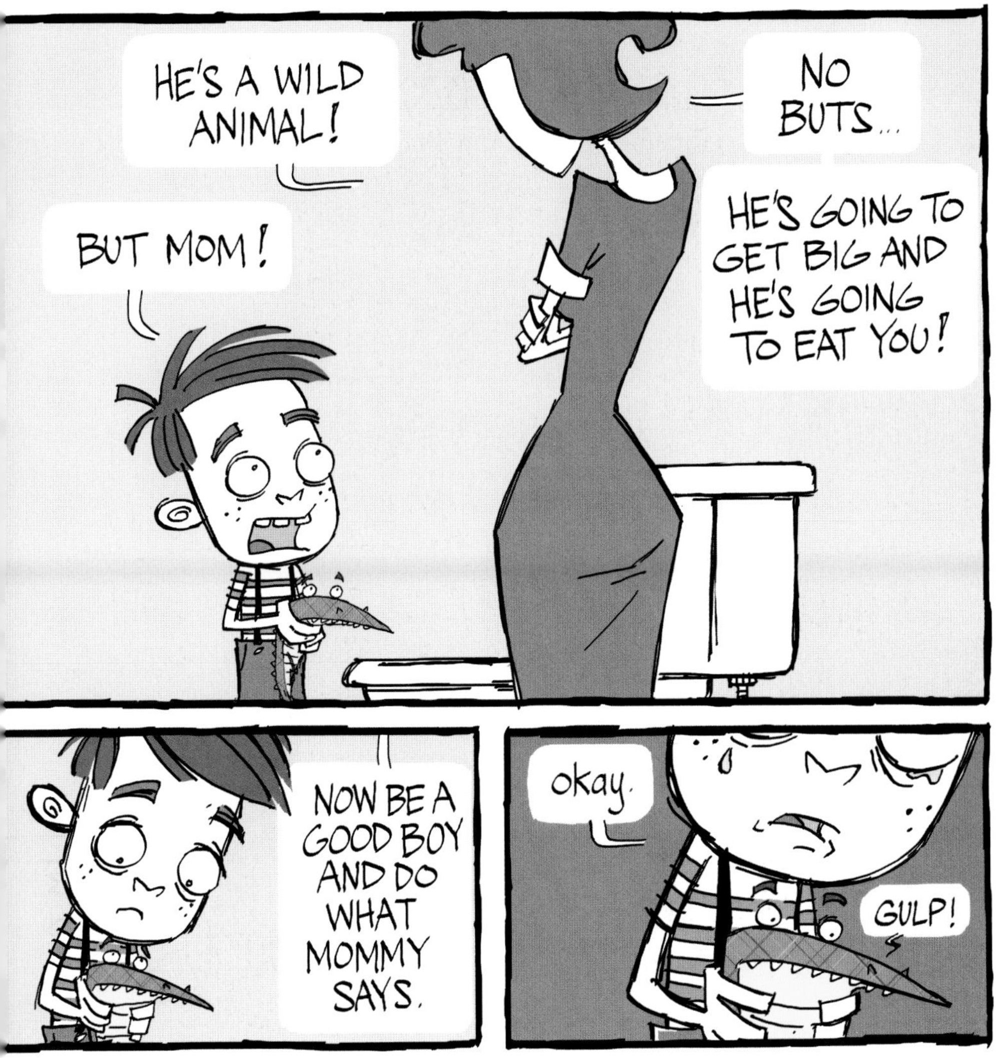
HE'S A WILD ANIMAL!
BUT MOM!
NO BUTS...
HE'S GOING TO GET BIG AND HE'S GOING TO EAT YOU!
NOW BE A GOOD BOY AND DO WHAT MOMMY SAYS.
okay.
GULP!

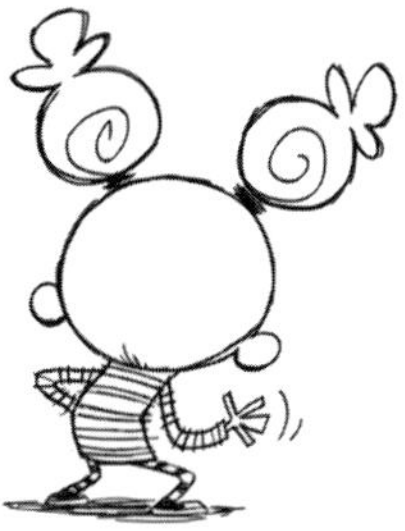

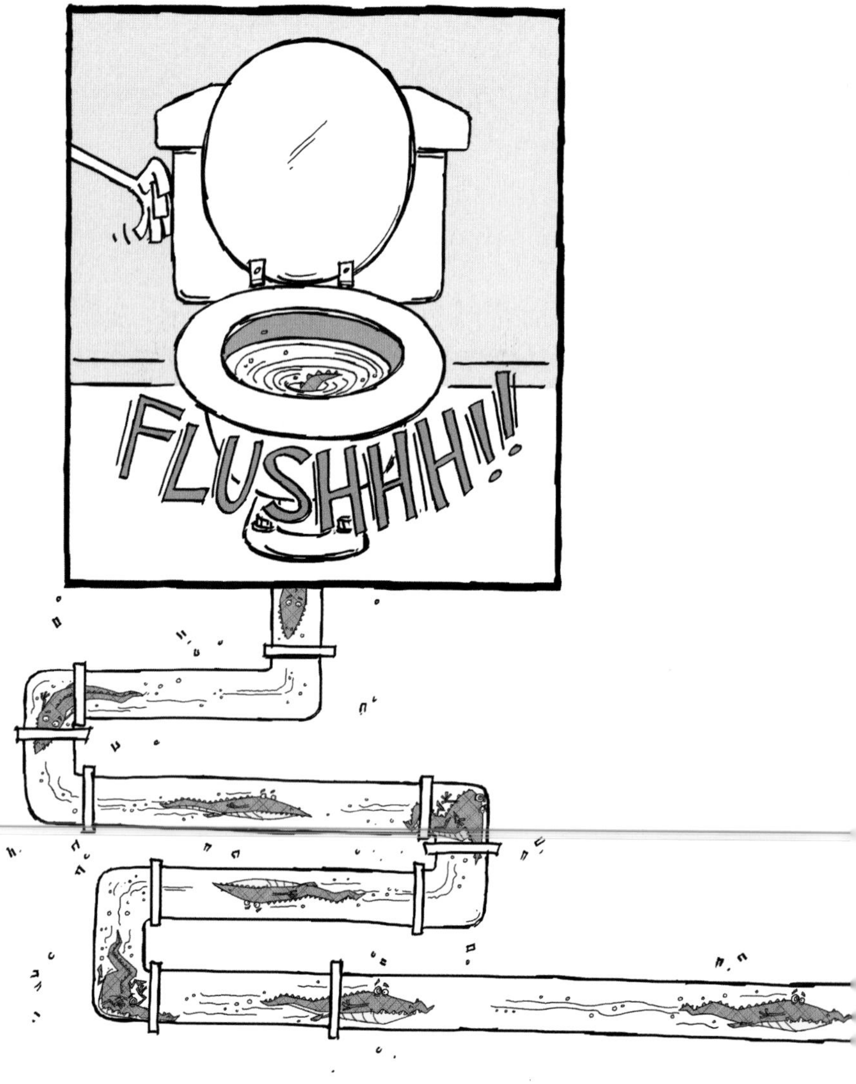
FLUSHHH!!

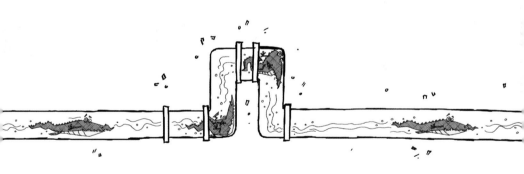

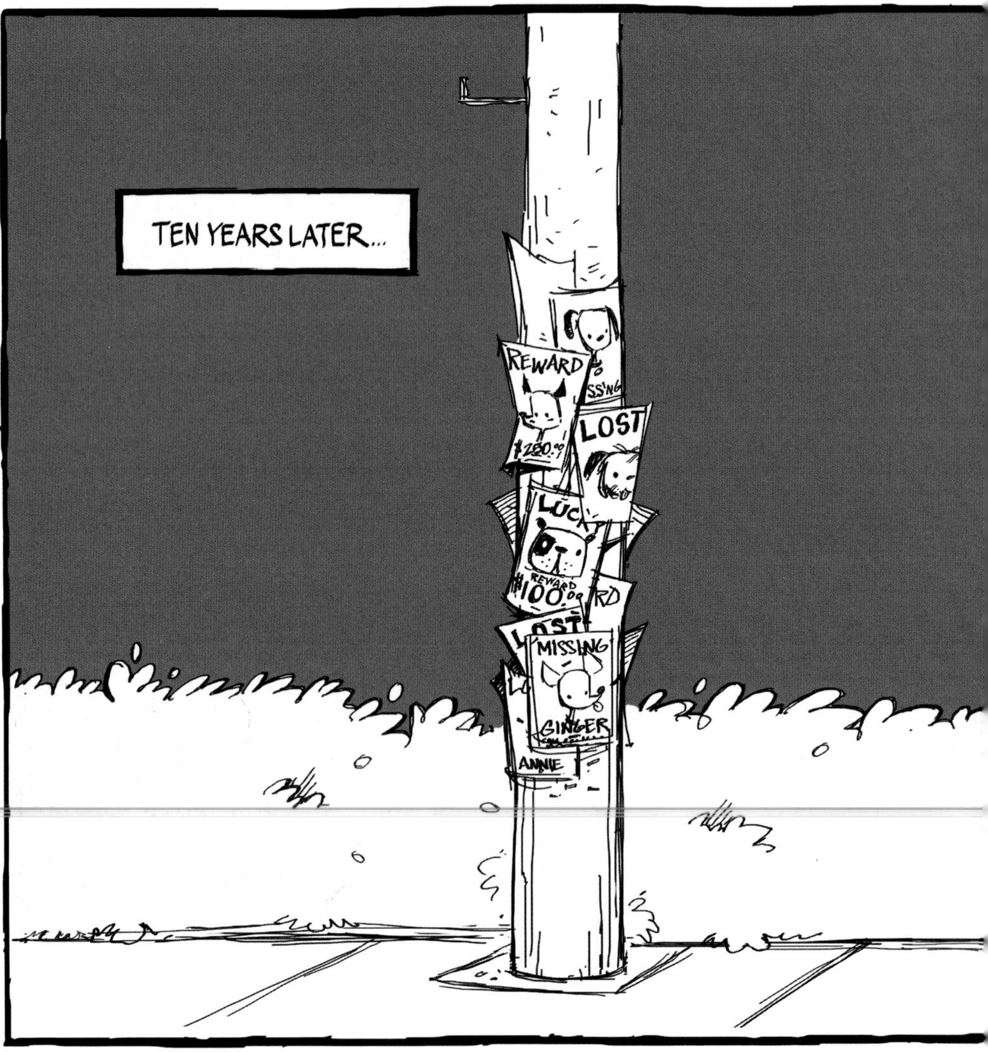
TEN YEARS LATER...
REWARD
LOST
MISSING
GINGER
ANNIE

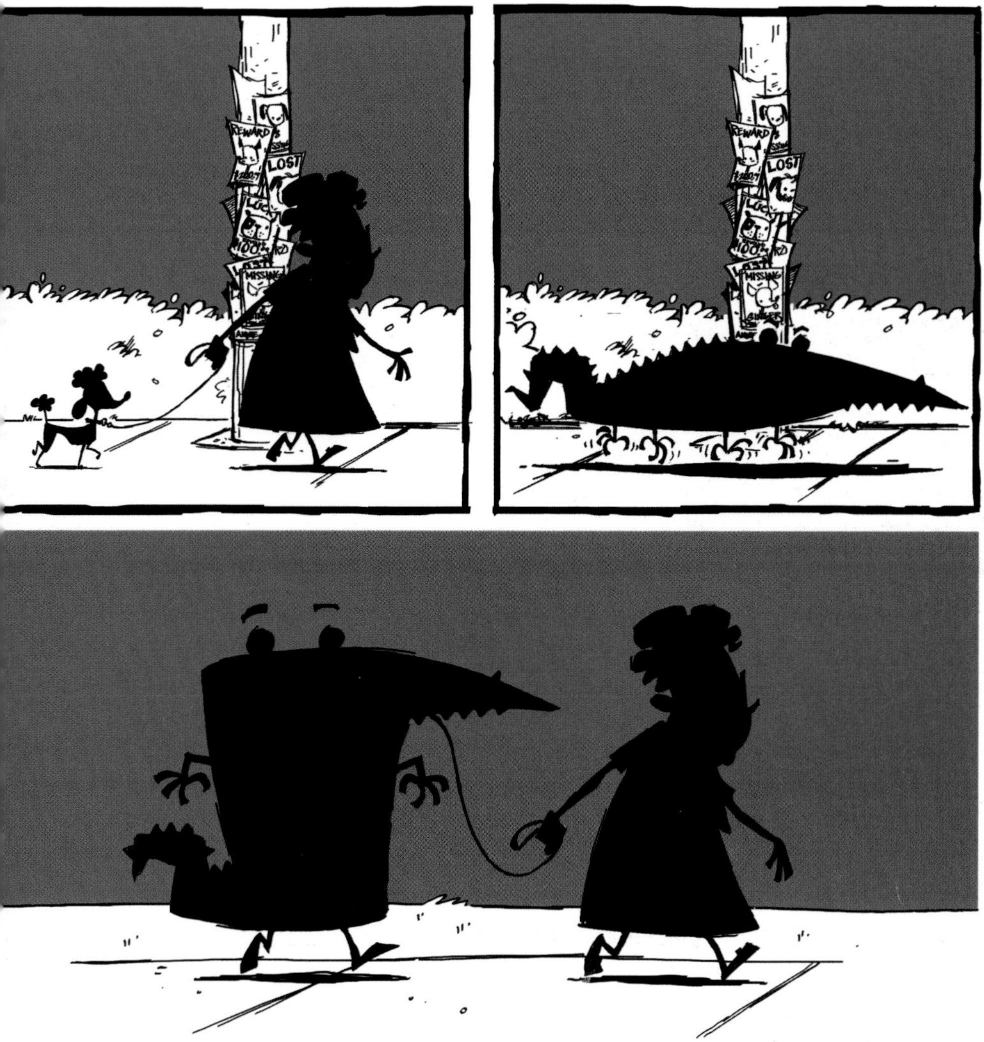
REWARD
LOST
MISSING

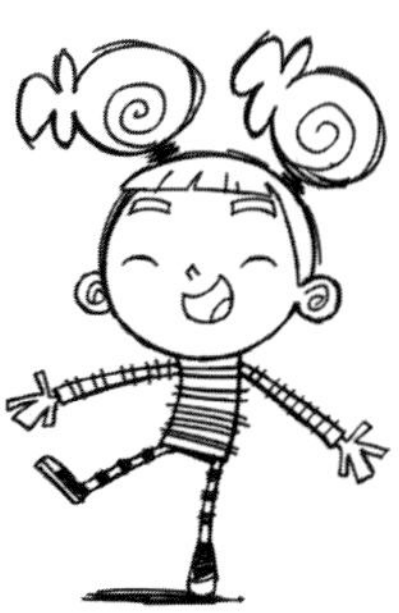

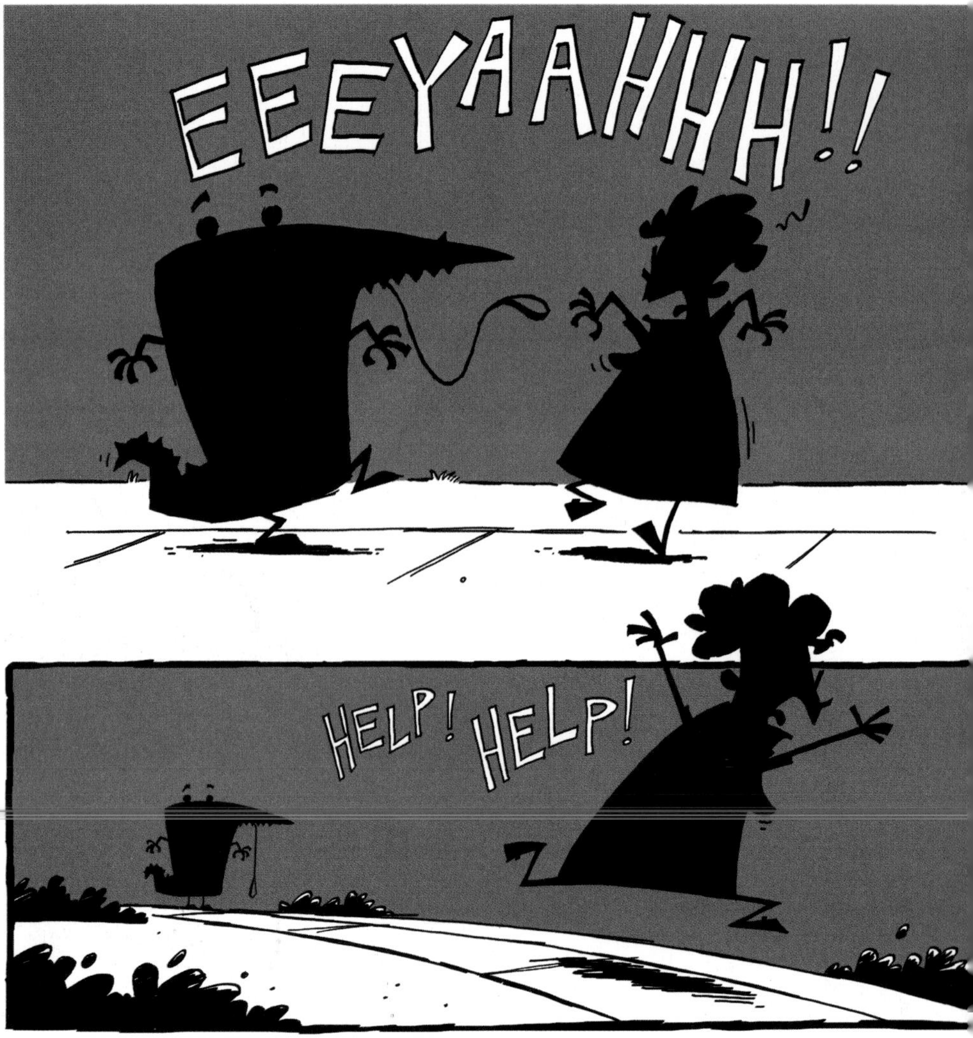
EEEYAAHHHH!!
HELP! HELP!

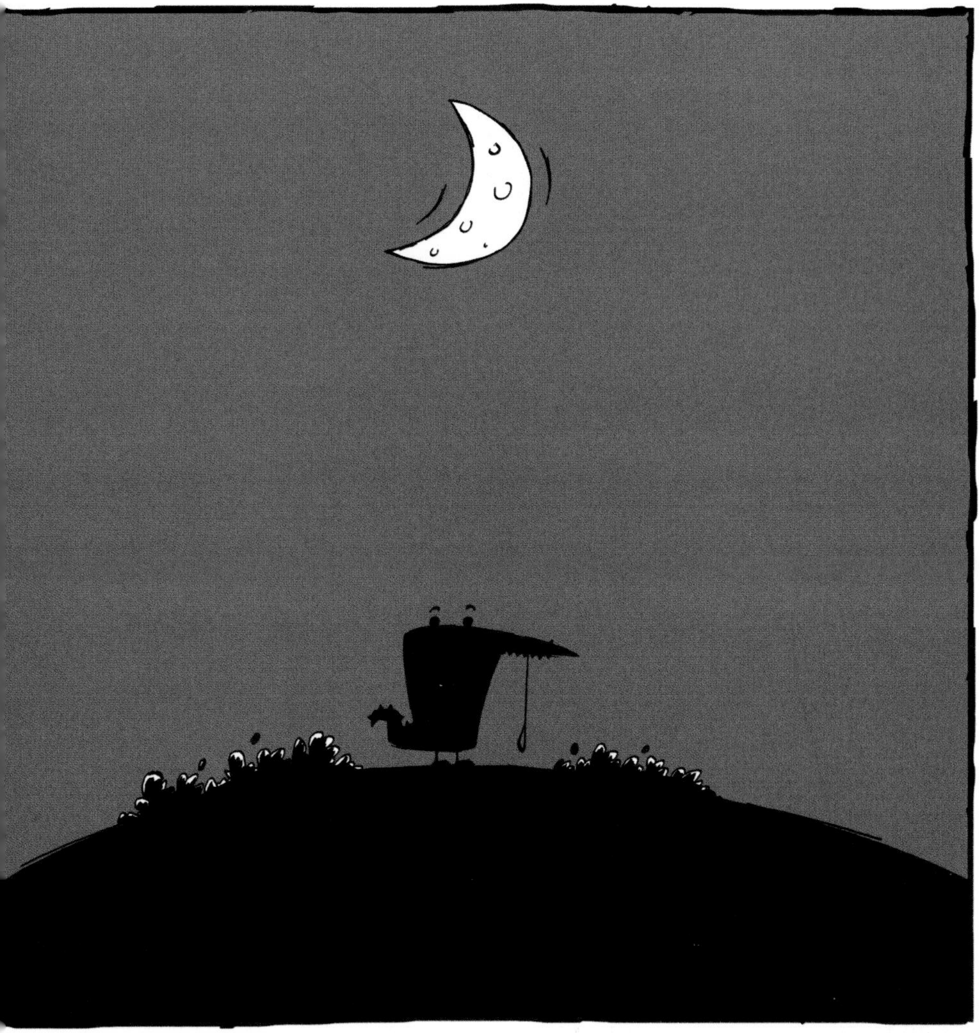

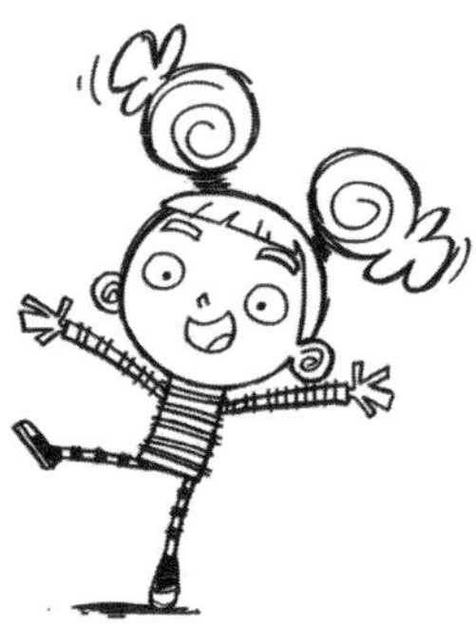

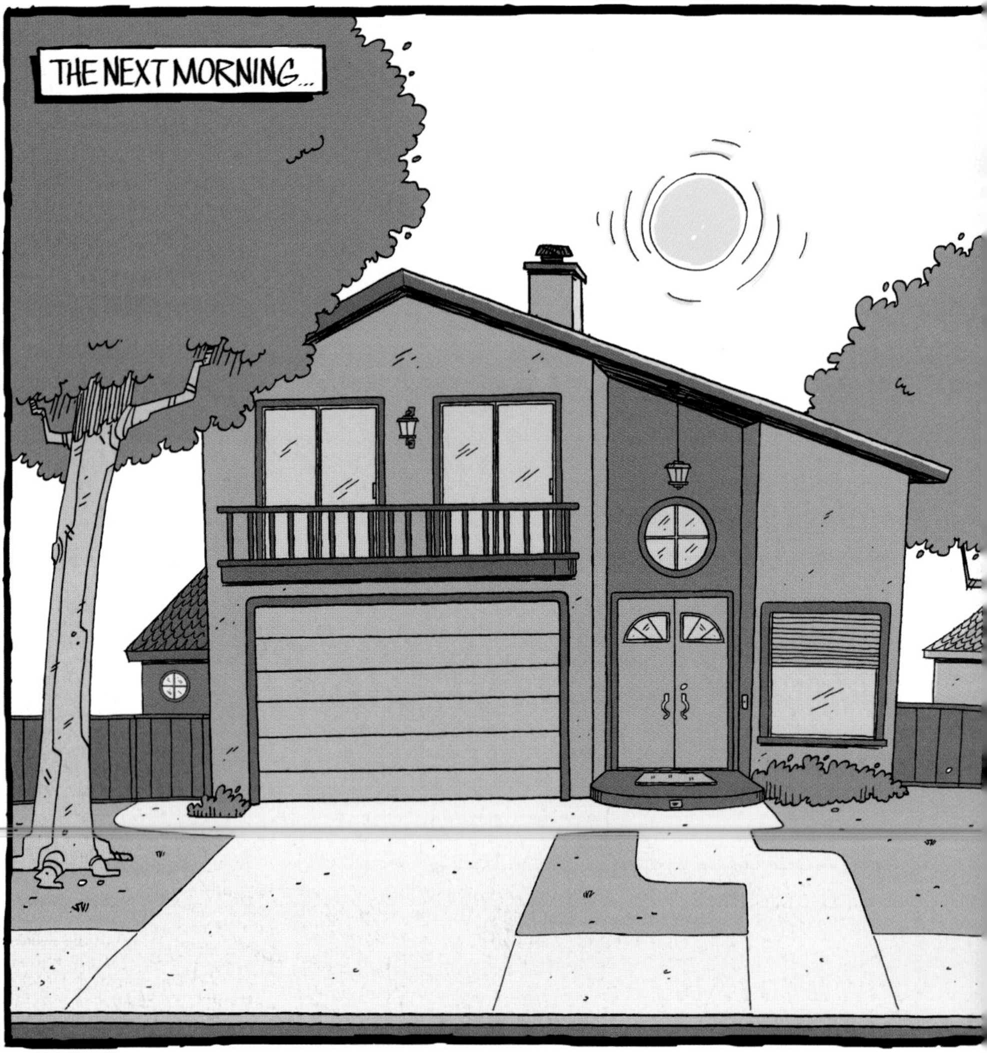
THE NEXT MORNING...

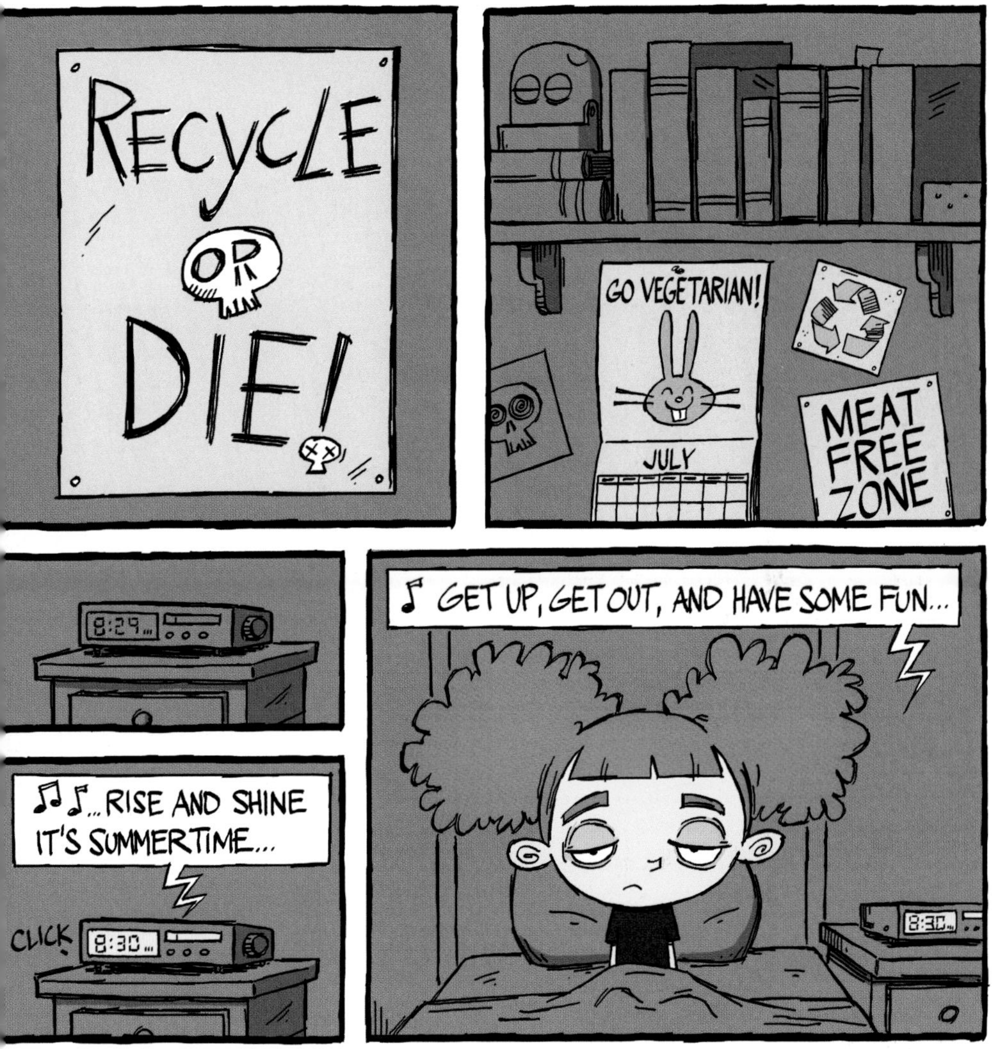
RECYCLE
OR
DIE!
GO VEGETARIAN!
JULY
MEAT FREE ZONE
8:29
...RISE AND SHINE IT'S SUMMERTIME...
CLICK
8:30
GET UP, GET OUT, AND HAVE SOME FUN...
8:30

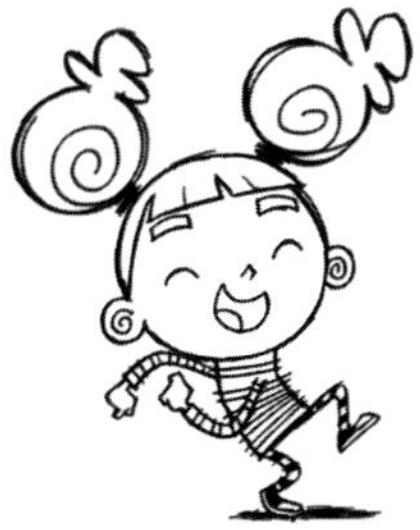

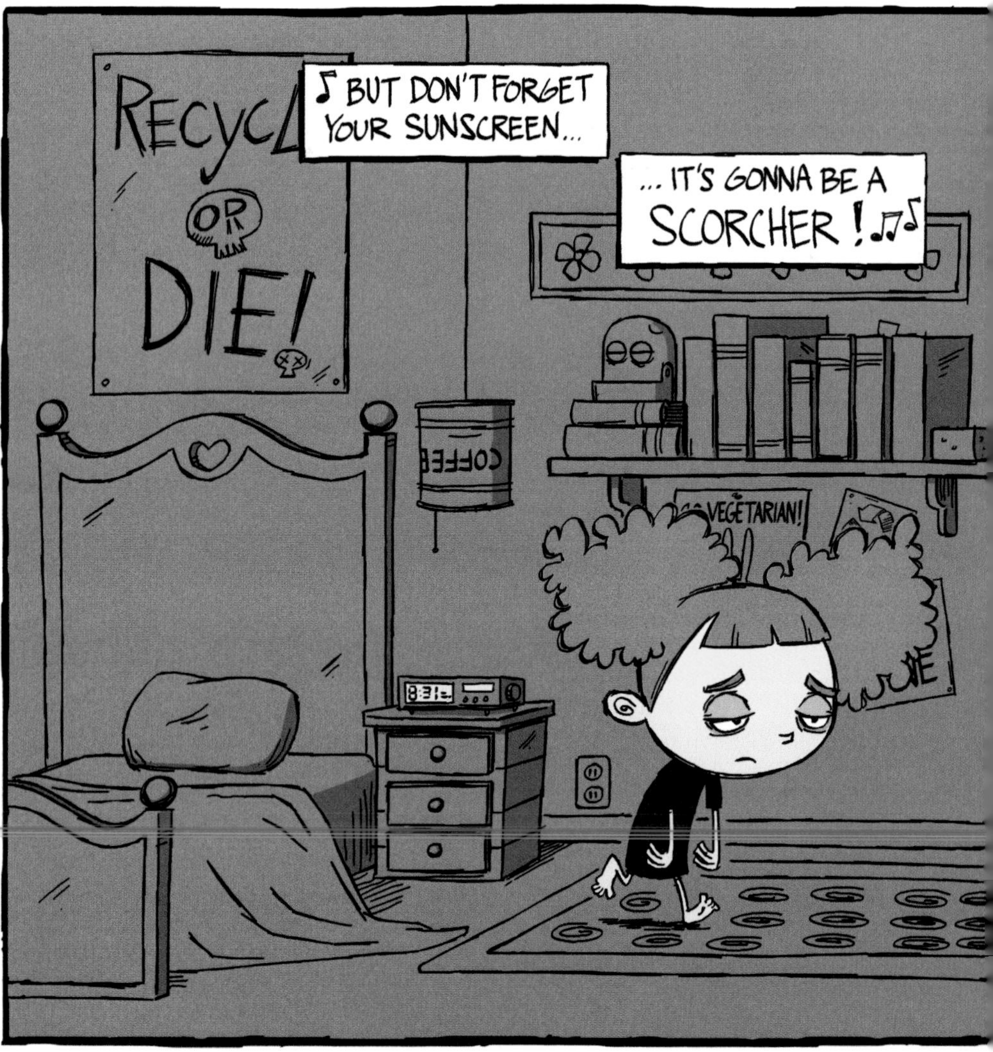
RECYCLE OR DIE!
♪ BUT DON'T FORGET YOUR SUNSCREEN...
... IT'S GONNA BE A SCORCHER! ♫♪
COFFEE
VEGETARIAN!

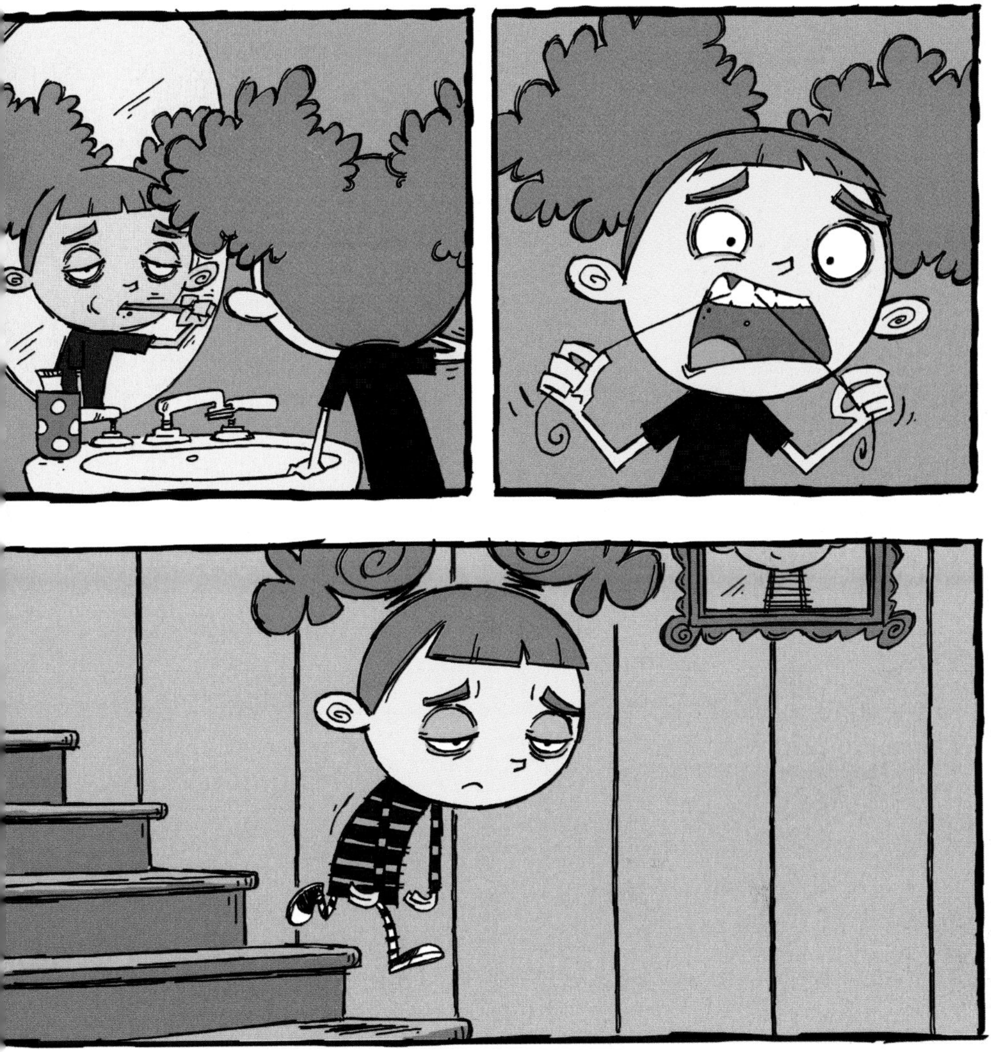

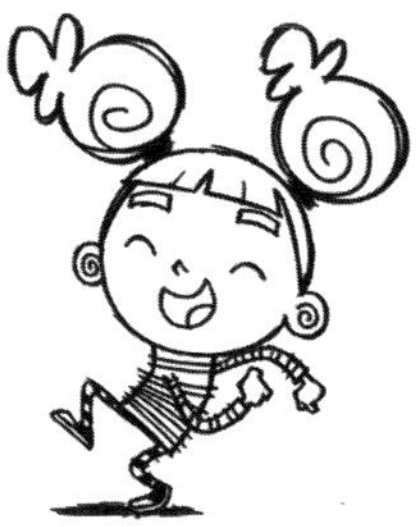

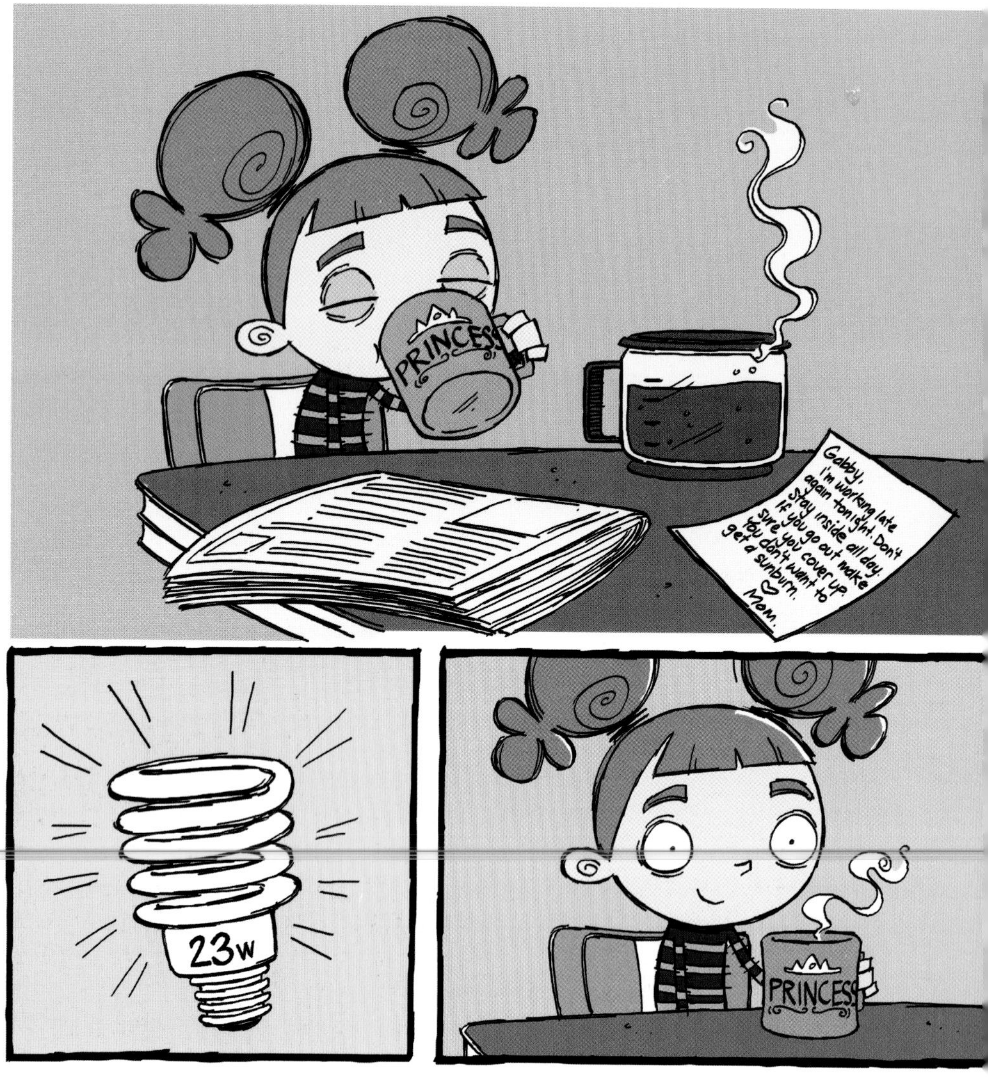
PRINCESS
Gabby,
I'm working late
again tonight. Don't
Stay inside all day.
If you go out make
sure you cover up.
You don't want to
get a sunburn.
Mom.
23w
PRINCESS

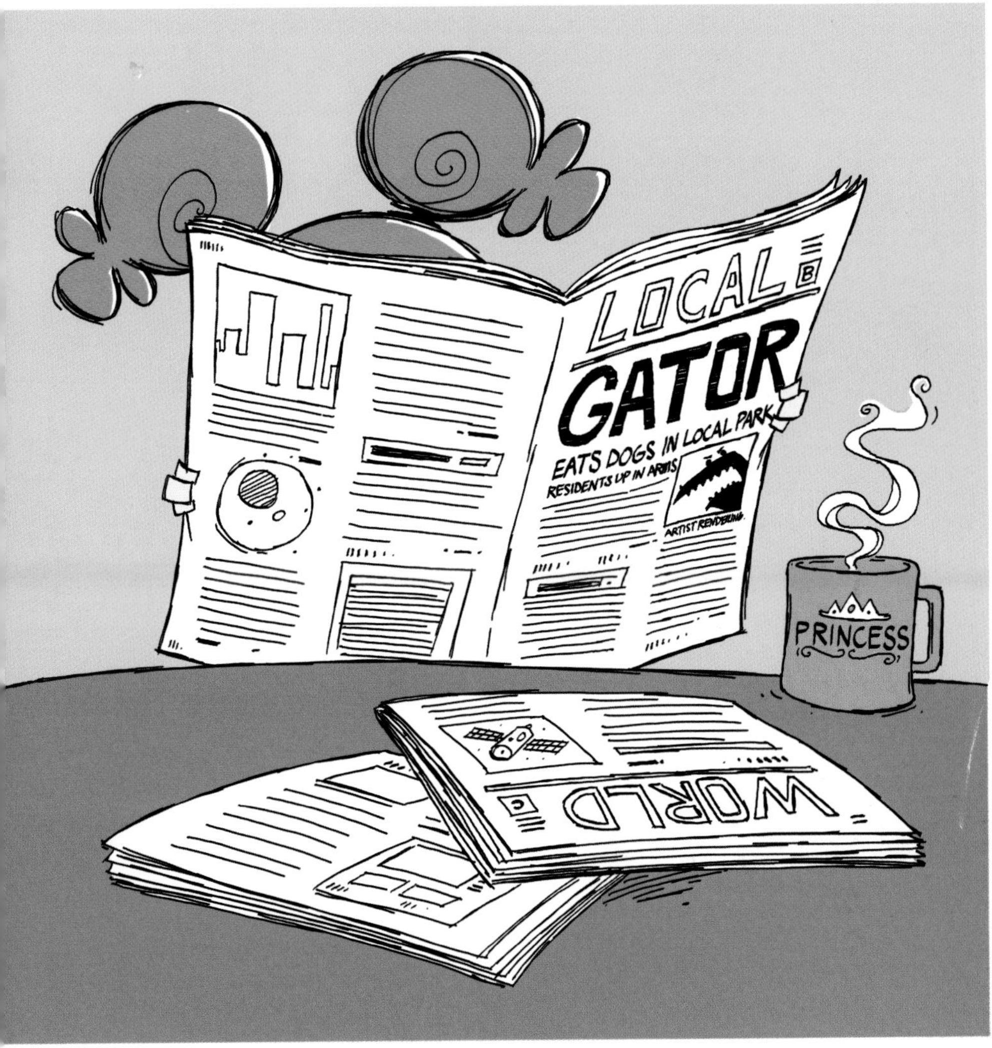
LOCAL B
GATOR
EATS DOGS IN LOCAL PARK
RESIDENTS UP IN ARMS
ARTIST RENDERING
PRINCESS
WORLD C

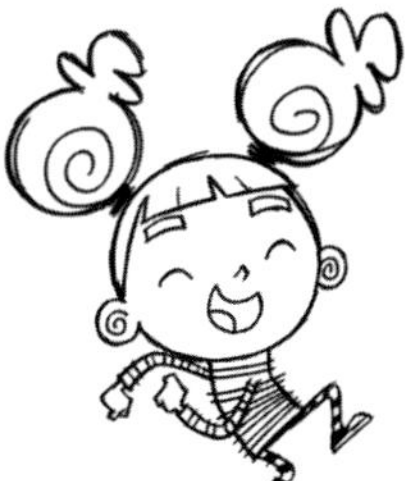

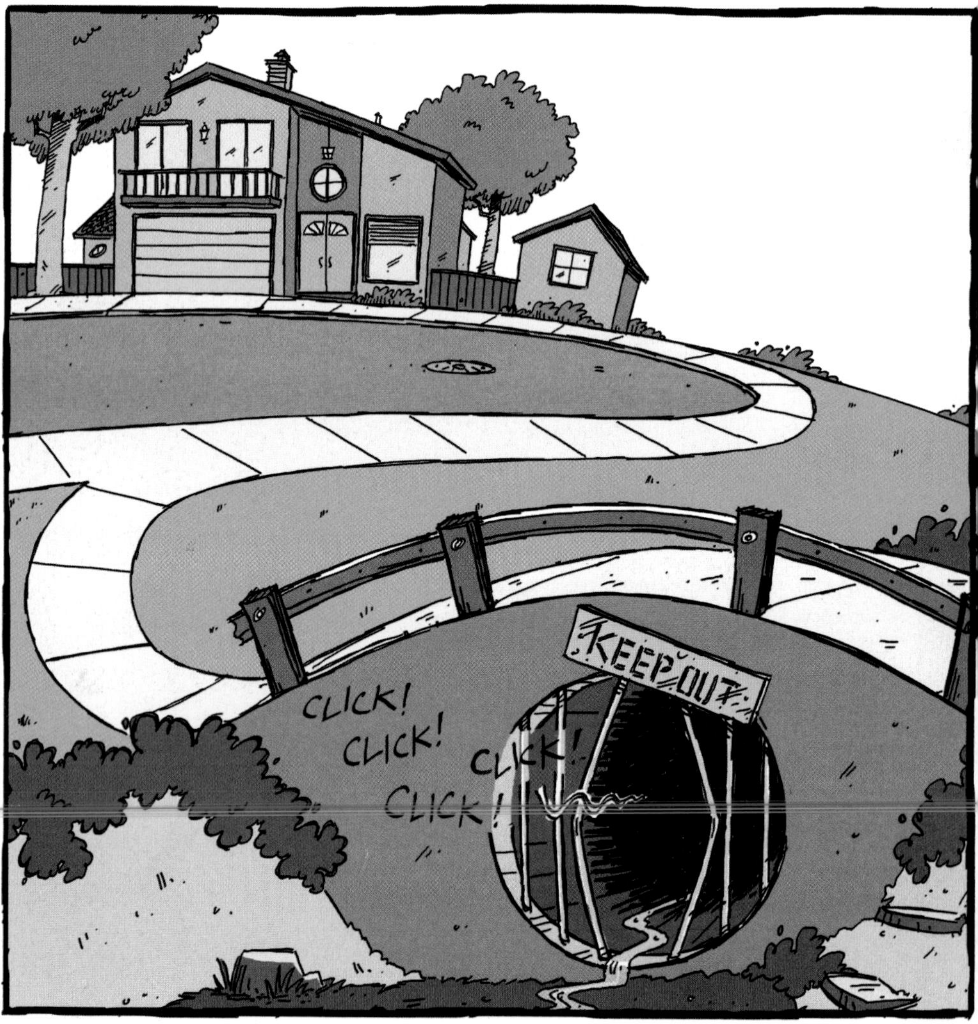
KEEP OUT
CLICK!
CLICK!
CLICK!
CLICK!

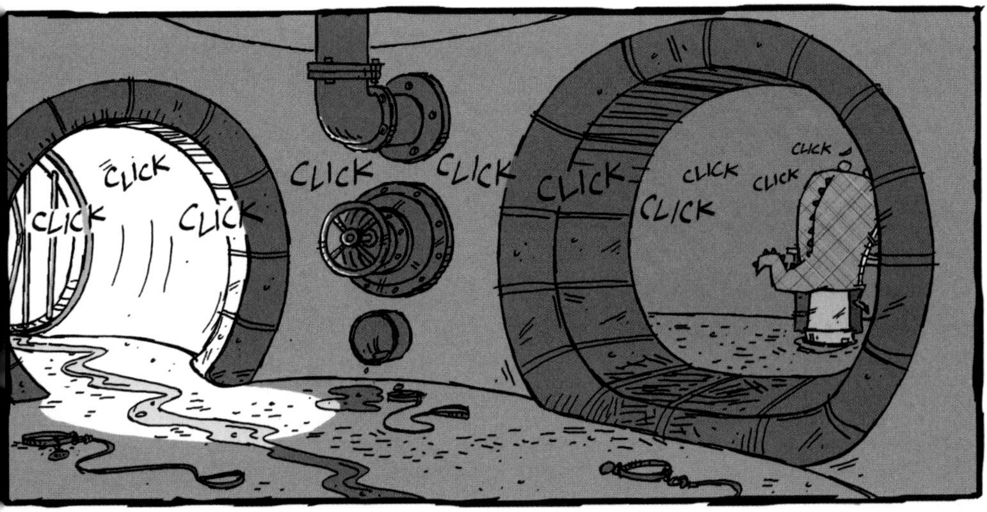
CLICK
CLICK
CLICK
CLICK
CLICK
CLICK
CLICK
CLICK
CLICK
CLICK

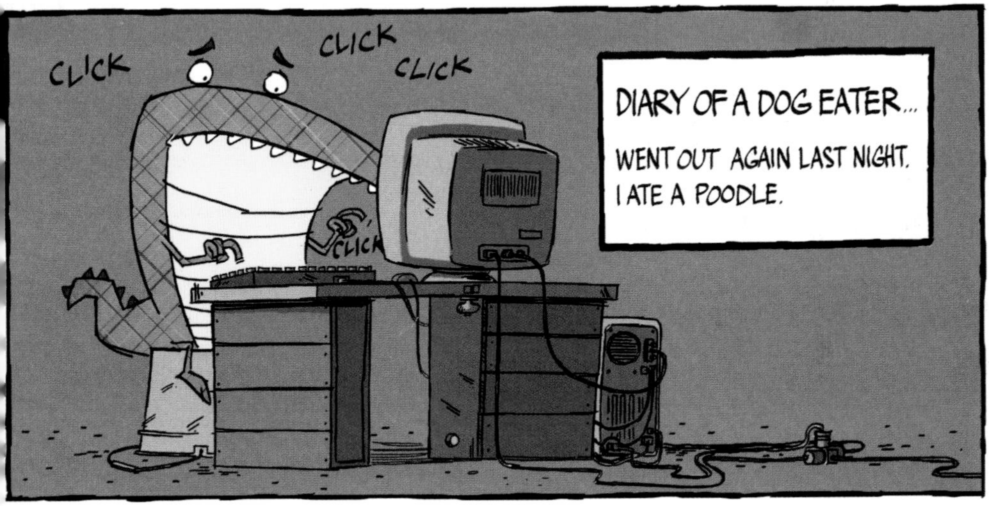
CLICK
CLICK
CLICK
CLICK
DIARY OF A DOG EATER...
WENT OUT AGAIN LAST NIGHT.
I ATE A POODLE.

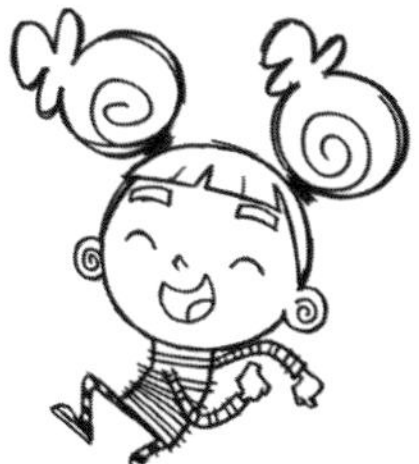

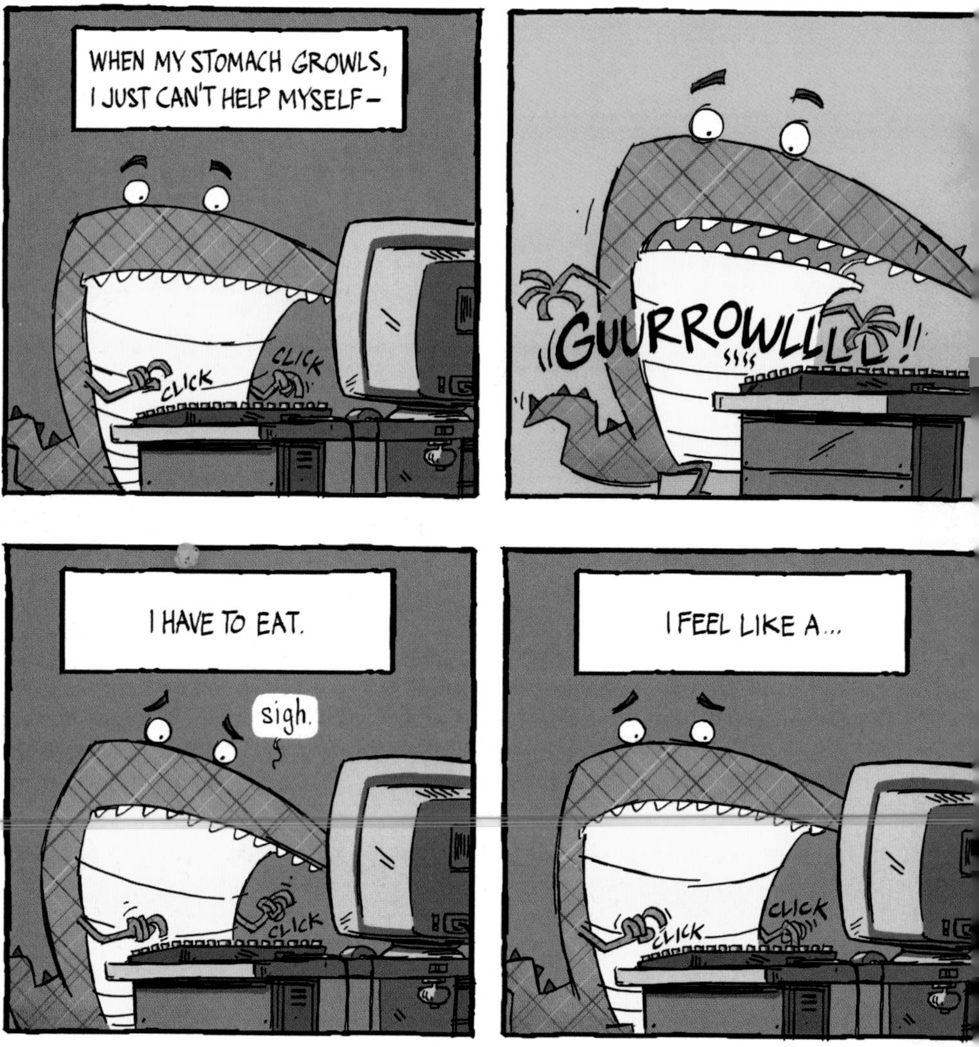
WHEN MY STOMACH GROWLS, I JUST CAN'T HELP MYSELF–
CLICK
CLICK
GUURROWLLLL!
I HAVE TO EAT.
sigh.
CLICK
I FEEL LIKE A...
CLICK
CLICK

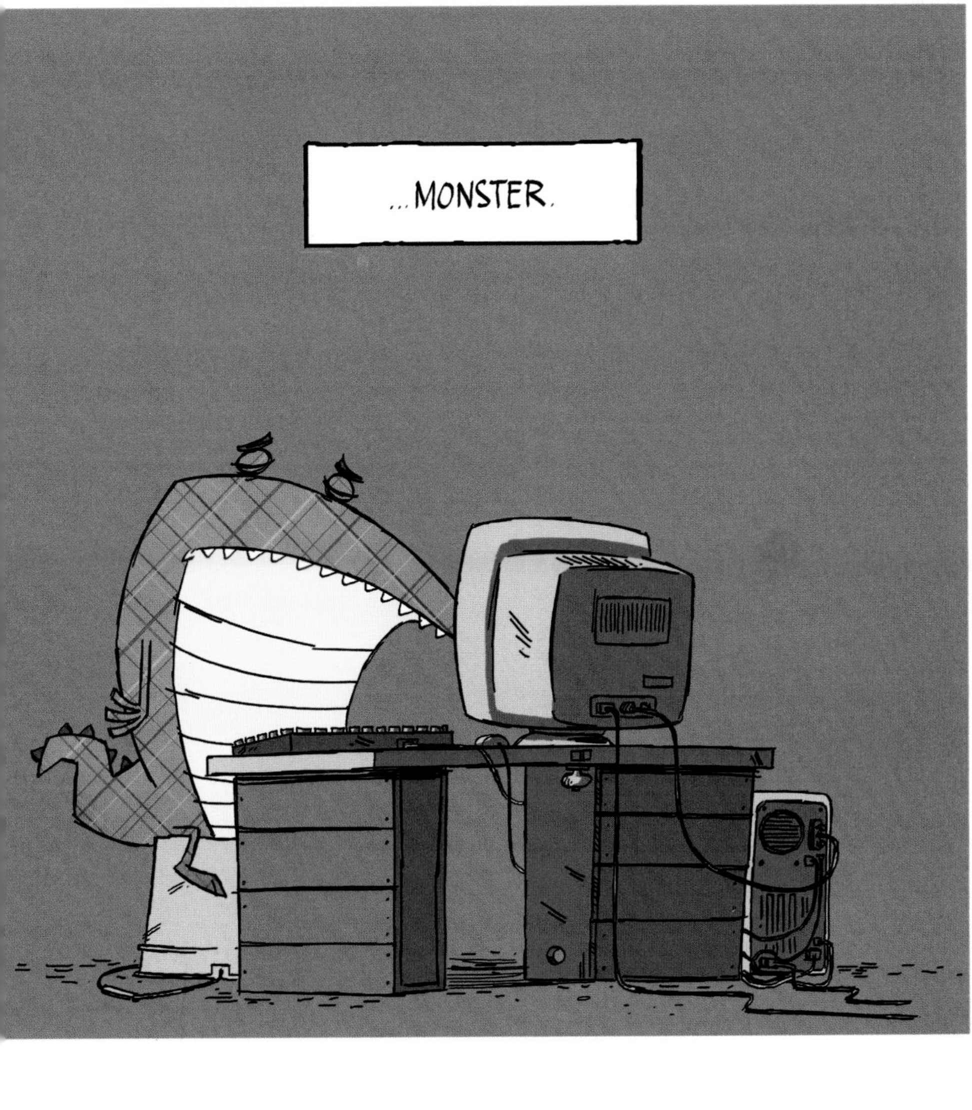
...MONSTER.

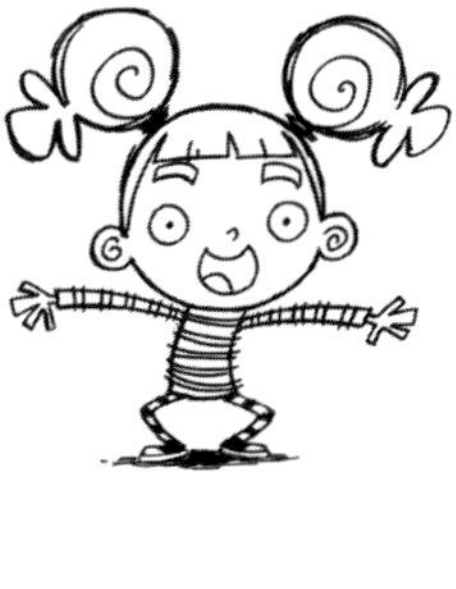

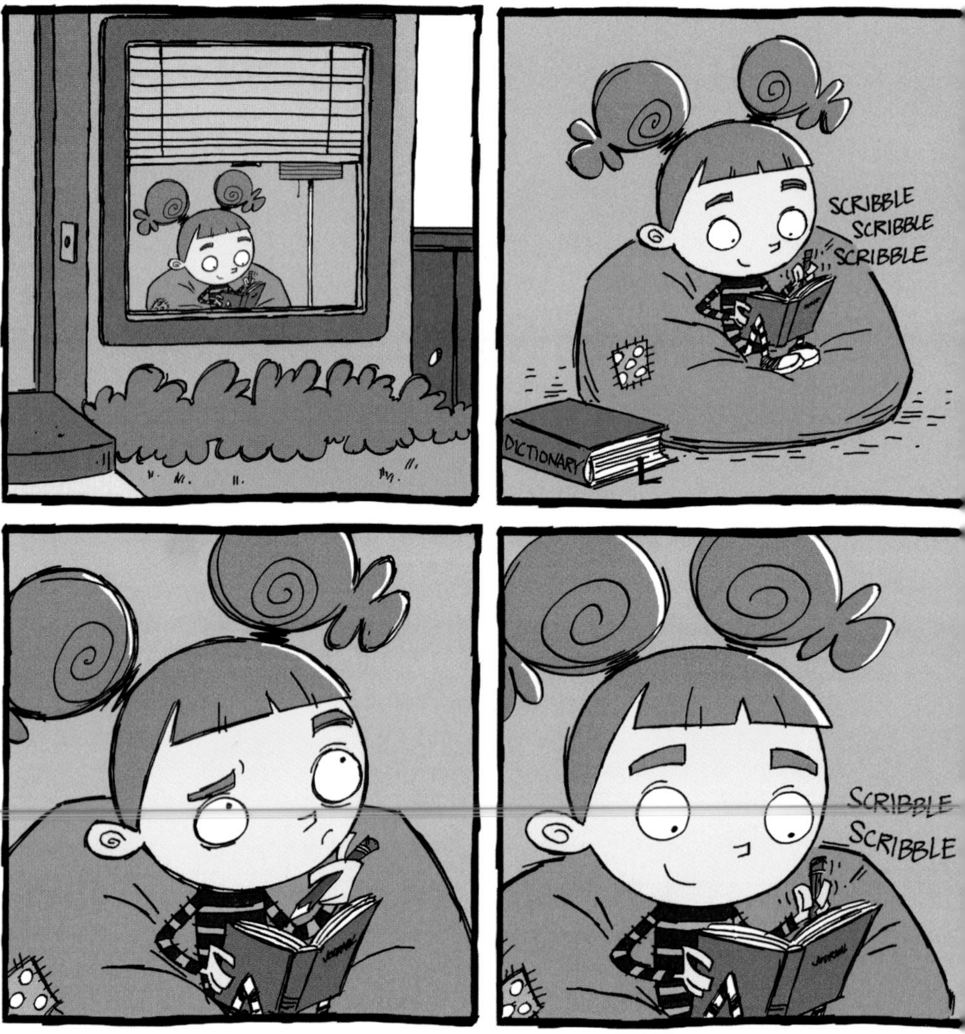
SCRIBBLE
SCRIBBLE
SCRIBBLE
DICTIONARY
SCRIBBLE
SCRIBBLE

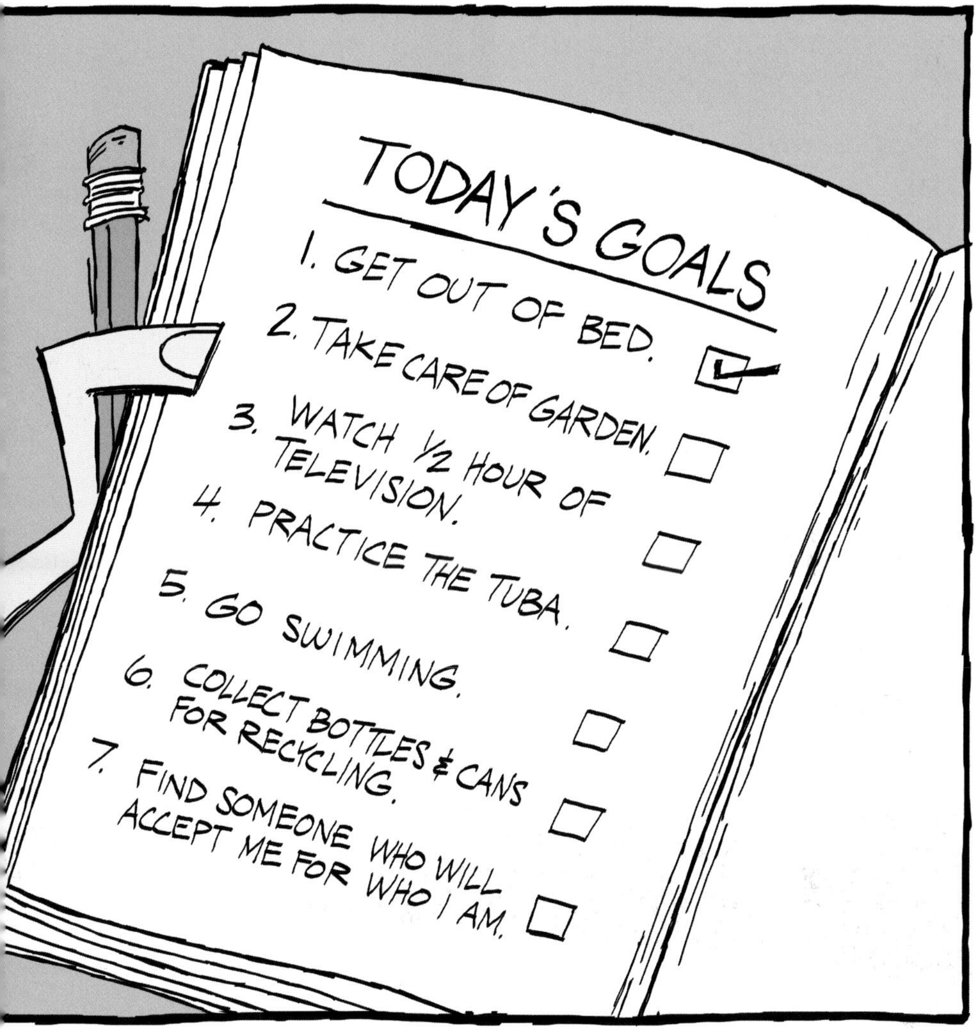
TODAY'S GOALS
1. GET OUT OF BED.
2. TAKE CARE OF GARDEN.
3. WATCH 1/2 HOUR OF TELEVISION.
4. PRACTICE THE TUBA.
5. GO SWIMMING.
6. COLLECT BOTTLES & CANS FOR RECYCLING.
7. FIND SOMEONE WHO WILL ACCEPT ME FOR WHO I AM.

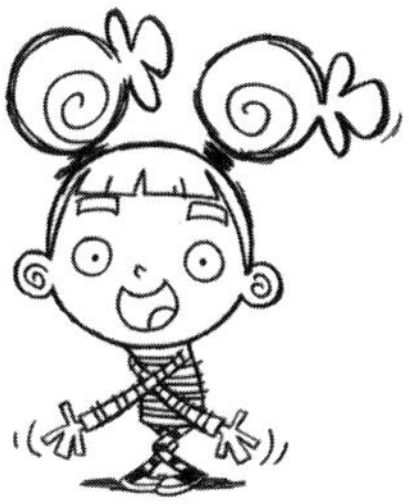

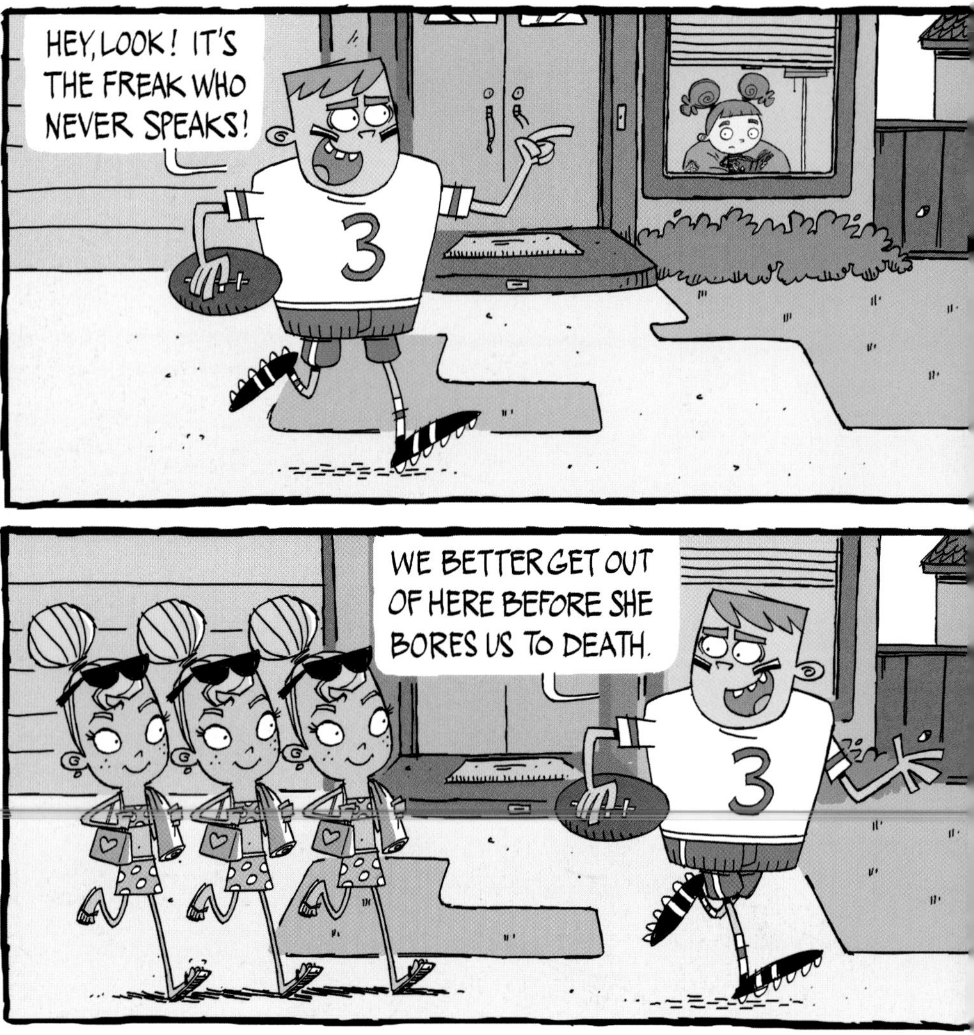
HEY, LOOK! IT'S THE FREAK WHO NEVER SPEAKS!
WE BETTER GET OUT OF HERE BEFORE SHE BORES US TO DEATH.

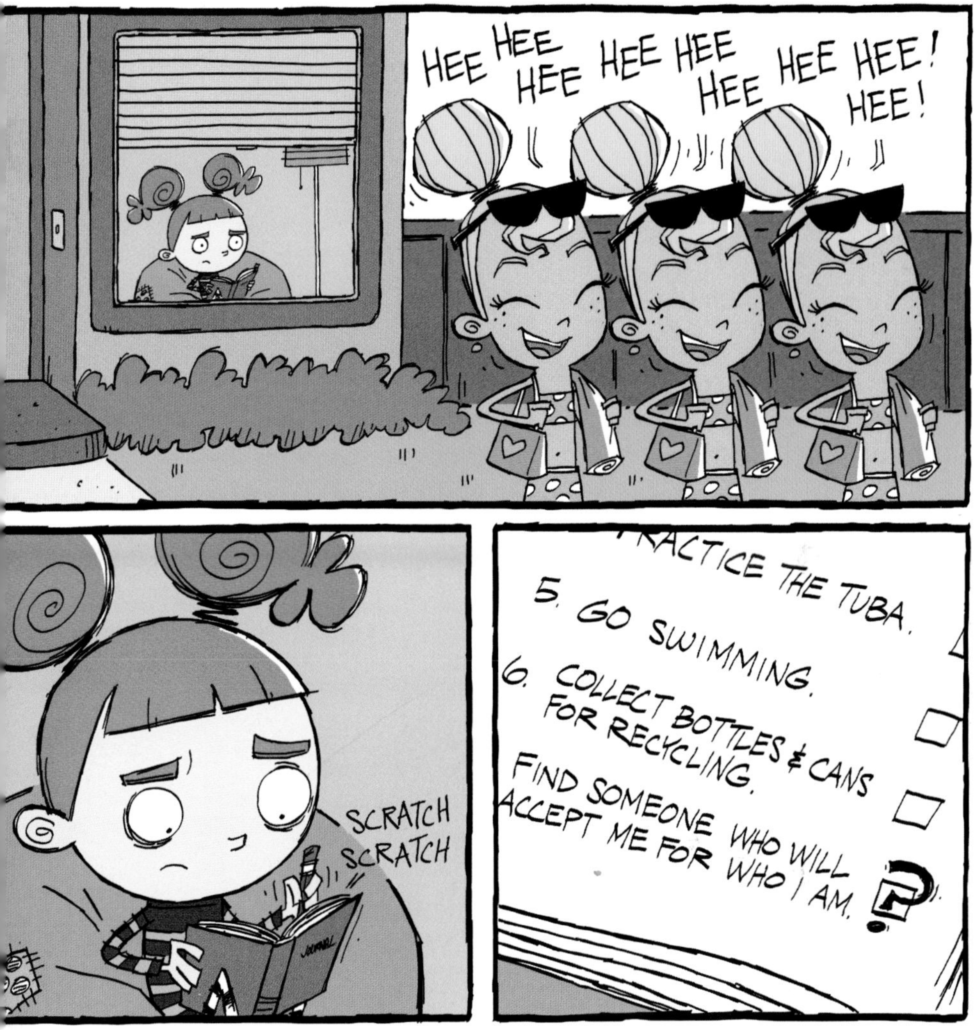
HEE HEE
HEE HEE HEE
HEE HEE HEE!
HEE!
SCRATCH
SCRATCH
RACTICE THE TUBA.
5. GO SWIMMING.
6. COLLECT BOTTLES & CANS FOR RECYCLING.
FIND SOMEONE WHO WILL ACCEPT ME FOR WHO I AM.

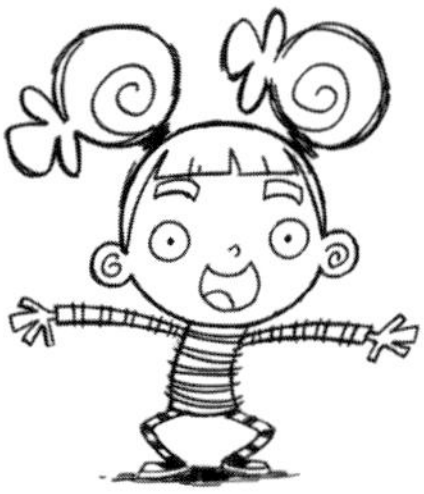

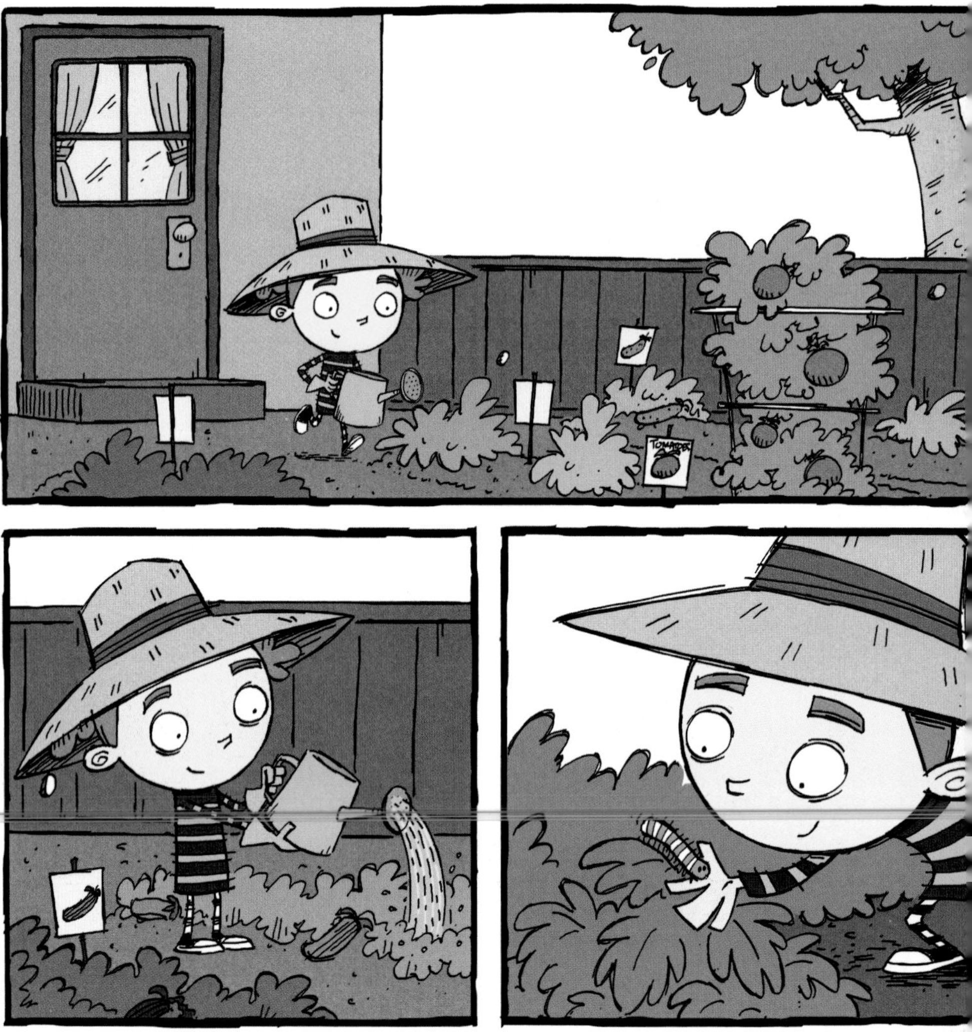
TOMATOES

TODAY'S GOALS

1. GET OUT OF BED. ☑
2. TAKE CARE OF GARDEN. ☑
3. WATCH ½ HOUR OF
   TELEVISION. ☐

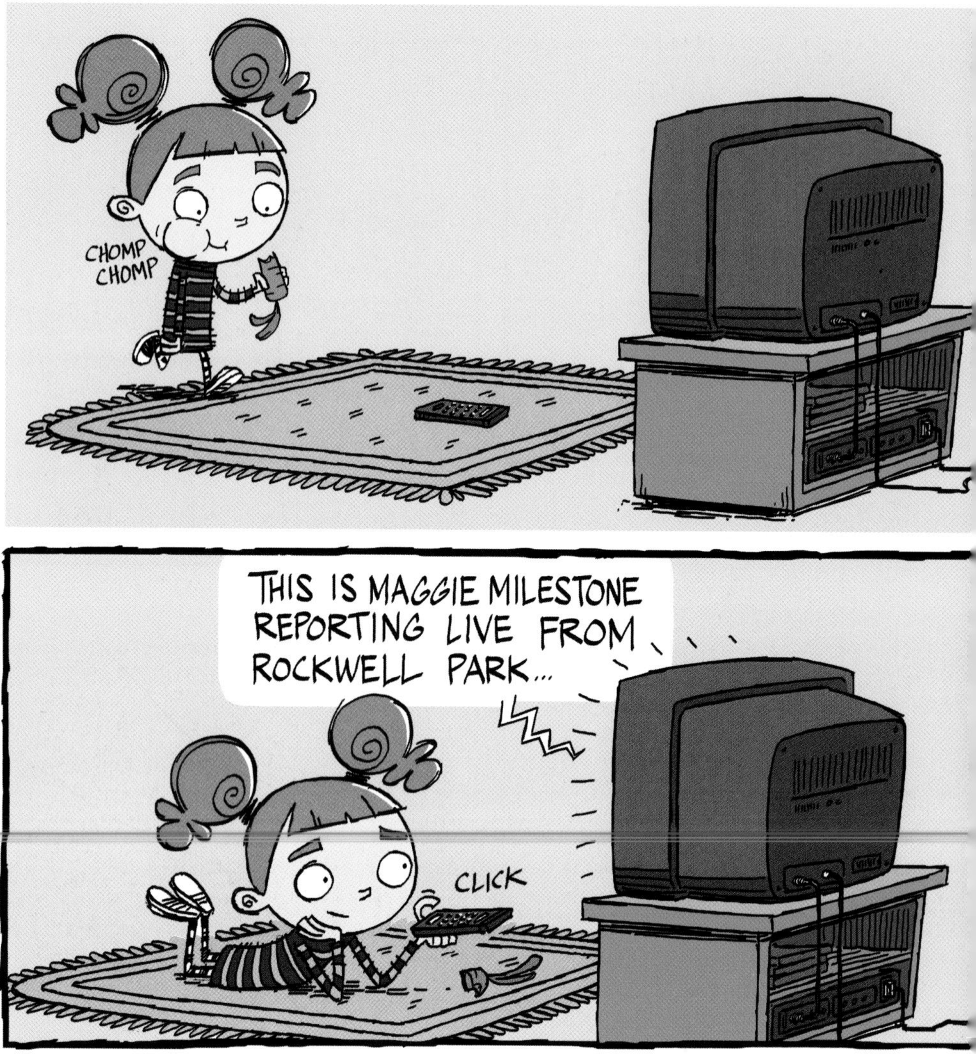
CHOMP
CHOMP
THIS IS MAGGIE MILESTONE REPORTING LIVE FROM ROCKWELL PARK...
CLICK

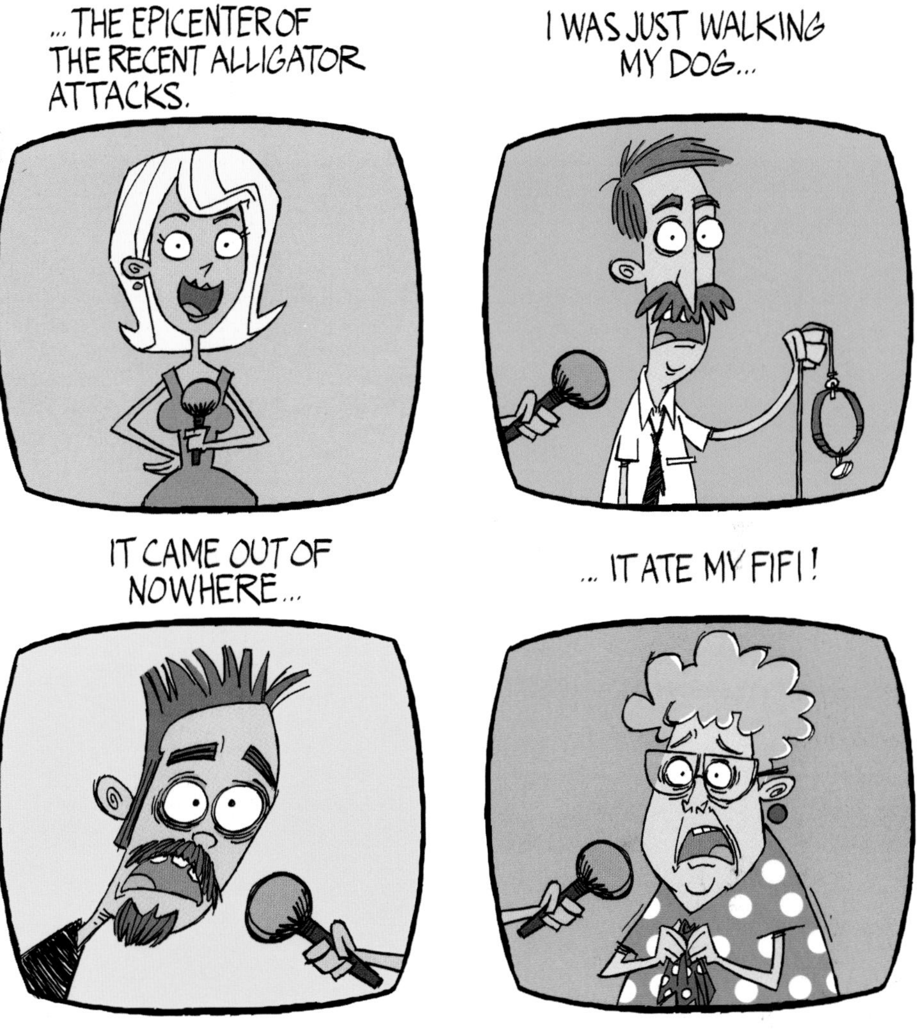
...THE EPICENTER OF THE RECENT ALLIGATOR ATTACKS.
I WAS JUST WALKING MY DOG...
IT CAME OUT OF NOWHERE...
... IT ATE MY FIFI!

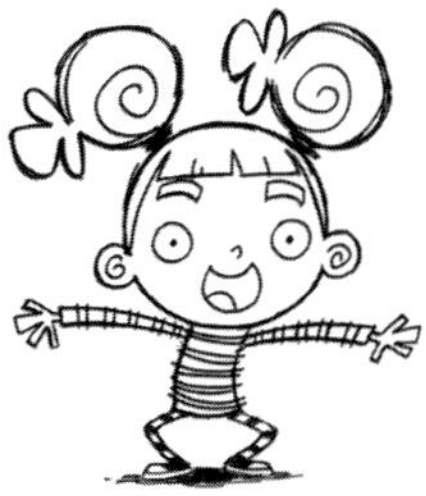

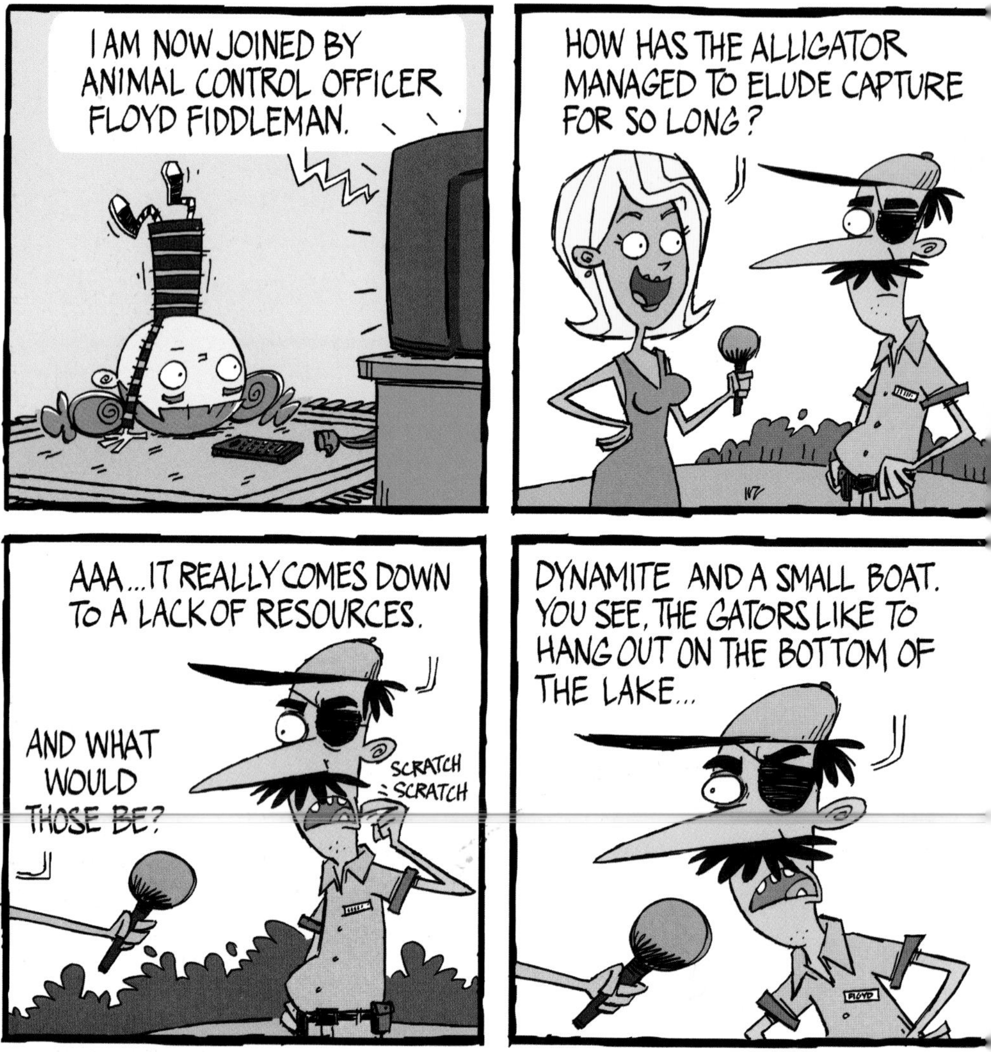
I AM NOW JOINED BY ANIMAL CONTROL OFFICER FLOYD FIDDLEMAN.
HOW HAS THE ALLIGATOR MANAGED TO ELUDE CAPTURE FOR SO LONG?
AAA...IT REALLY COMES DOWN TO A LACK OF RESOURCES.
AND WHAT WOULD THOSE BE?
SCRATCH SCRATCH
DYNAMITE AND A SMALL BOAT. YOU SEE, THE GATORS LIKE TO HANG OUT ON THE BOTTOM OF THE LAKE...
FLOYD

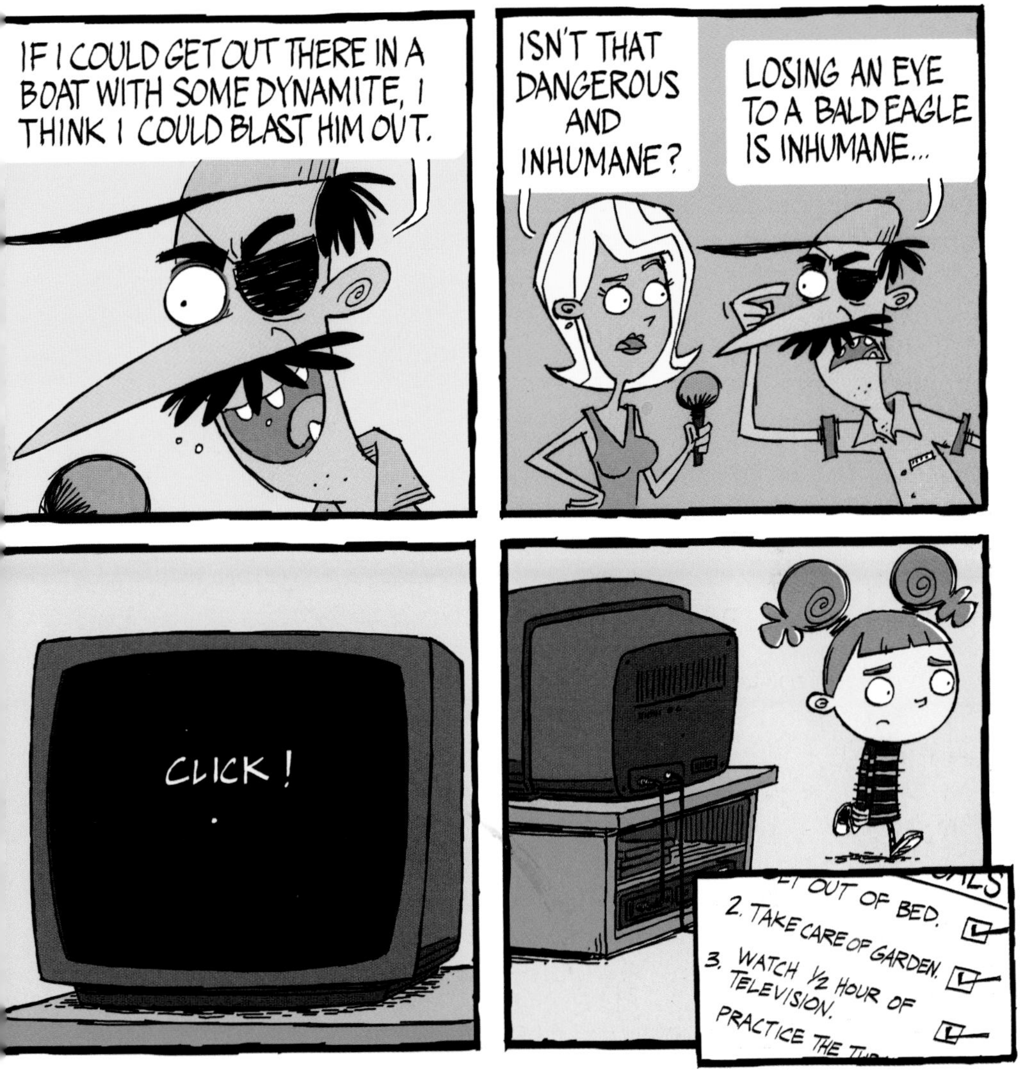
IF I COULD GET OUT THERE IN A BOAT WITH SOME DYNAMITE, I THINK I COULD BLAST HIM OUT.
ISN'T THAT DANGEROUS AND INHUMANE?
LOSING AN EYE TO A BALD EAGLE IS INHUMANE...
CLICK!
OUT OF BED.
2. TAKE CARE OF GARDEN.
3. WATCH ½ HOUR OF TELEVISION.
PRACTICE THE

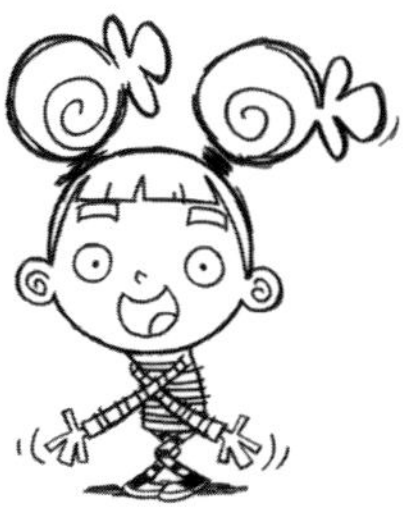

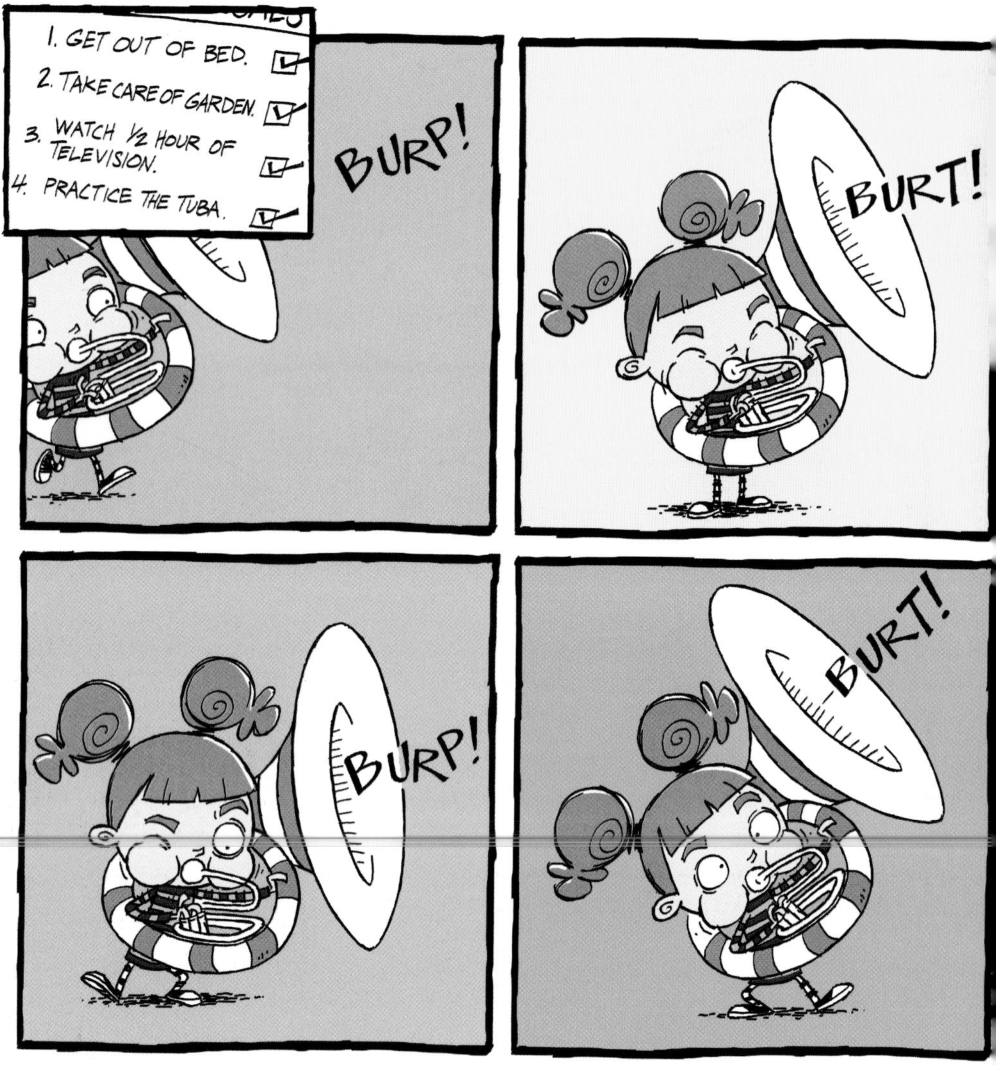
1. GET OUT OF BED.
2. TAKE CARE OF GARDEN.
3. WATCH ½ HOUR OF TELEVISION.
4. PRACTICE THE TUBA.
BURP!
BURT!
BURP!
BURT!

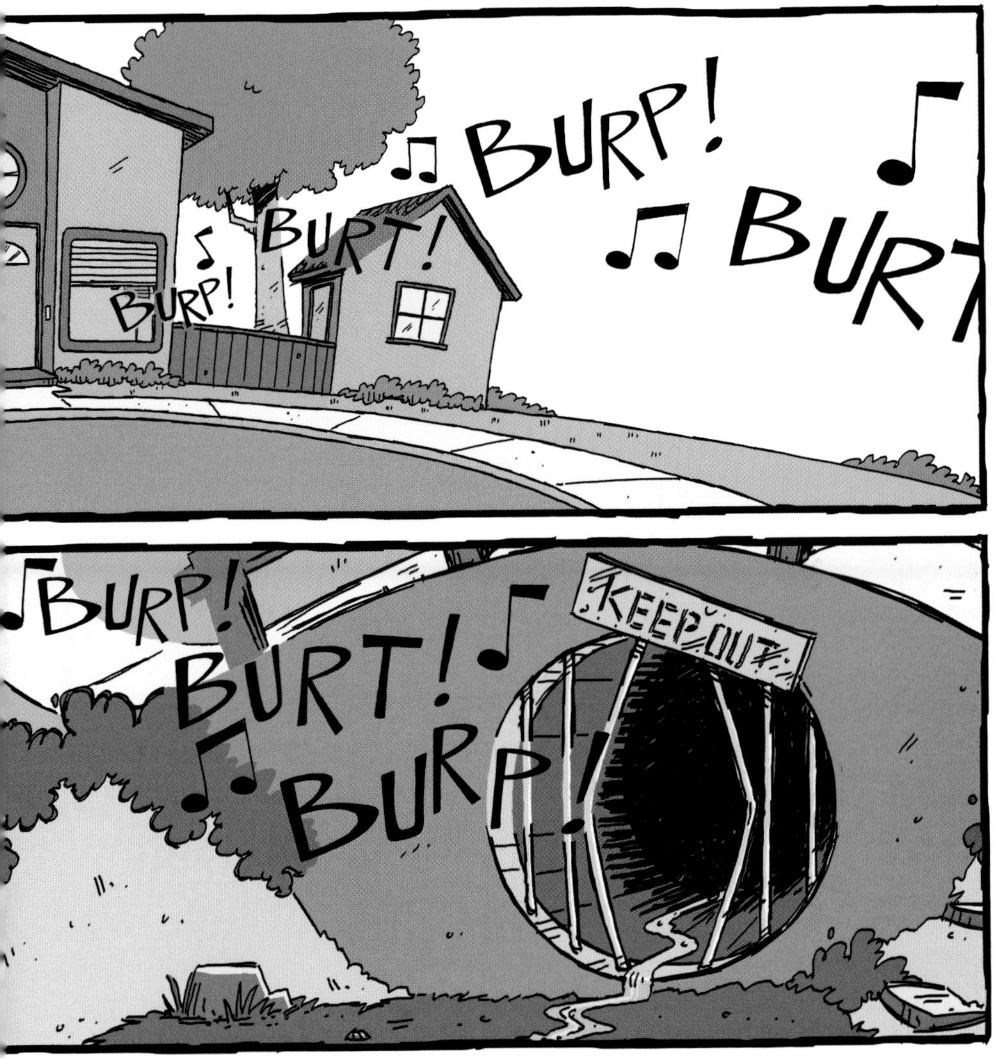
BURP!
BURT!
BURP!
BURT
BURP!
BURT!
BURP!
KEEP OUT

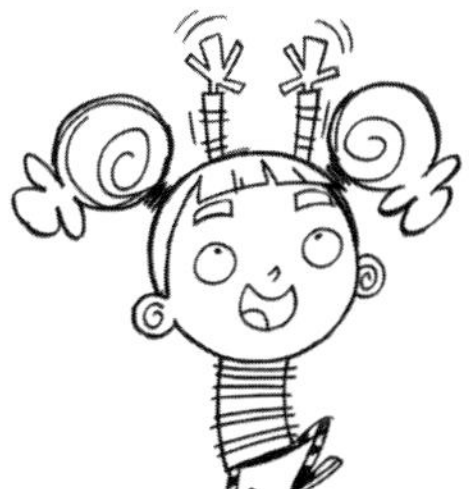

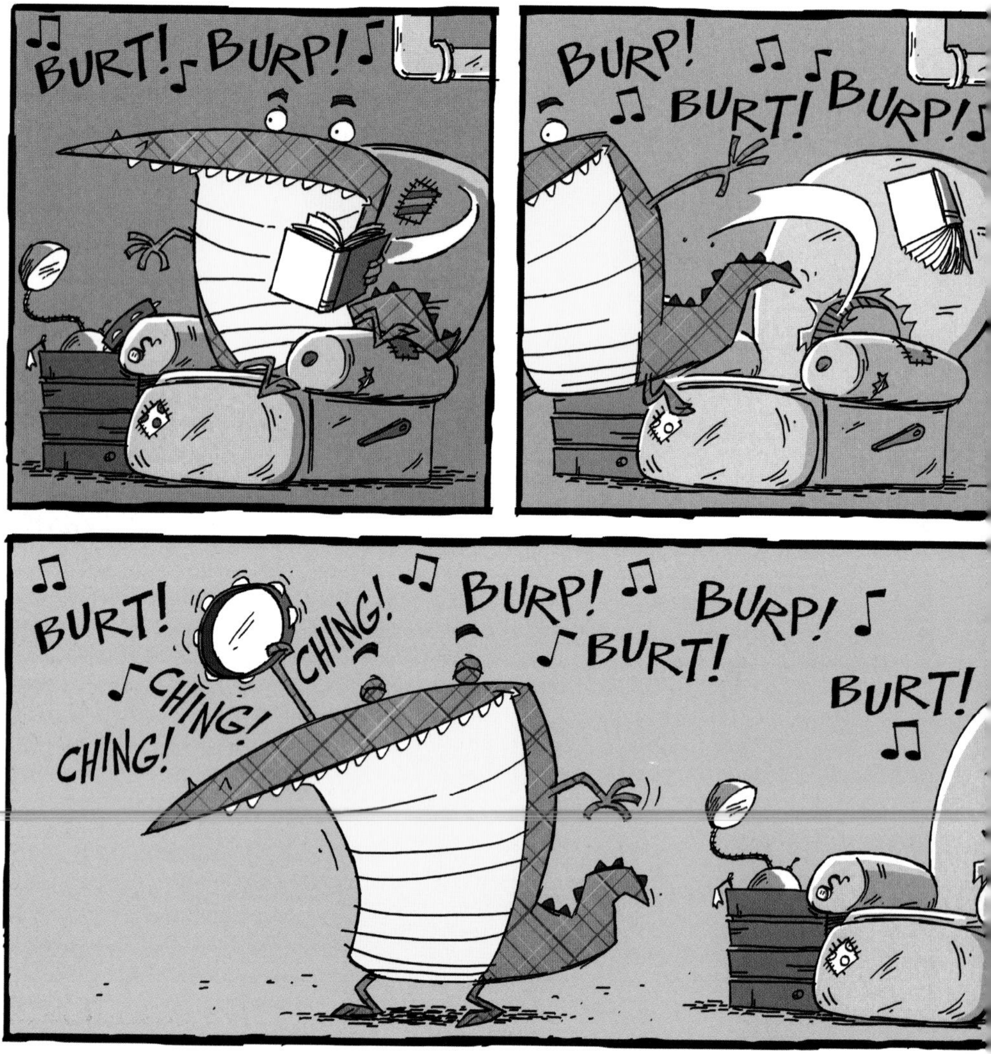
BURT!
BURP!
BURP!
BURT!
BURP!
BURT!
CHING!
CHING!
CHING!
BURP!
BURP!
BURT!
BURT!

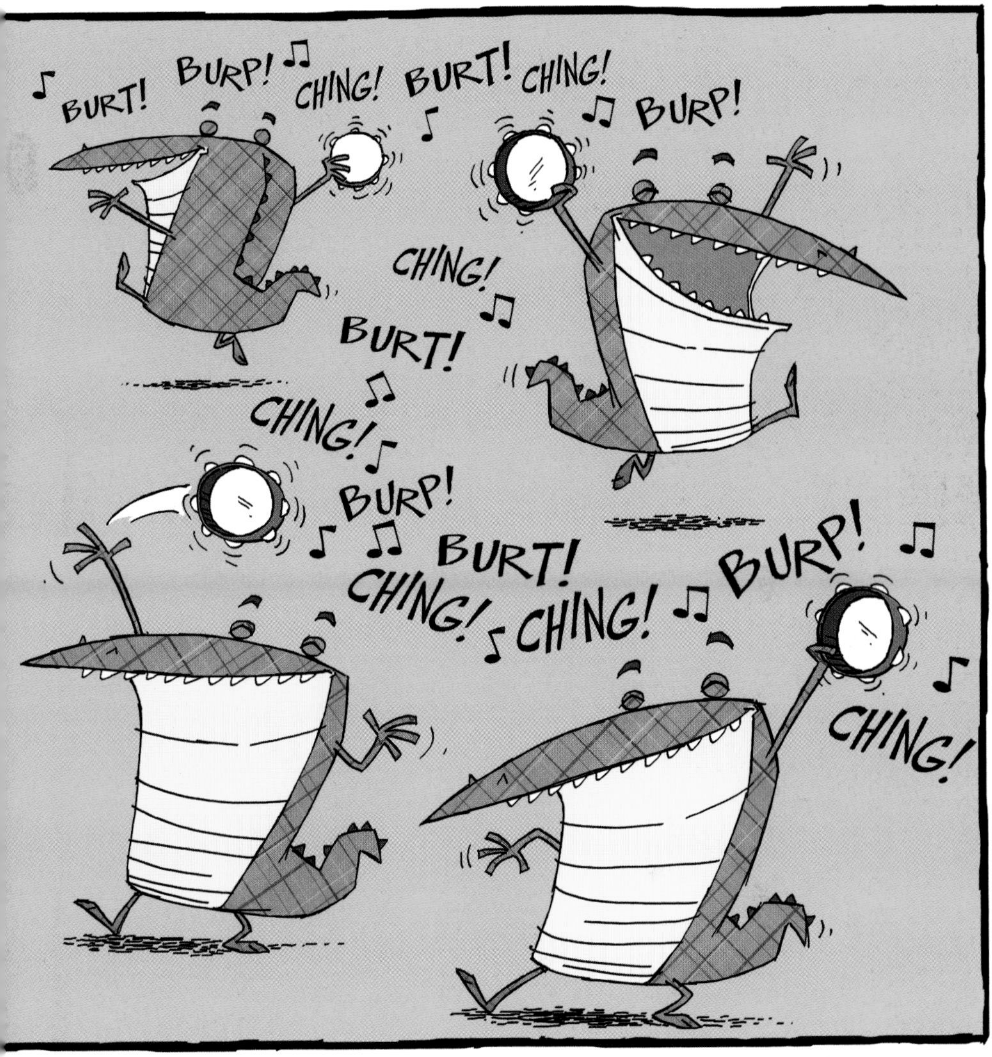
BURT!
BURP!
CHING!
BURT!
CHING!
BURP!
CHING!
BURT!
CHING!
BURP!
BURT!
CHING!
CHING!
BURP!
CHING!

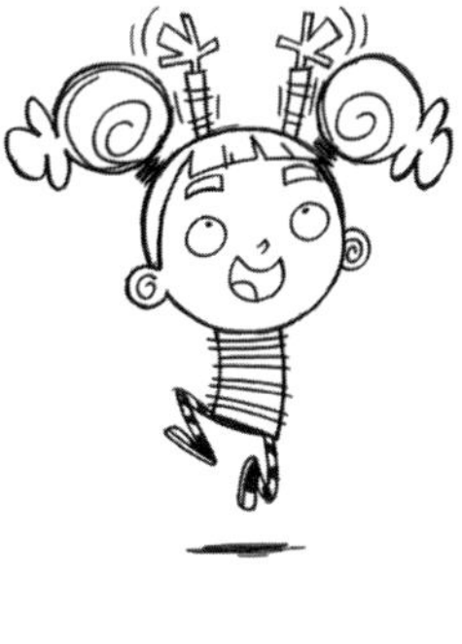

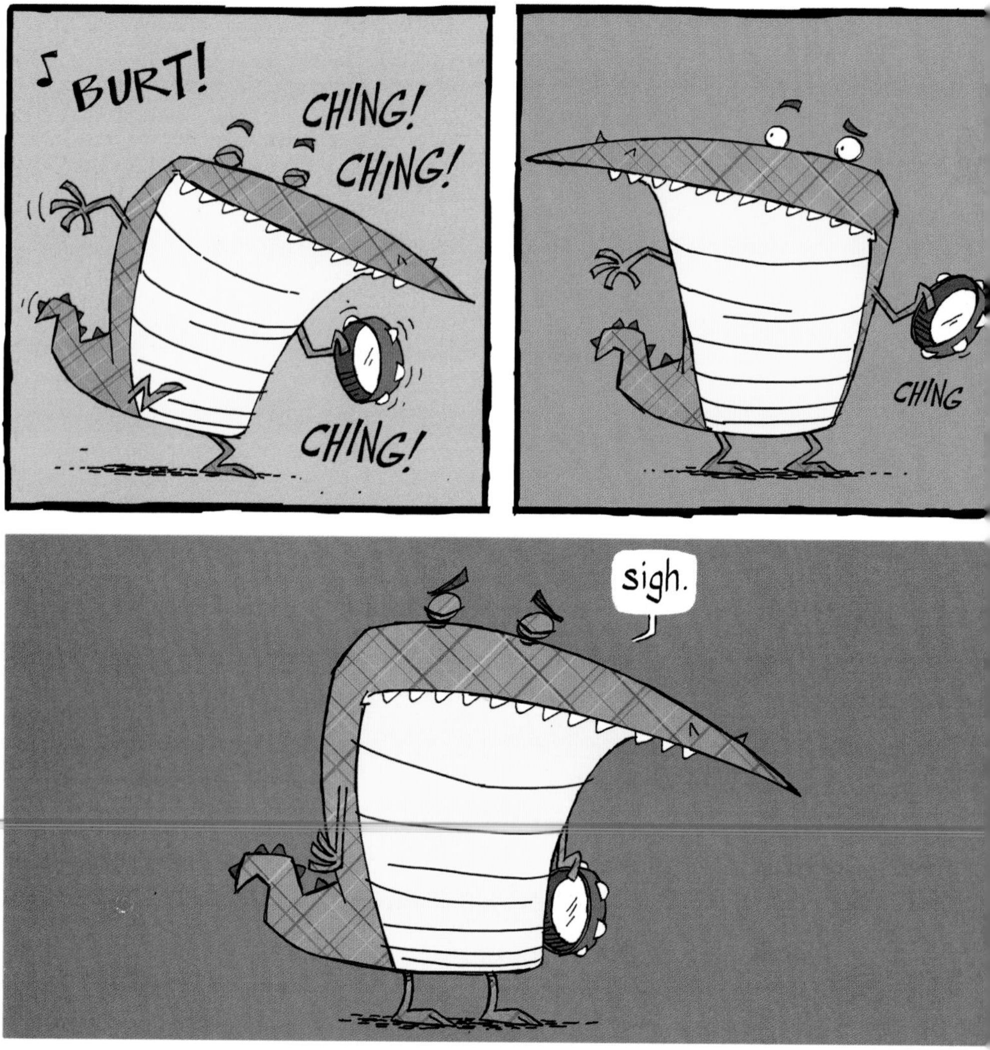

♪ BURT!
CHING! CHING!
CHING!
CHING
sigh.

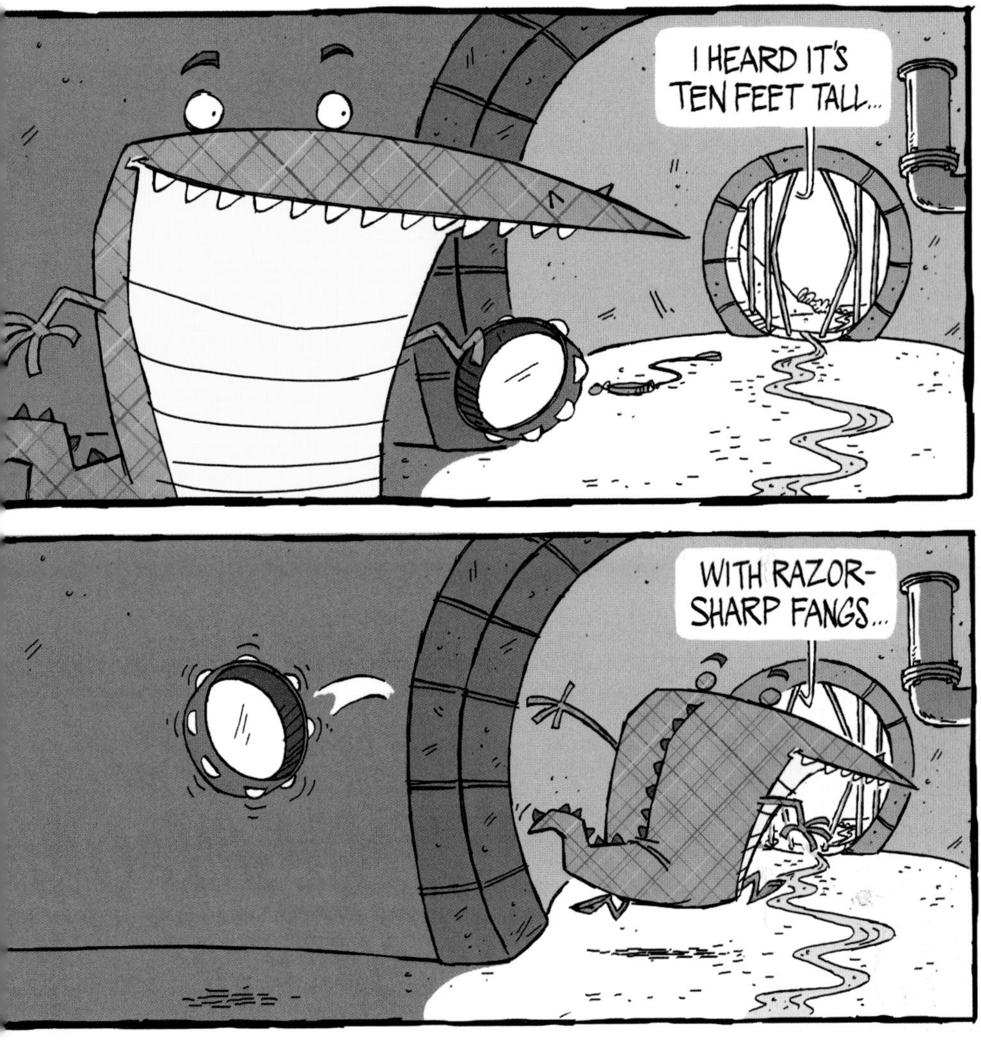
I HEARD IT'S TEN FEET TALL...
WITH RAZOR-SHARP FANGS...

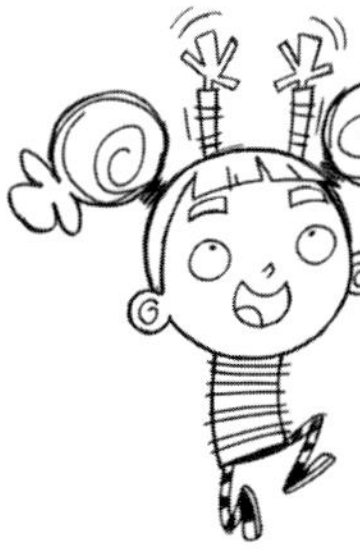

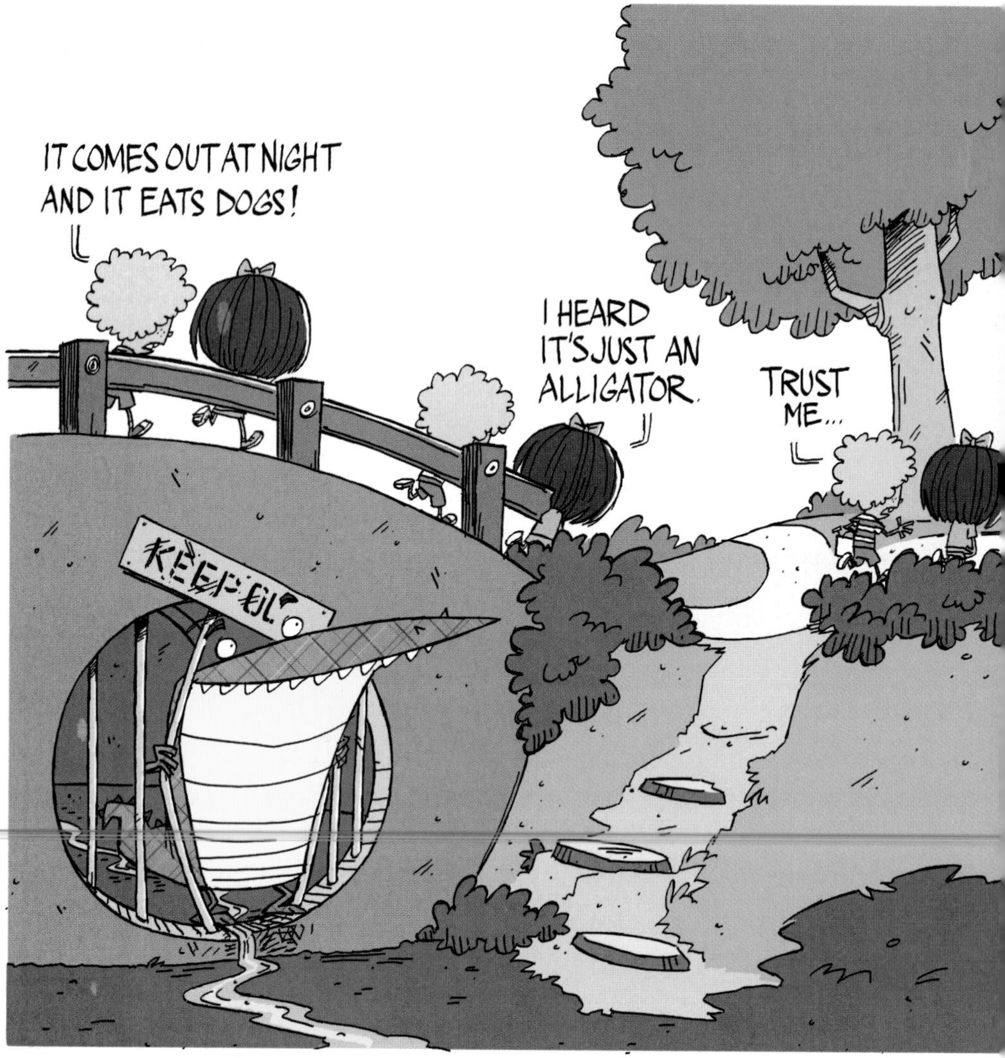
IT COMES OUT AT NIGHT AND IT EATS DOGS!
I HEARD IT'S JUST AN ALLIGATOR.
TRUST ME...
KEEP OUT

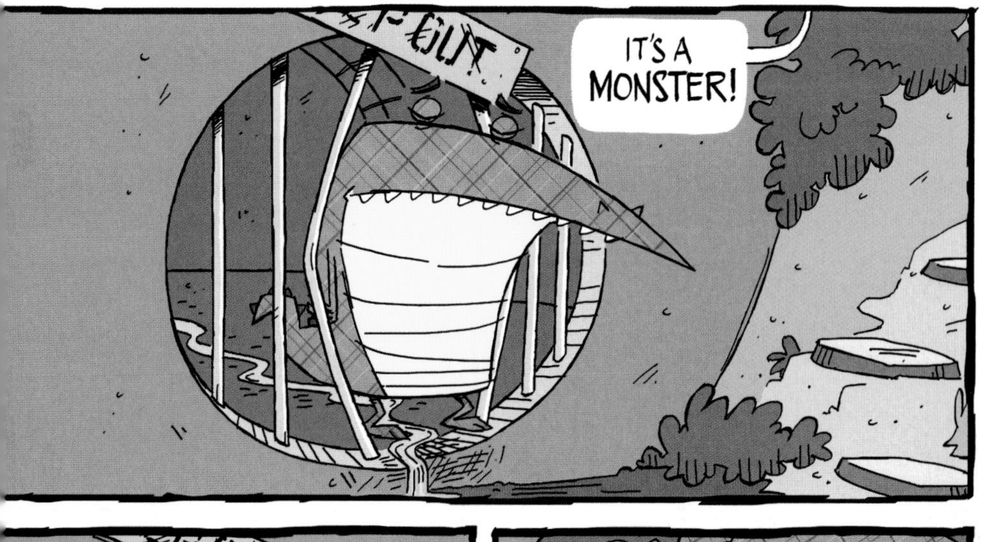
IT'S A MONSTER!
GUURROWLLLL!

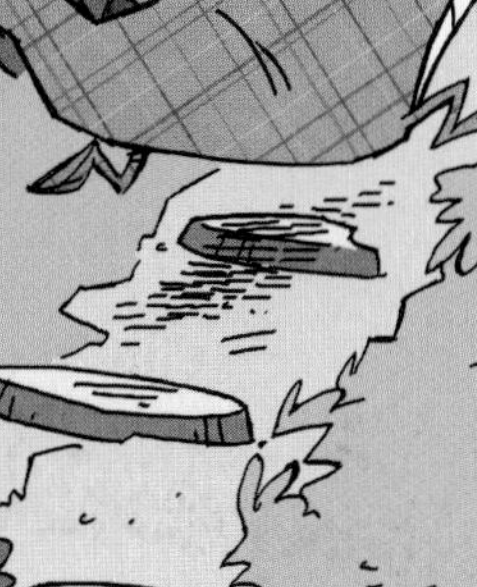

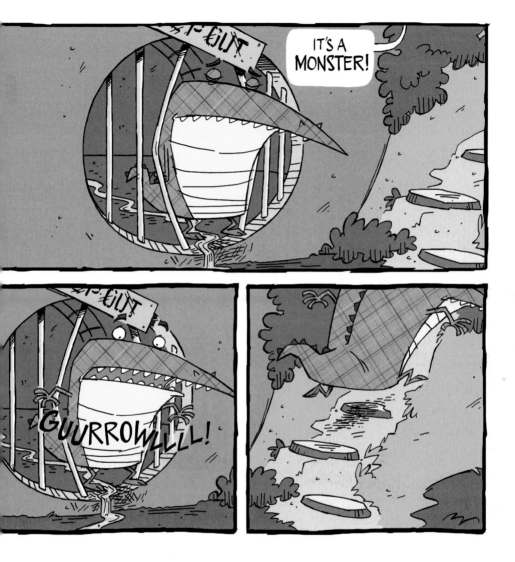

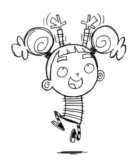

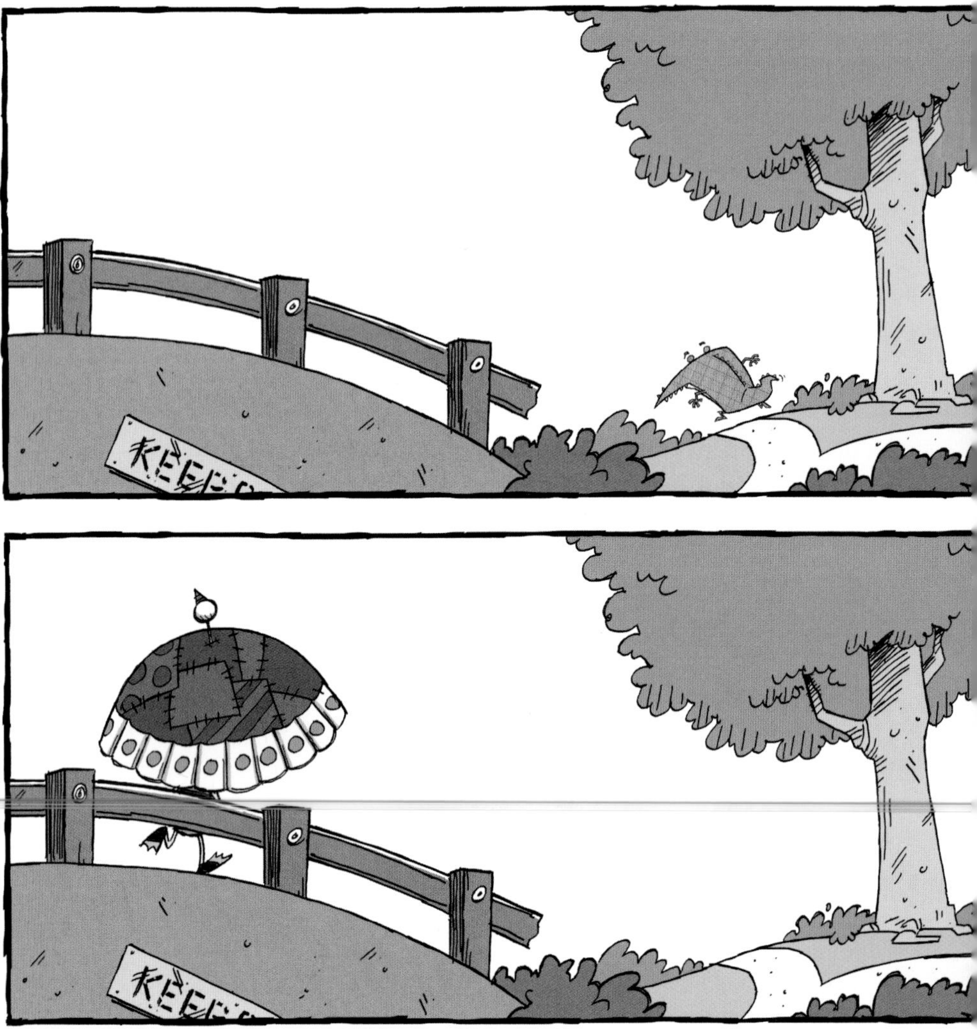

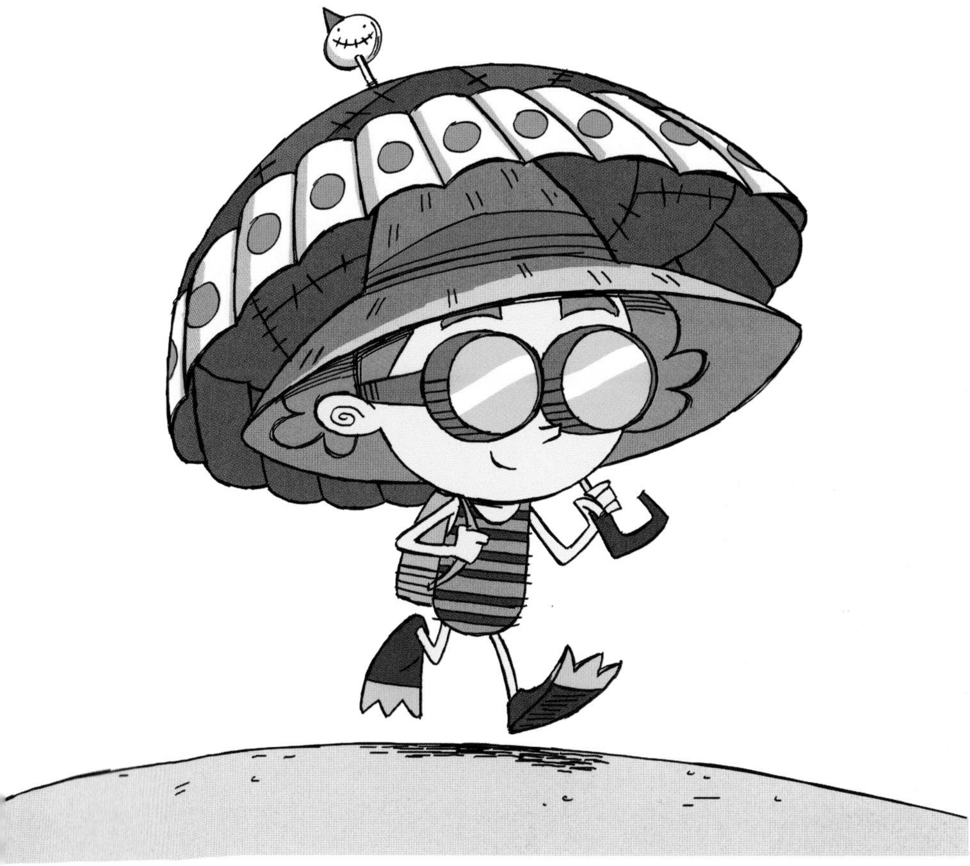

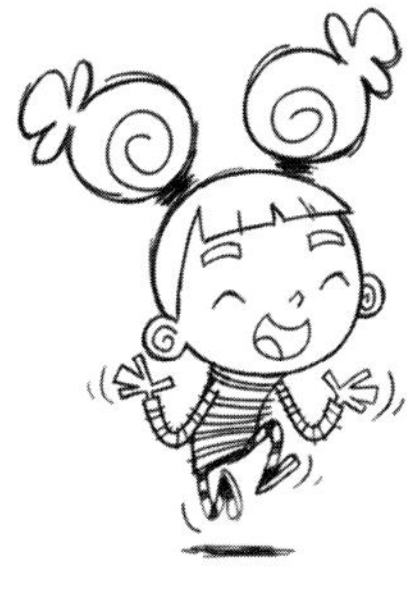

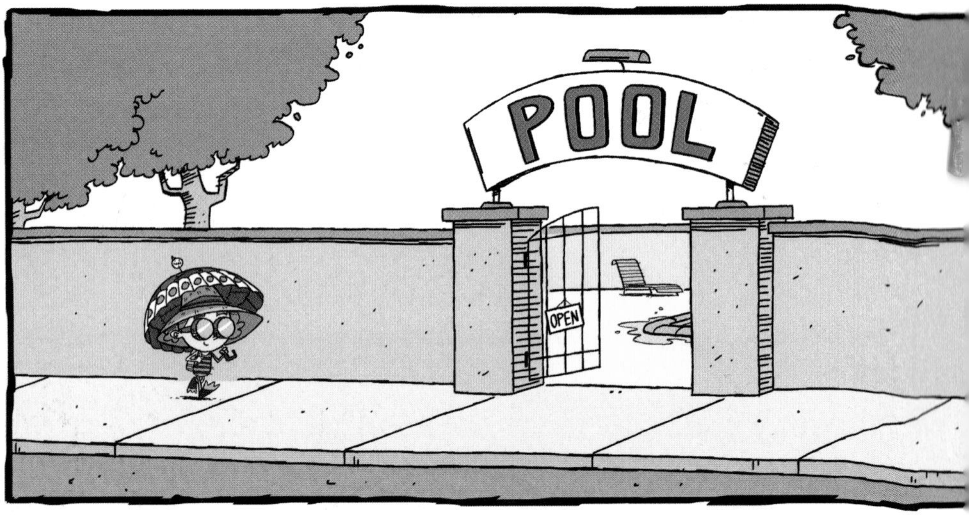
POOL
OPEN

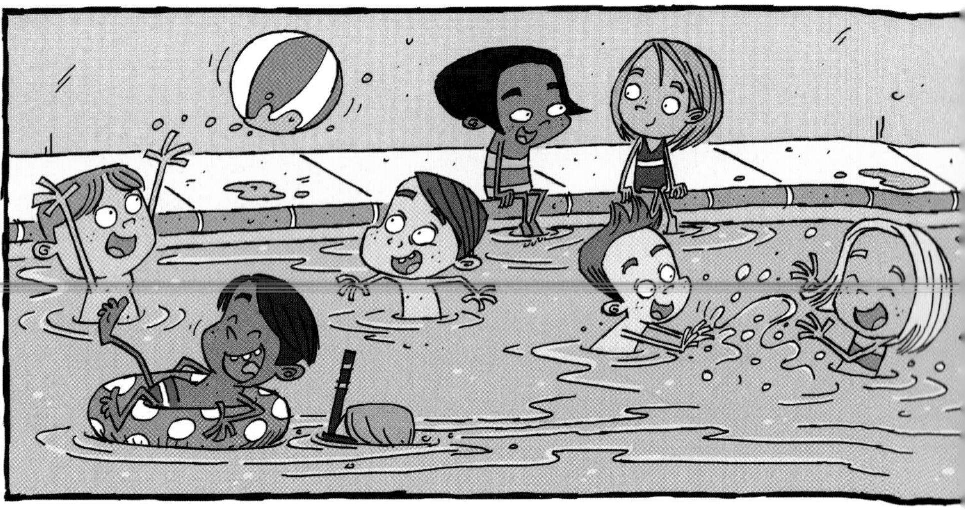

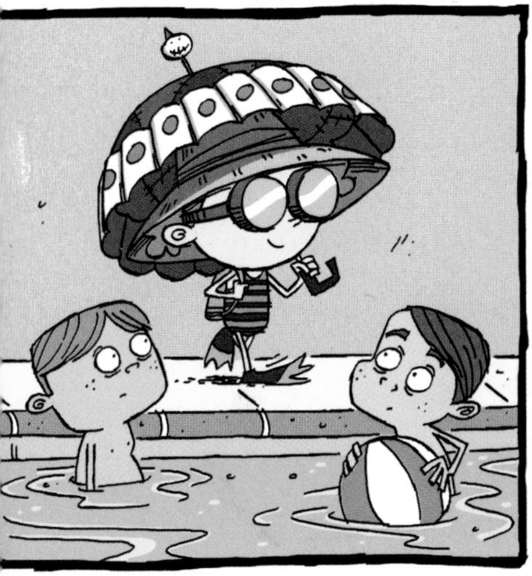

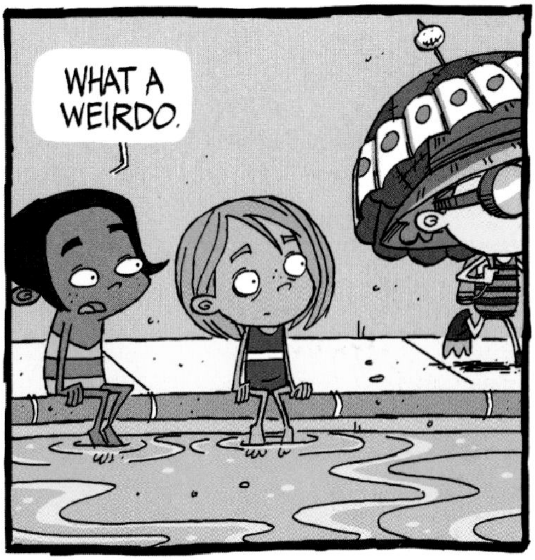
WHAT A WEIRDO.

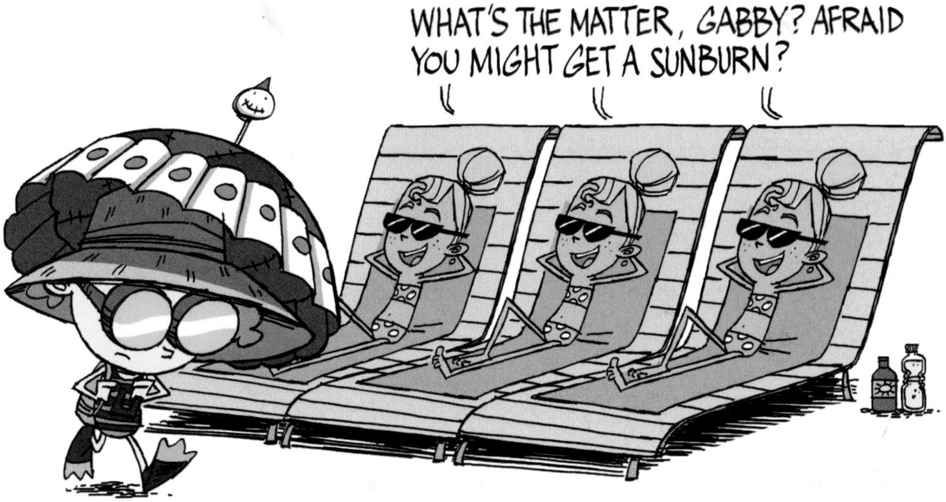
WHAT'S THE MATTER, GABBY? AFRAID YOU MIGHT GET A SUNBURN?

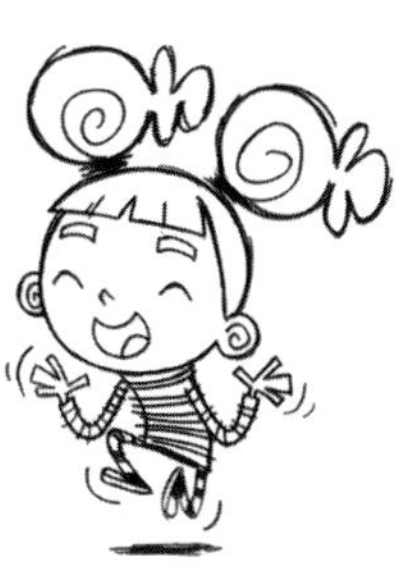

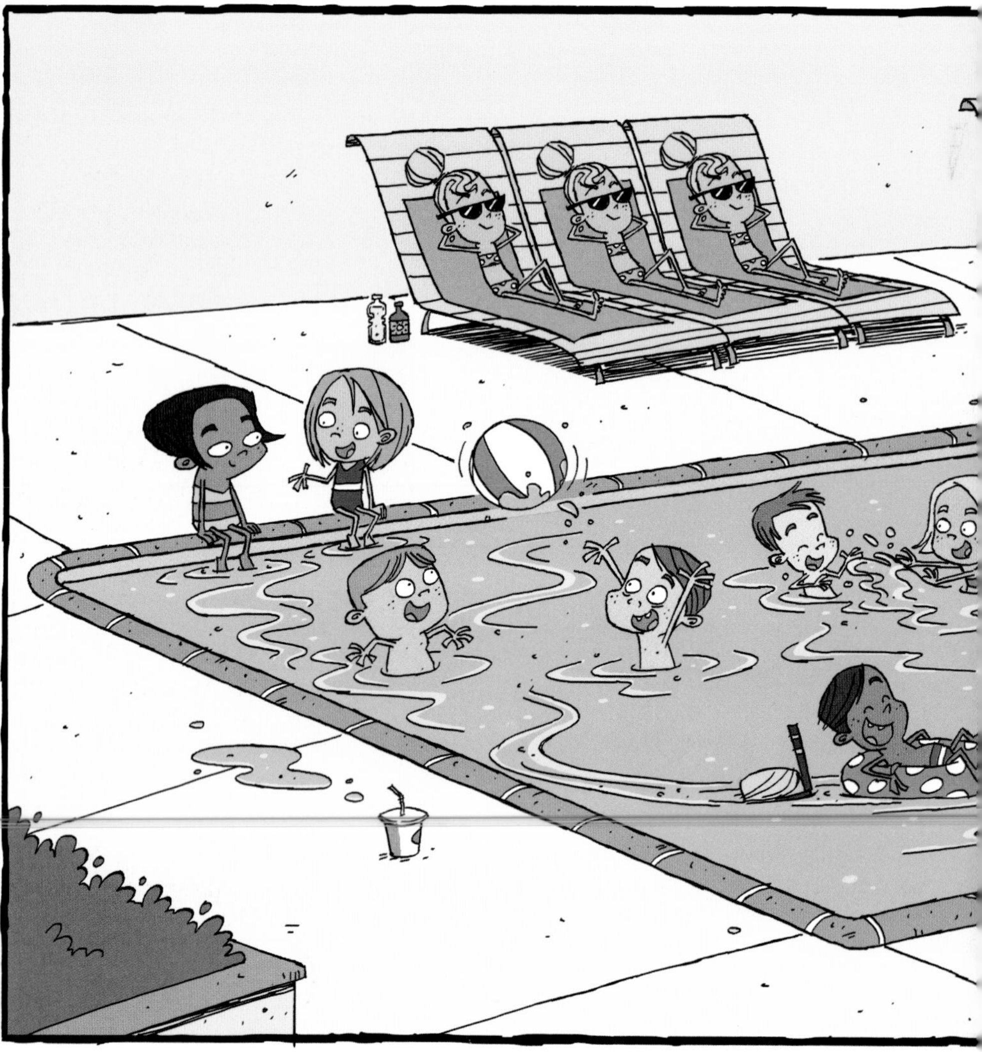

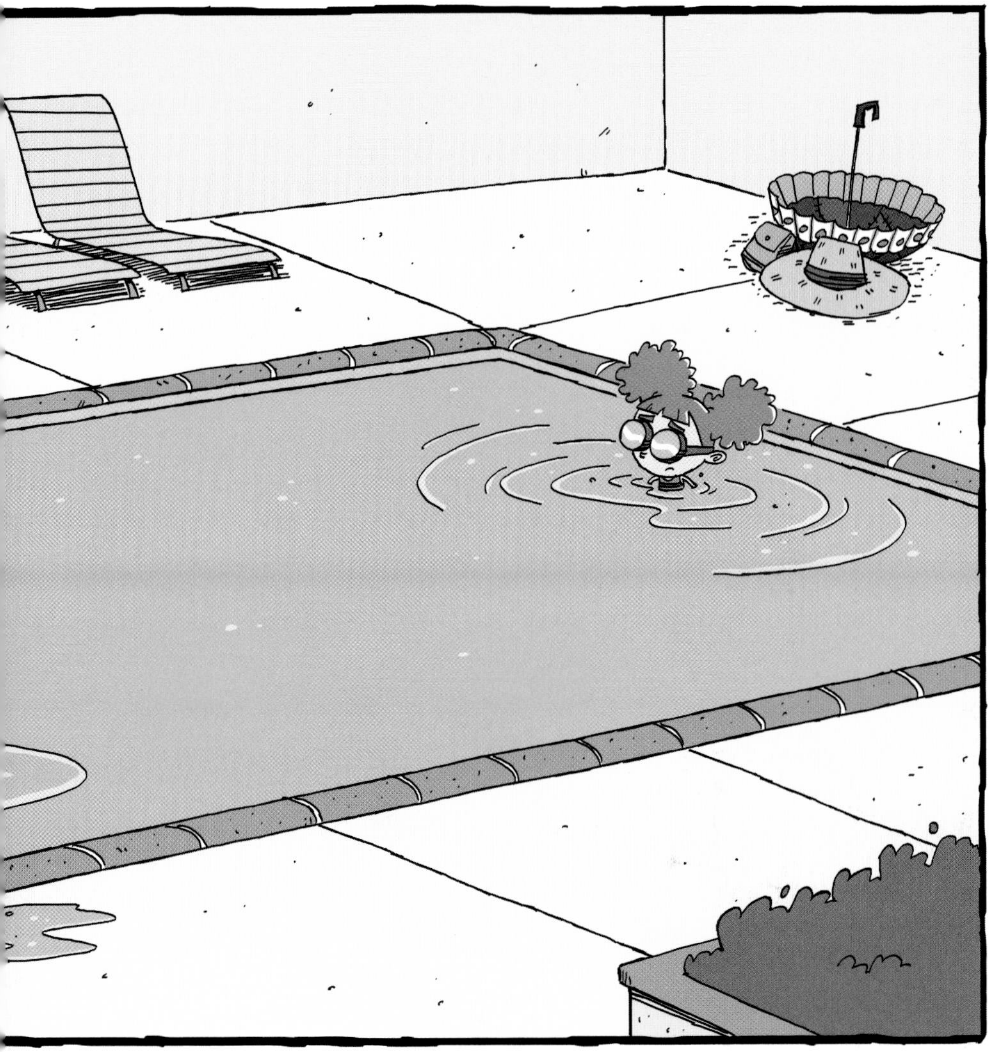

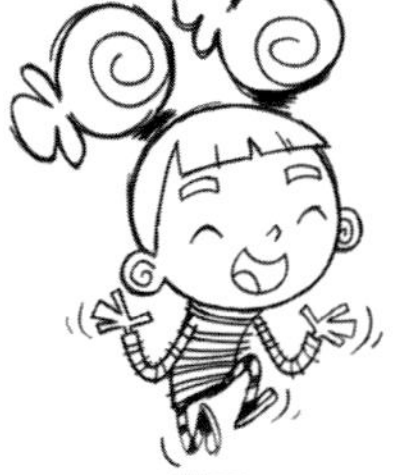

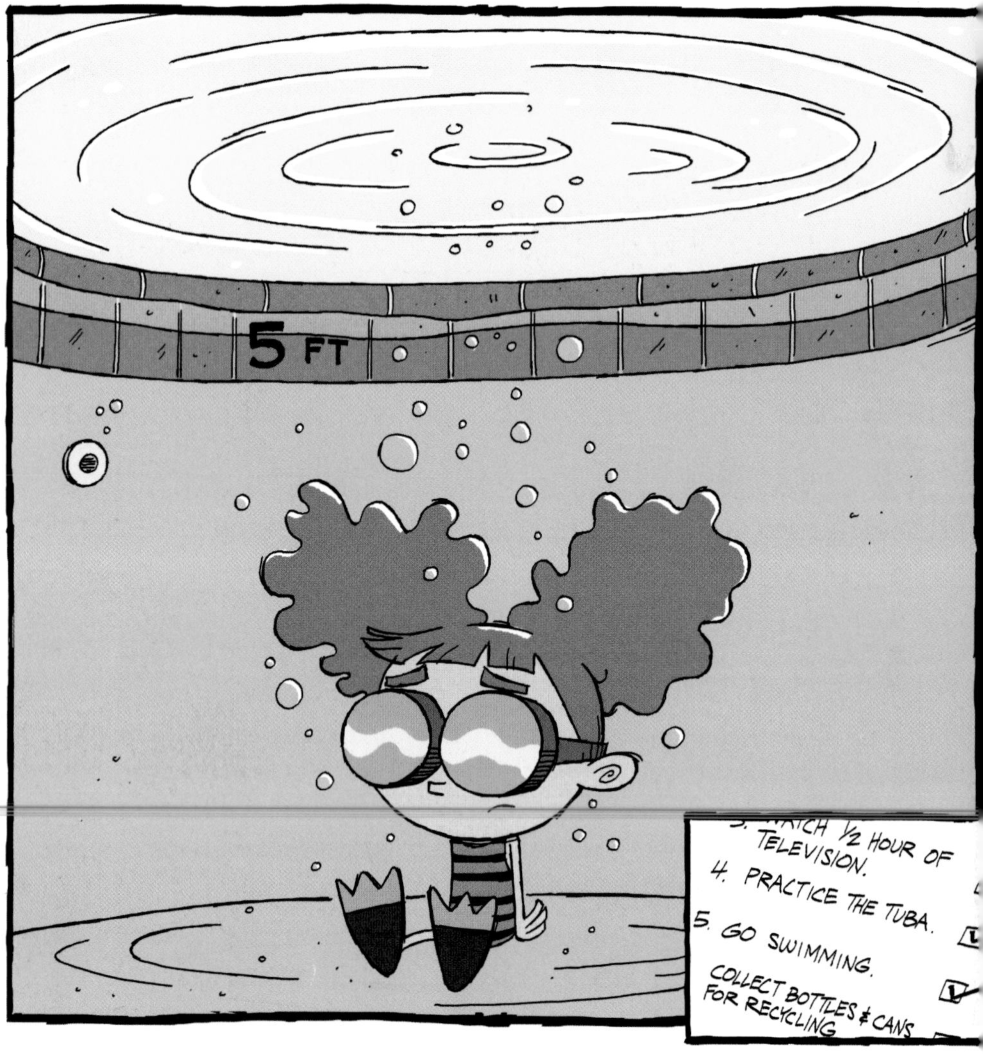
5 FT
WATCH ½ HOUR OF TELEVISION.
4. PRACTICE THE TUBA.
5. GO SWIMMING.
COLLECT BOTTLES & CANS FOR RECYCLING

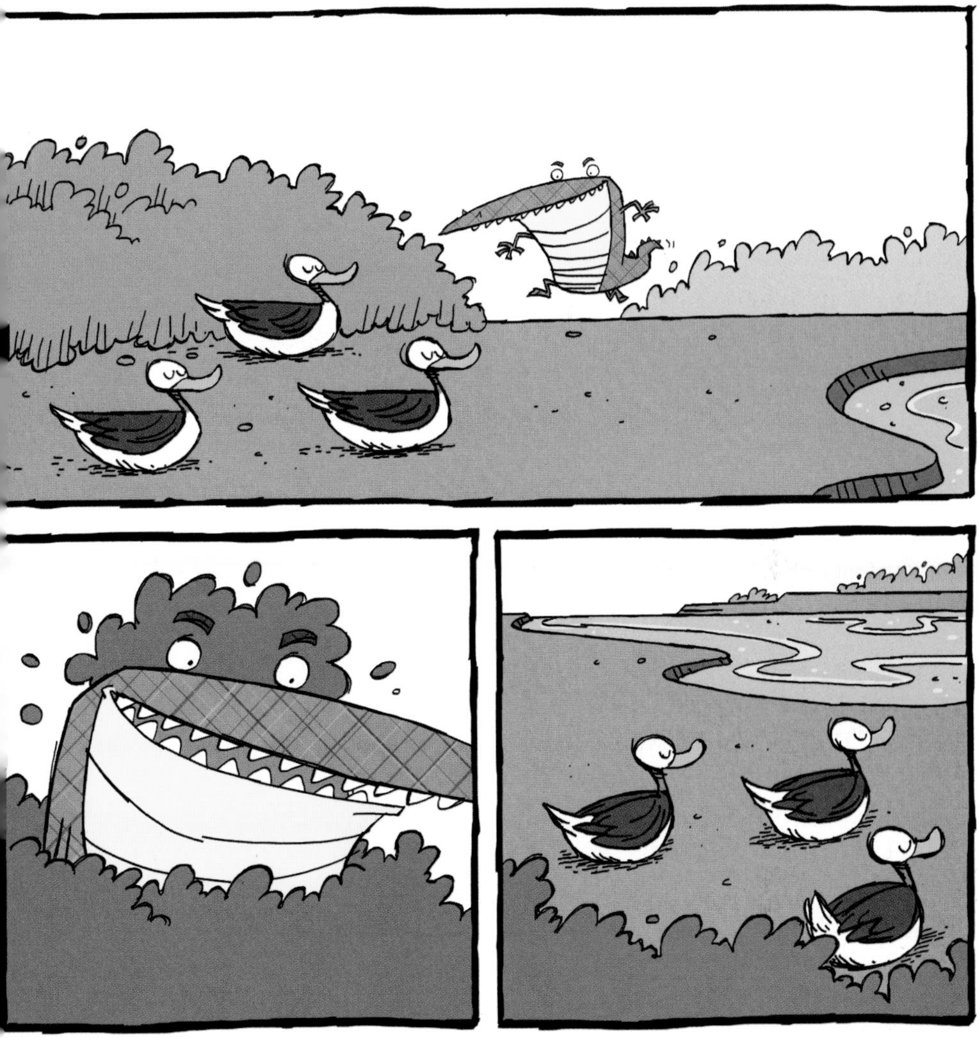

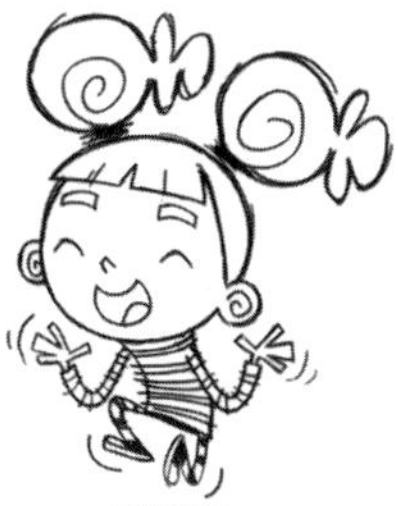

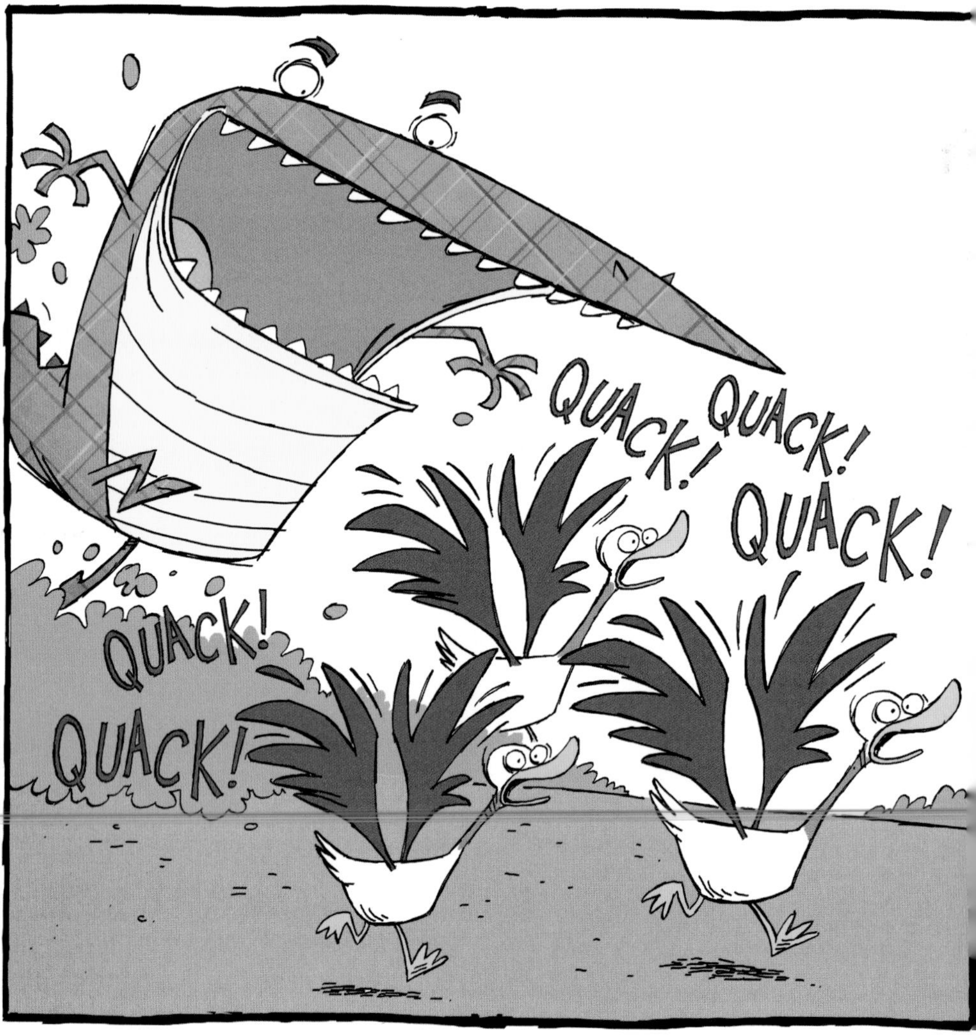
QUACK!
QUACK!
QUACK!
QUACK!
QUACK!

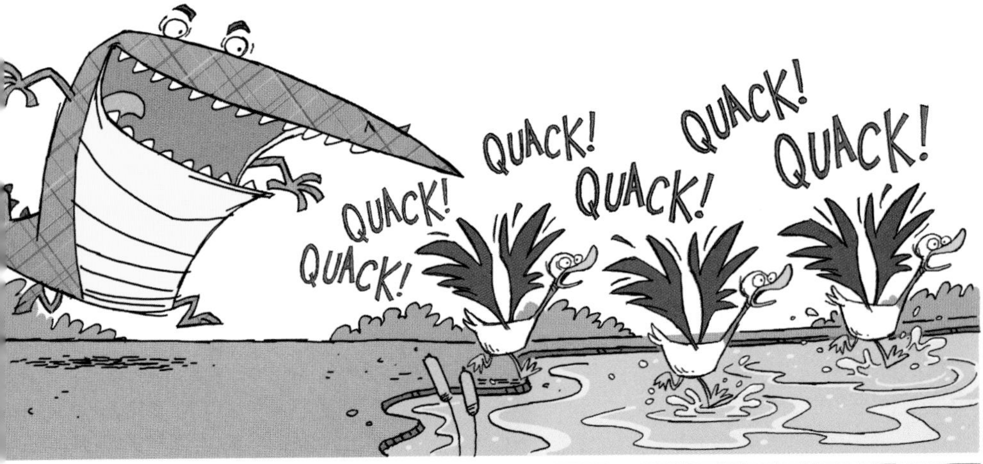
QUACK!
QUACK!
QUACK!
QUACK!
QUACK!
QUACK!

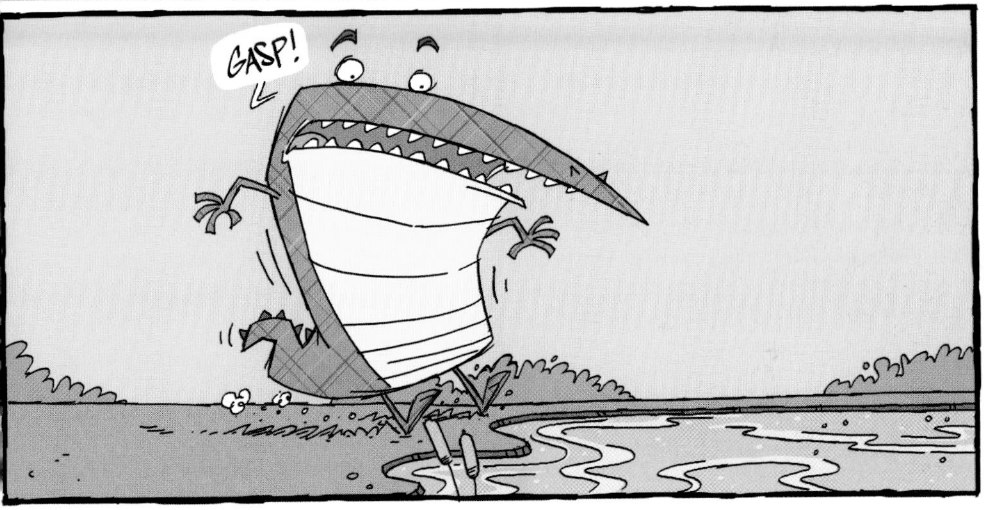
GASP!

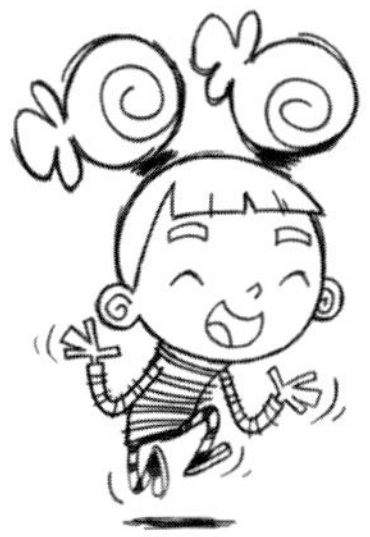

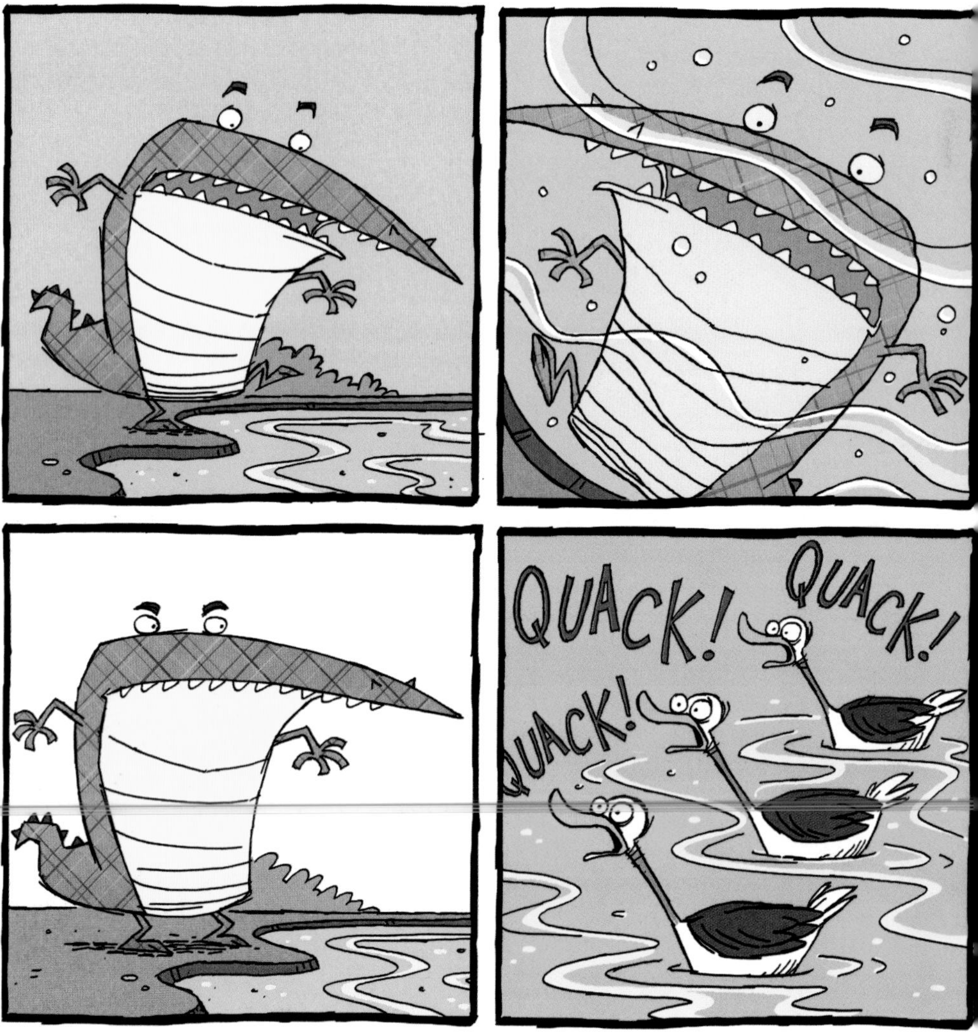
QUACK!
QUACK!
QUACK!

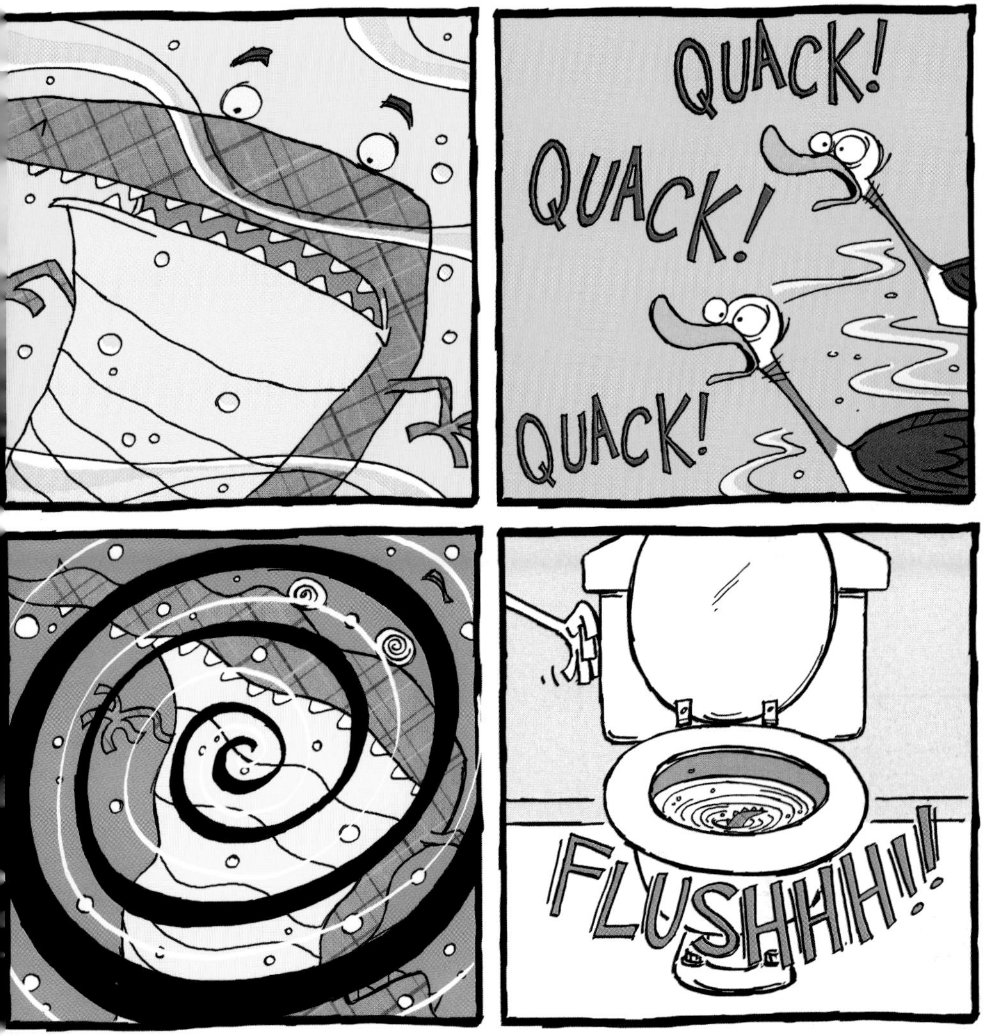
QUACK!
QUACK!
QUACK!
FLUSHHH!!!

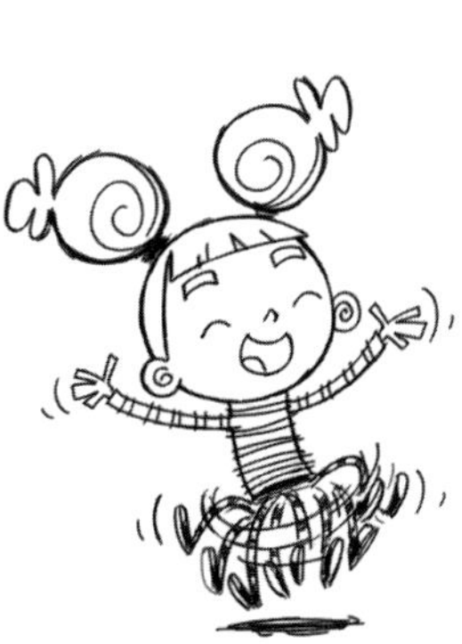

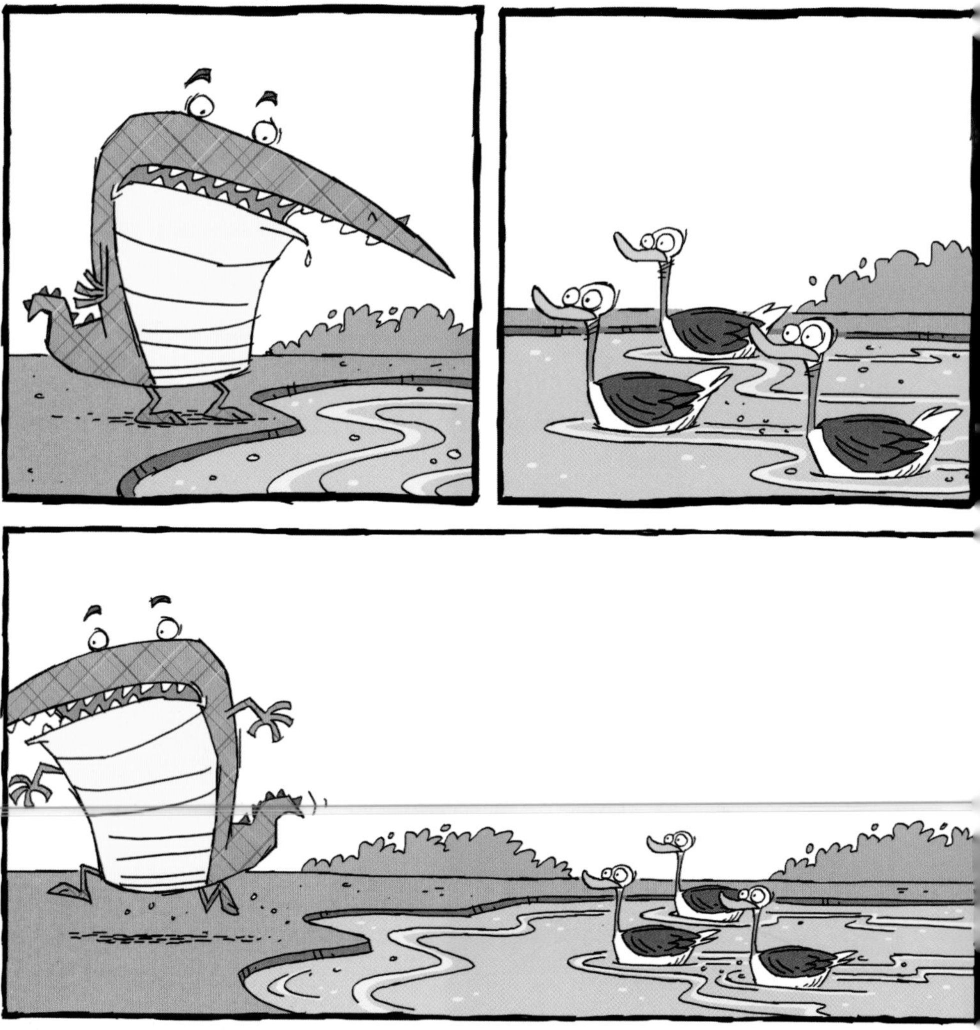

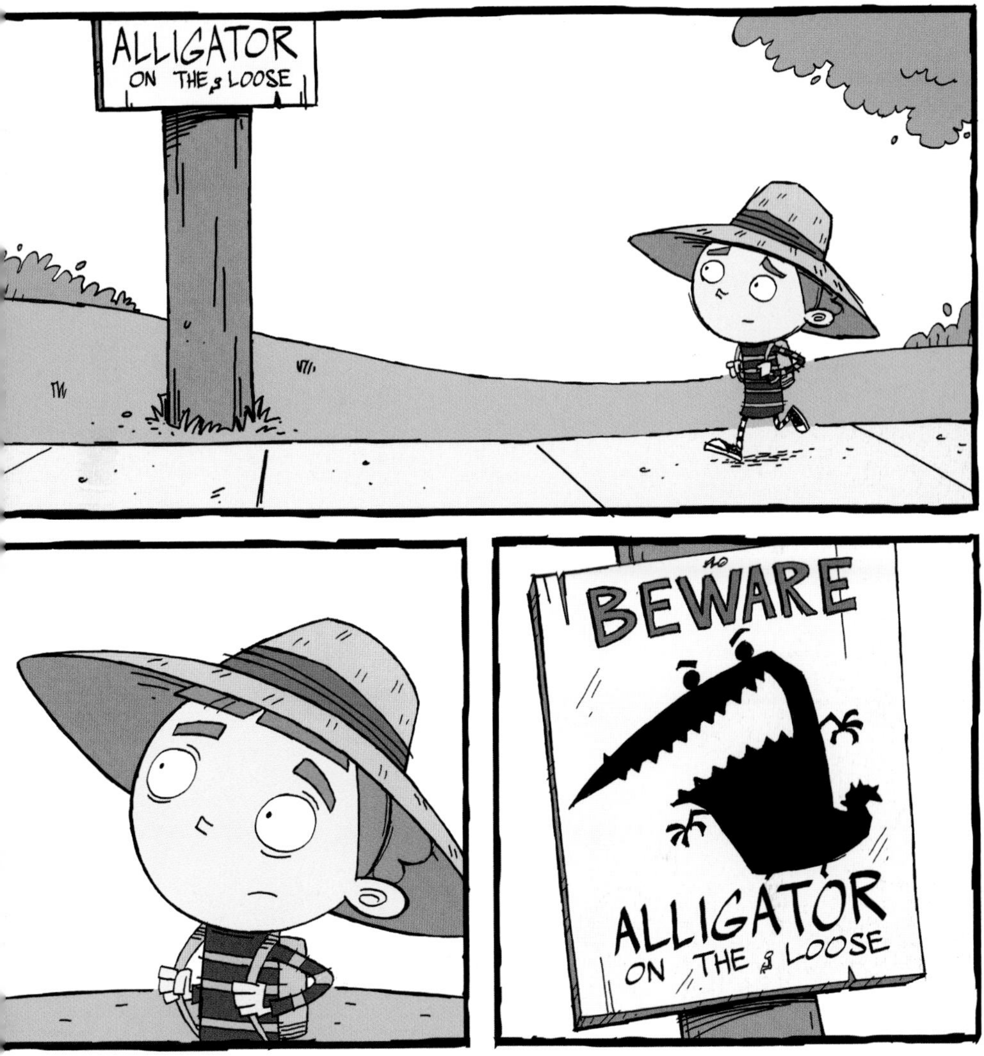
ALLIGATOR
ON THE LOOSE
BEWARE
ALLIGATOR
ON THE LOOSE

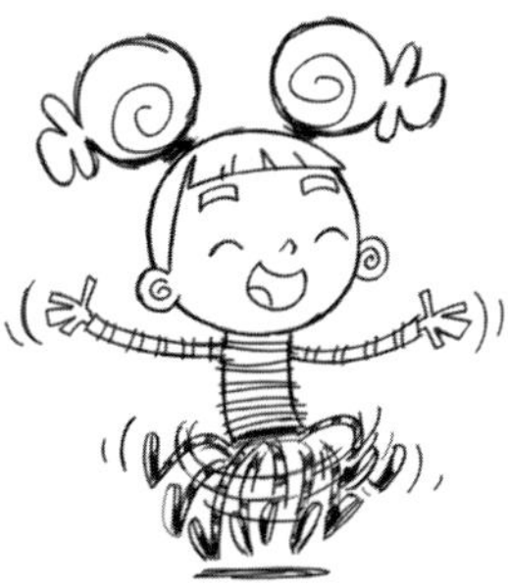

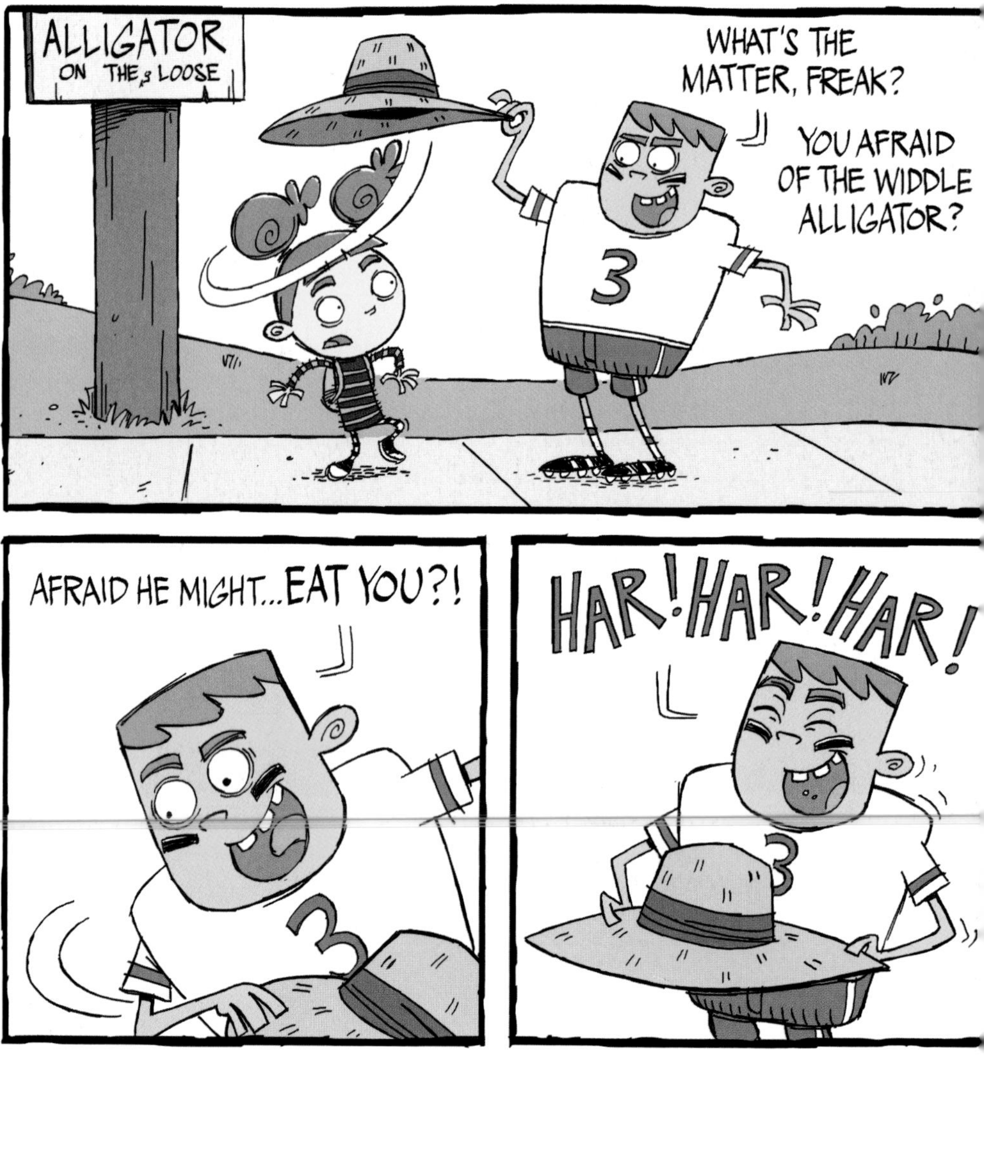
ALLIGATOR ON THE LOOSE
WHAT'S THE MATTER, FREAK?
YOU AFRAID OF THE WIDDLE ALLIGATOR?
AFRAID HE MIGHT...EAT YOU?!
HAR! HAR! HAR!

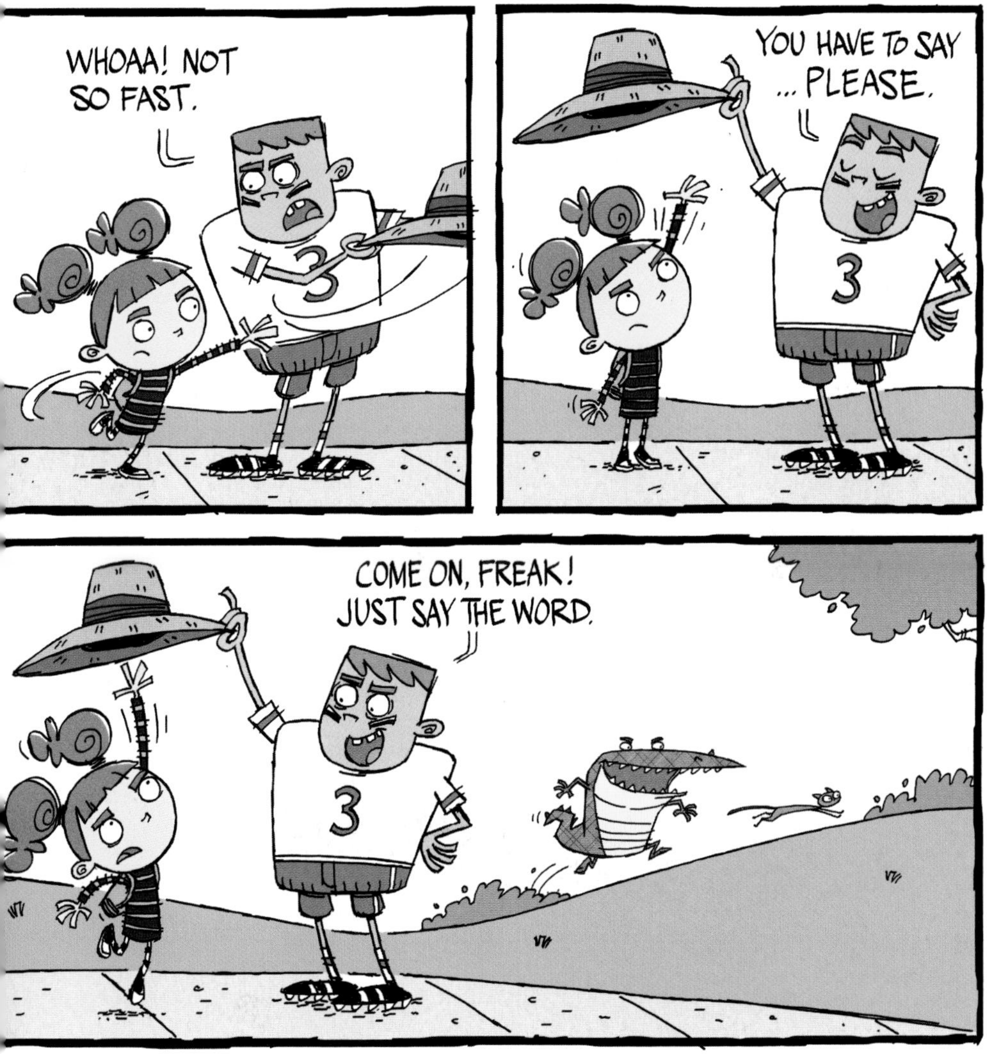
WHOAA! NOT SO FAST.
YOU HAVE TO SAY ...PLEASE.
COME ON, FREAK! JUST SAY THE WORD.

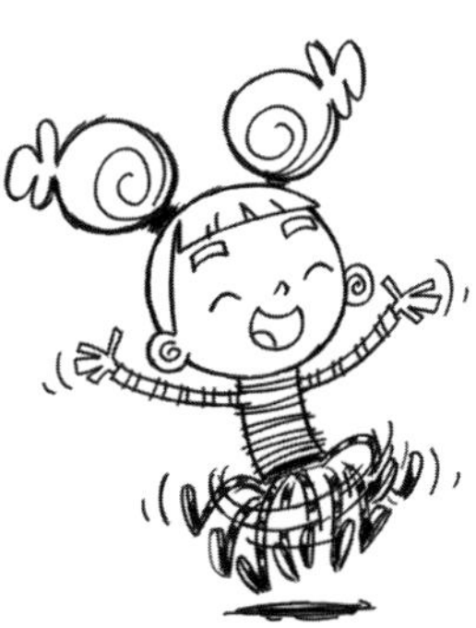

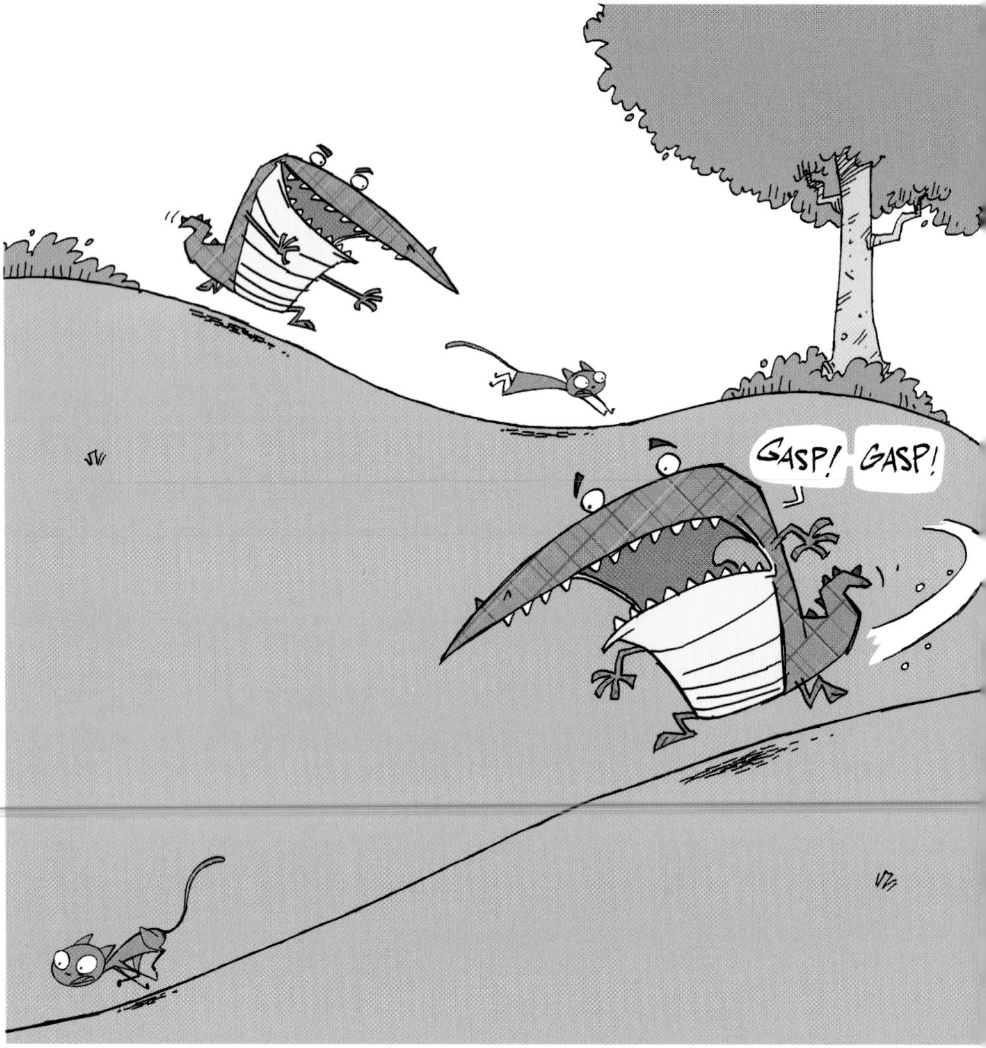
GASP! GASP!

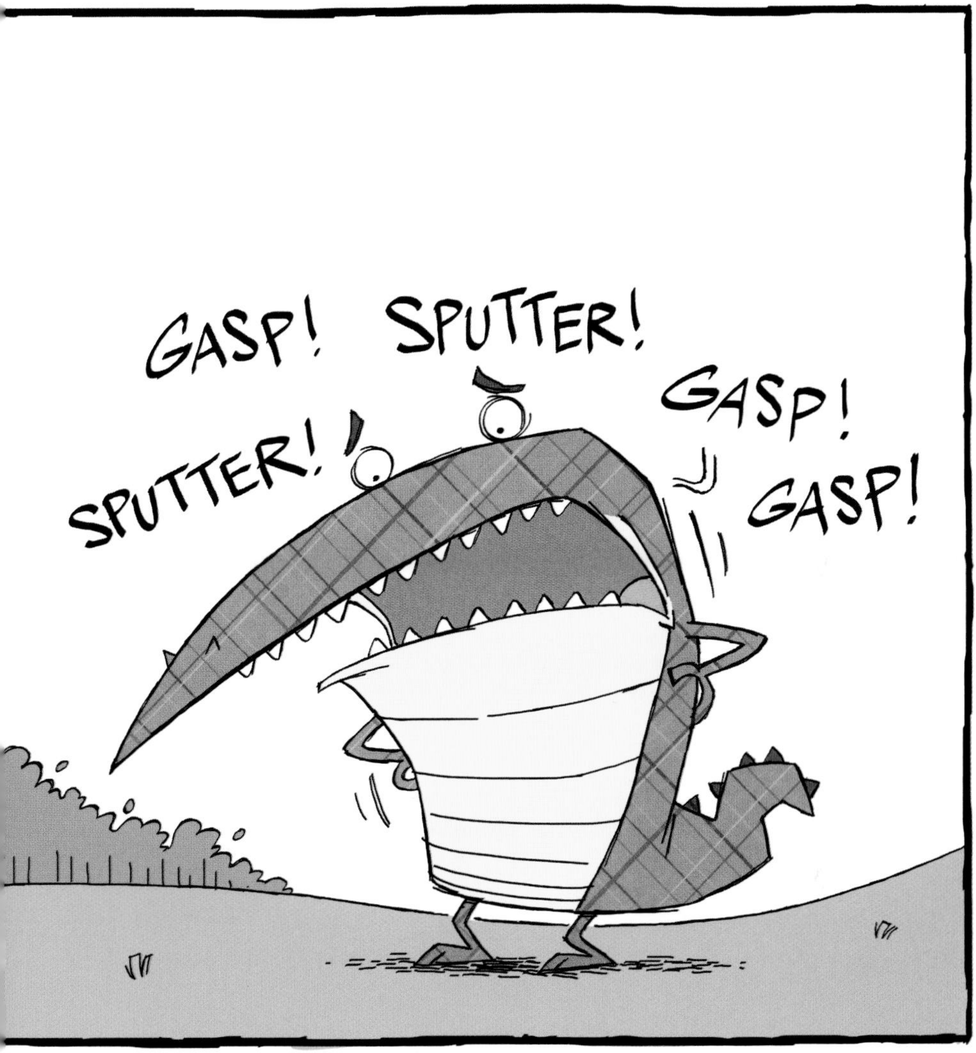
GASP!
SPUTTER!
SPUTTER!
GASP!
GASP!

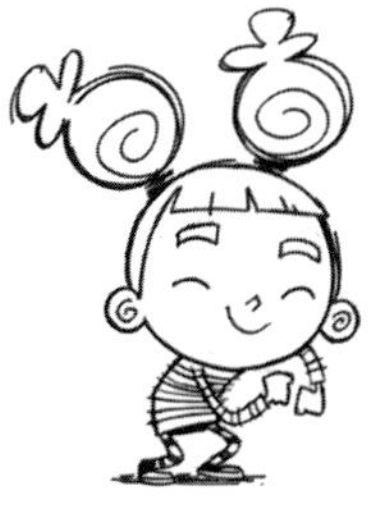

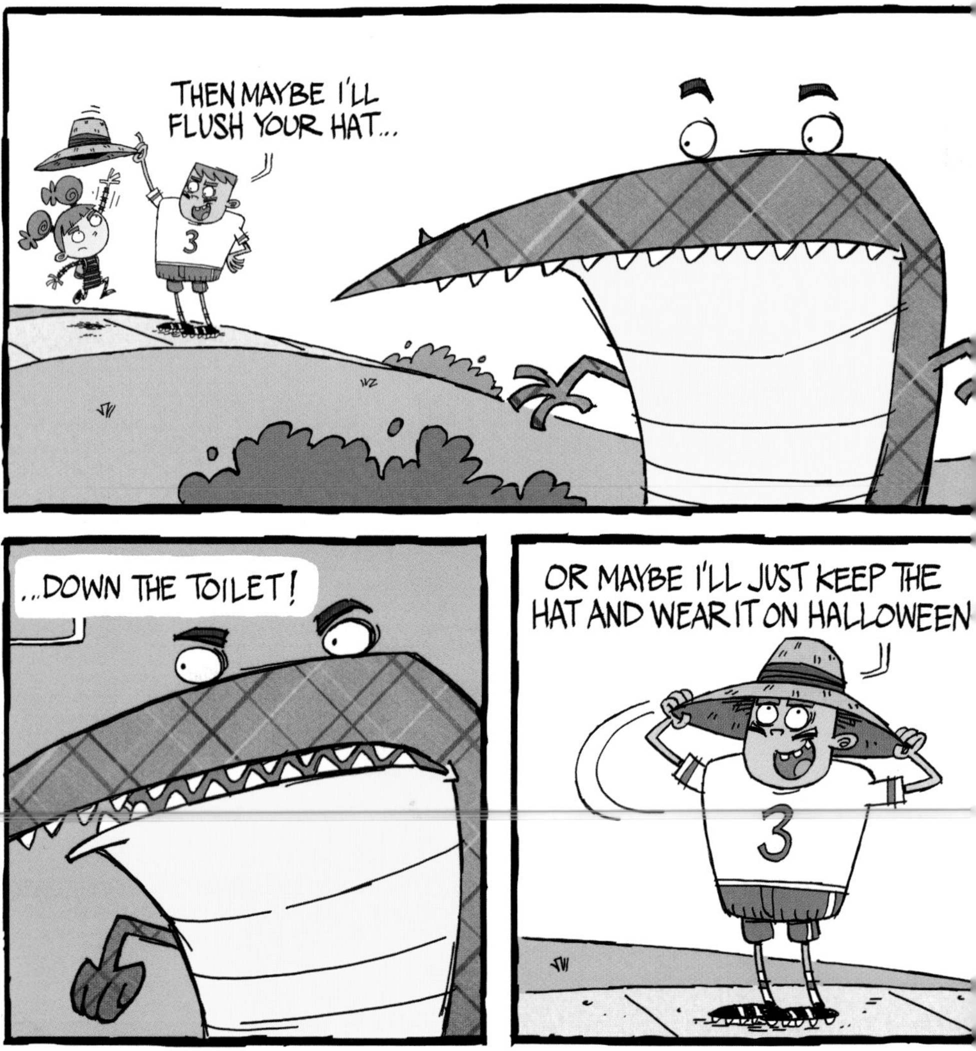
THEN MAYBE I'LL FLUSH YOUR HAT...
...DOWN THE TOILET!
OR MAYBE I'LL JUST KEEP THE HAT AND WEAR IT ON HALLOWEEN

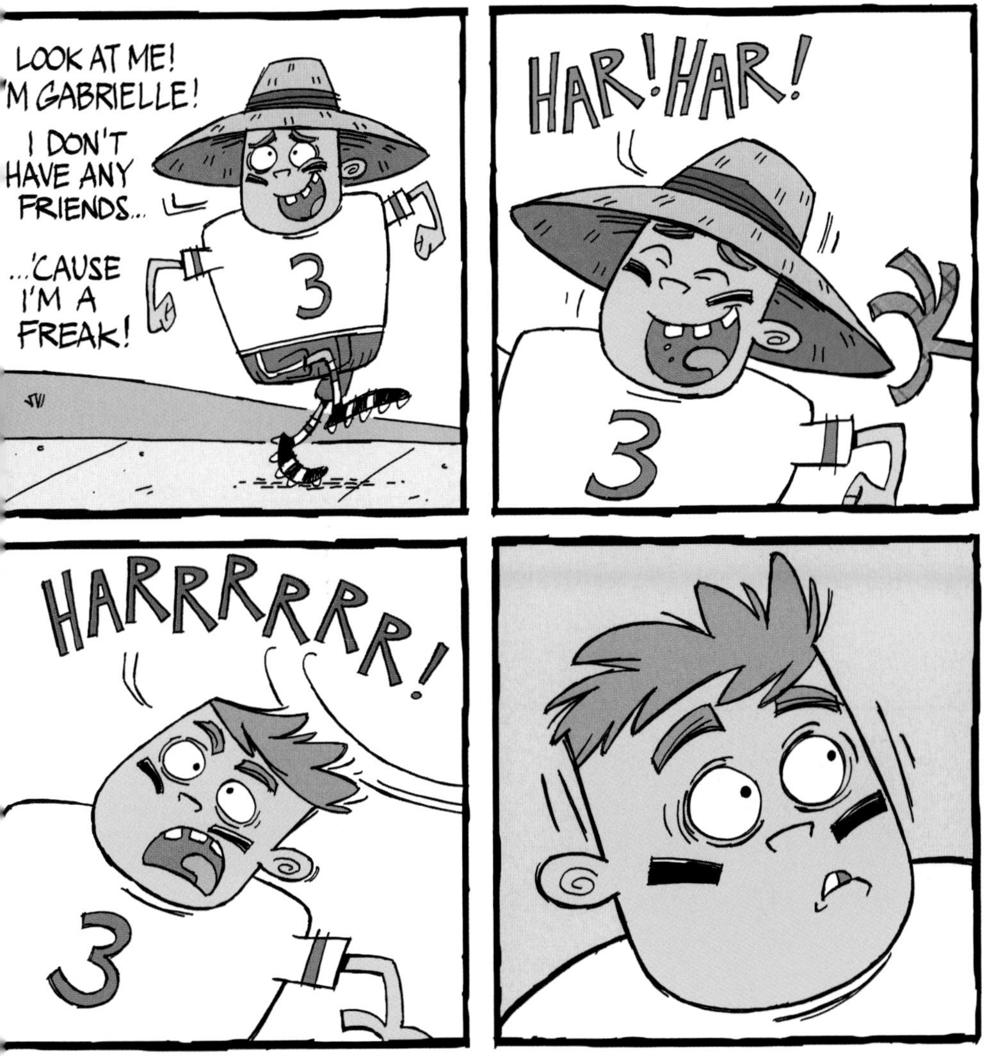
LOOK AT ME!
'M GABRIELLE!
I DON'T HAVE ANY FRIENDS...
...'CAUSE I'M A FREAK!
3
HAR! HAR!
3
HARRRRRR!
3

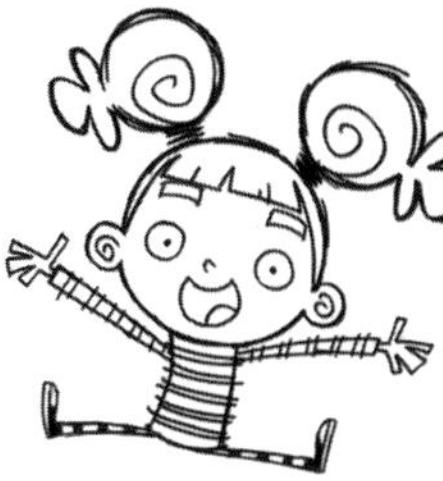

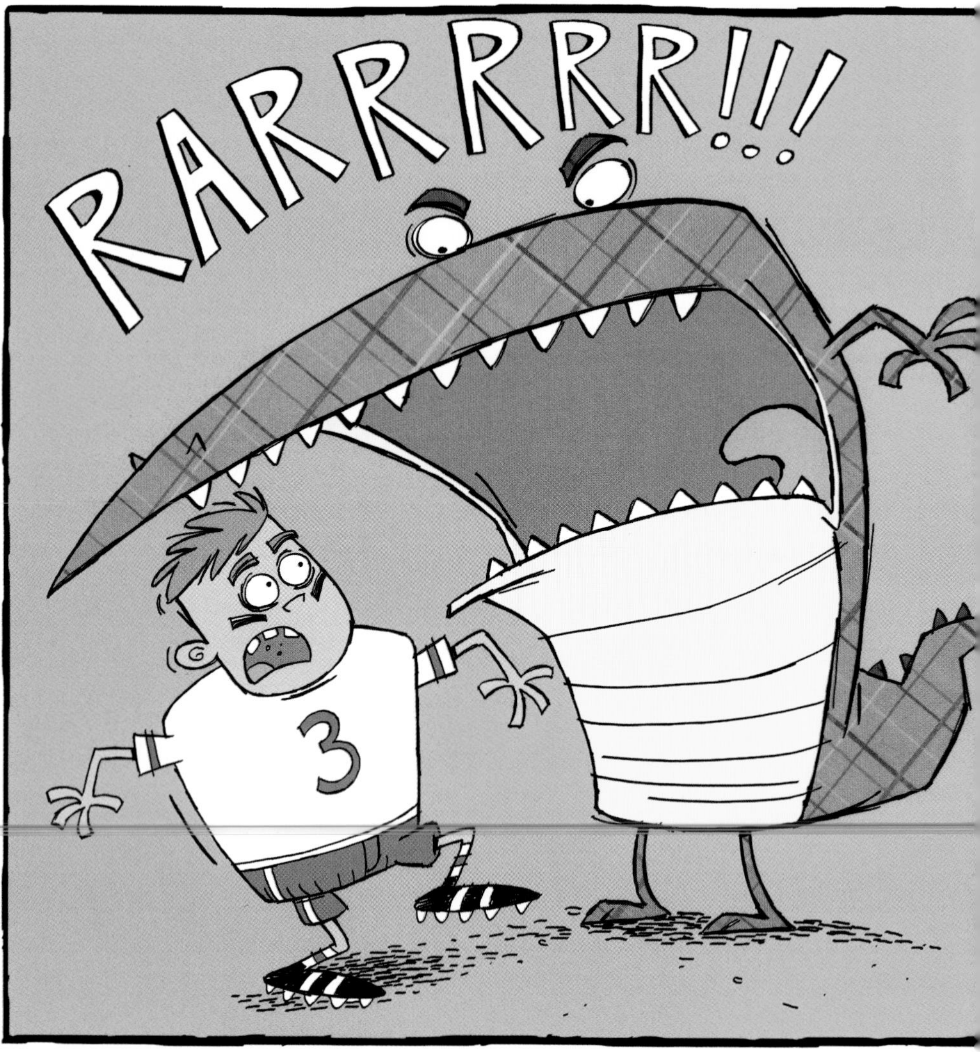
RARRRRRR!!!
3

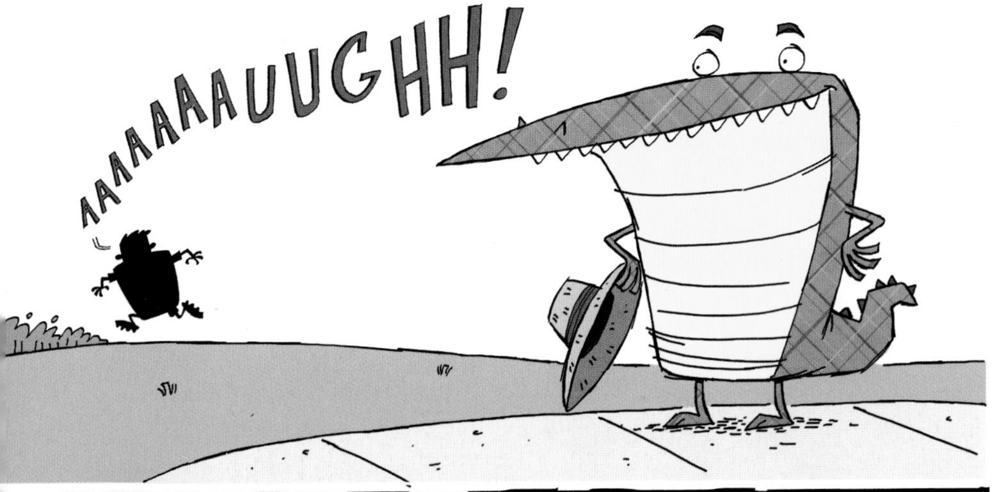
AAAAAAAUUGHH!

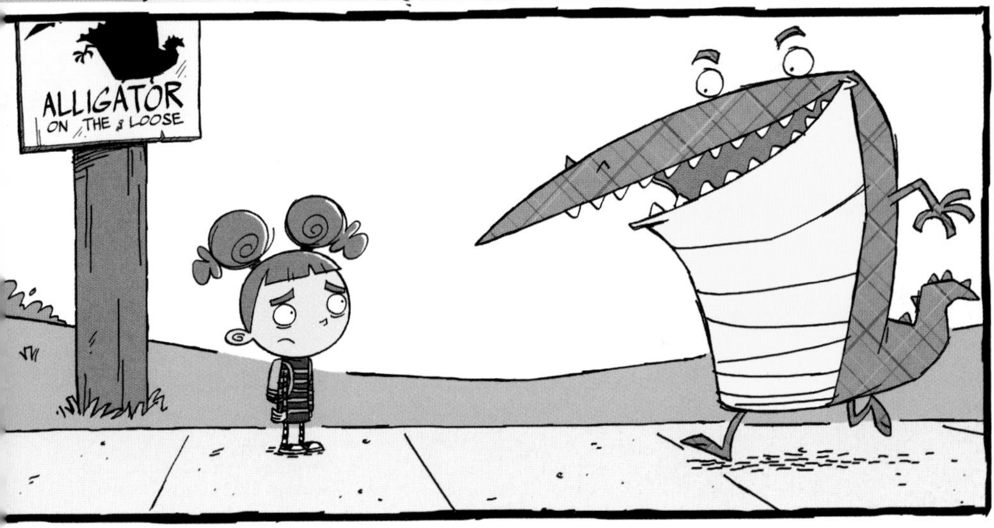
ALLIGATOR ON THE LOOSE

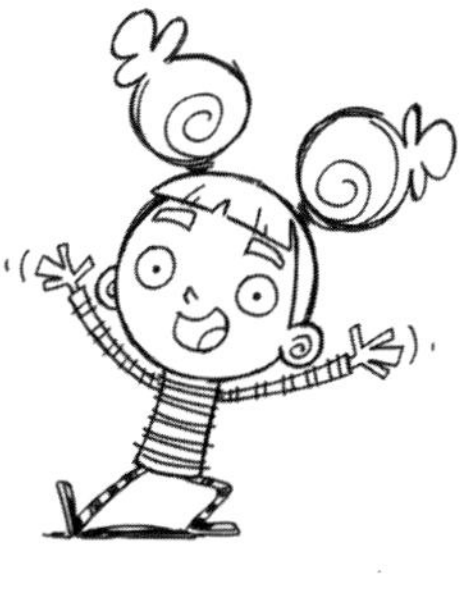

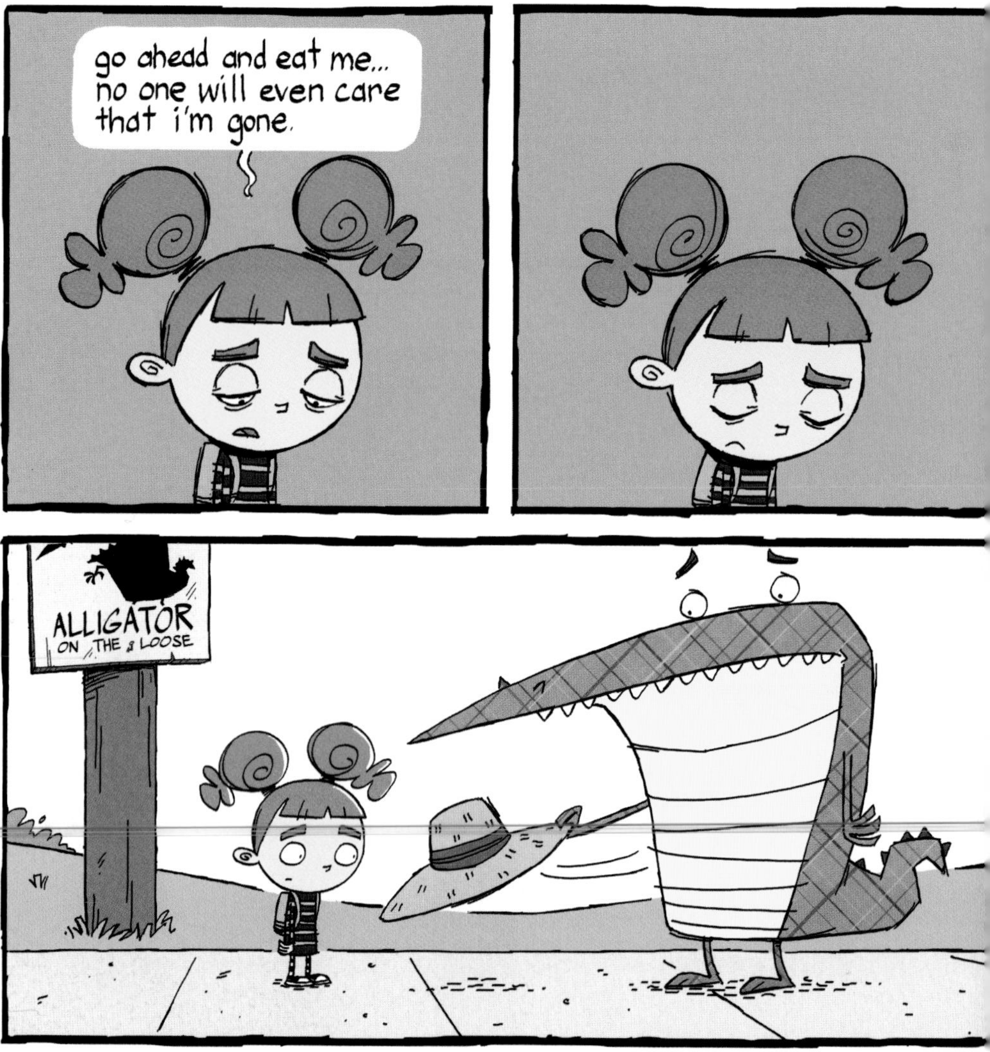
go ahead and eat me...
no one will even care
that i'm gone.
ALLIGATOR
ON THE LOOSE

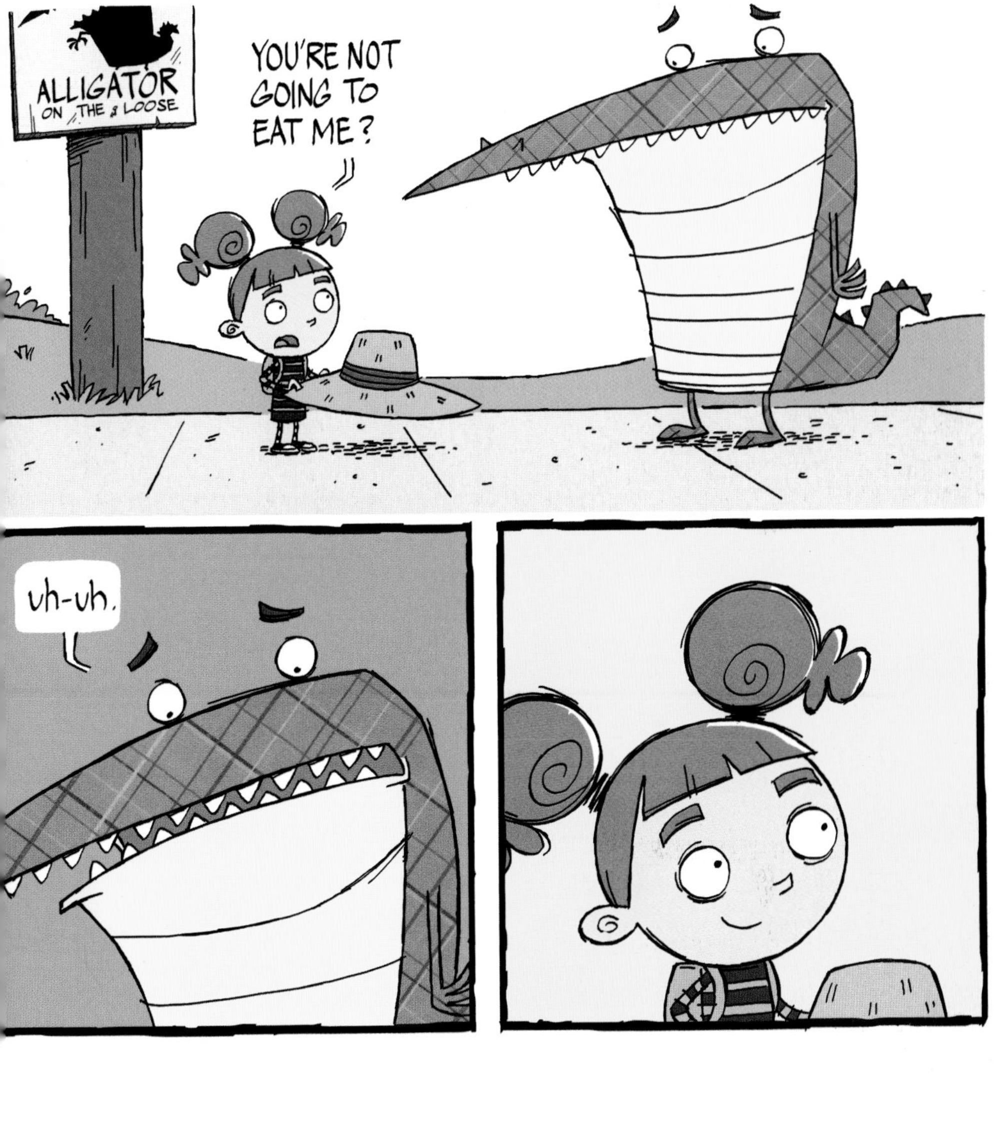
ALLIGATOR ON THE LOOSE
YOU'RE NOT GOING TO EAT ME?
uh-uh.

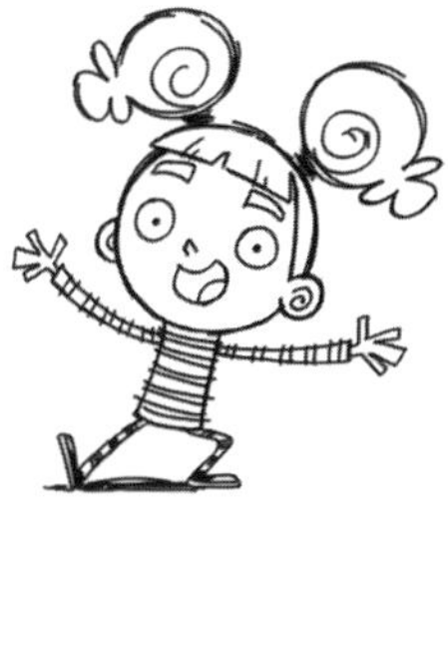

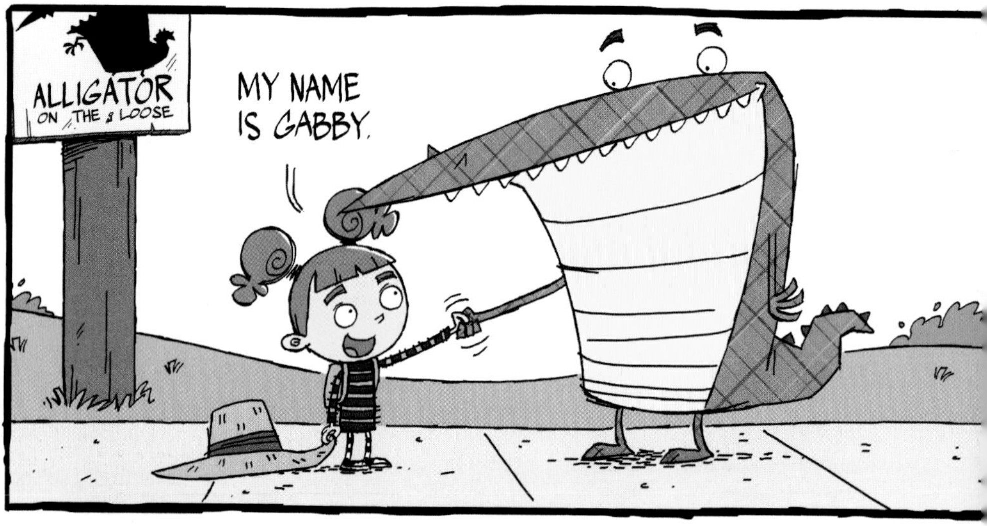
ALLIGATOR ON THE LOOSE
MY NAME IS GABBY.

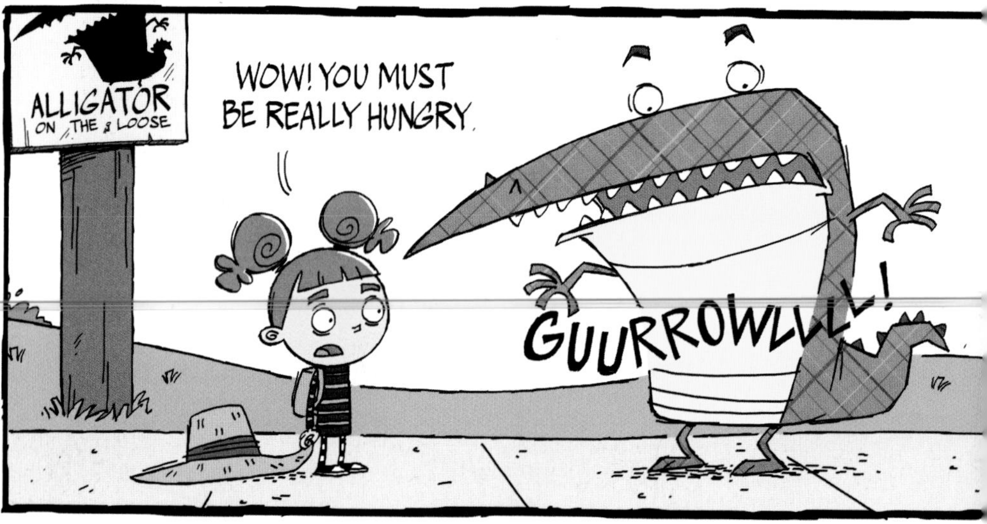
ALLIGATOR ON THE LOOSE
WOW! YOU MUST BE REALLY HUNGRY.
GUURROWLLLL!

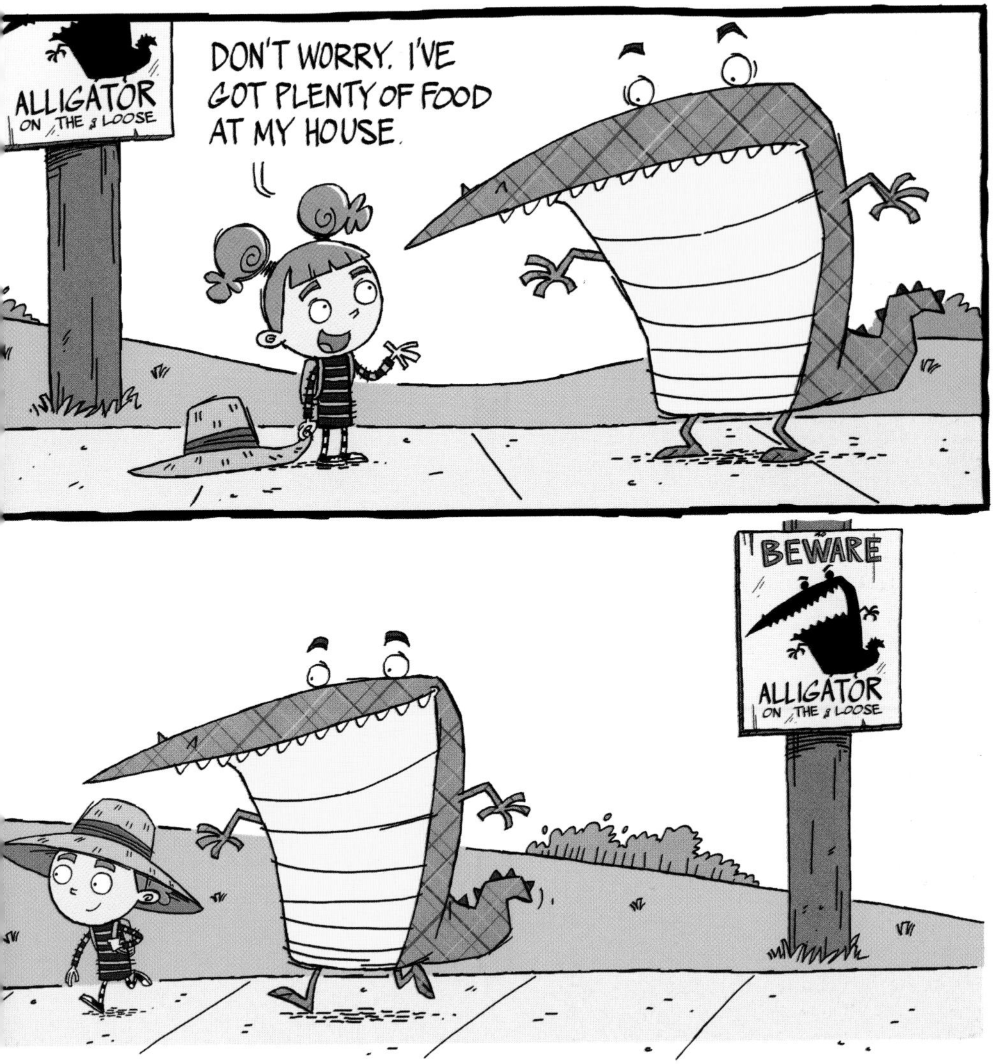
ALLIGATOR
ON THE LOOSE
DON'T WORRY. I'VE GOT PLENTY OF FOOD AT MY HOUSE.
BEWARE
ALLIGATOR
ON THE LOOSE

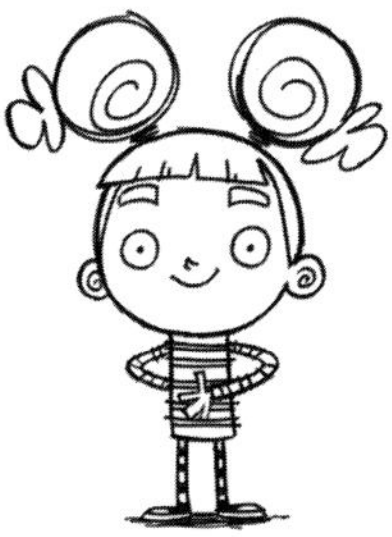

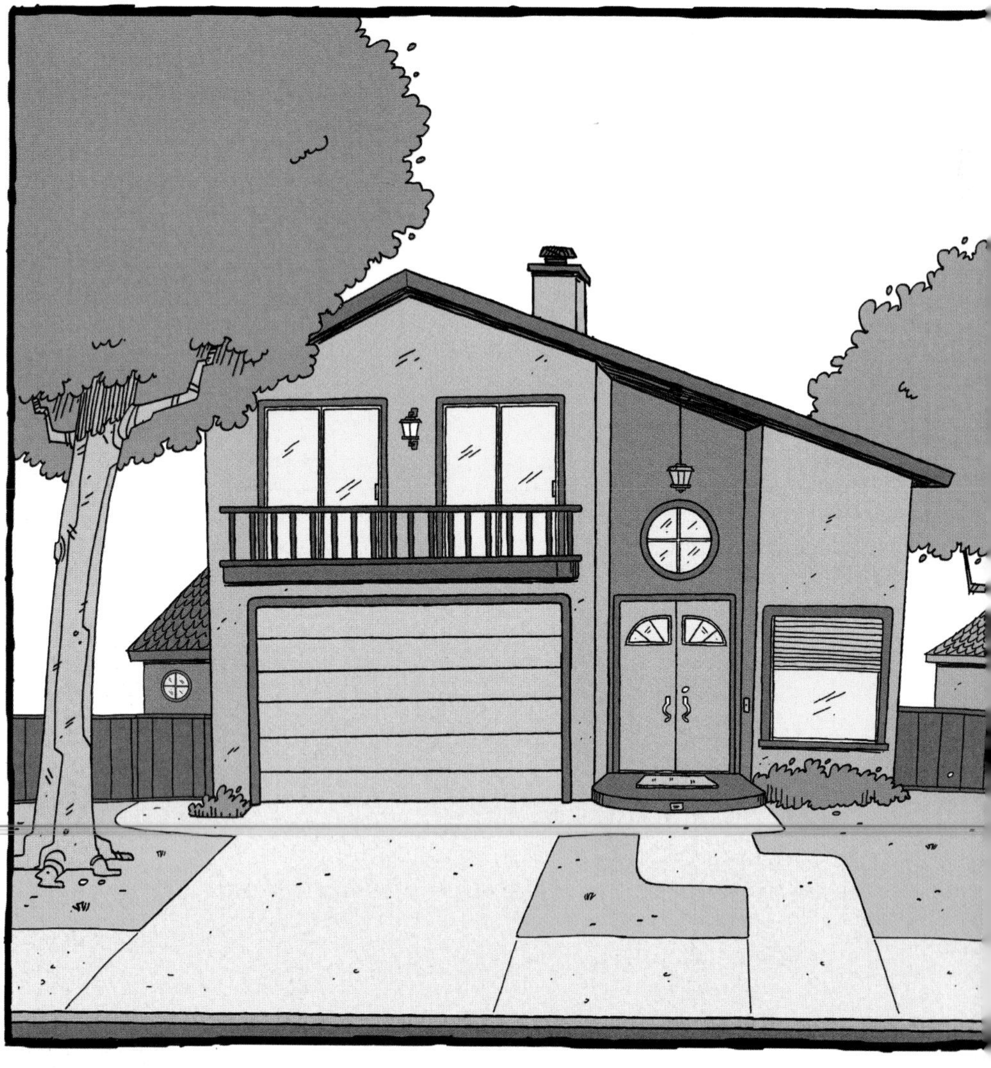

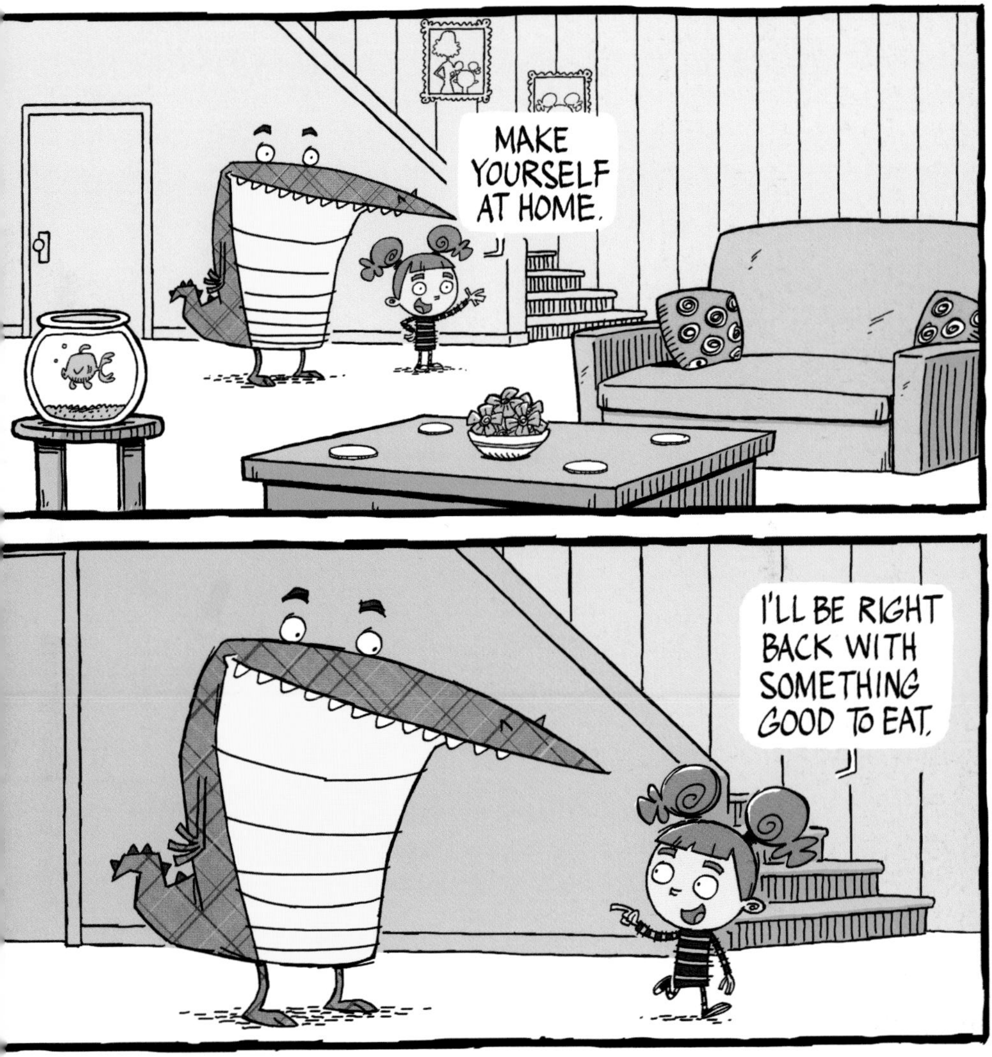
MAKE YOURSELF AT HOME.
I'LL BE RIGHT BACK WITH SOMETHING GOOD TO EAT.

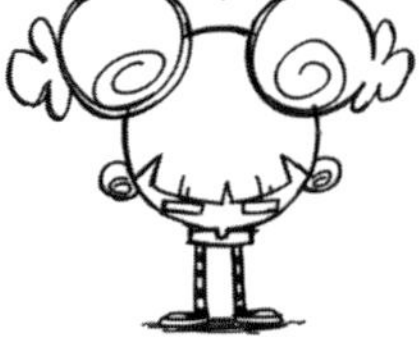

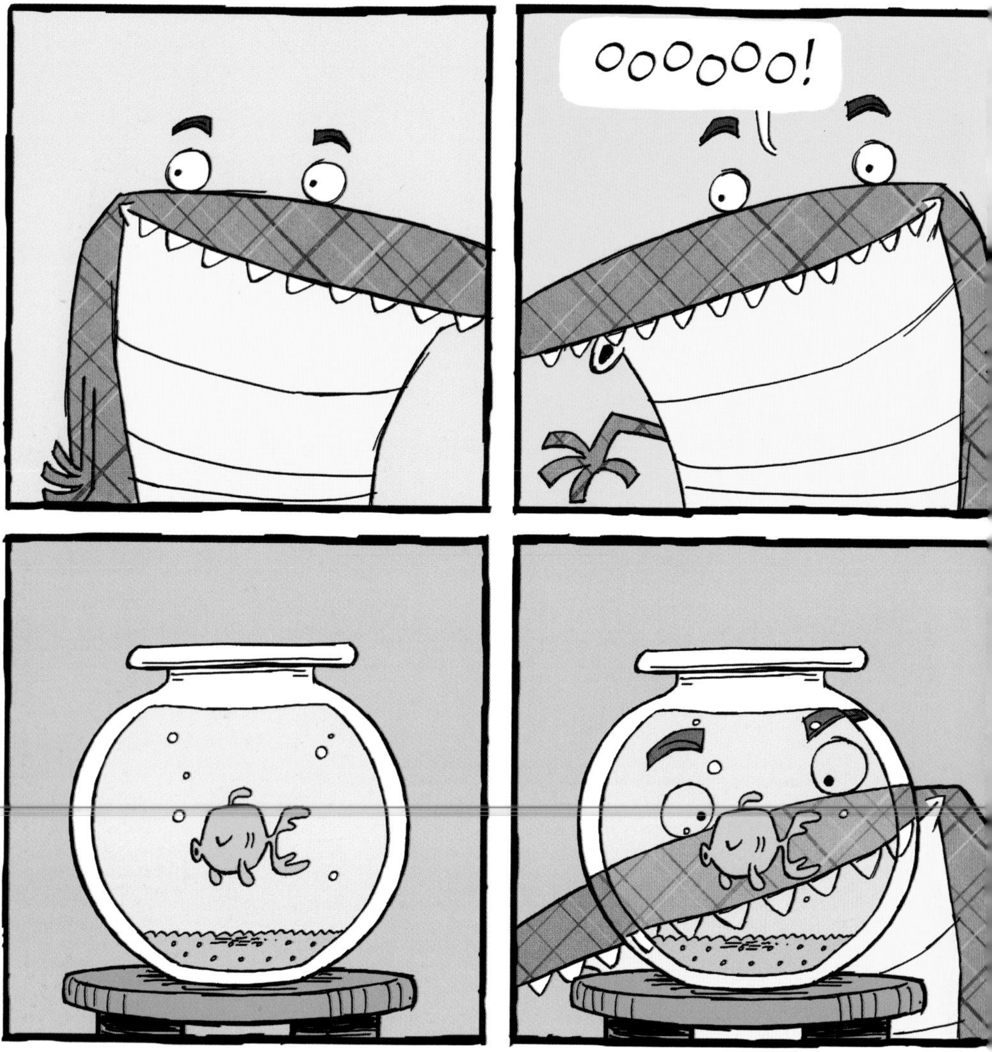
OOOOOO!

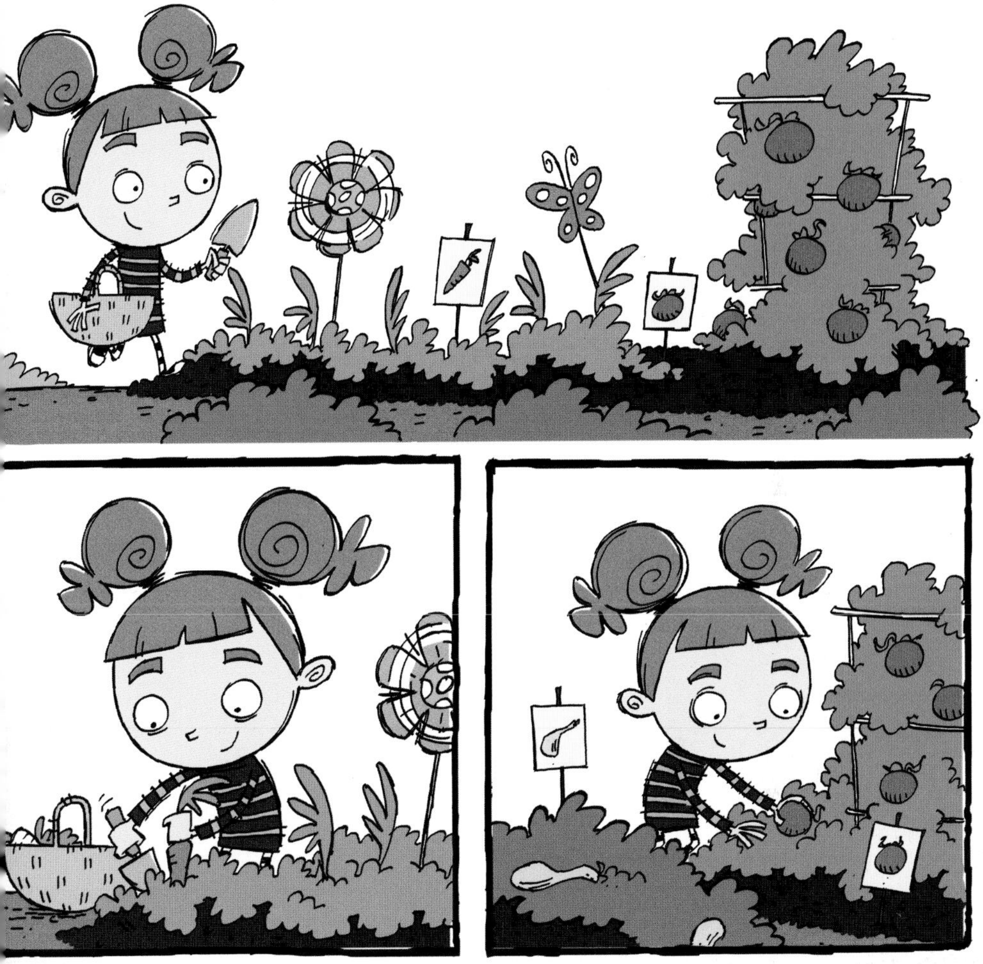

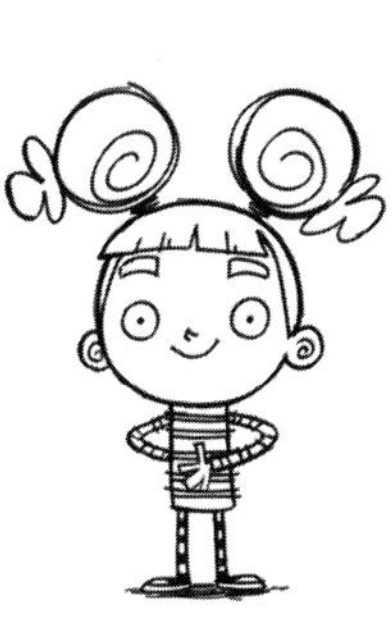

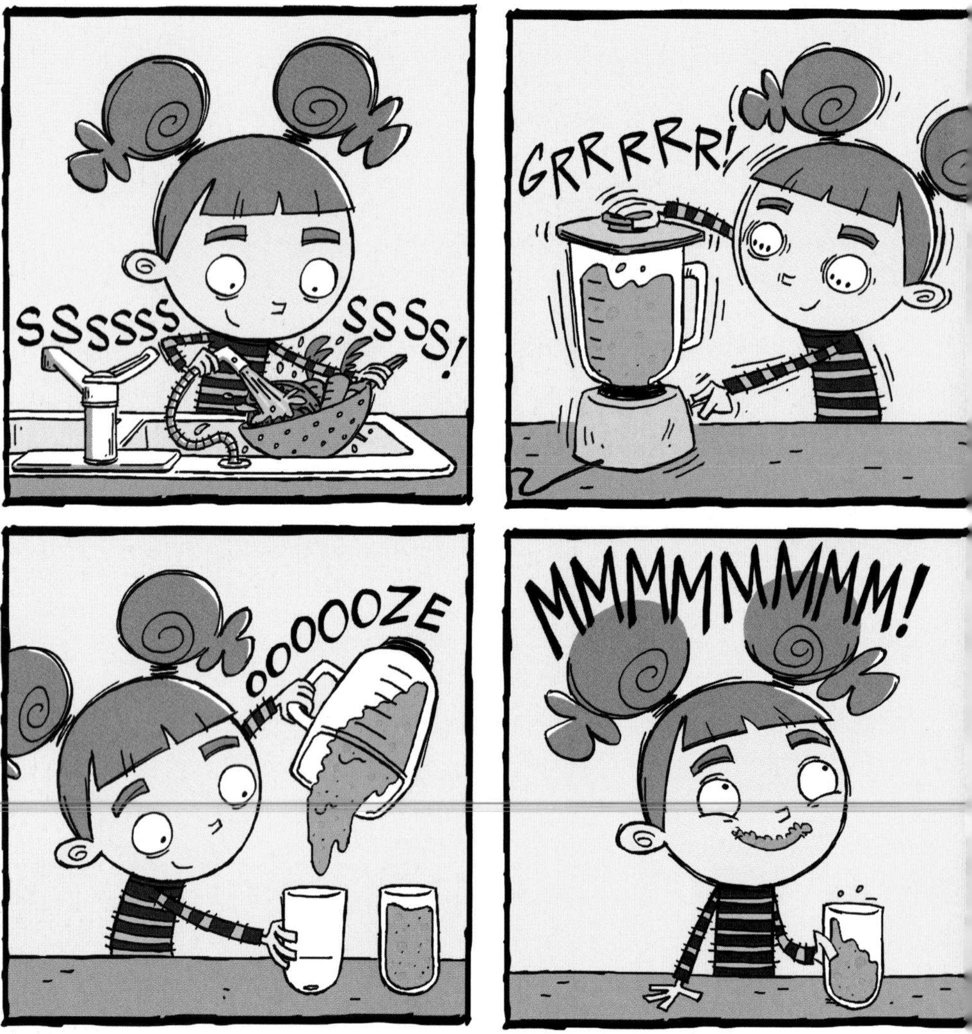
SSSSSS
SSSS!
GRRRRR!
OOOOOZE
MMMMMMMM!

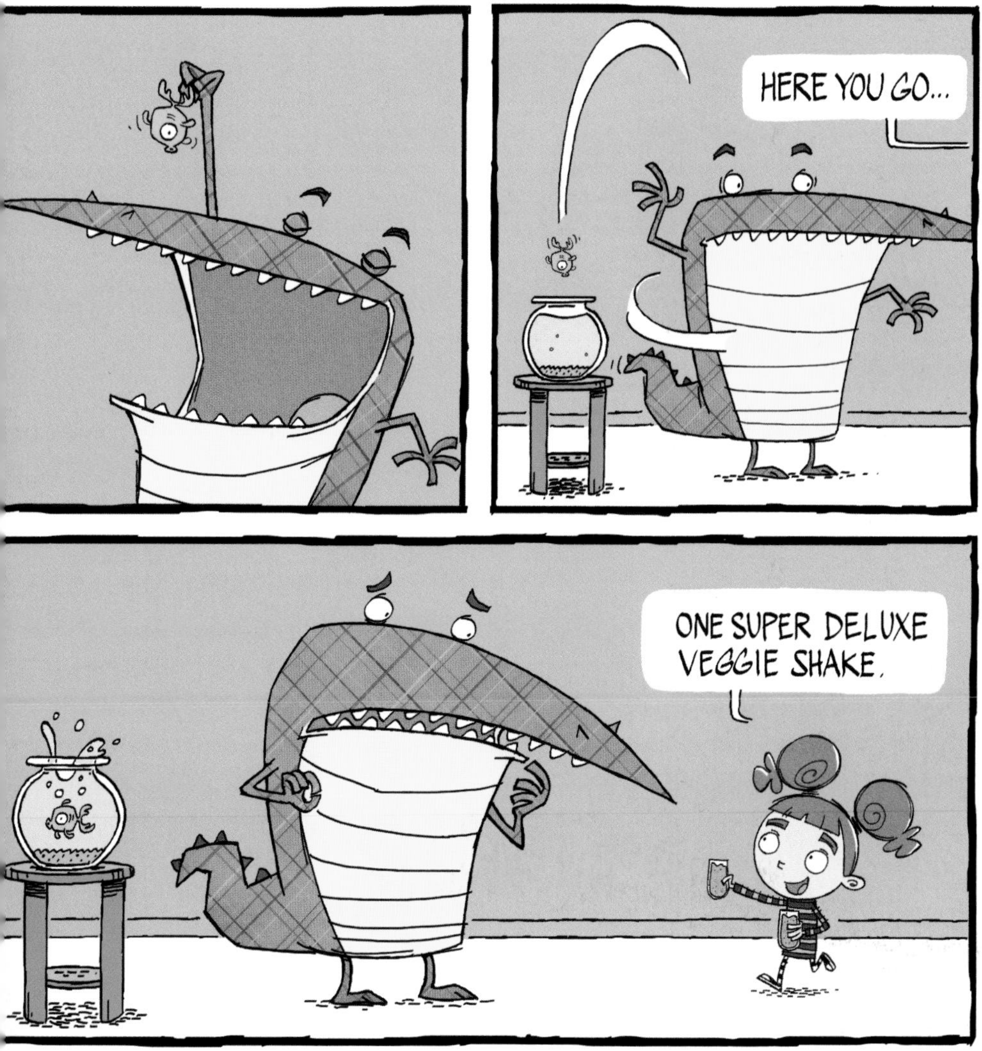
HERE YOU GO...
ONE SUPER DELUXE VEGGIE SHAKE.

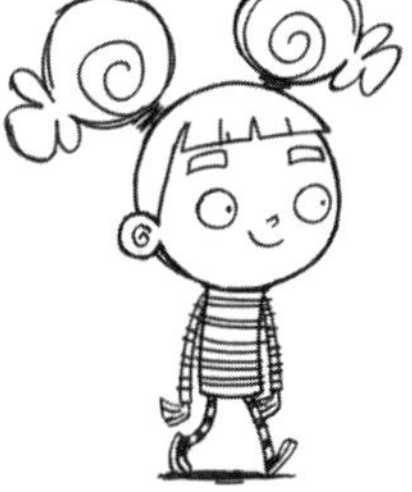

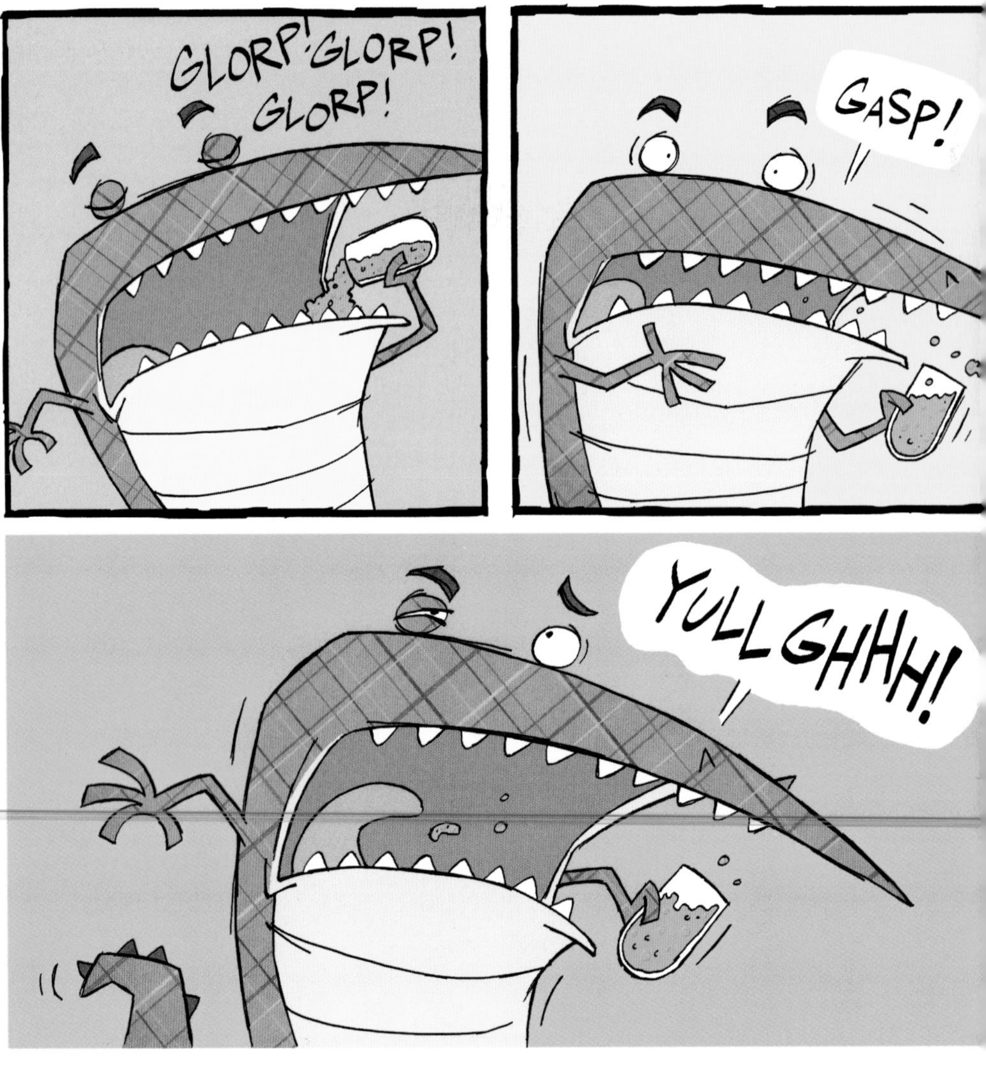
GLORP! GLORP!
GLORP!
GASP!
YULLGHHH!

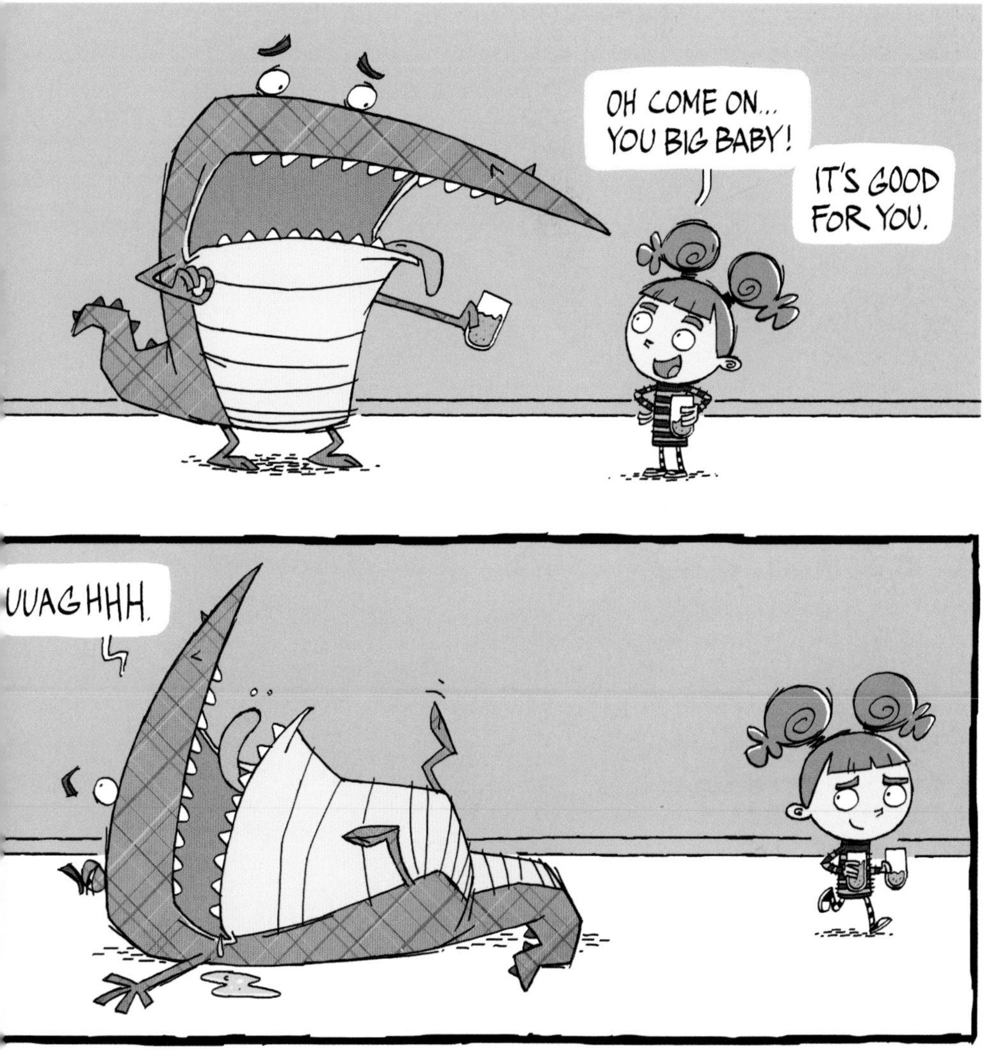
OH COME ON...
YOU BIG BABY!
IT'S GOOD
FOR YOU.
UUAGHHH.

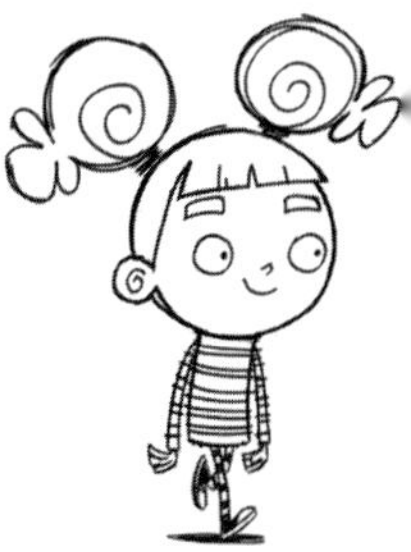

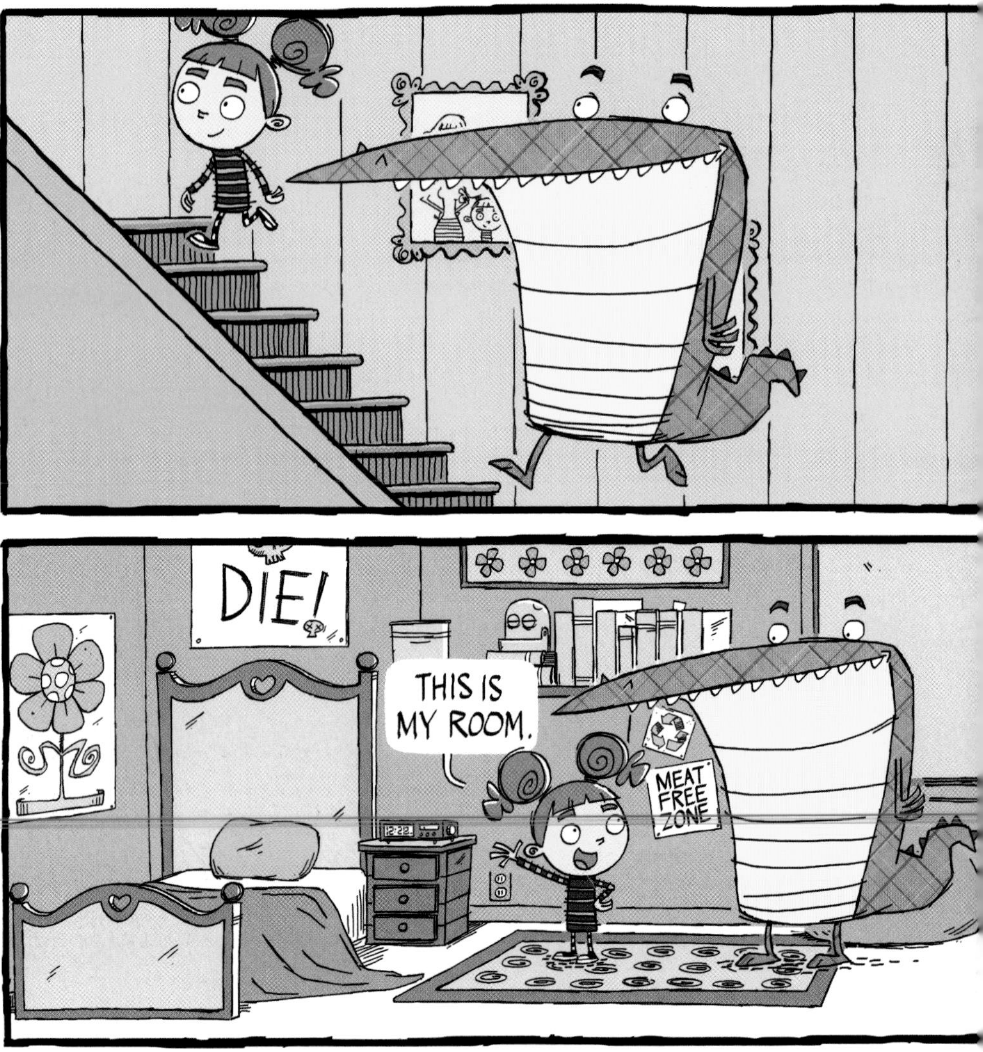
DIE!
THIS IS MY ROOM.
MEAT FREE ZONE

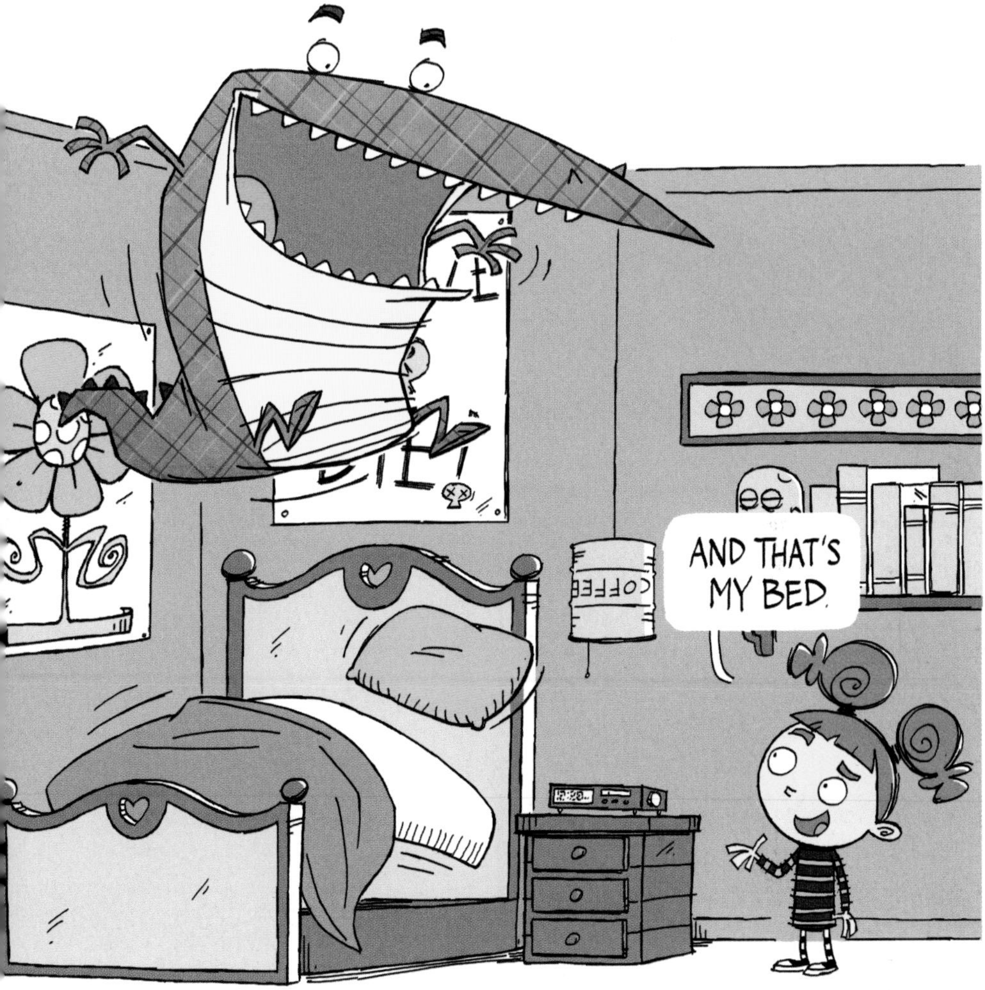
AND THAT'S MY BED.

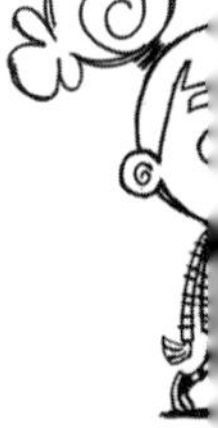

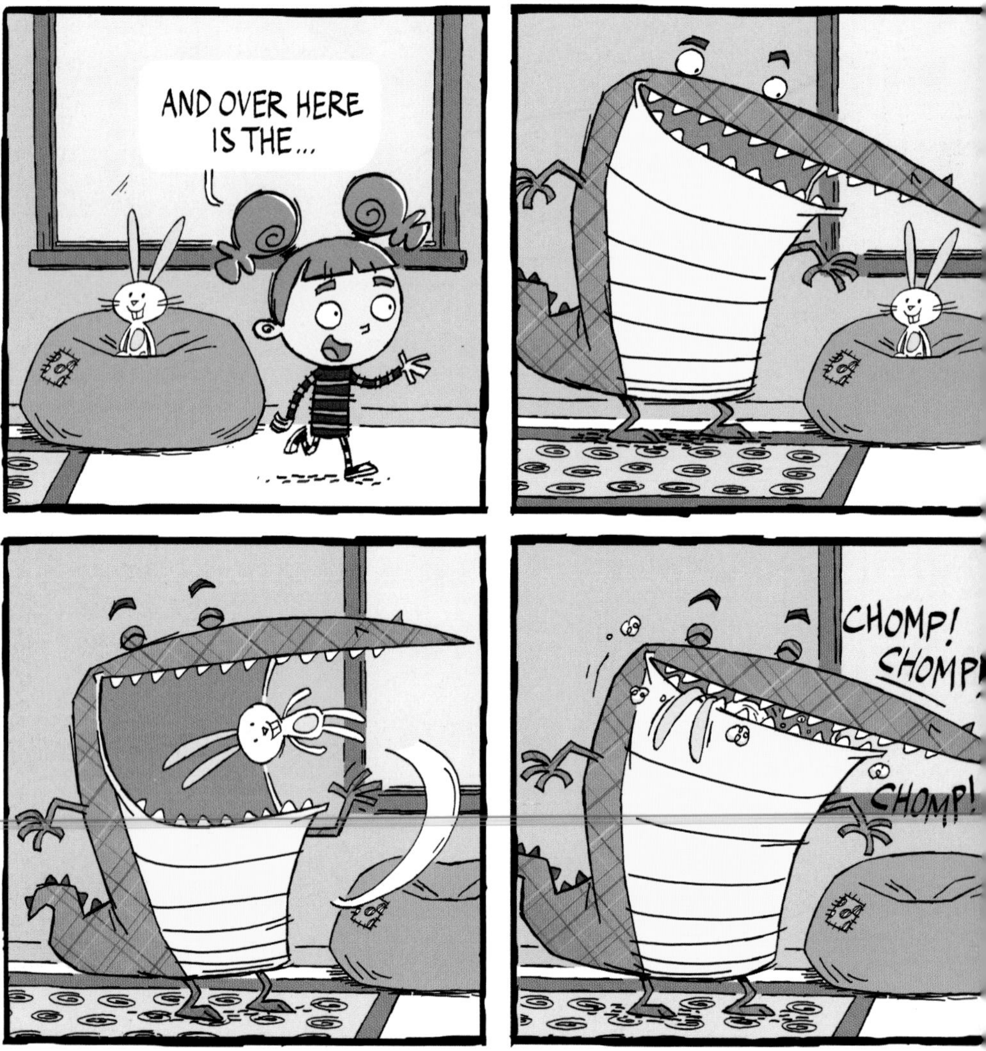
AND OVER HERE IS THE...
CHOMP!
CHOMP!
CHOMP!

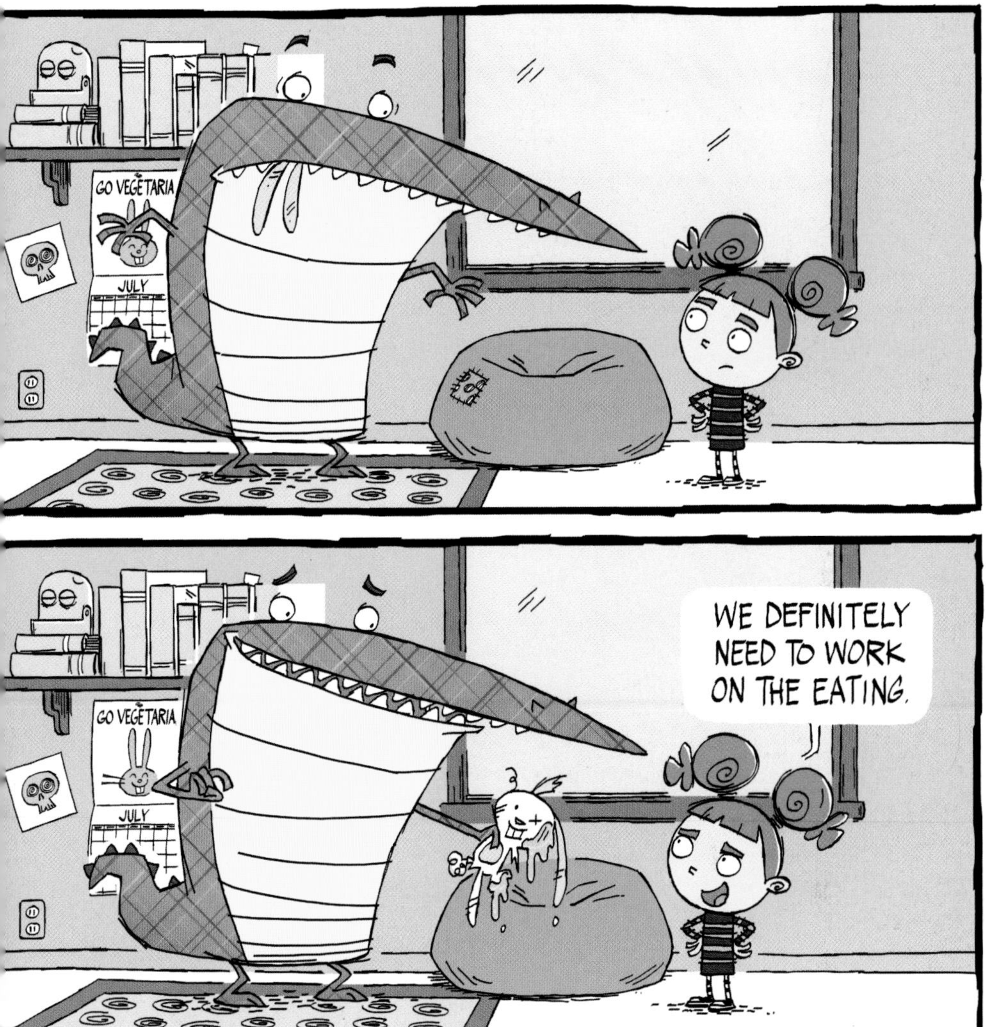
GO VEGETARIA
JULY
GO VEGETARIA
JULY
WE DEFINITELY NEED TO WORK ON THE EATING.

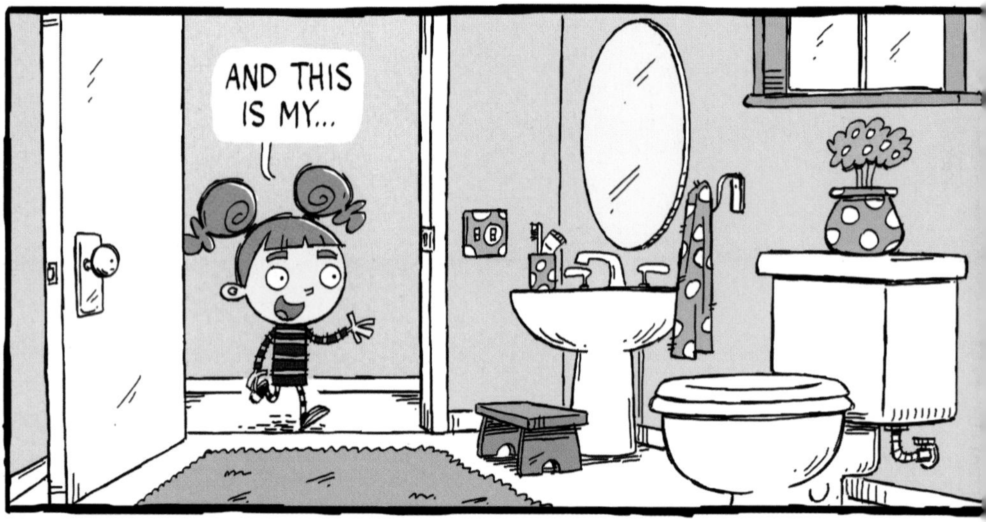
AND THIS IS MY...

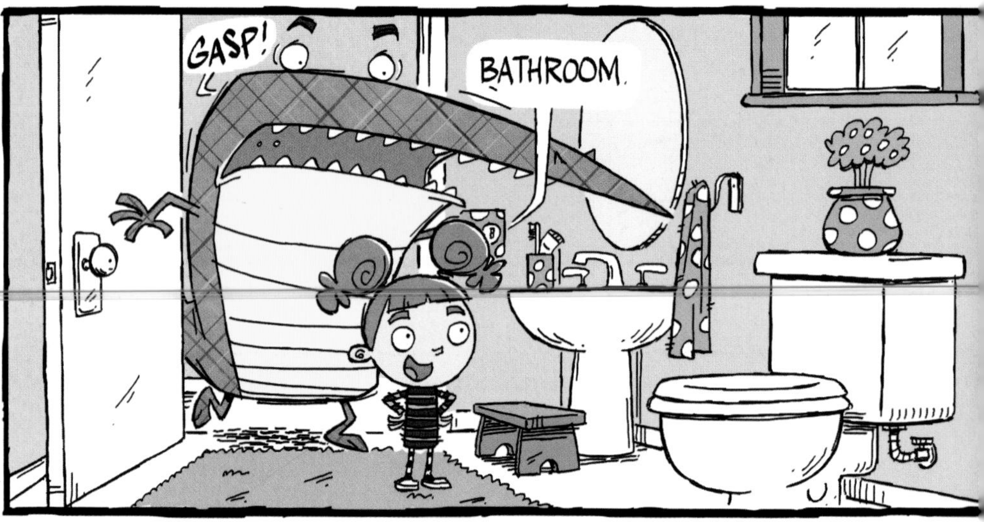
GASP!
BATHROOM.

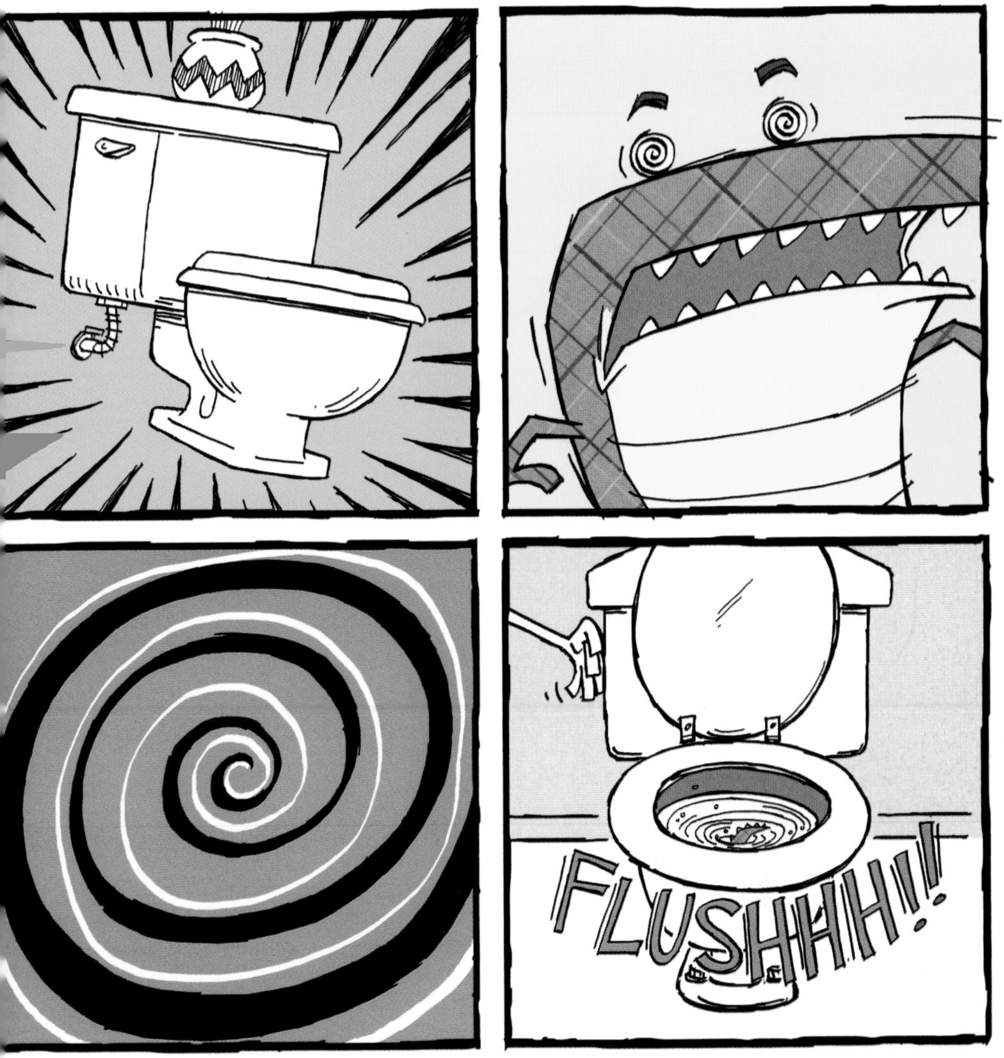
FLUSHHH!!!

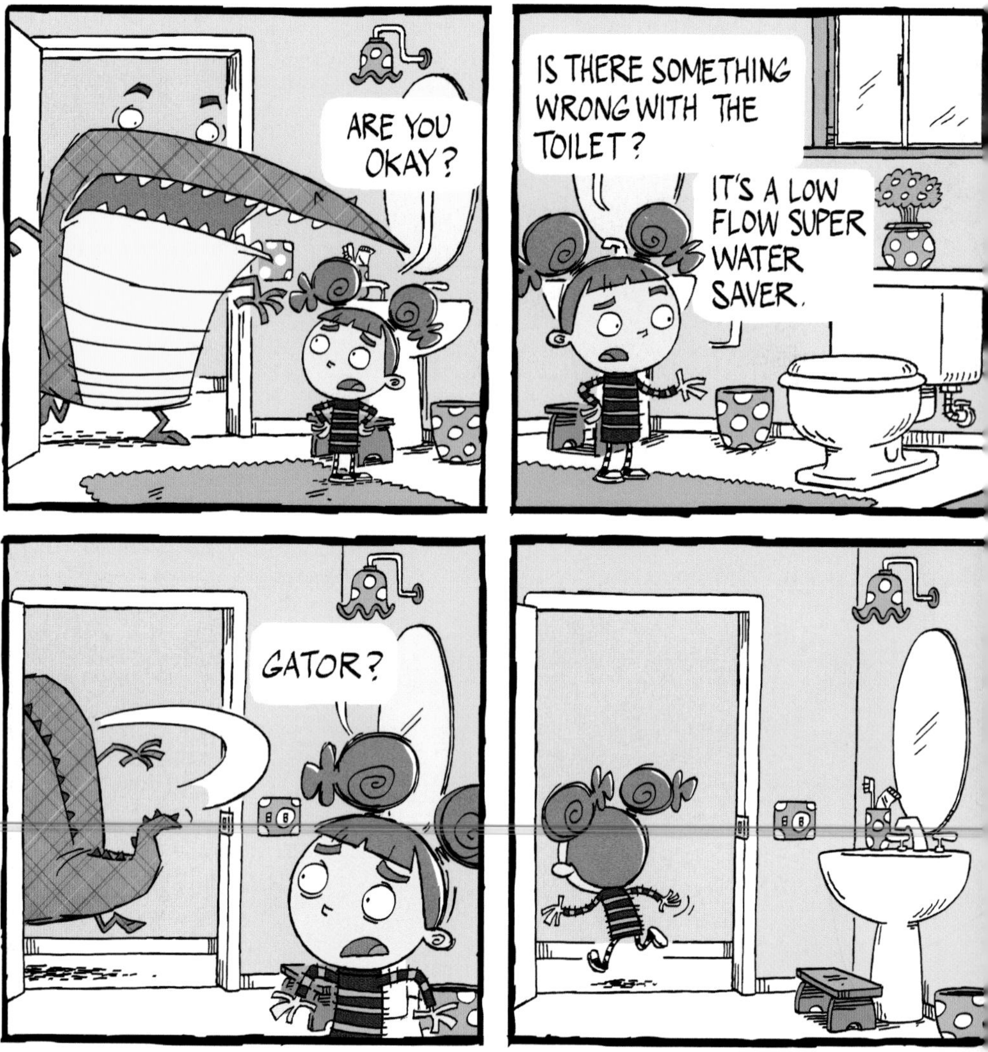
ARE YOU OKAY?
IS THERE SOMETHING WRONG WITH THE TOILET?
IT'S A LOW FLOW SUPER WATER SAVER.
GATOR?

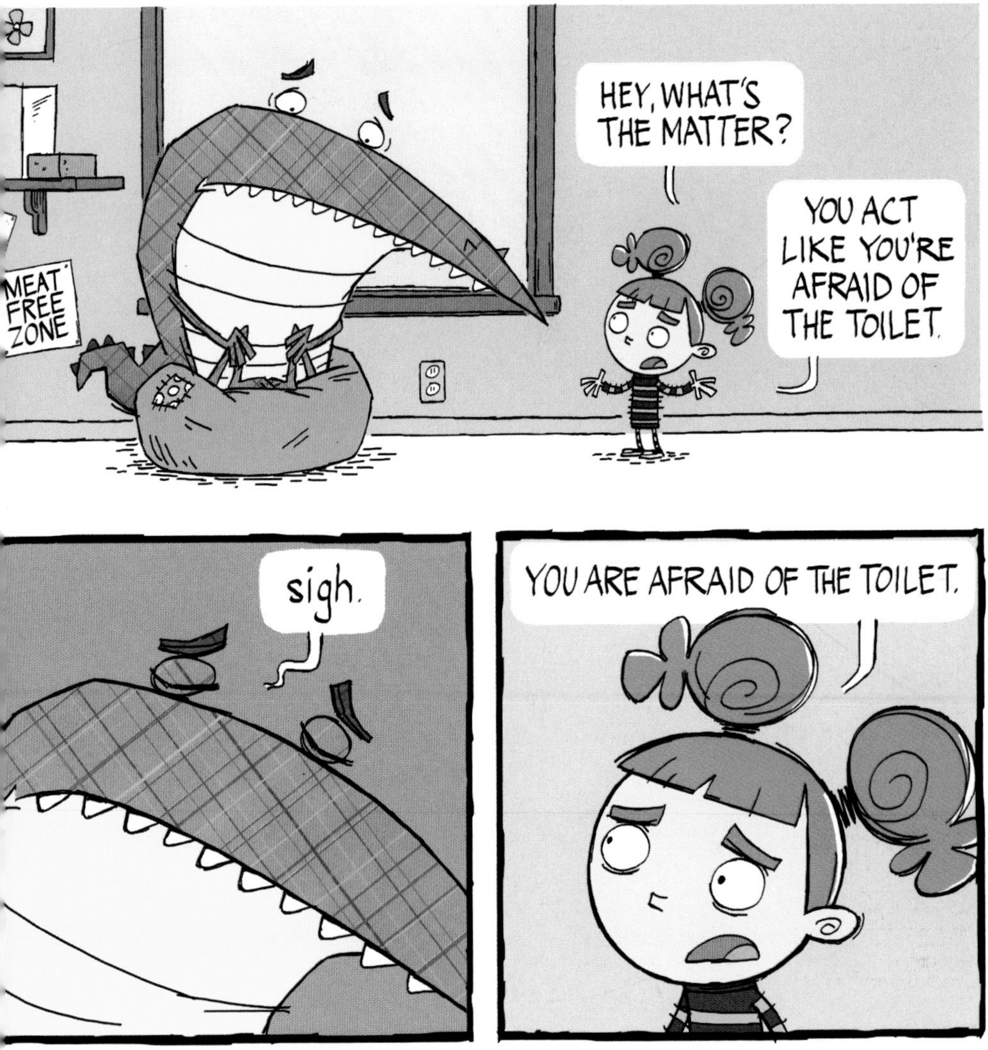
MEAT FREE ZONE
HEY, WHAT'S THE MATTER?
YOU ACT LIKE YOU'RE AFRAID OF THE TOILET.
sigh.
YOU ARE AFRAID OF THE TOILET.

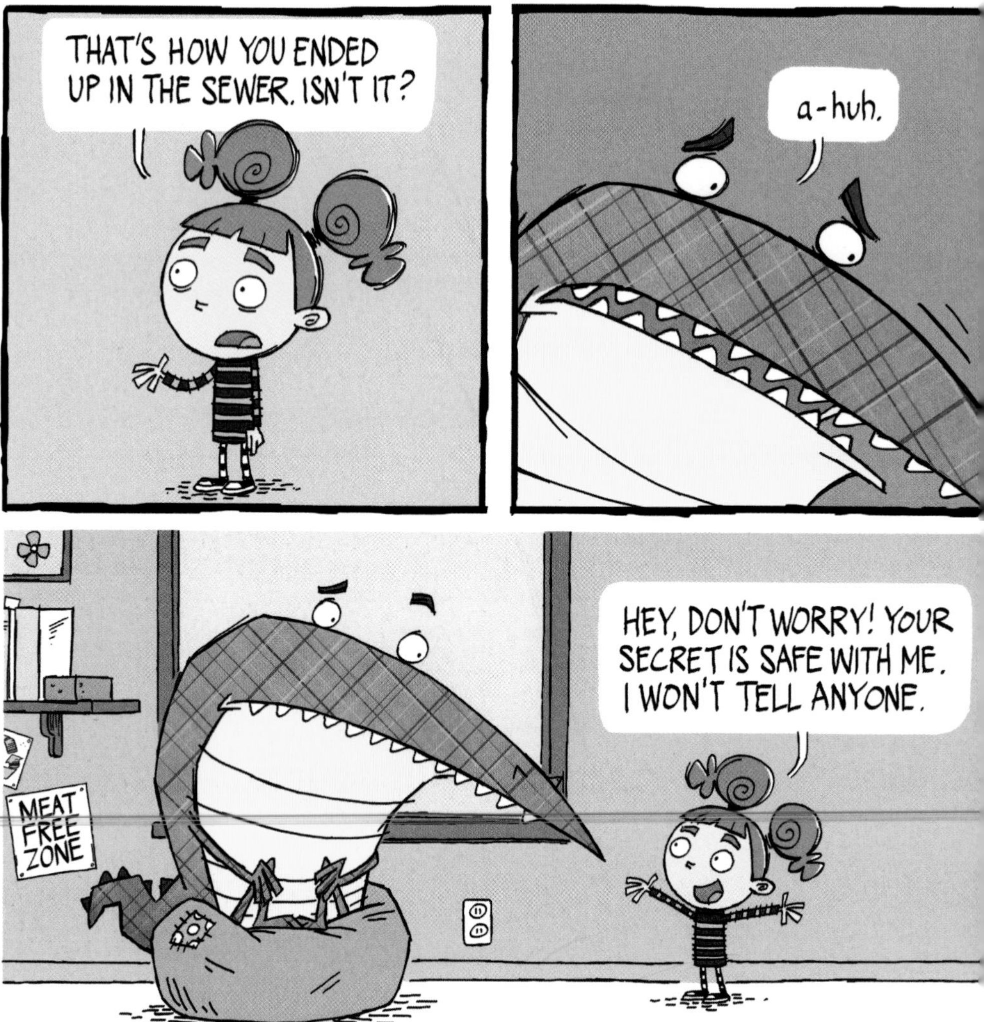
THAT'S HOW YOU ENDED UP IN THE SEWER, ISN'T IT?
a-huh.
MEAT FREE ZONE
HEY, DON'T WORRY! YOUR SECRET IS SAFE WITH ME. I WON'T TELL ANYONE.

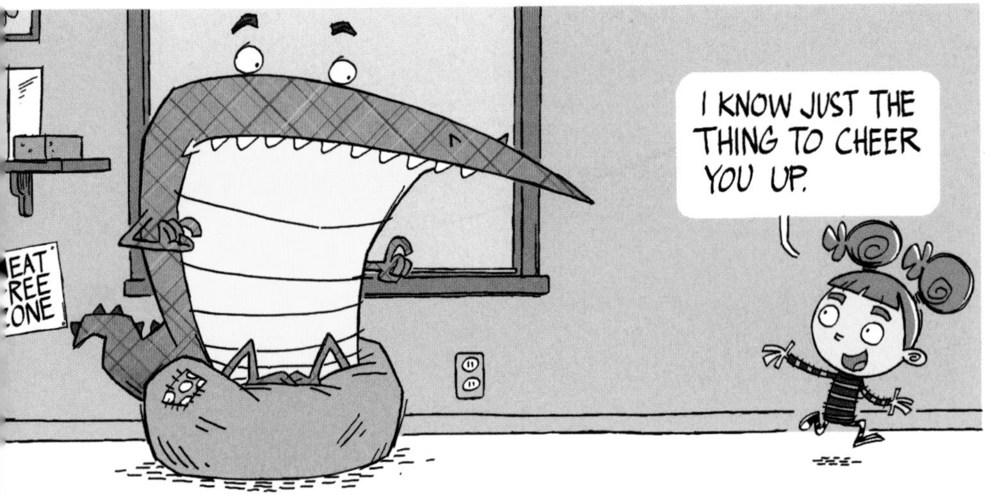
I KNOW JUST THE THING TO CHEER YOU UP.

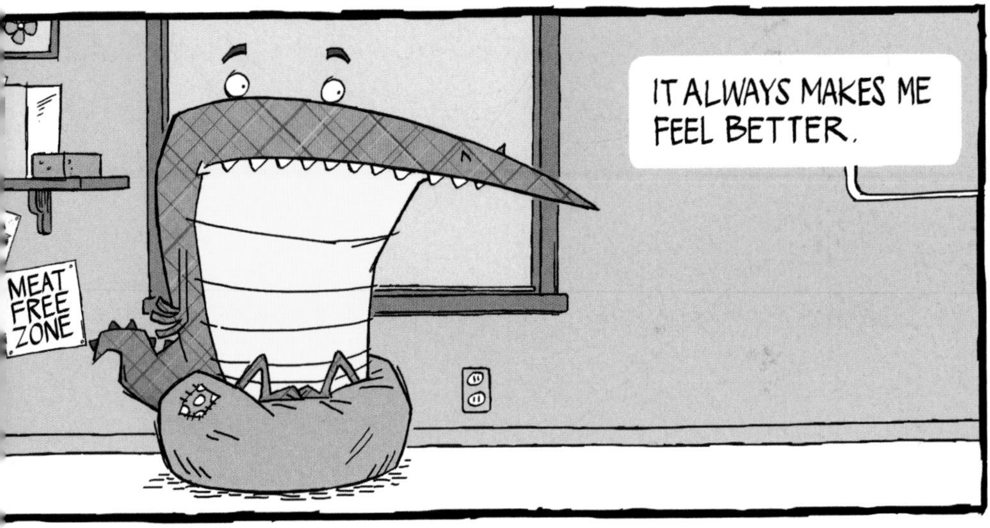
MEAT FREE ZONE
IT ALWAYS MAKES ME FEEL BETTER.

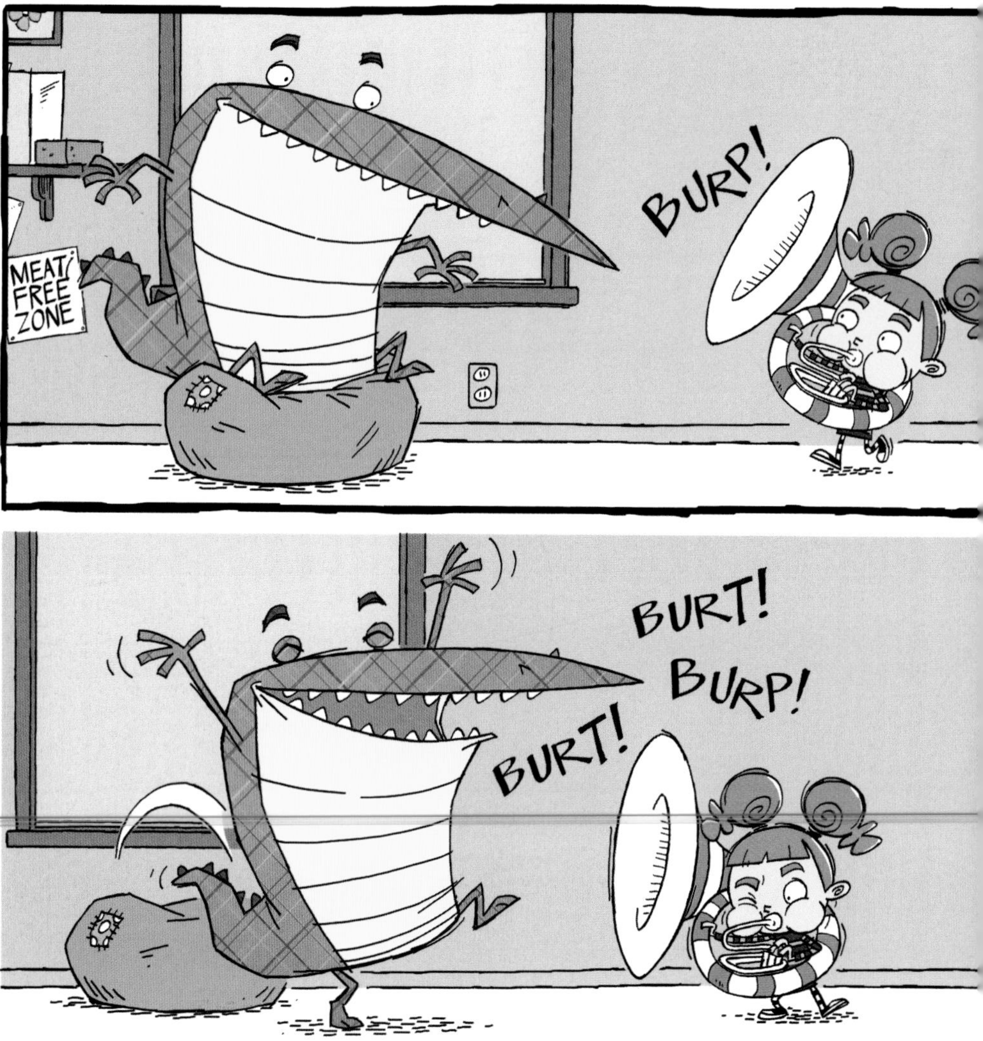
MEAT FREE ZONE
BURP!
BURT!
BURP!
BURT!

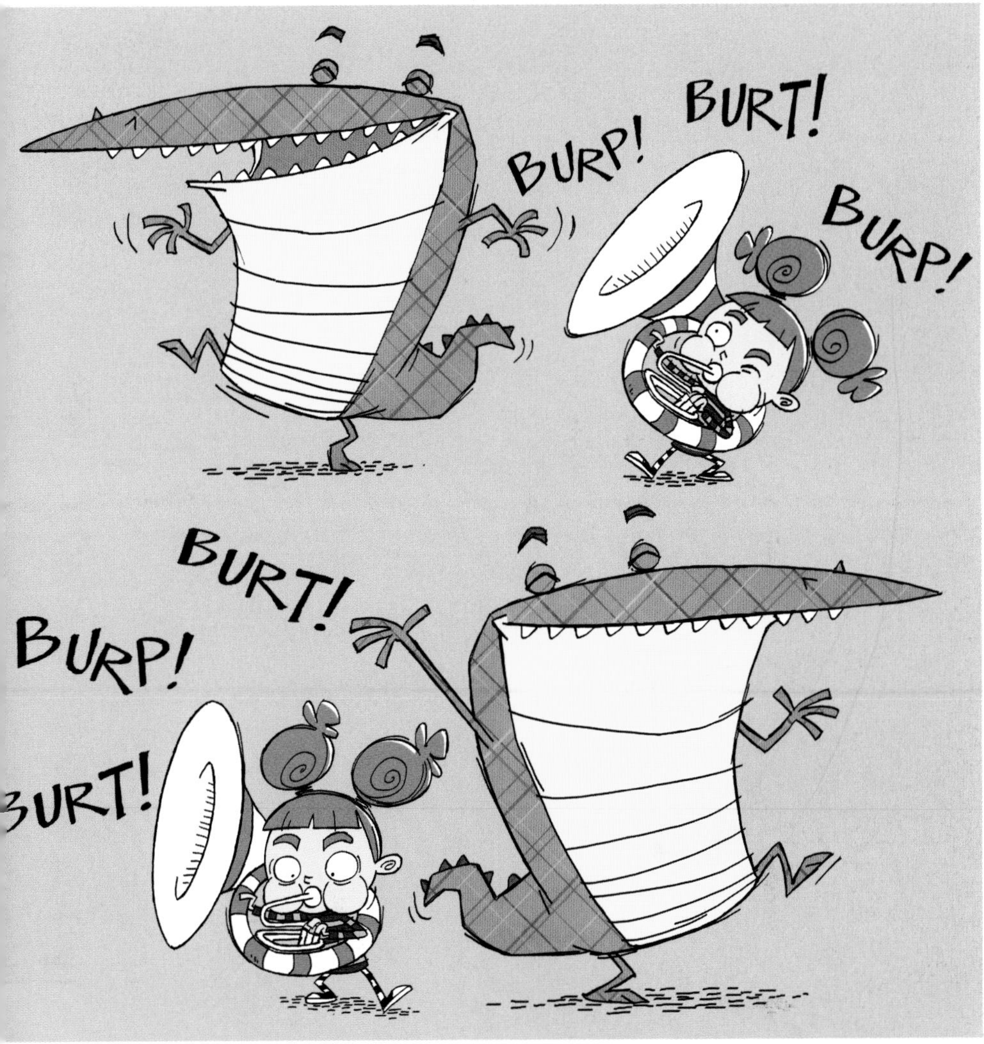
BURP!
BURT!
BURP!
BURT!
BURP!
BURT!

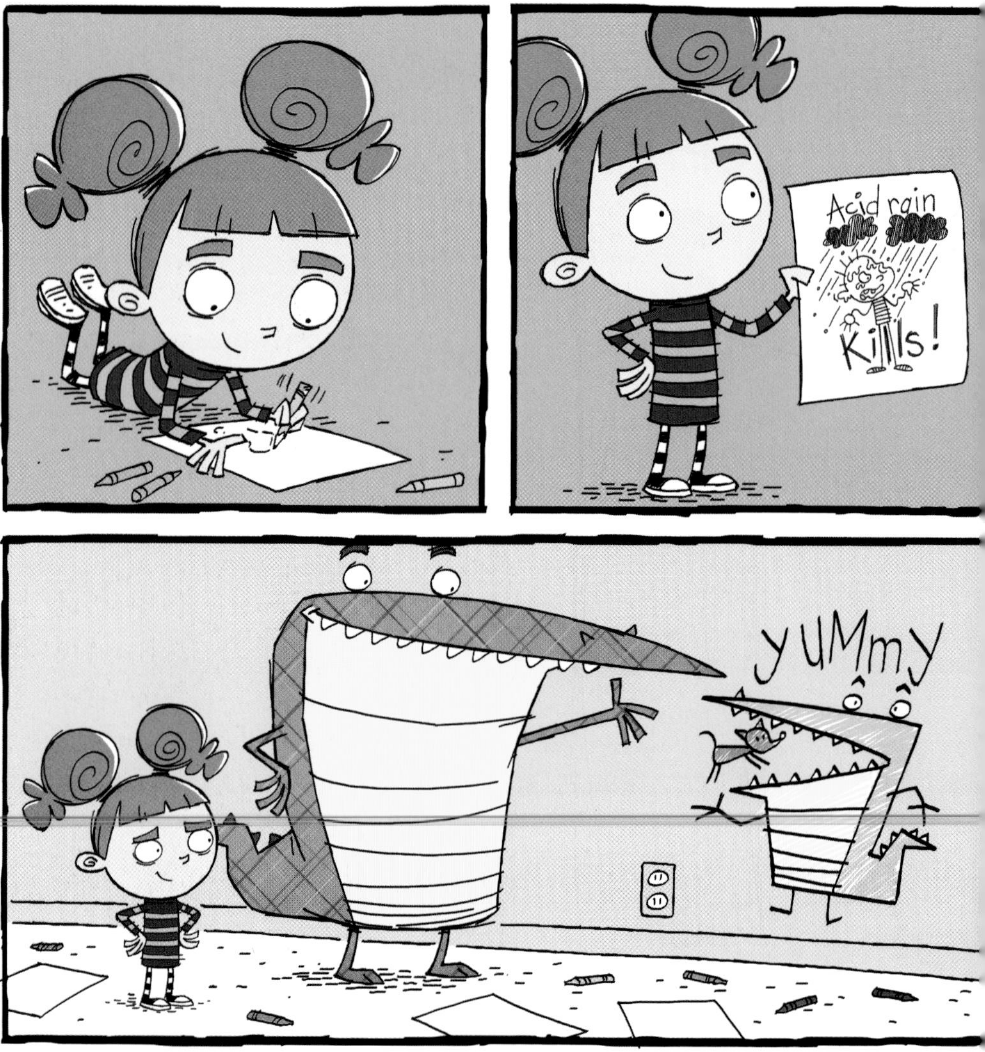
Acid rain
Kills!
yUMmy

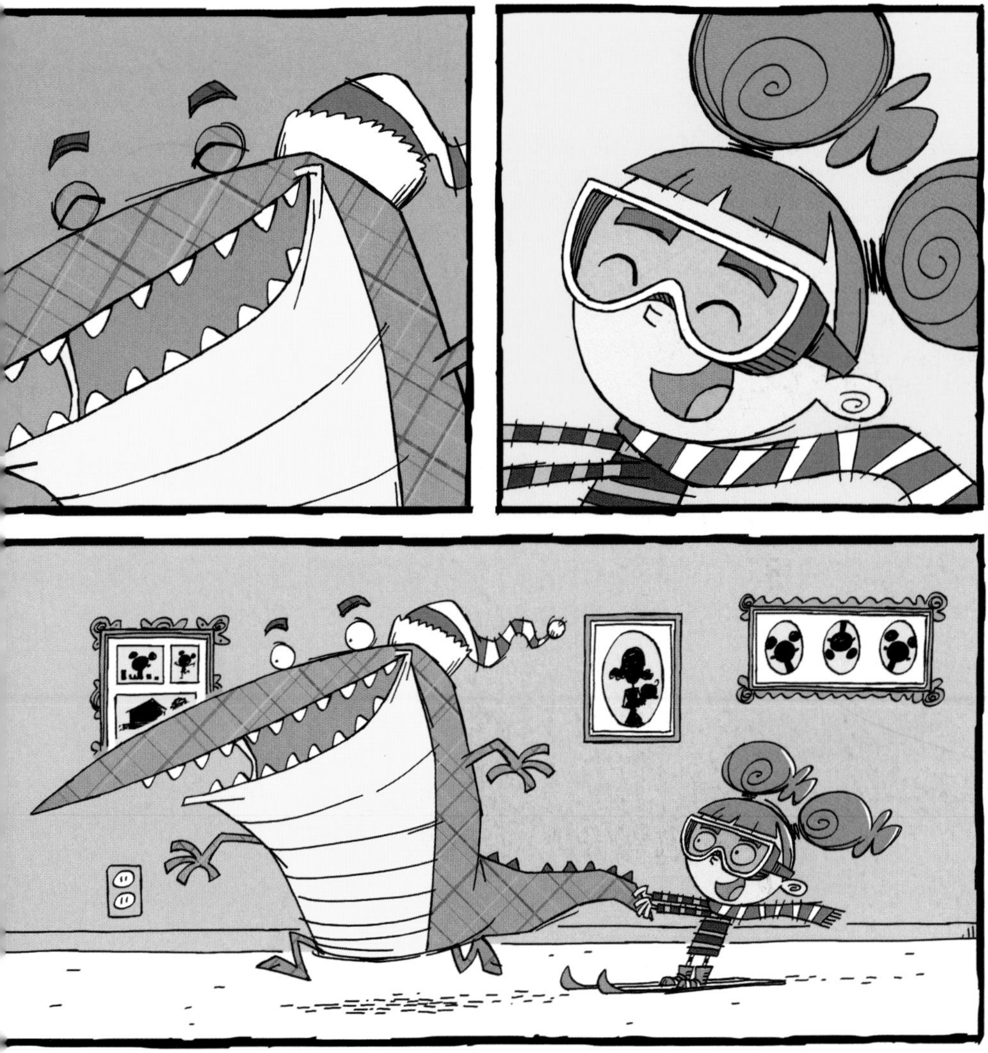

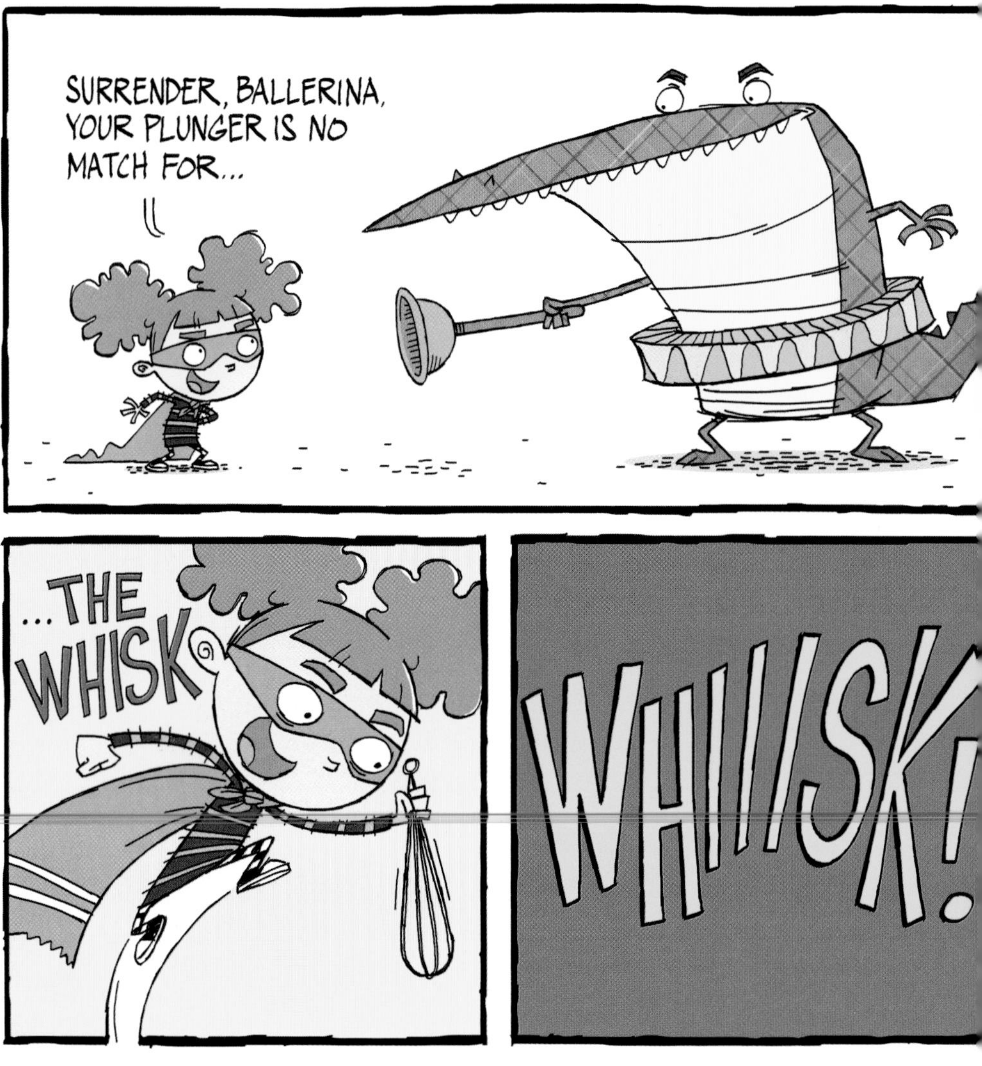

SURRENDER, BALLERINA, YOUR PLUNGER IS NO MATCH FOR...
...THE WHISK
WHIIISK!

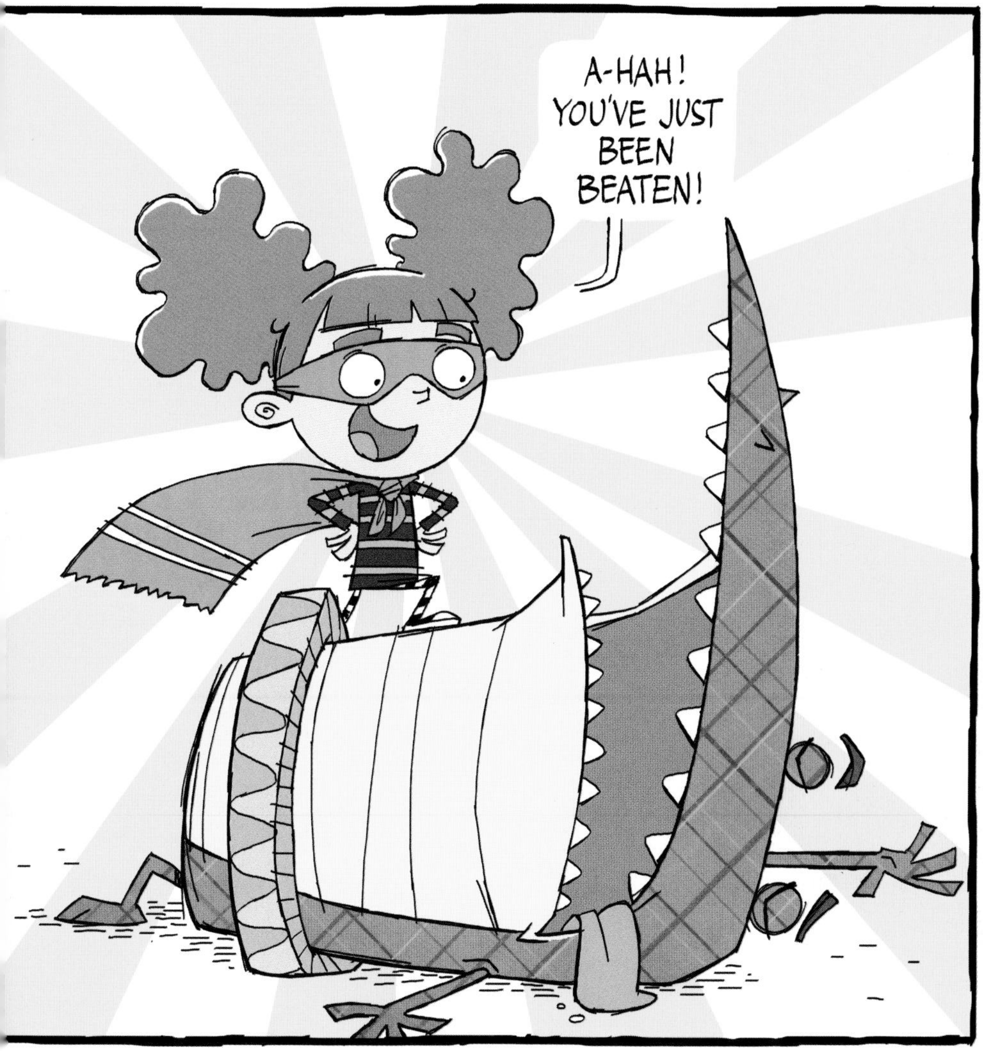
A-HAH! YOU'VE JUST BEEN BEATEN!

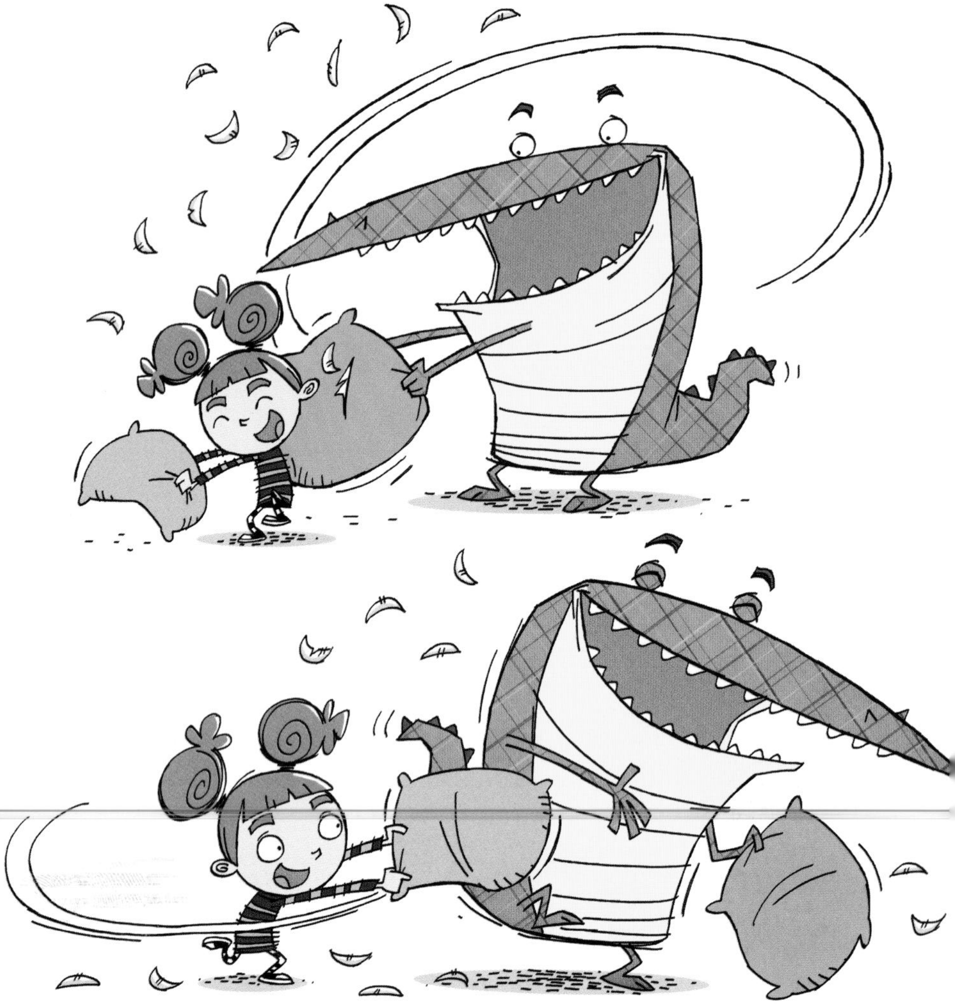

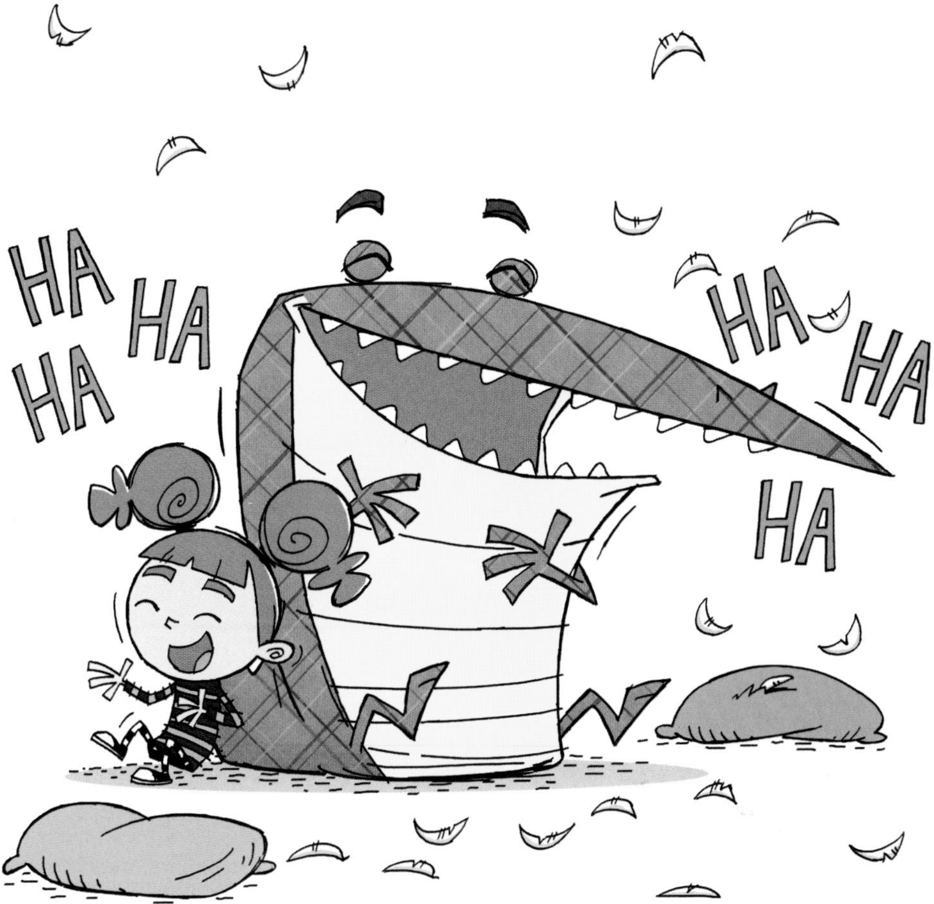
HA
HA
HA
HA
HA
HA

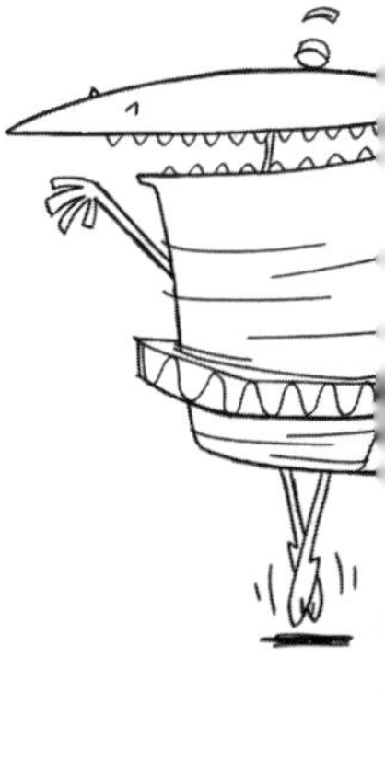

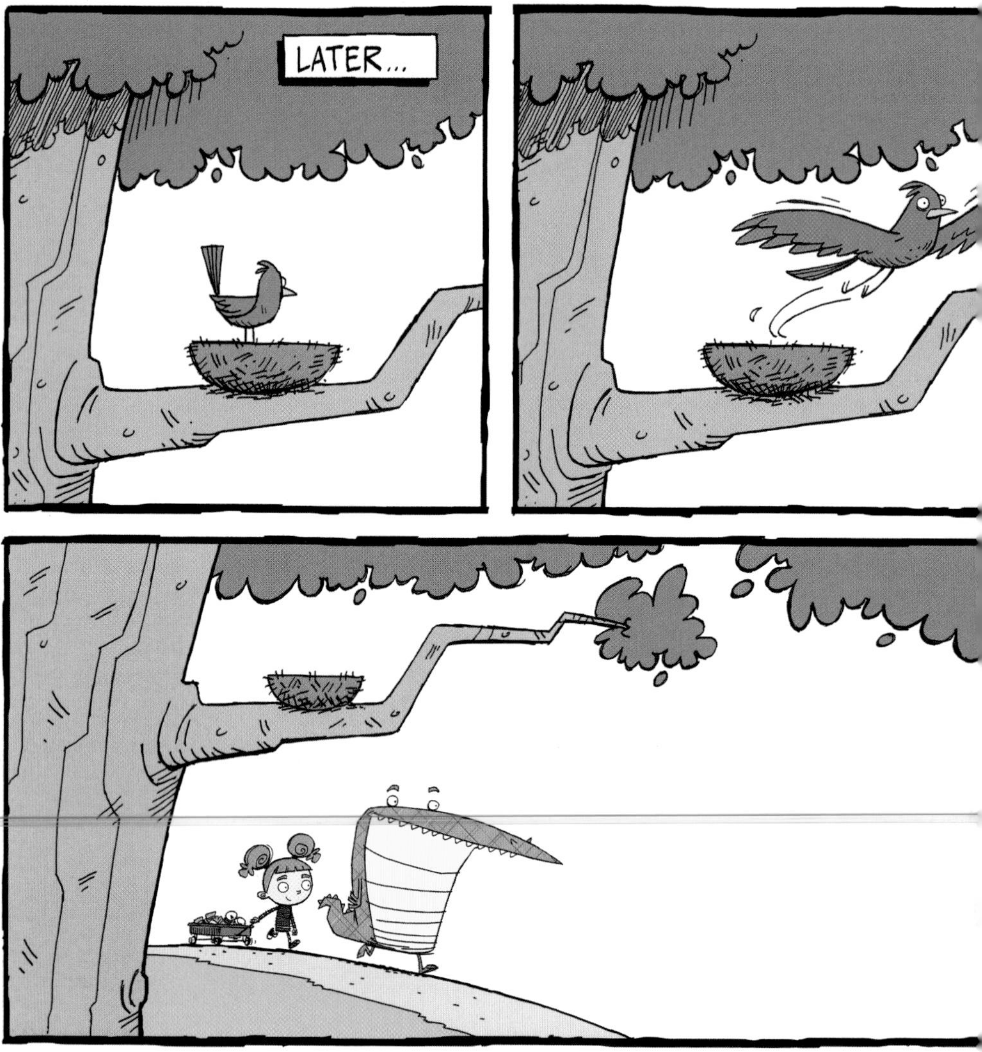
LATER...

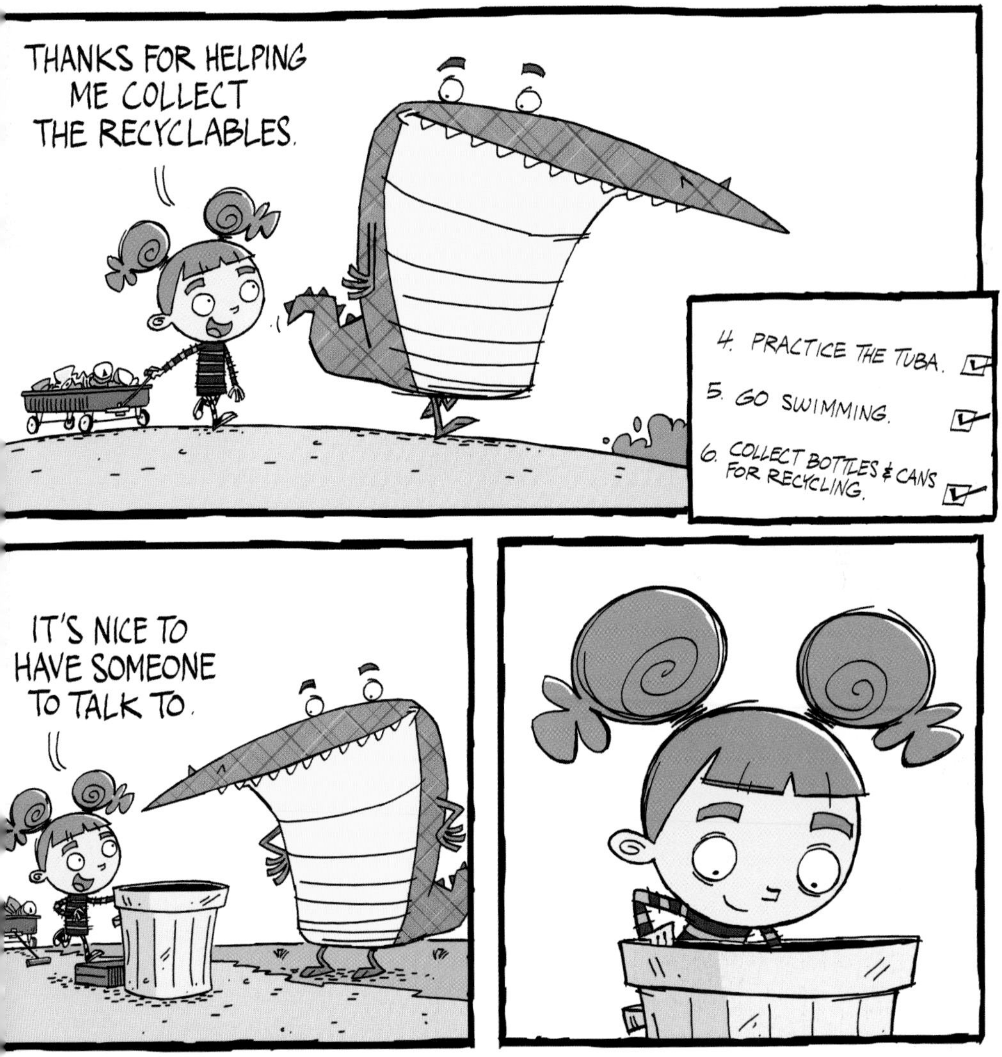
THANKS FOR HELPING ME COLLECT THE RECYCLABLES.
4. PRACTICE THE TUBA.
5. GO SWIMMING.
6. COLLECT BOTTLES & CANS FOR RECYCLING.
IT'S NICE TO HAVE SOMEONE TO TALK TO.

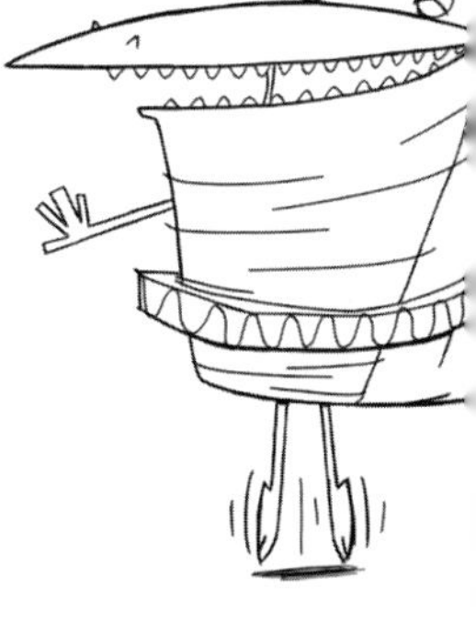

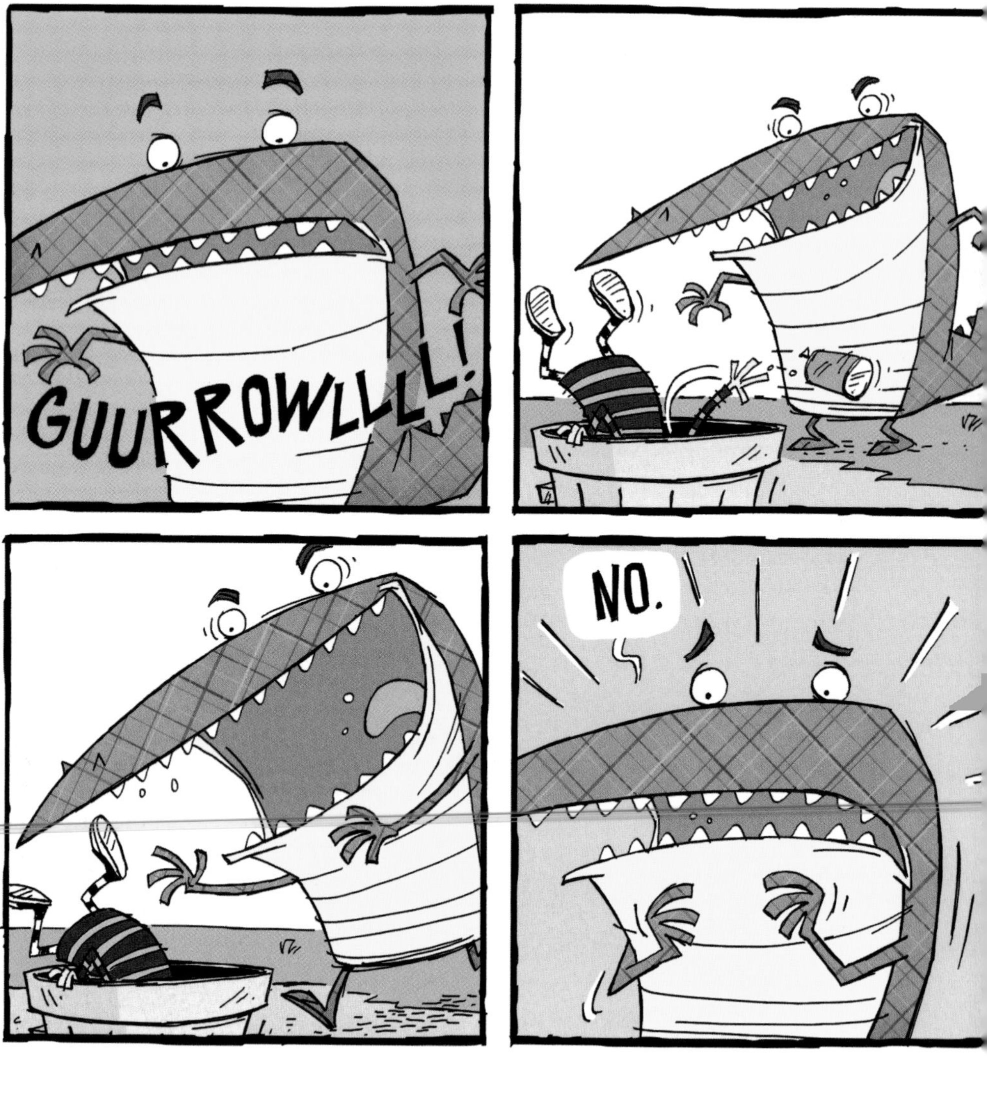
GUURROWLLLL!
NO.

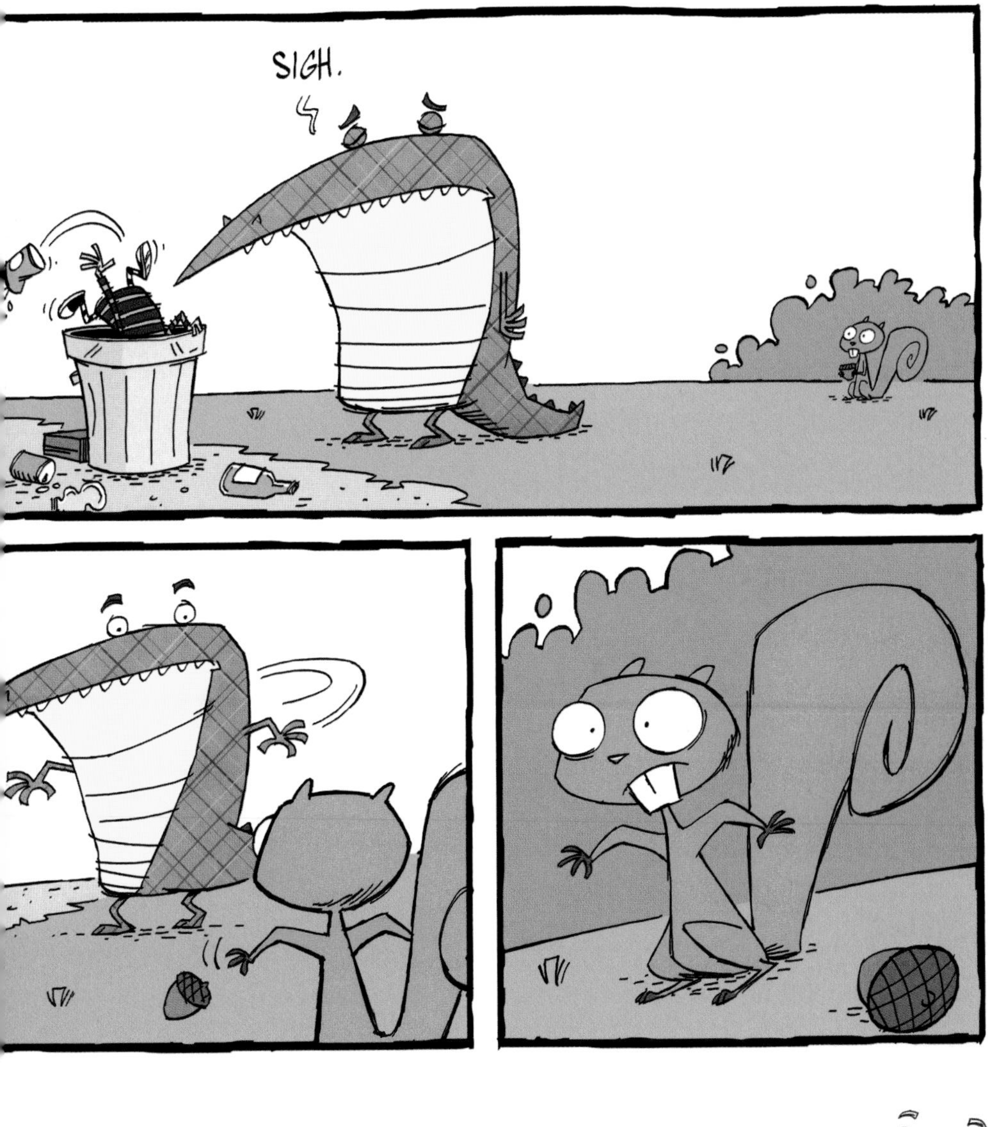
SIGH.

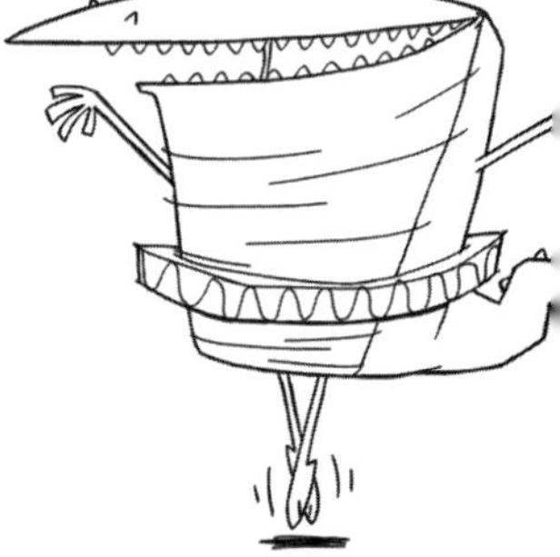

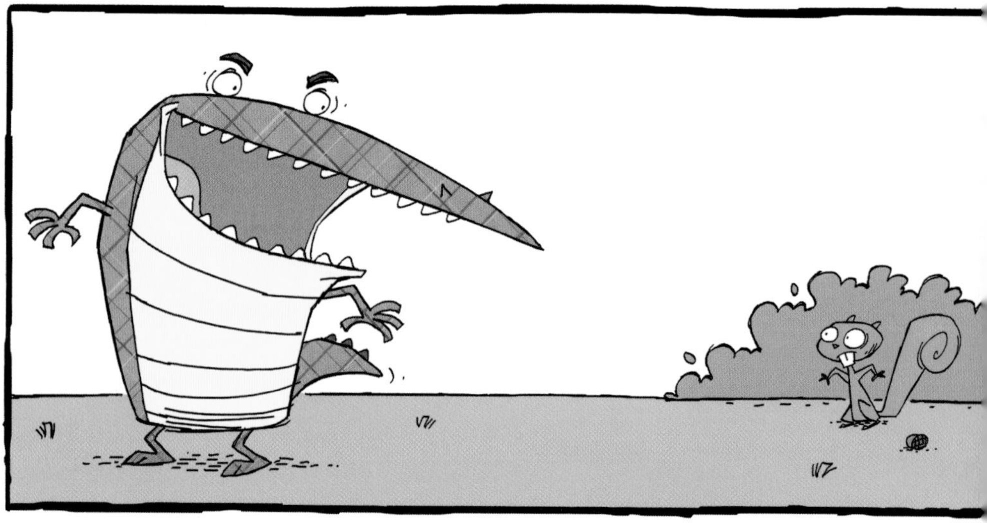

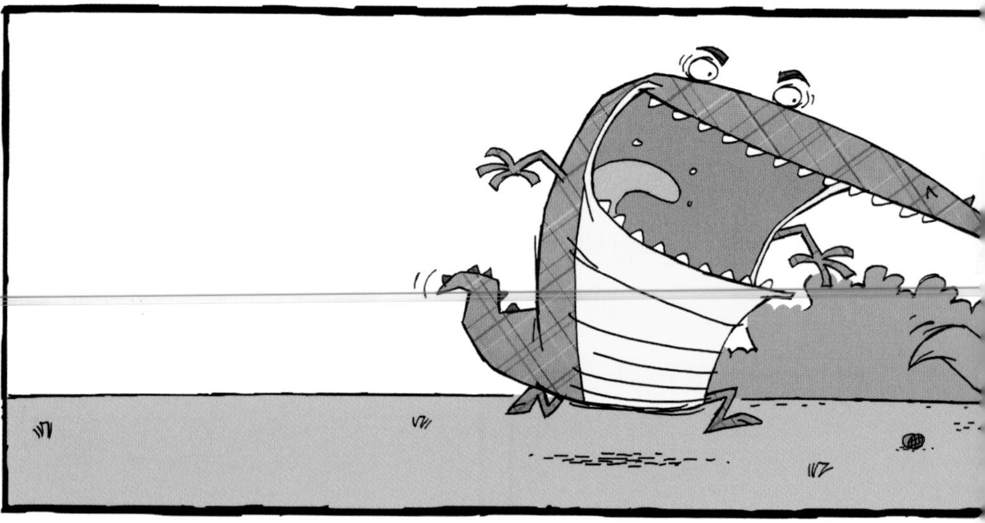

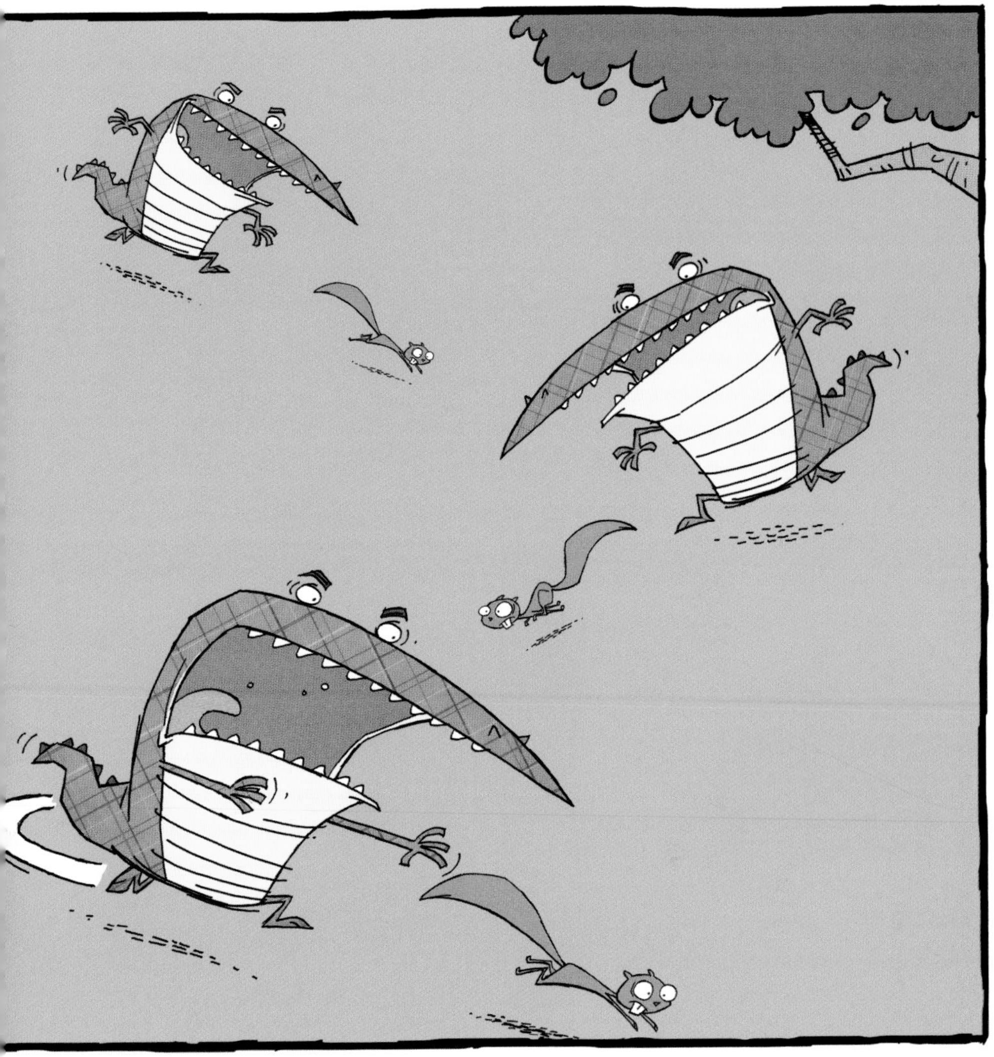

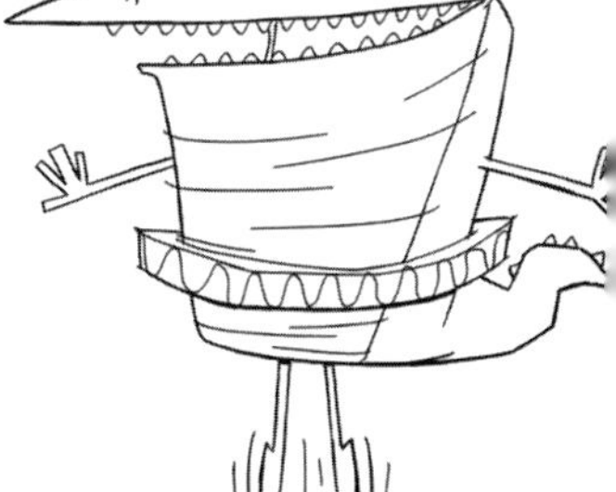

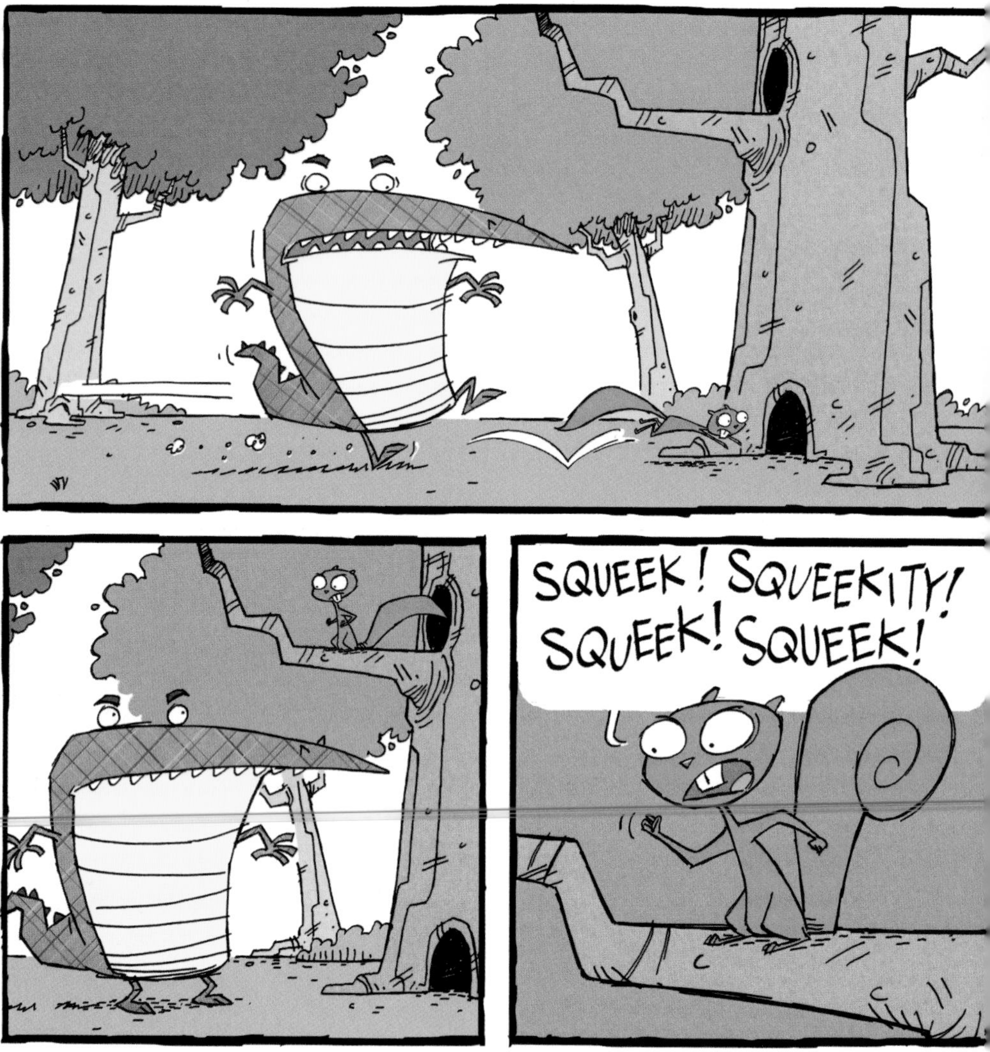
SQUEEK! SQUEEKITY! SQUEEK! SQUEEK!

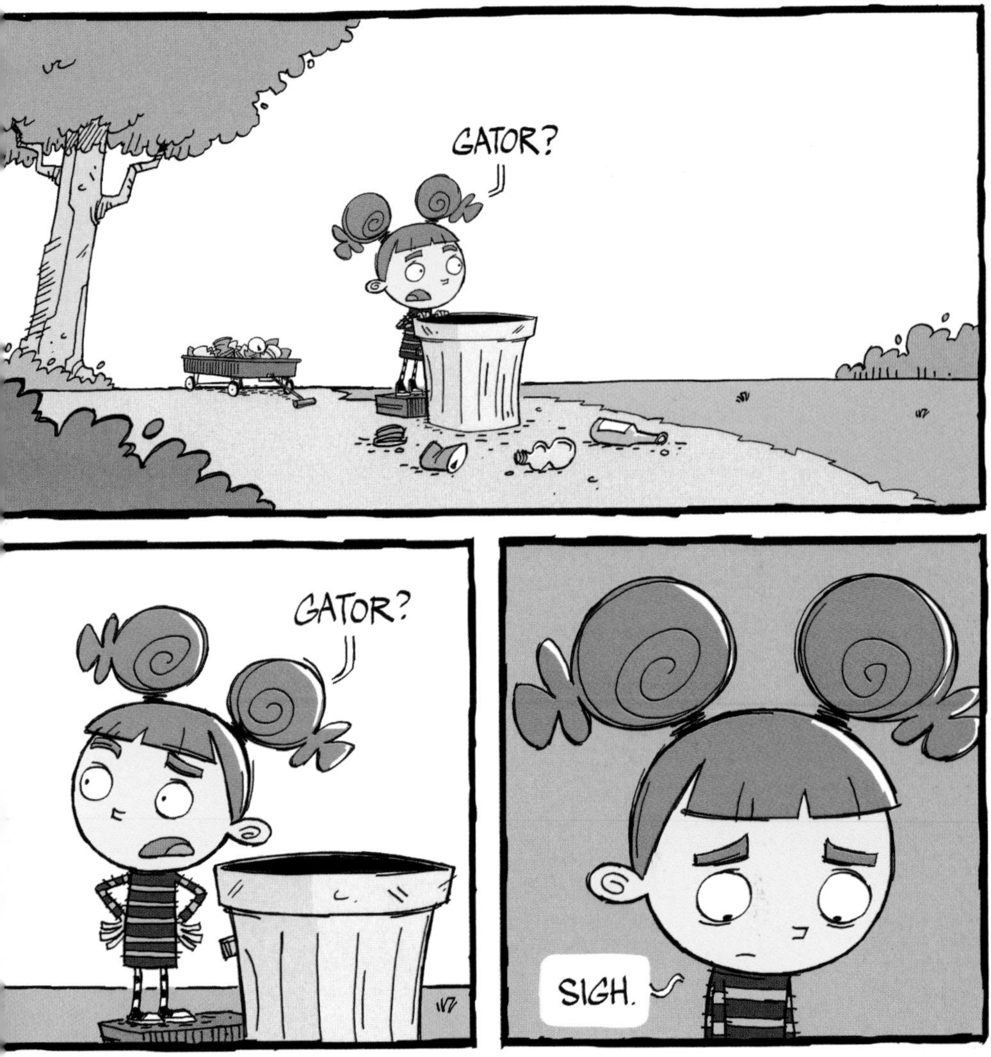
GATOR?
GATOR?
SIGH.

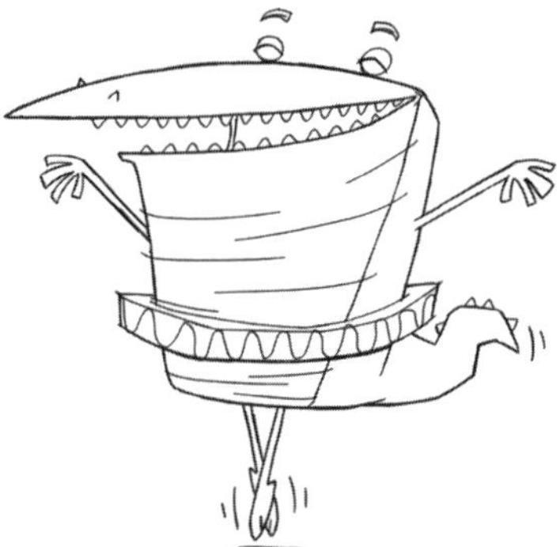

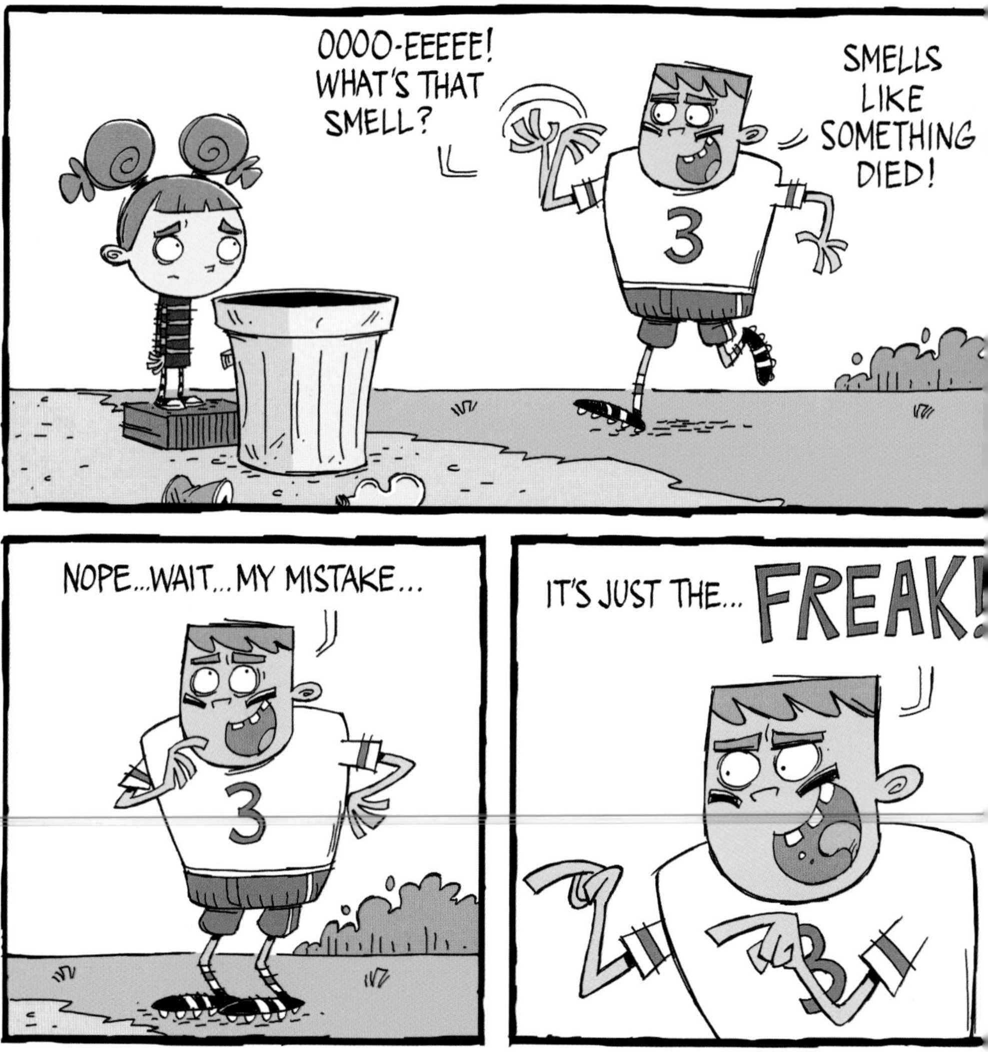
OOOO-EEEEE! WHAT'S THAT SMELL?
SMELLS LIKE SOMETHING DIED!
NOPE...WAIT...MY MISTAKE...
IT'S JUST THE... FREAK!

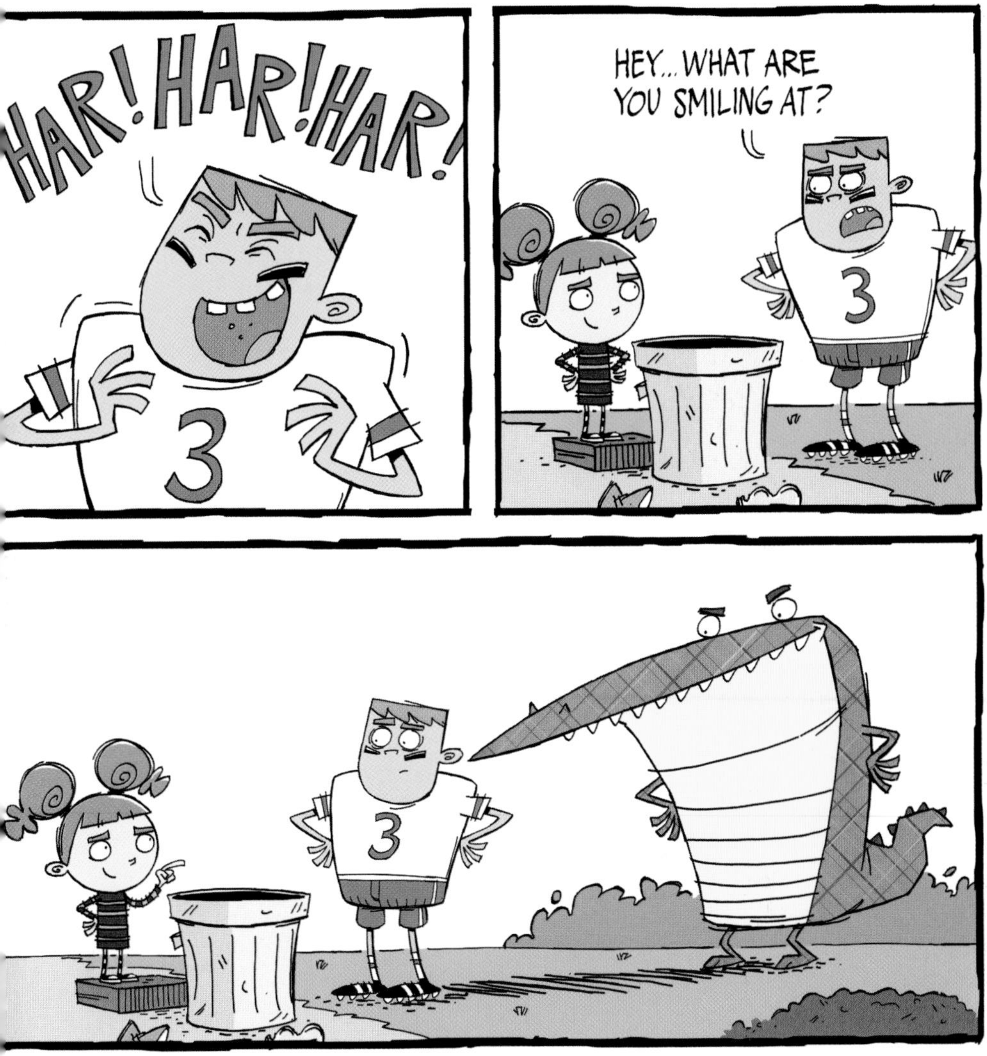
HAR! HAR! HAR!
HEY... WHAT ARE YOU SMILING AT?

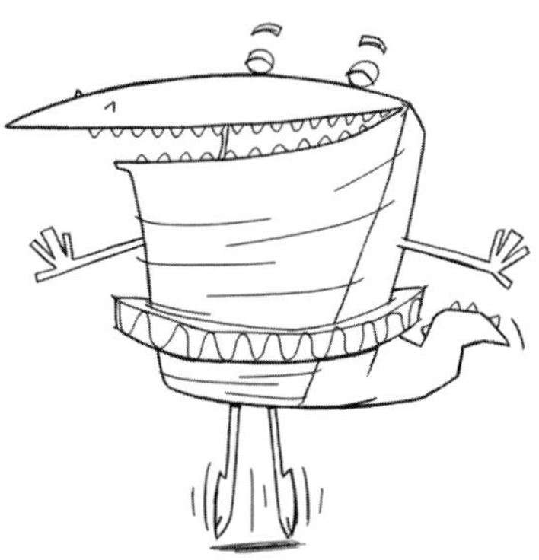

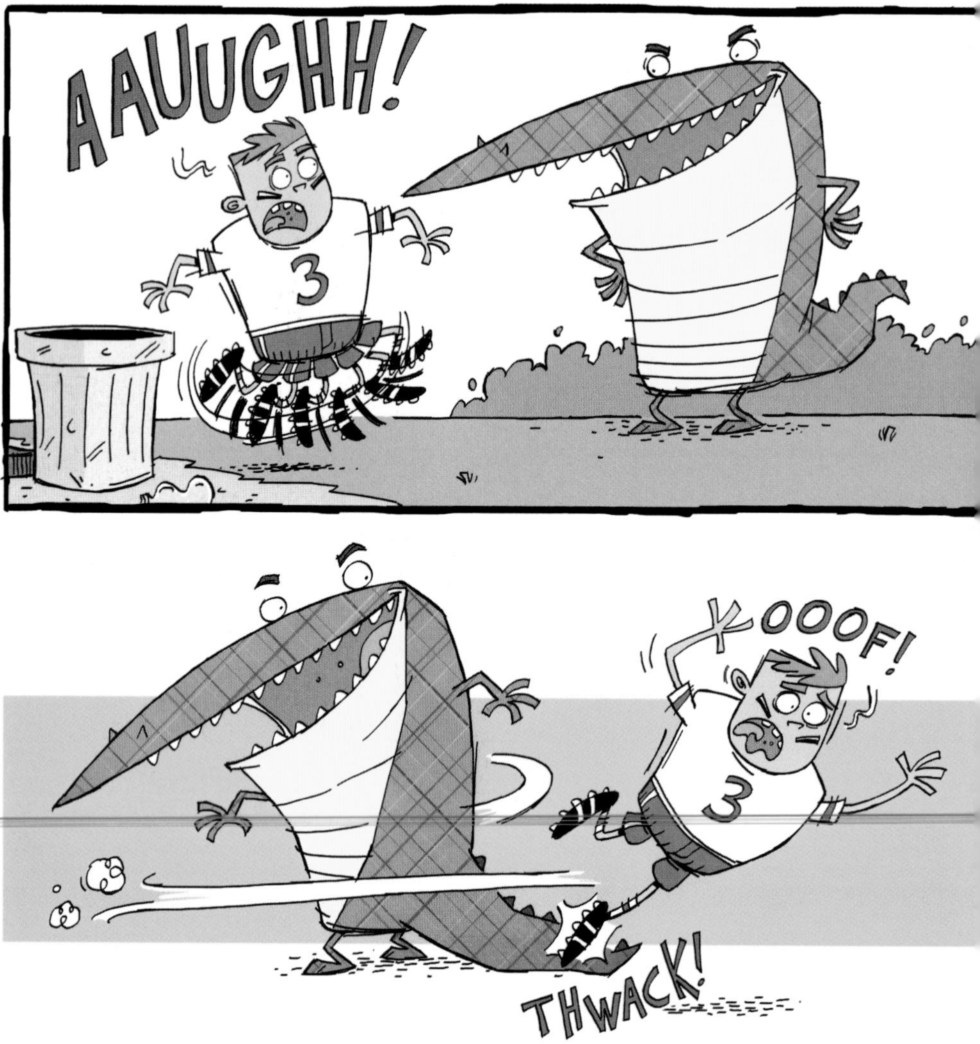
AAUUGHH!
3
OOOF!
3
THWACK!

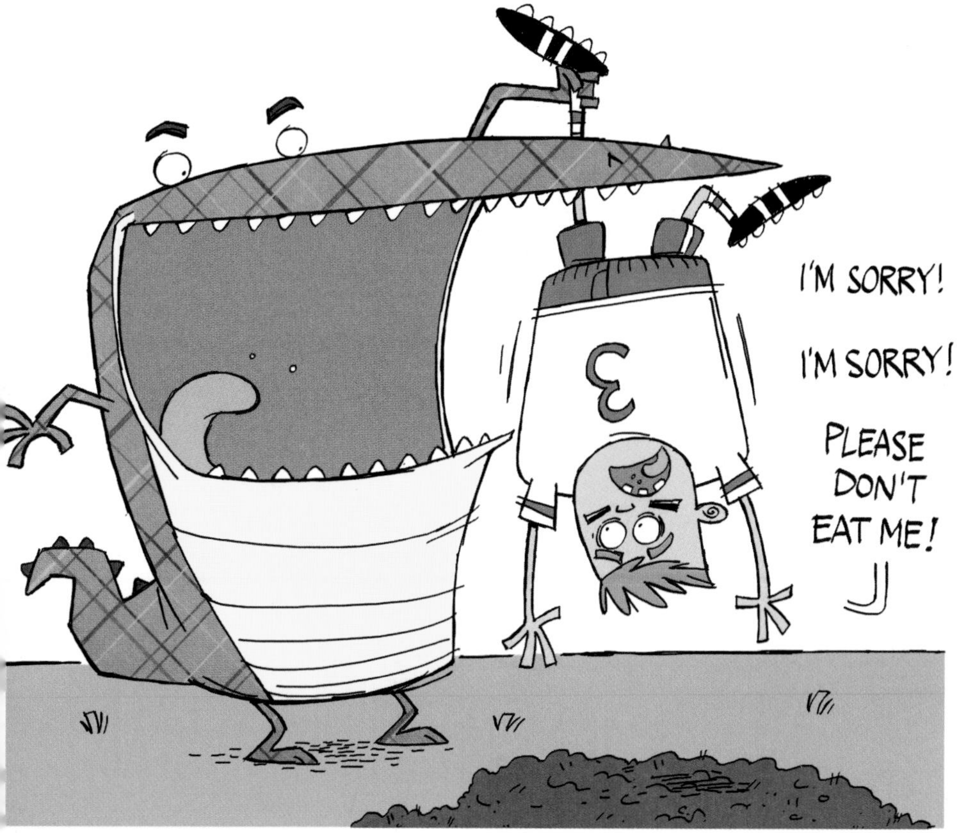
I'M SORRY!
I'M SORRY!
PLEASE DON'T EAT ME!

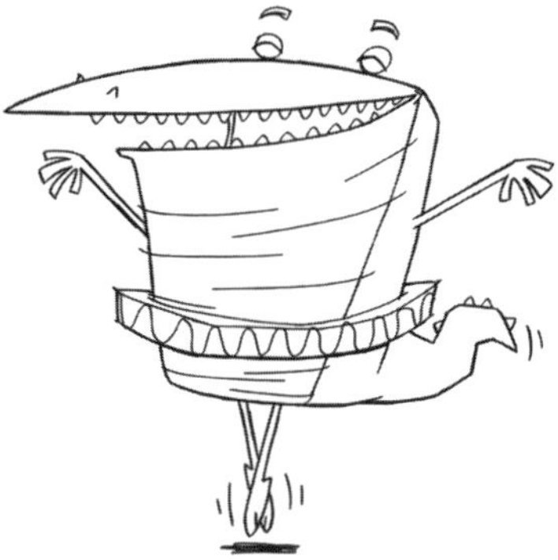

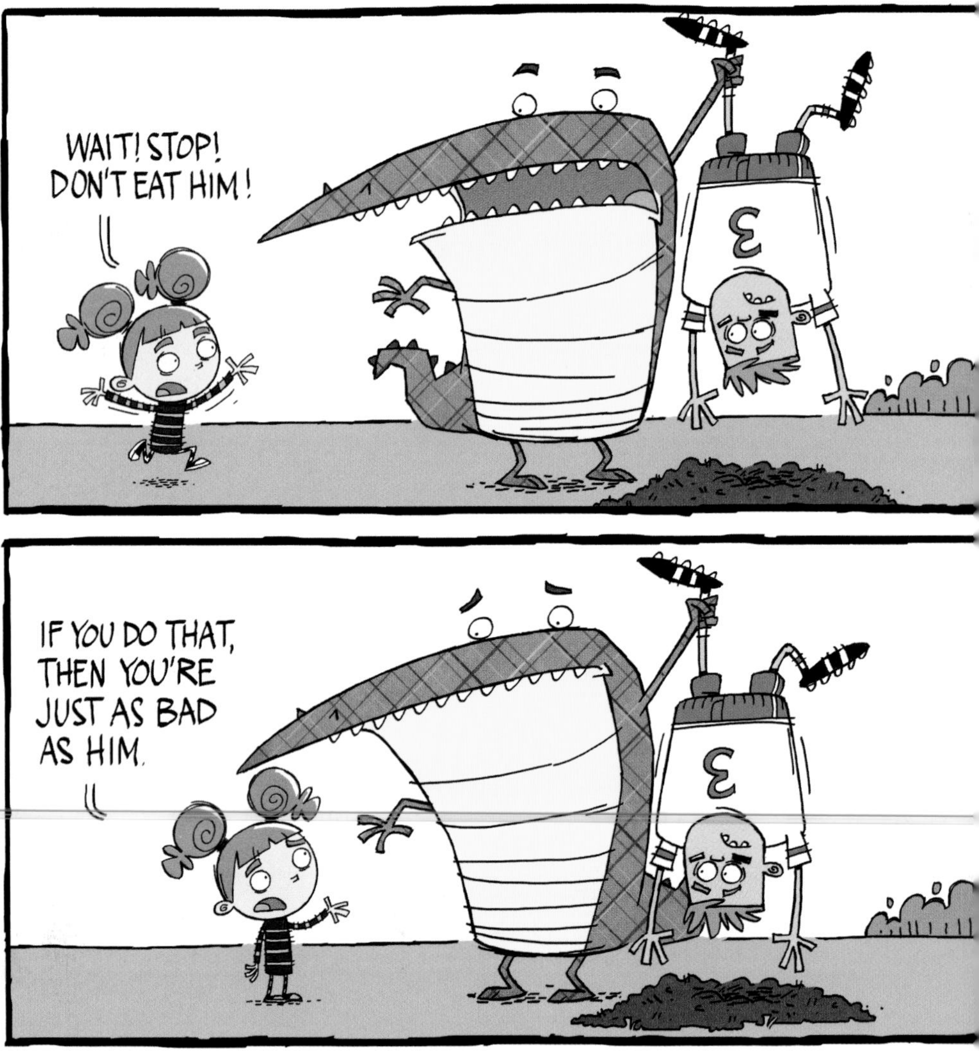
WAIT! STOP! DON'T EAT HIM!
IF YOU DO THAT, THEN YOU'RE JUST AS BAD AS HIM.

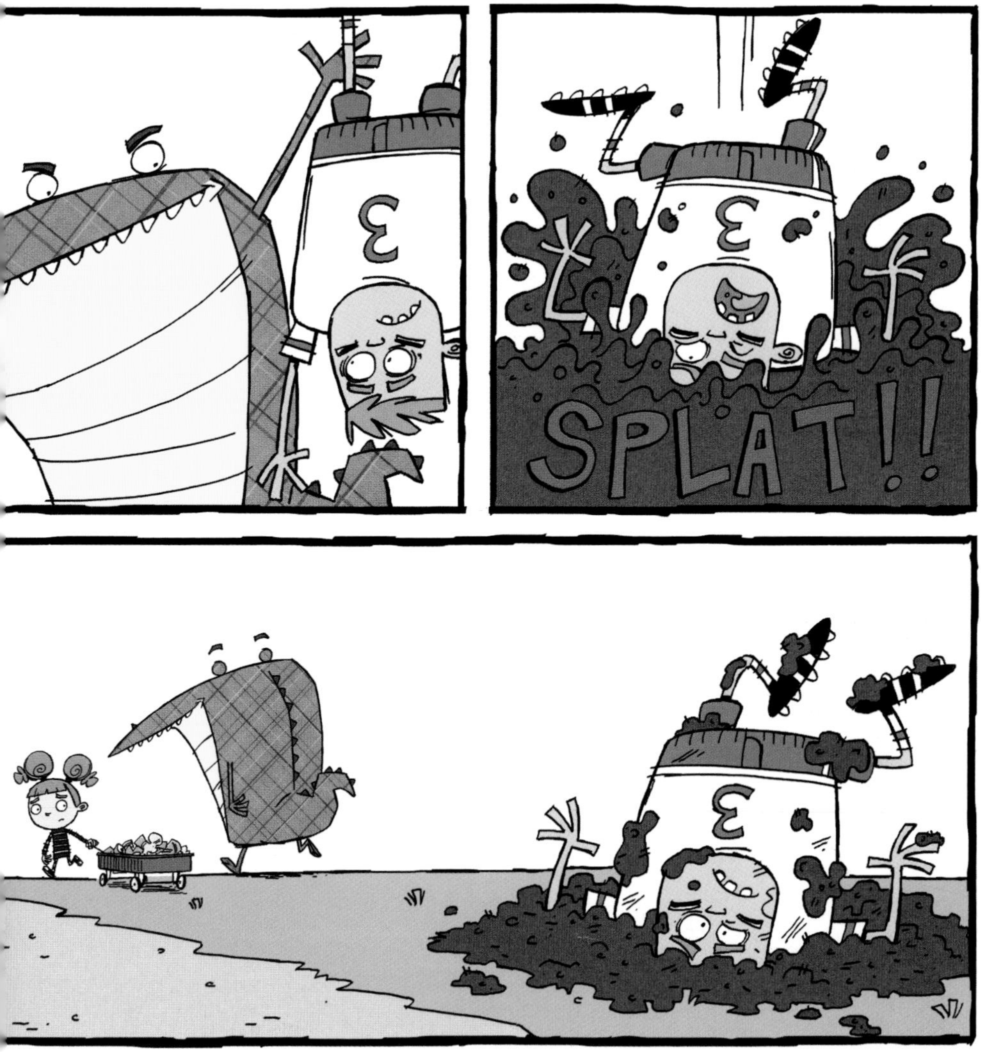
SPLAT!!

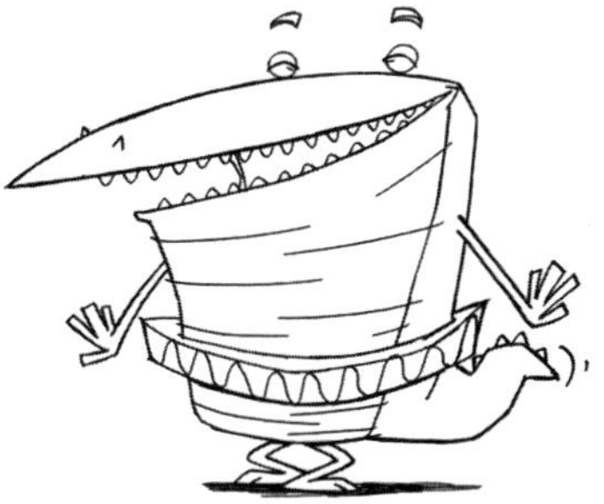

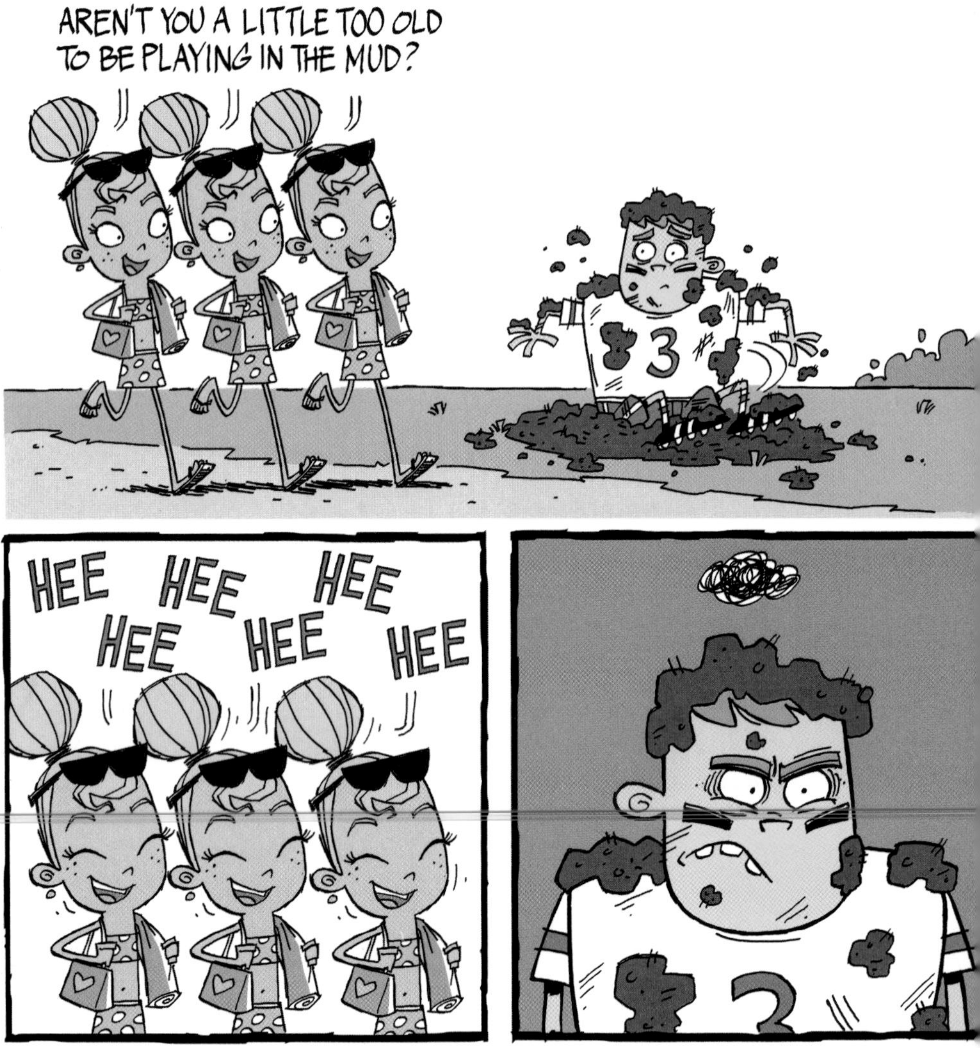
AREN'T YOU A LITTLE TOO OLD TO BE PLAYING IN THE MUD?
HEE HEE HEE HEE HEE HEE

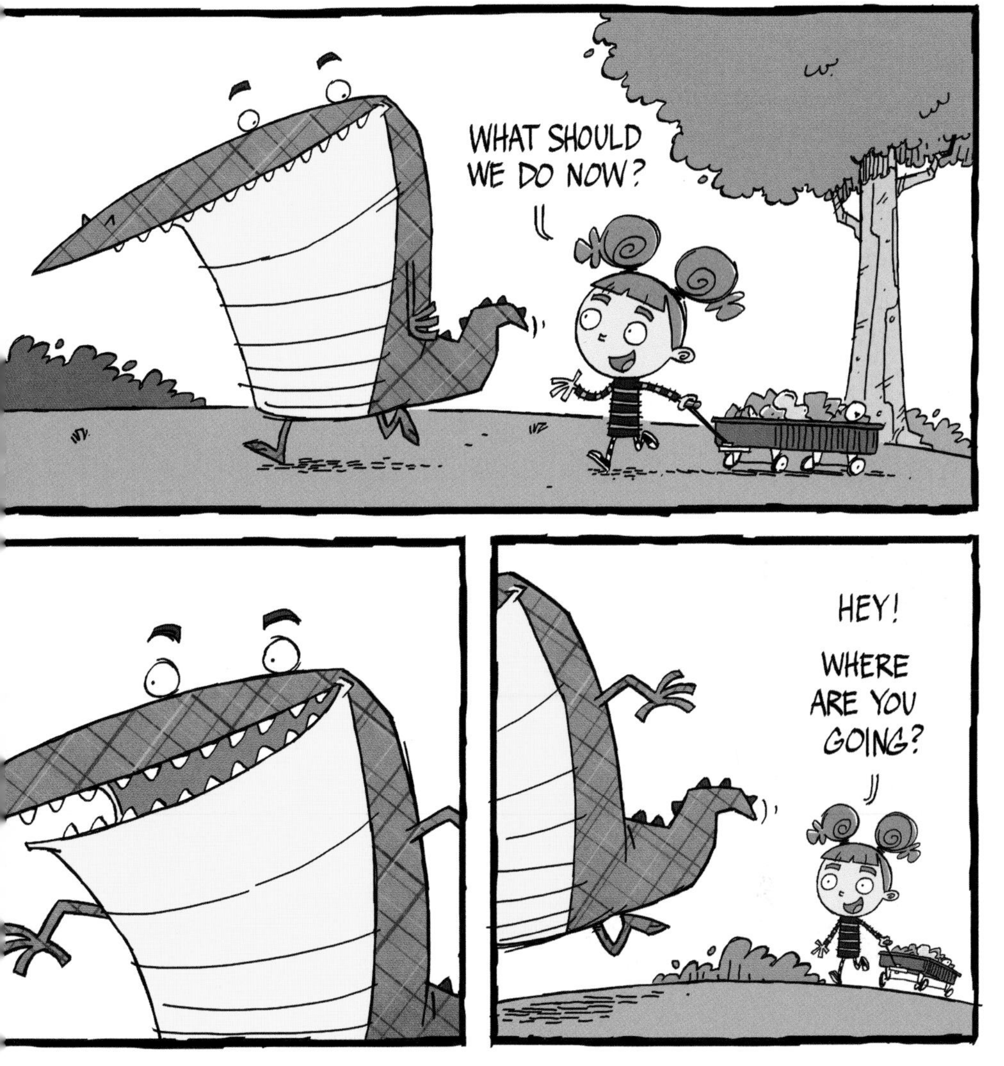
WHAT SHOULD WE DO NOW?
HEY!
WHERE ARE YOU GOING?

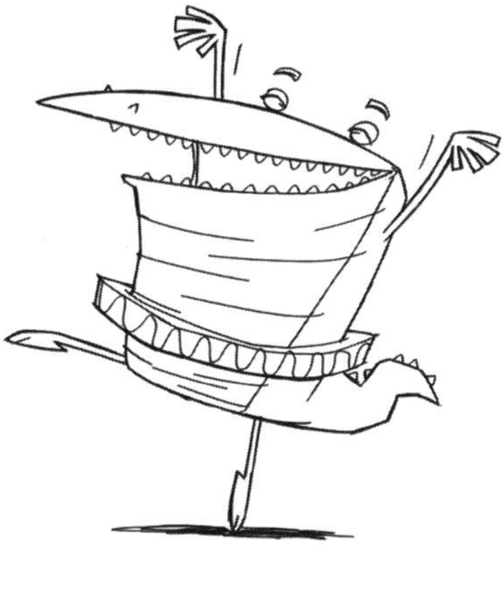

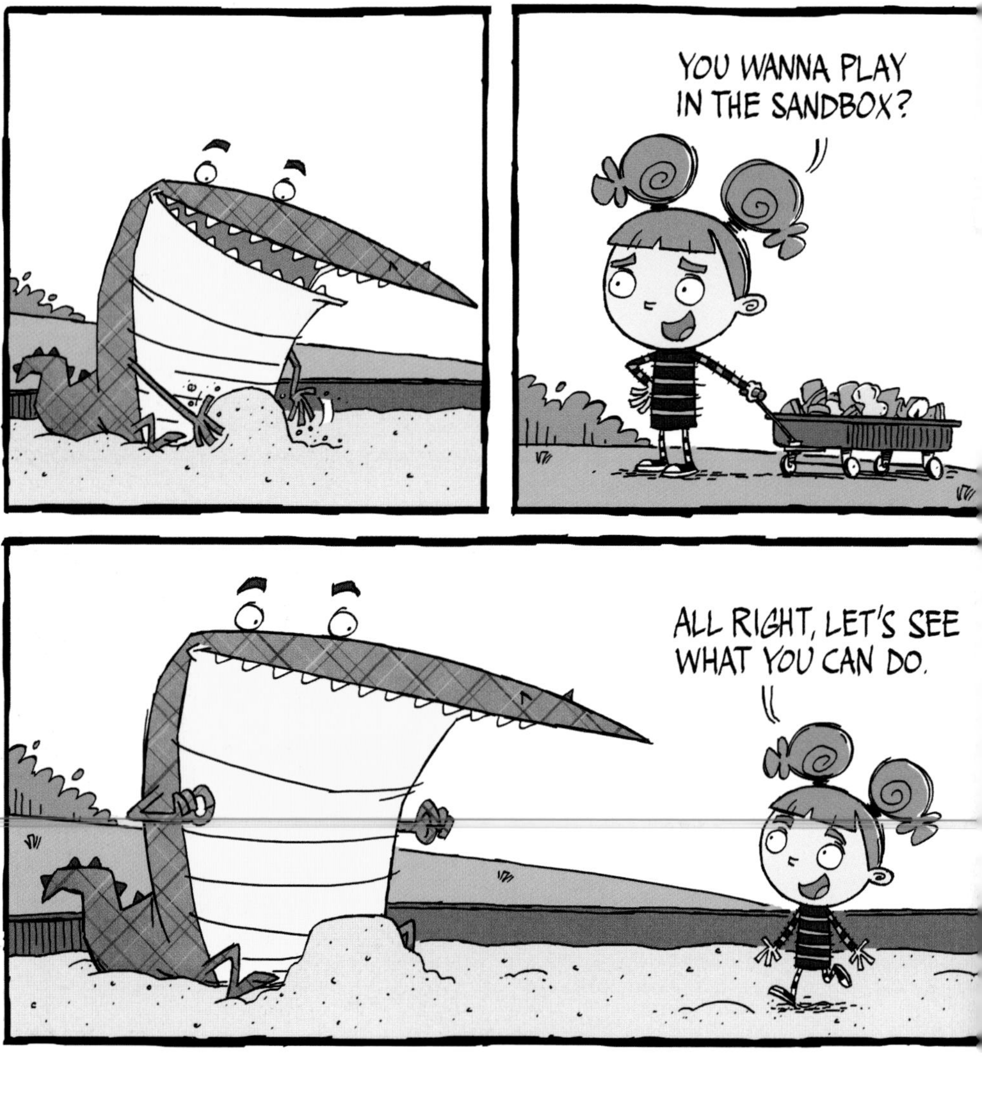
YOU WANNA PLAY IN THE SANDBOX?
ALL RIGHT, LET'S SEE WHAT YOU CAN DO.

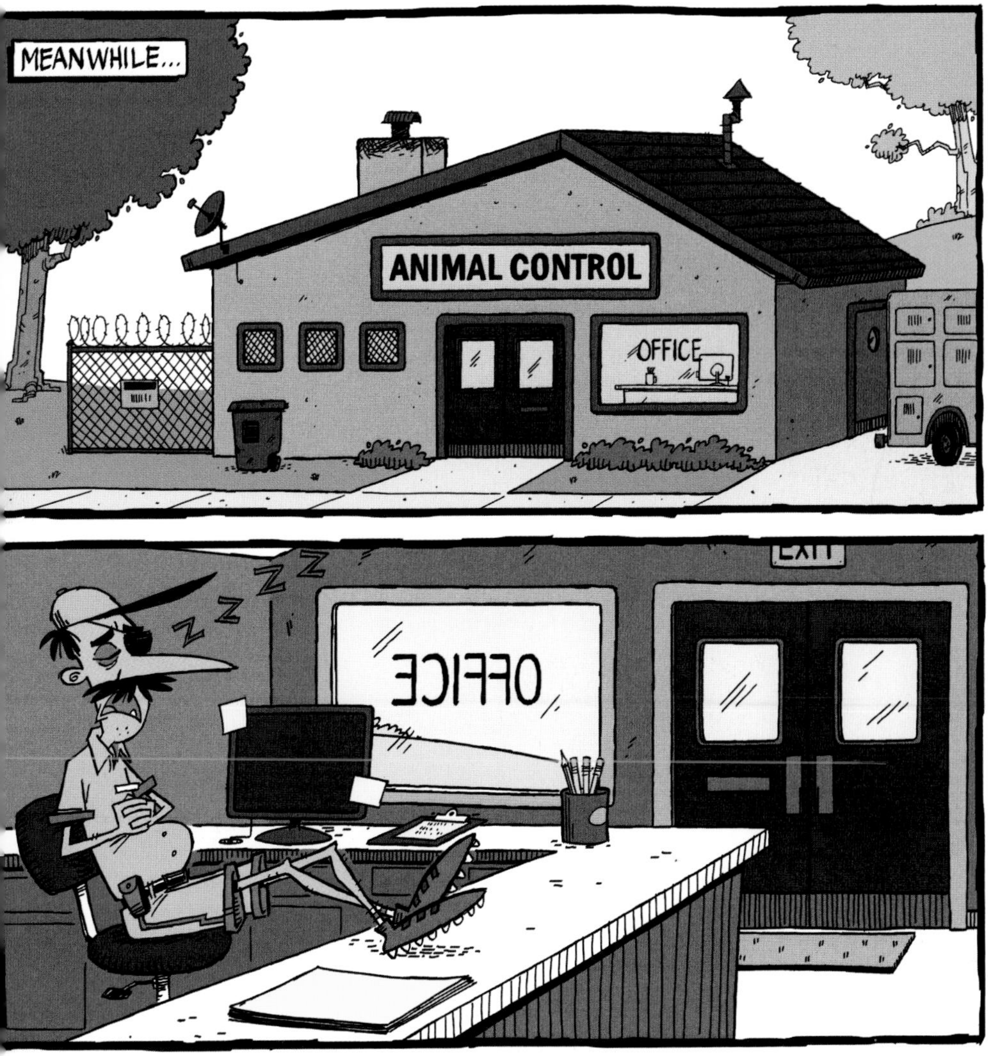
MEANWHILE...
ANIMAL CONTROL
OFFICE

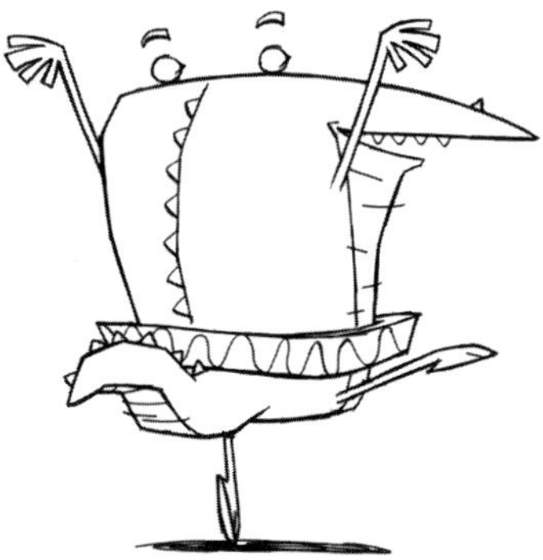

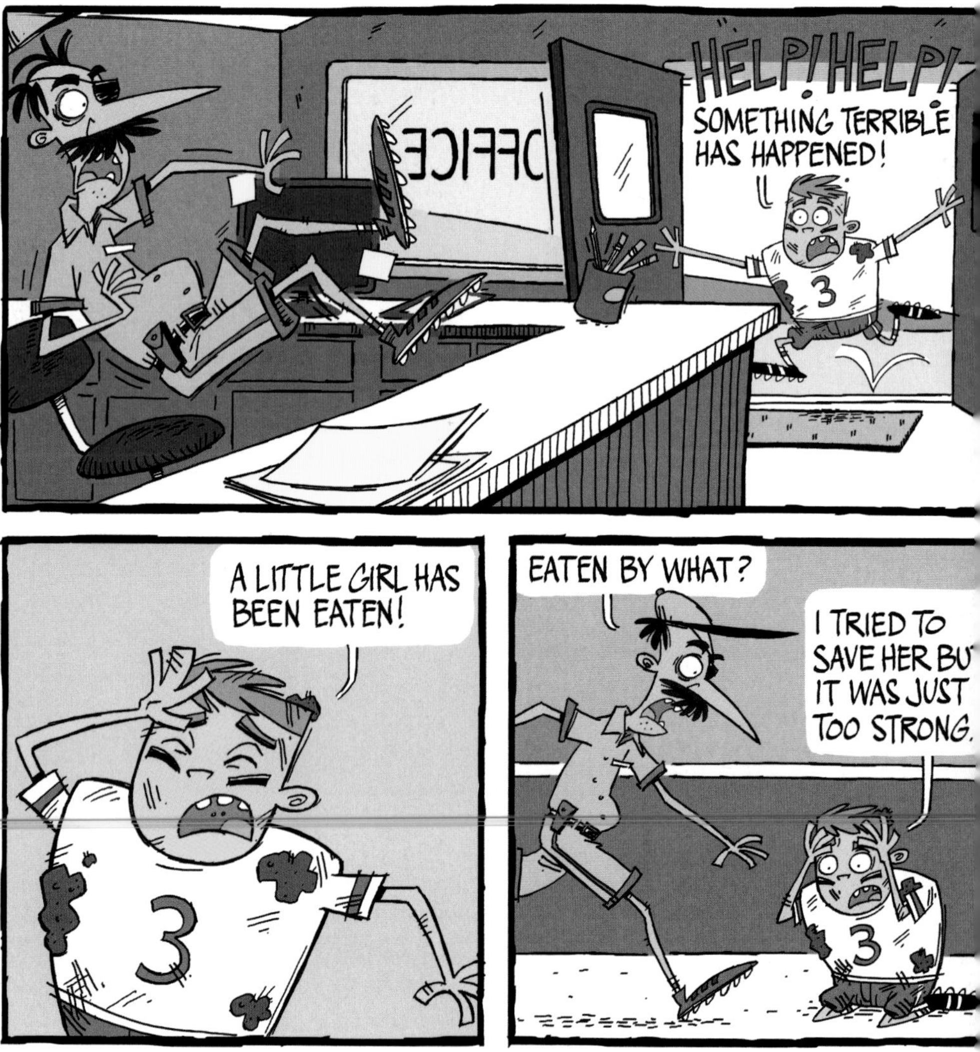
HELP! HELP!
SOMETHING TERRIBLE HAS HAPPENED!
A LITTLE GIRL HAS BEEN EATEN!
EATEN BY WHAT?
I TRIED TO SAVE HER BU IT WAS JUST TOO STRONG.

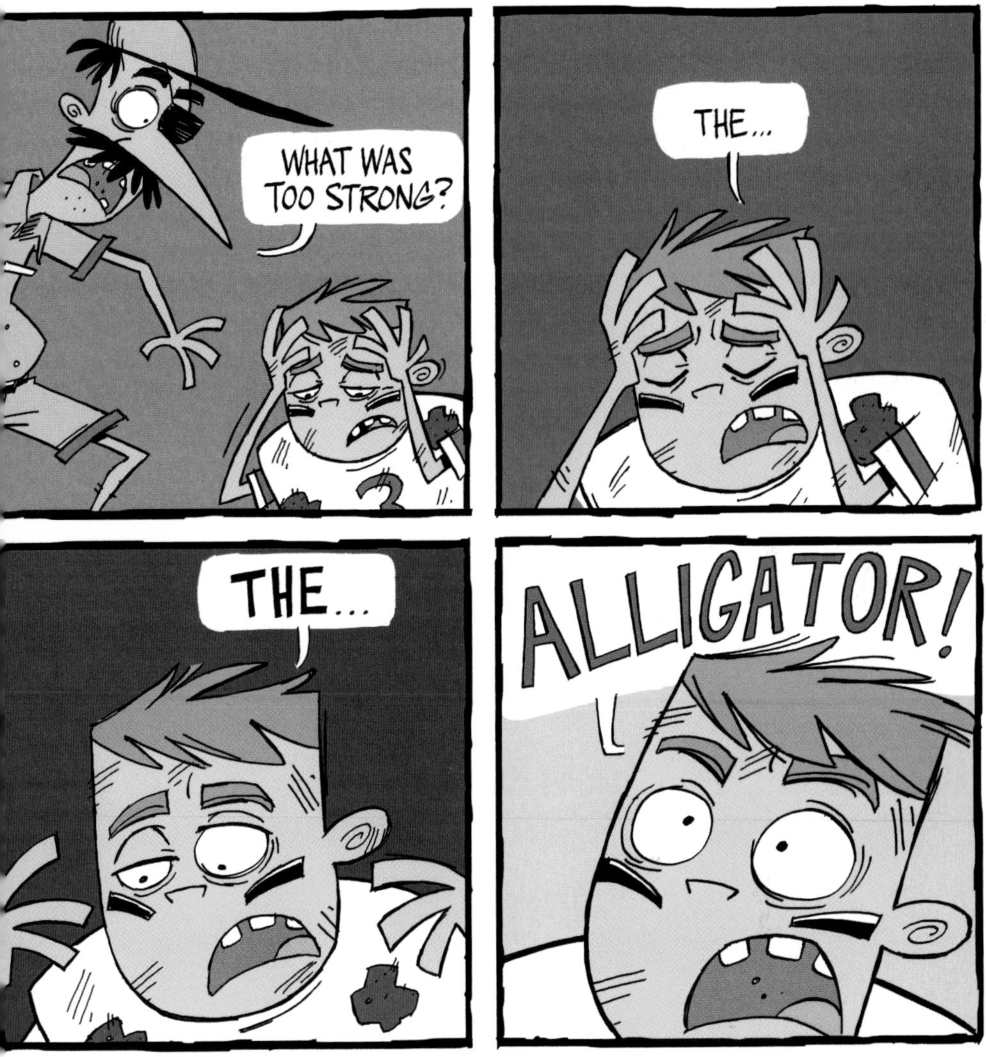
WHAT WAS TOO STRONG?
THE...
THE...
ALLIGATOR!

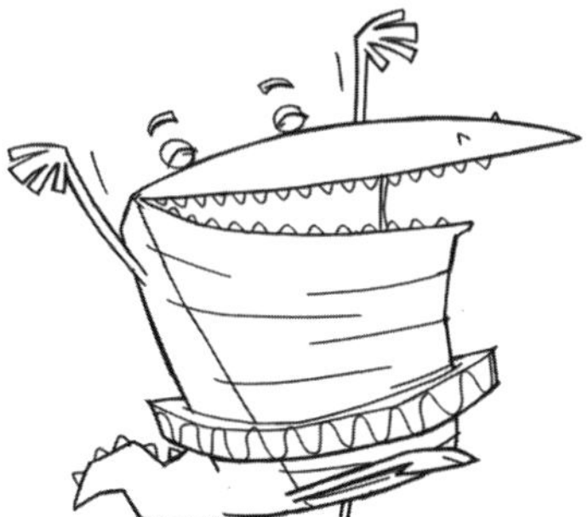

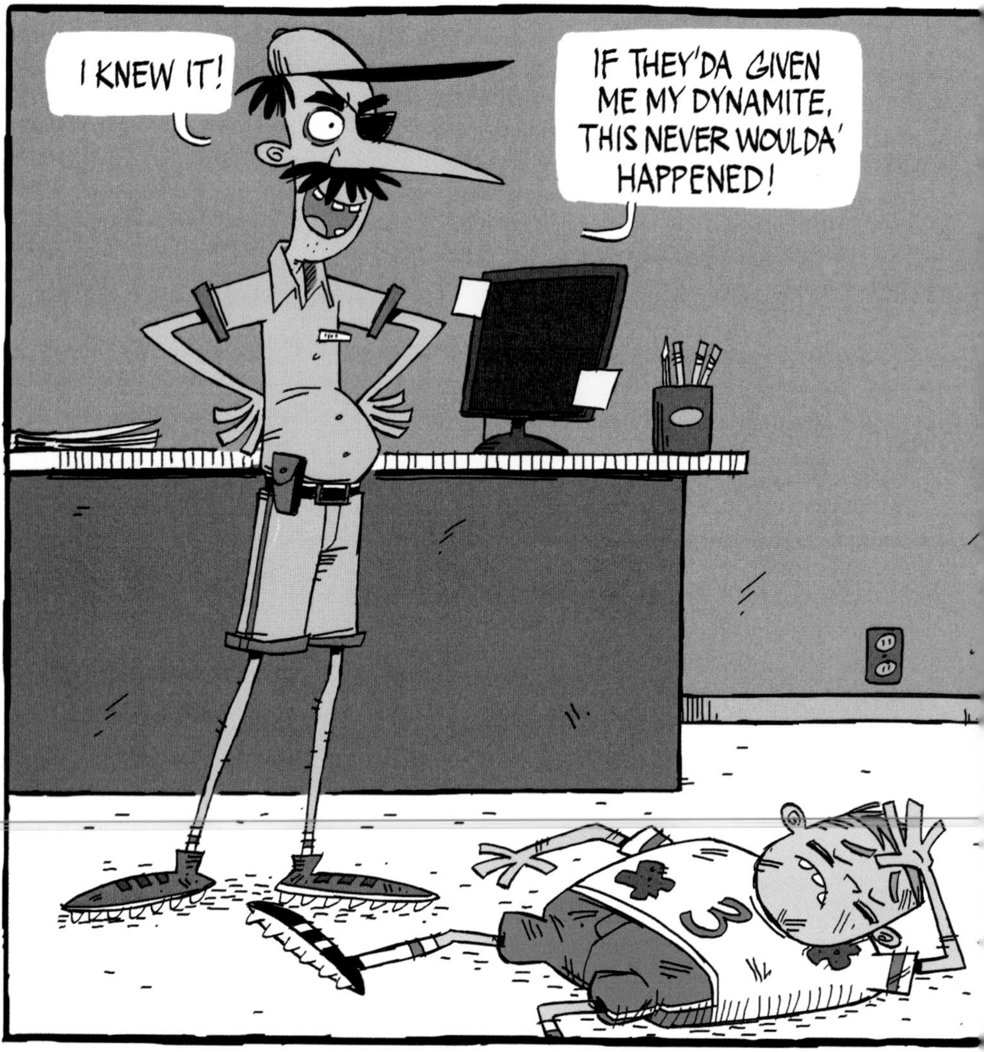
I KNEW IT!
IF THEY'DA GIVEN ME MY DYNAMITE, THIS NEVER WOULDA' HAPPENED!

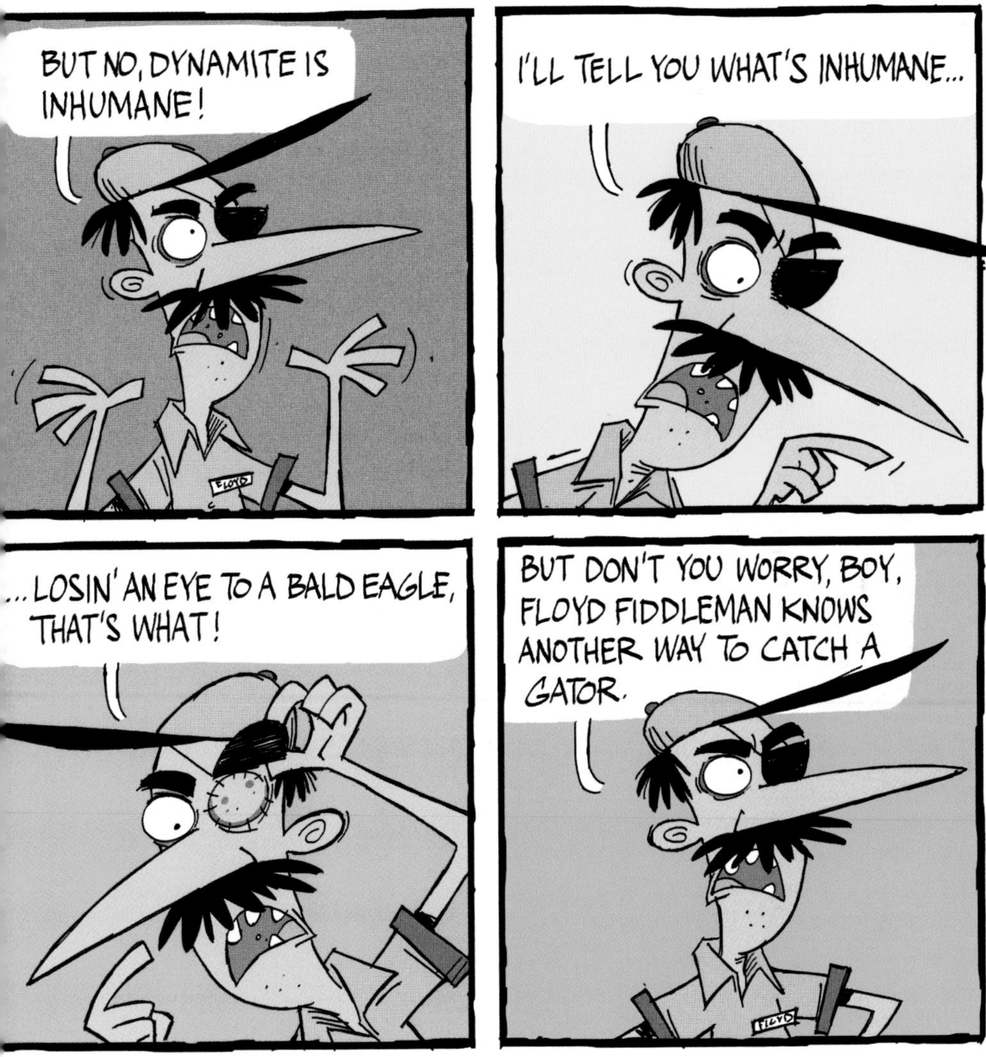
BUT NO, DYNAMITE IS INHUMANE!
I'LL TELL YOU WHAT'S INHUMANE...
...LOSIN' AN EYE TO A BALD EAGLE, THAT'S WHAT!
BUT DON'T YOU WORRY, BOY, FLOYD FIDDLEMAN KNOWS ANOTHER WAY TO CATCH A GATOR.

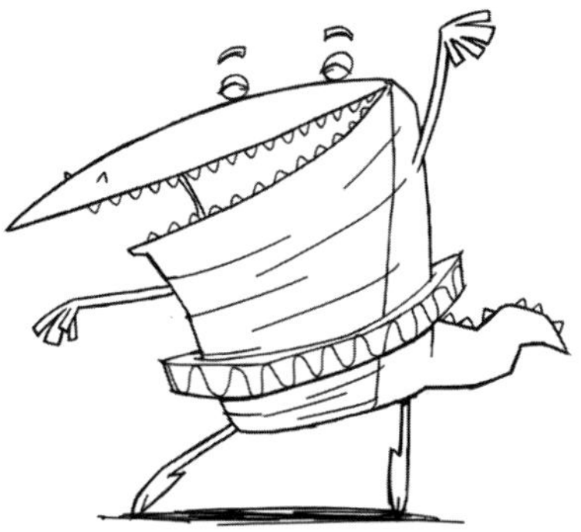

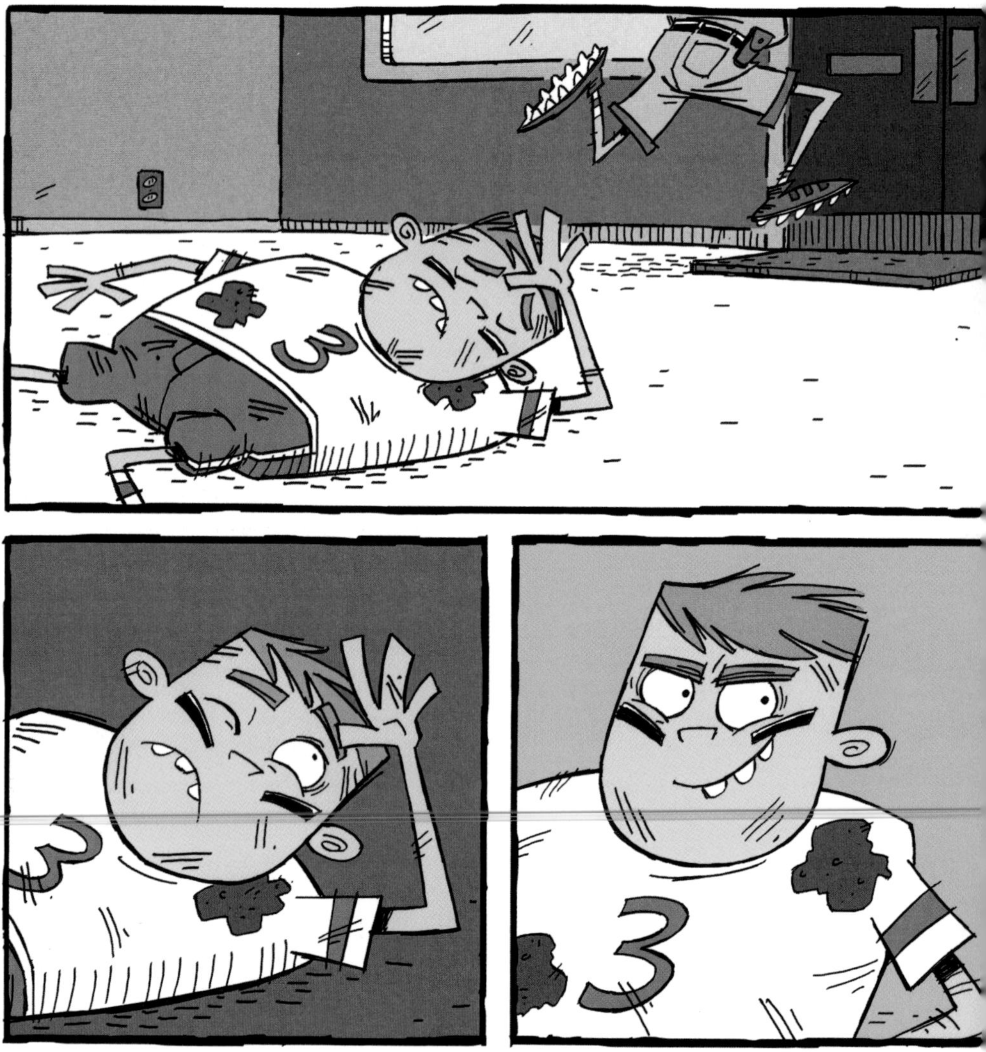

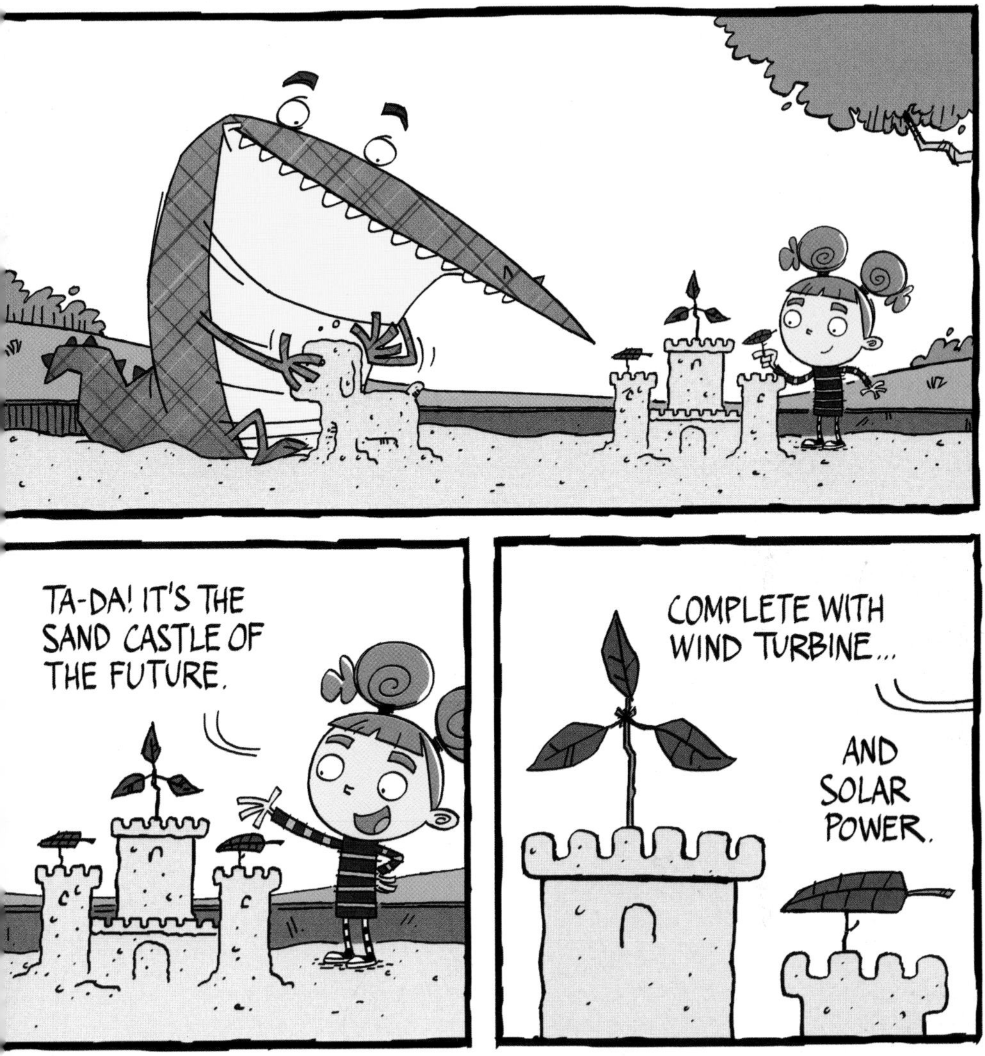
TA-DA! IT'S THE SAND CASTLE OF THE FUTURE.
COMPLETE WITH WIND TURBINE...
AND SOLAR POWER.

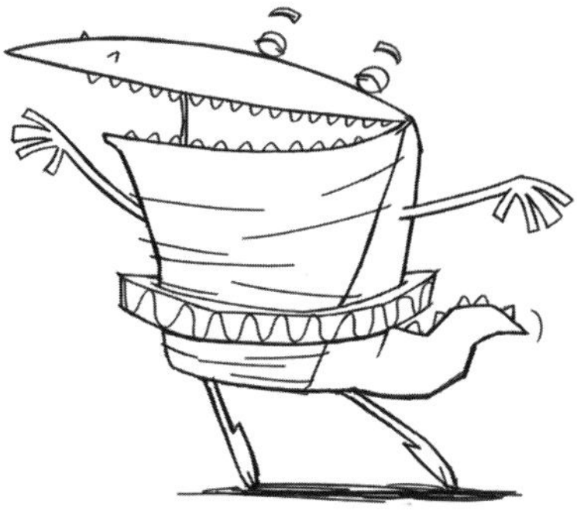

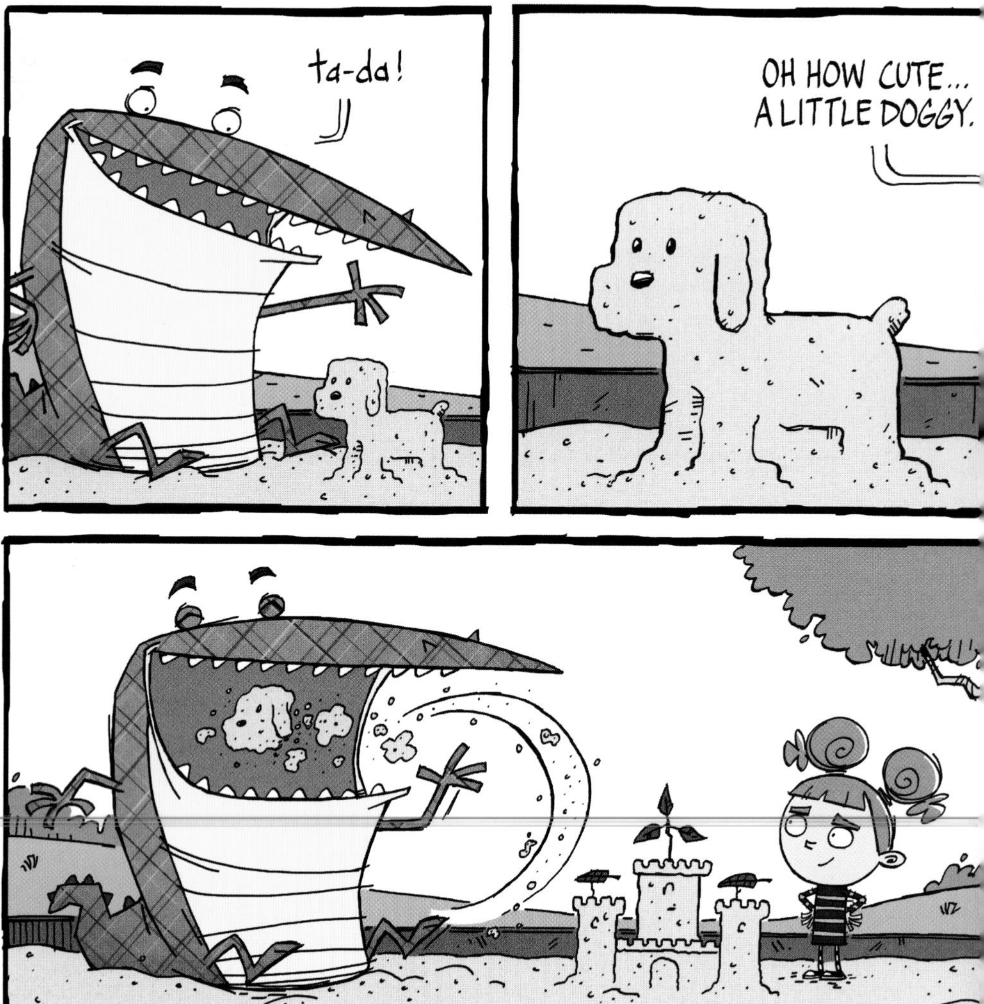
ta-da!
OH HOW CUTE...
A LITTLE DOGGY.

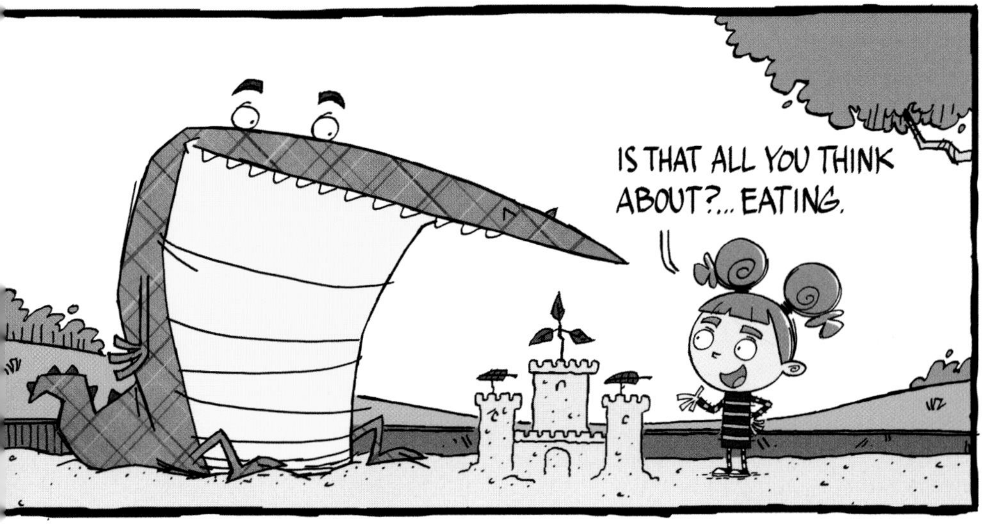
IS THAT ALL YOU THINK ABOUT?... EATING.

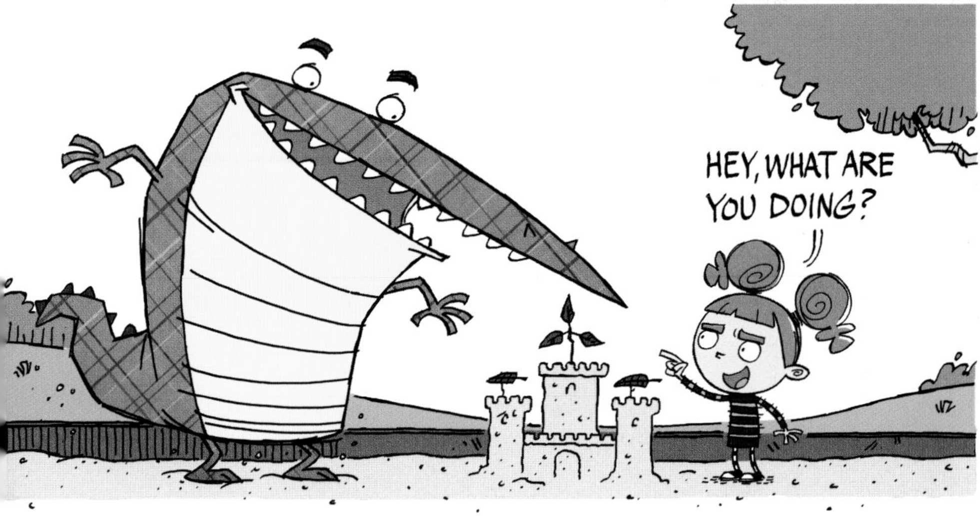
HEY, WHAT ARE YOU DOING?

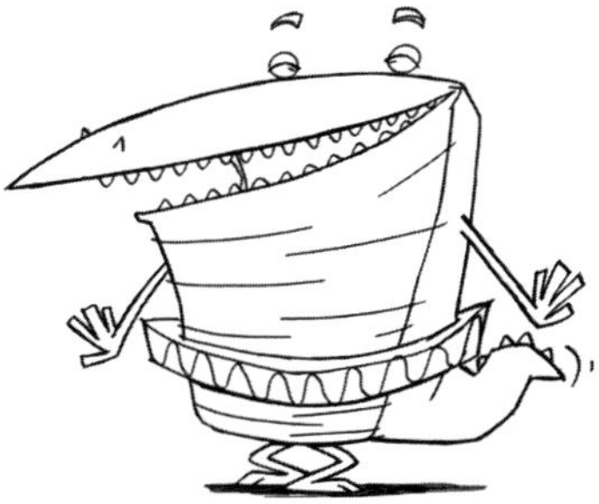

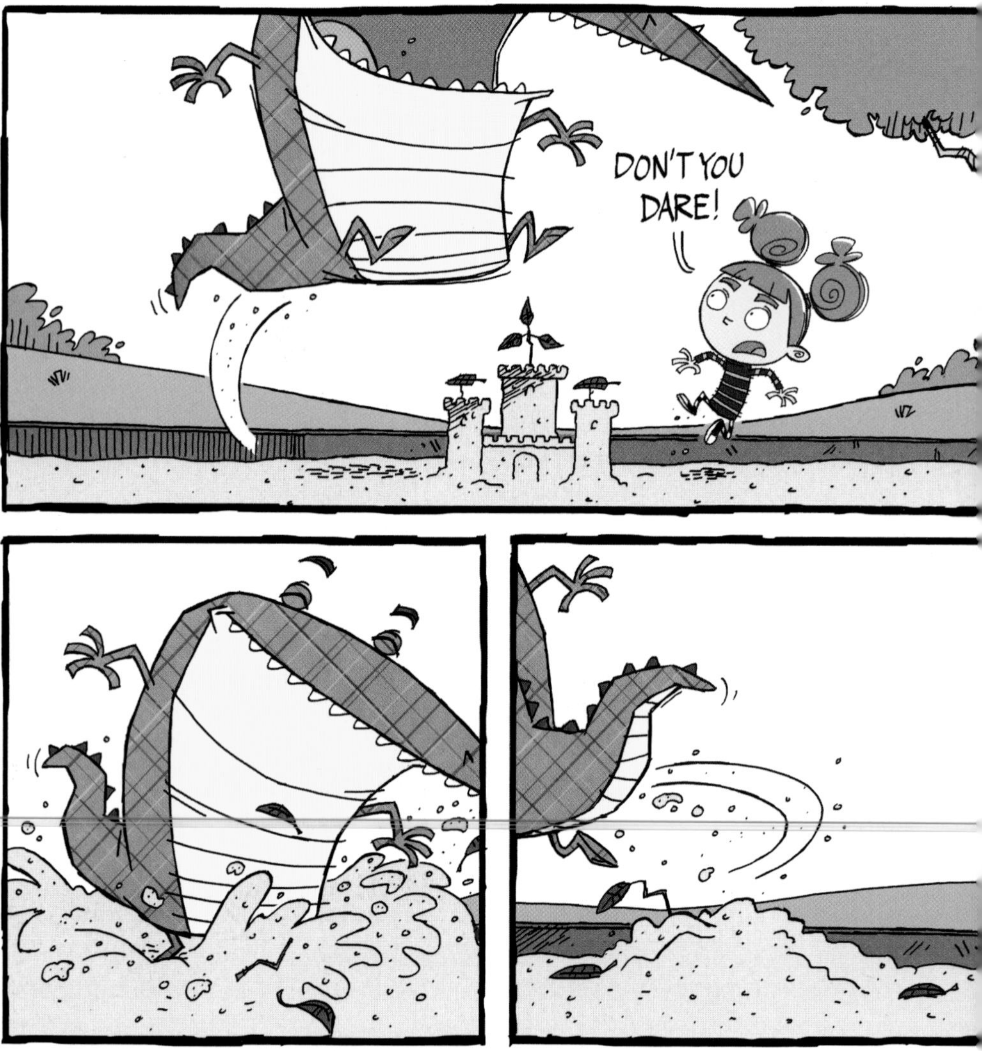
DON'T YOU DARE!

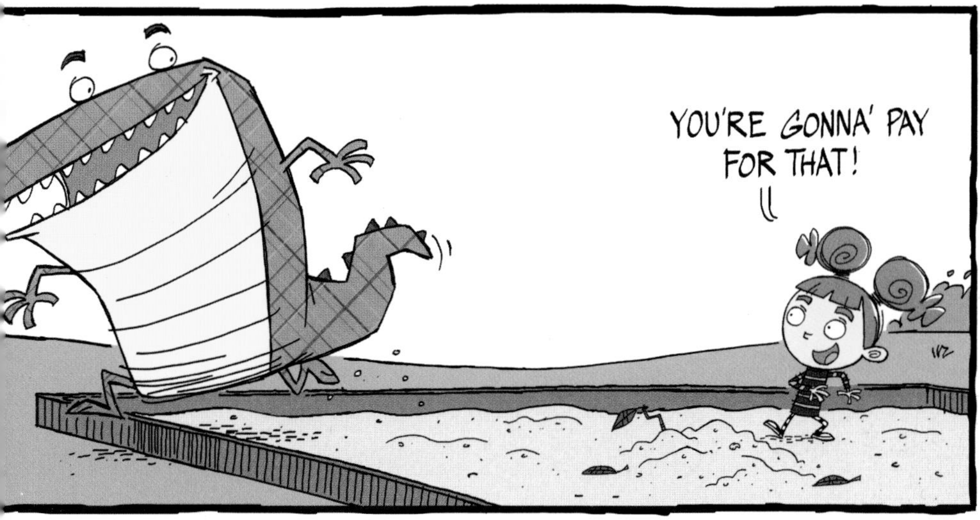
YOU'RE GONNA' PAY FOR THAT!

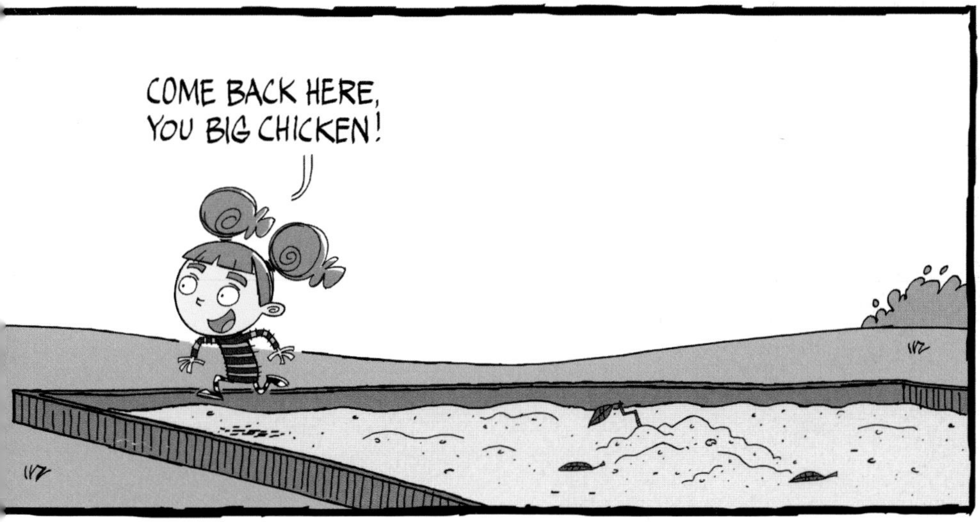
COME BACK HERE, YOU BIG CHICKEN!

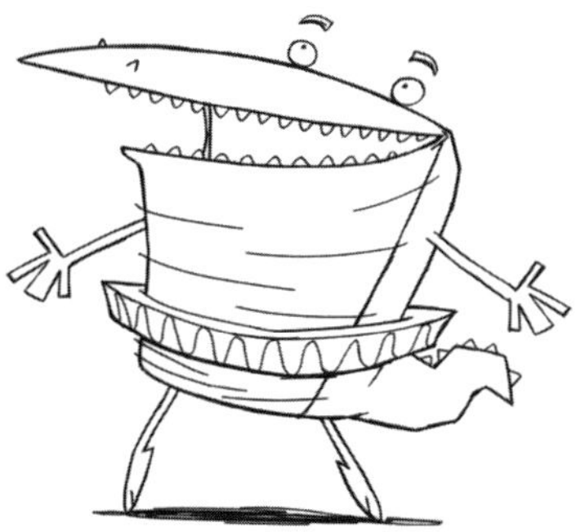

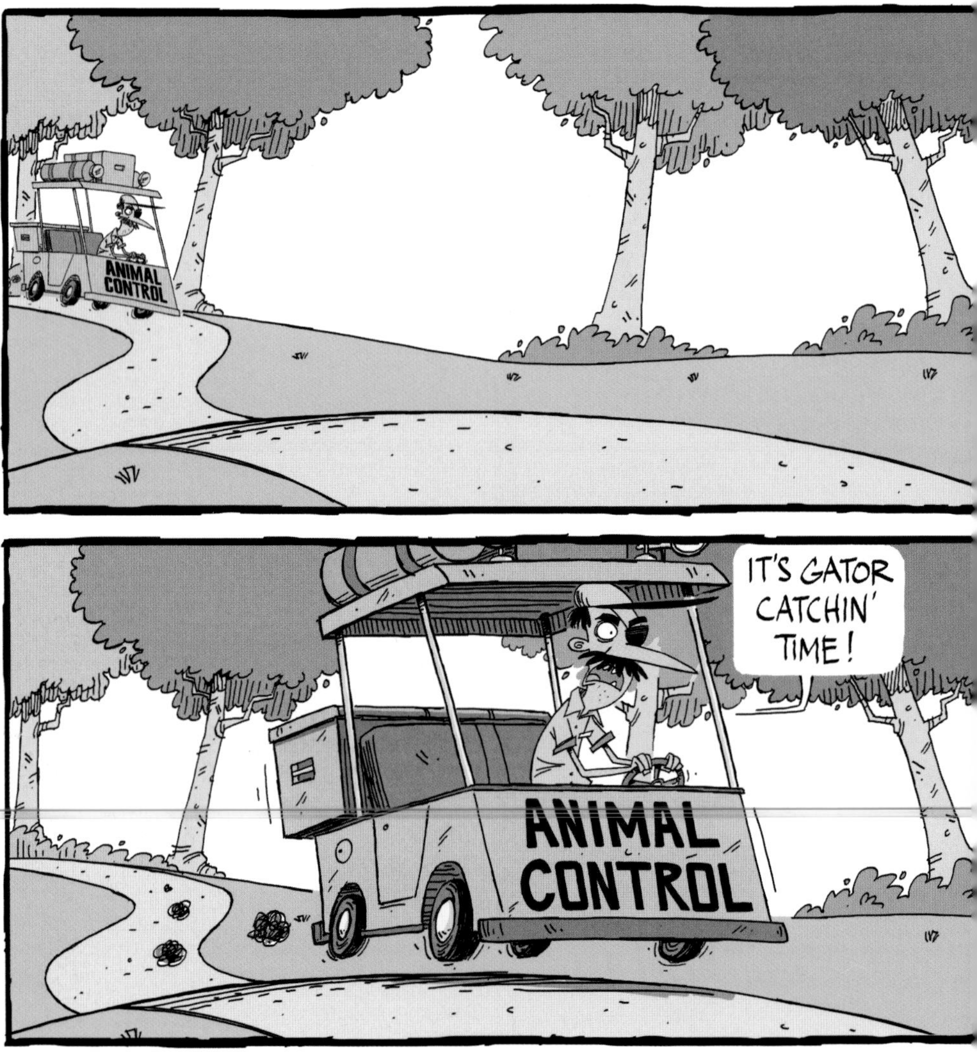
ANIMAL CONTROL
ANIMAL CONTROL
IT'S GATOR CATCHIN' TIME!

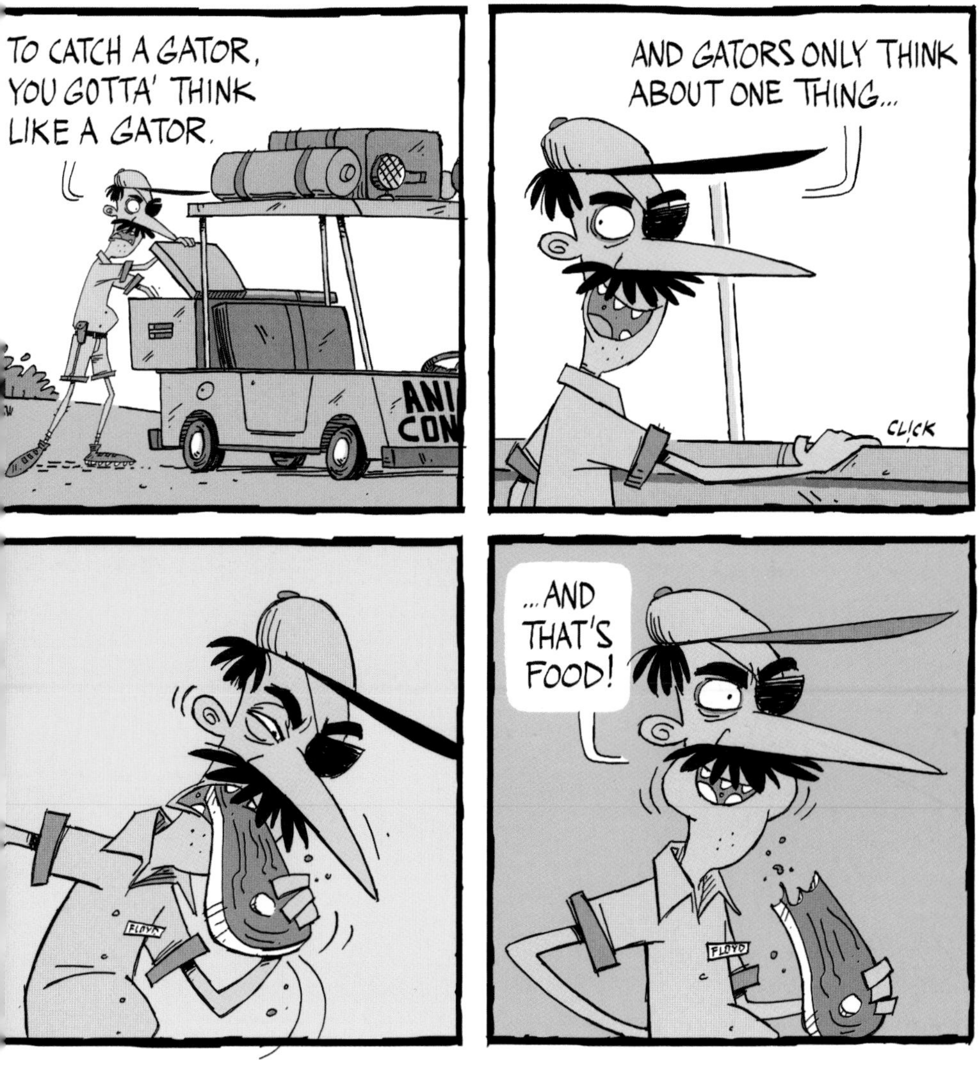
TO CATCH A GATOR, YOU GOTTA' THINK LIKE A GATOR.
AND GATORS ONLY THINK ABOUT ONE THING...
CLICK
...AND THAT'S FOOD!

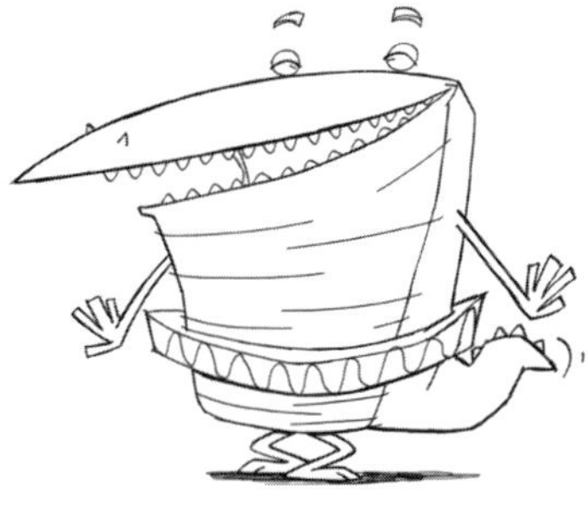

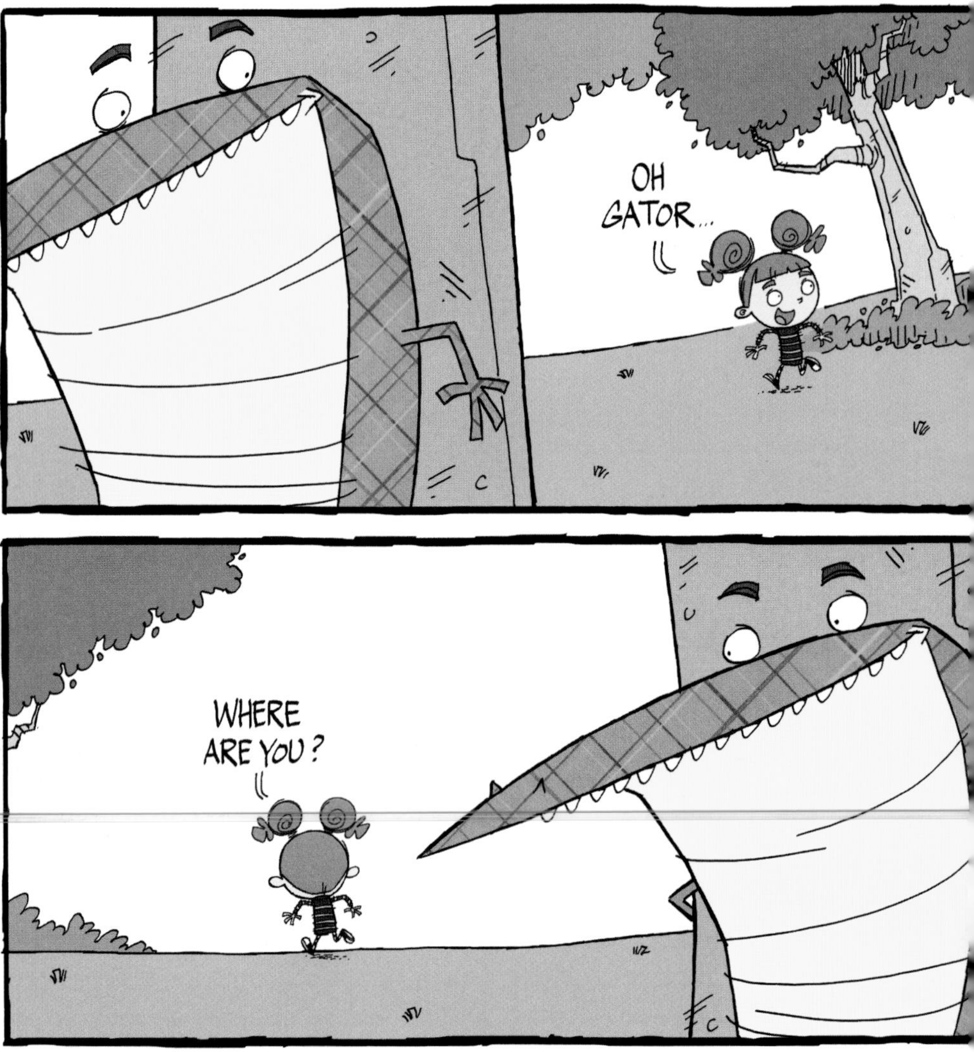
OH GATOR...
WHERE ARE YOU?

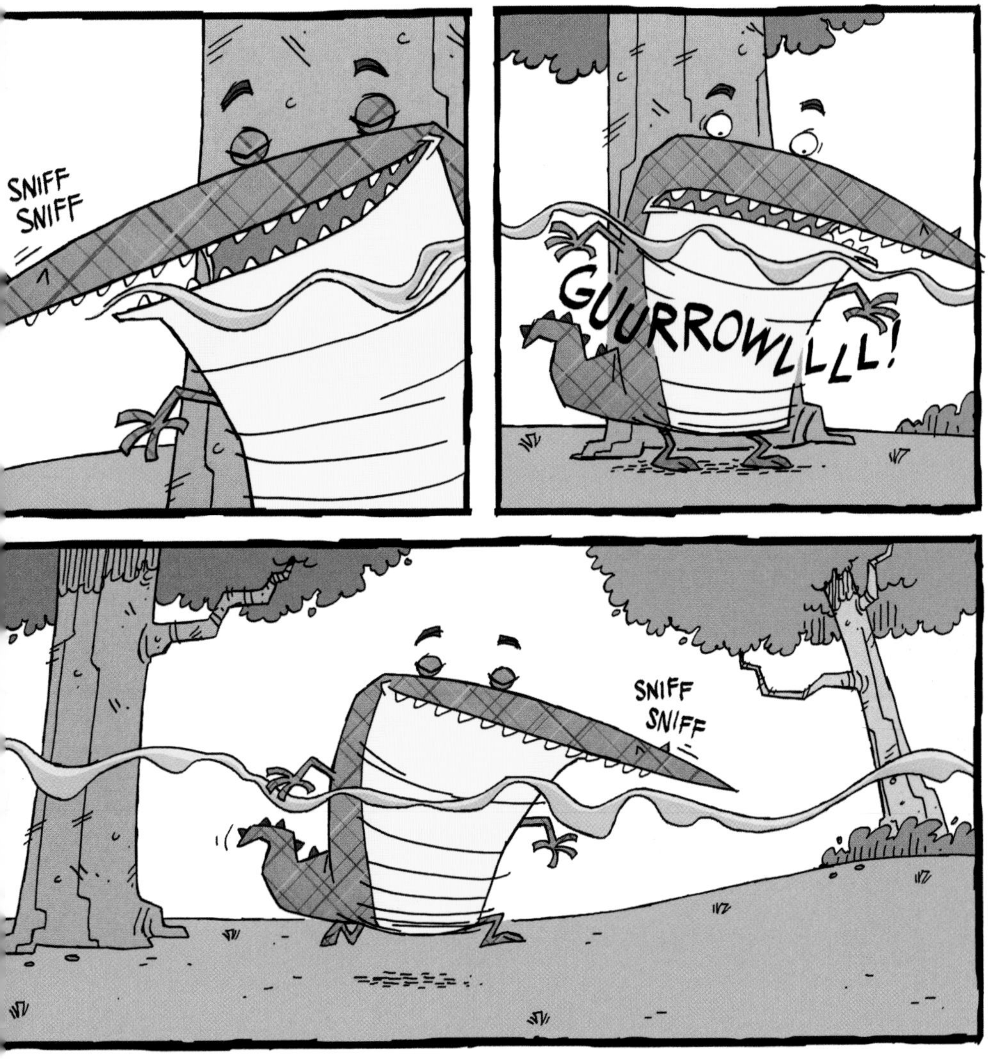
SNIFF
SNIFF
GUURROWLLLL!
SNIFF
SNIFF

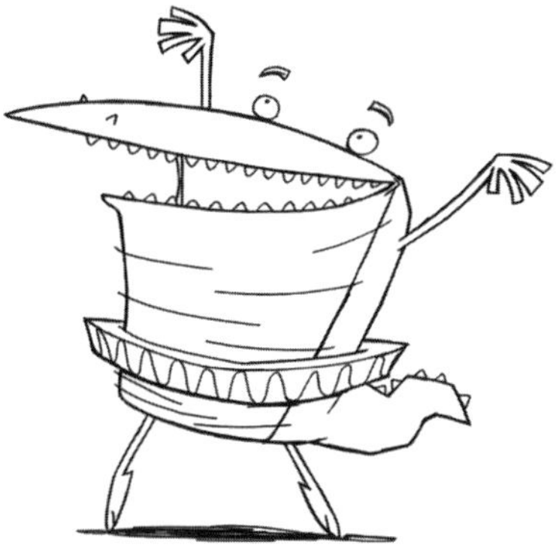

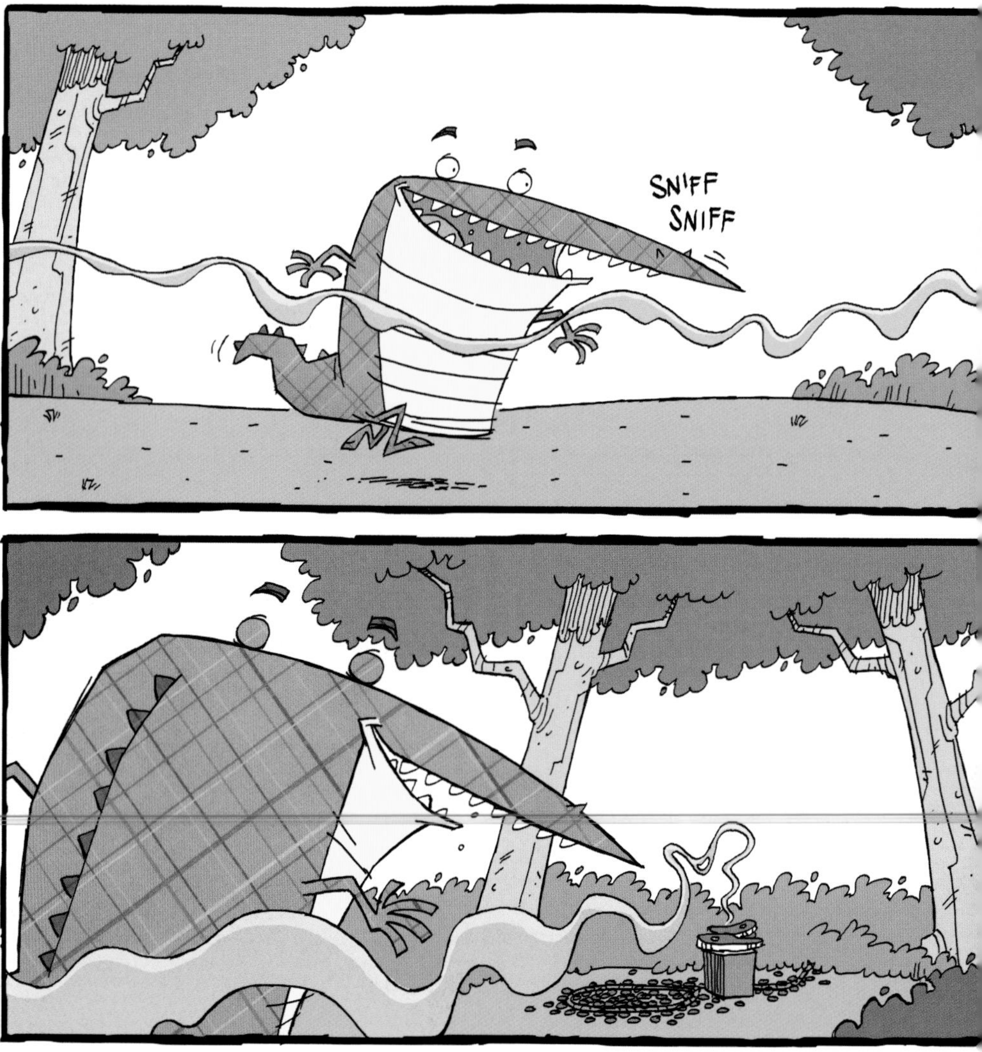
SNIFF
SNIFF

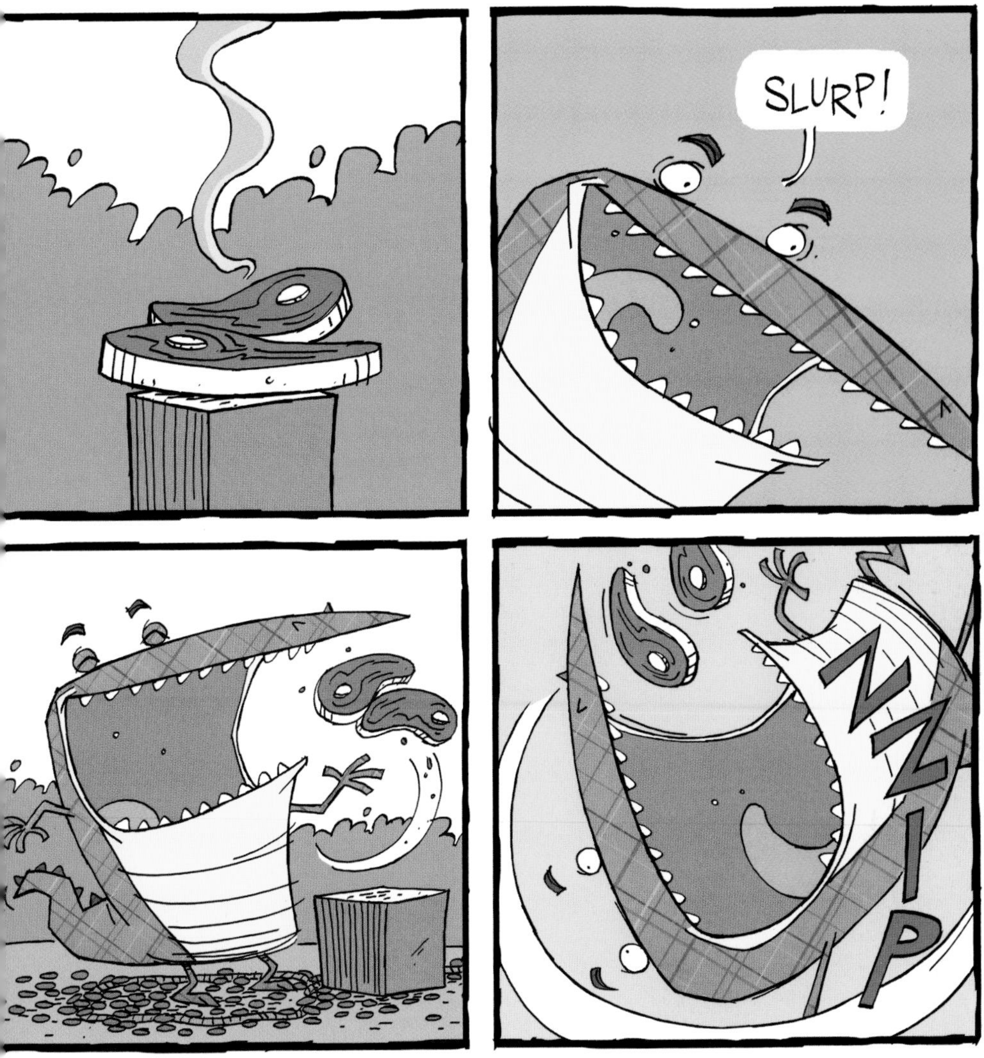
SLURP!
NNIP

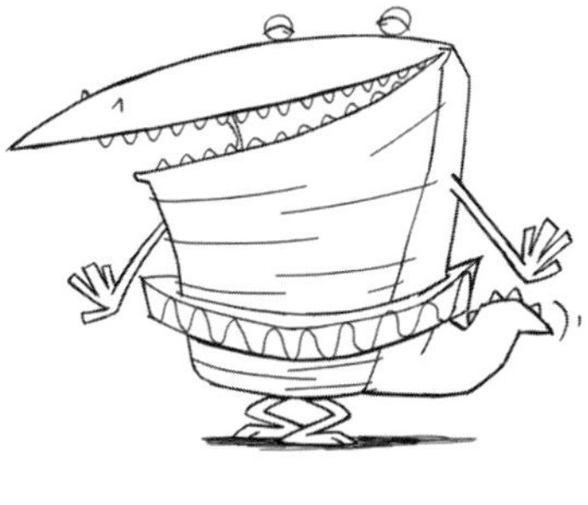

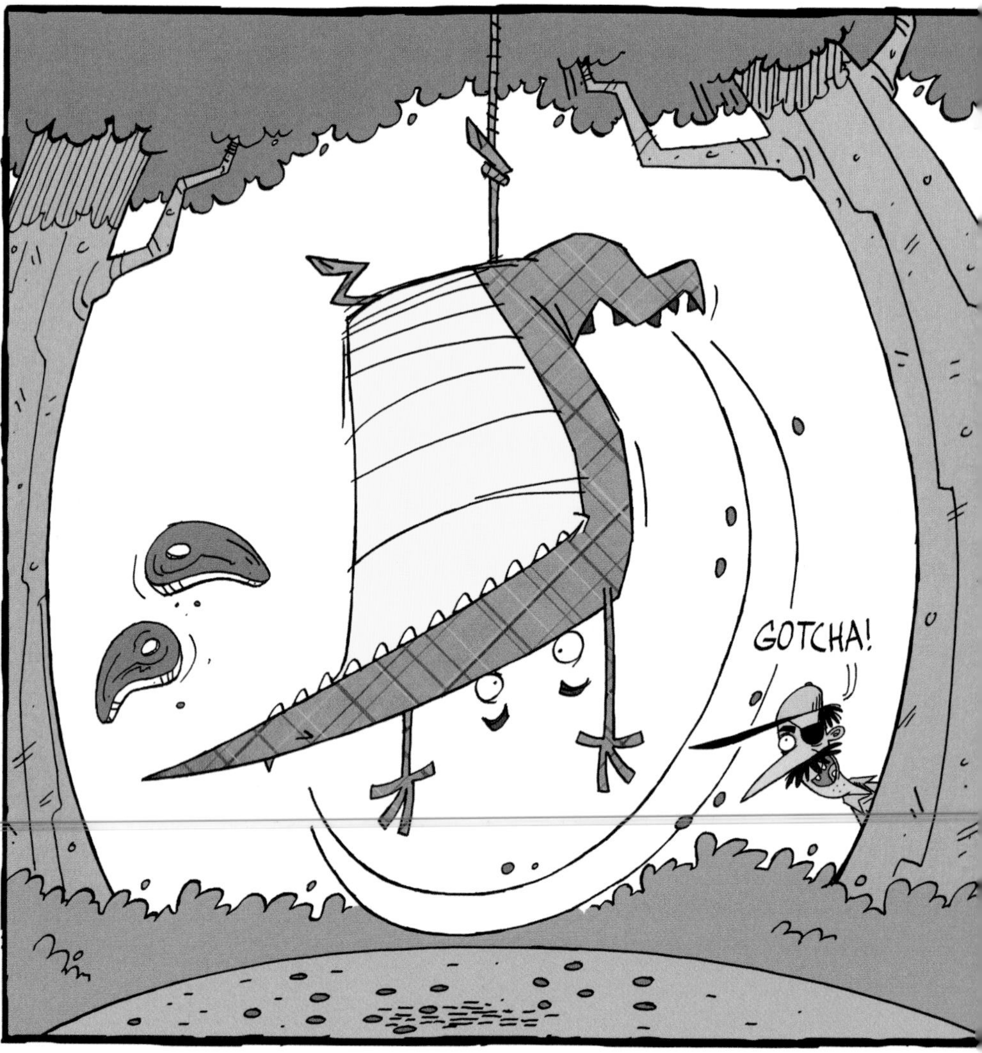
GOTCHA!

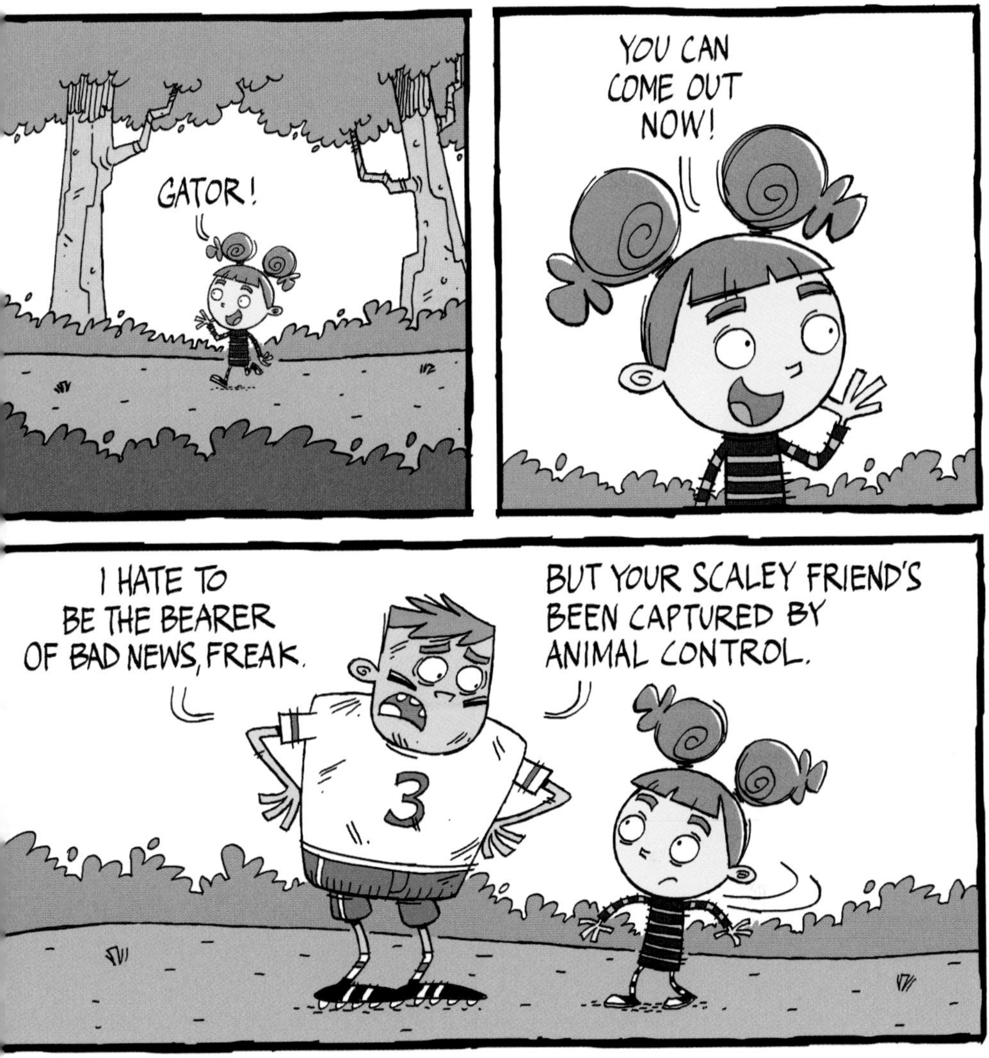
GATOR!
YOU CAN COME OUT NOW!
I HATE TO BE THE BEARER OF BAD NEWS, FREAK.
BUT YOUR SCALEY FRIEND'S BEEN CAPTURED BY ANIMAL CONTROL.

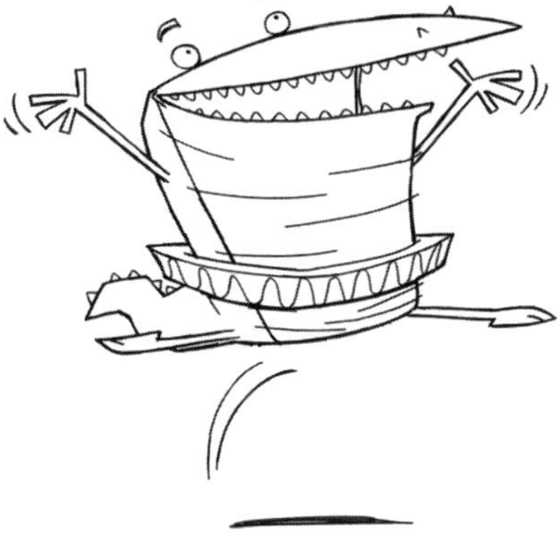

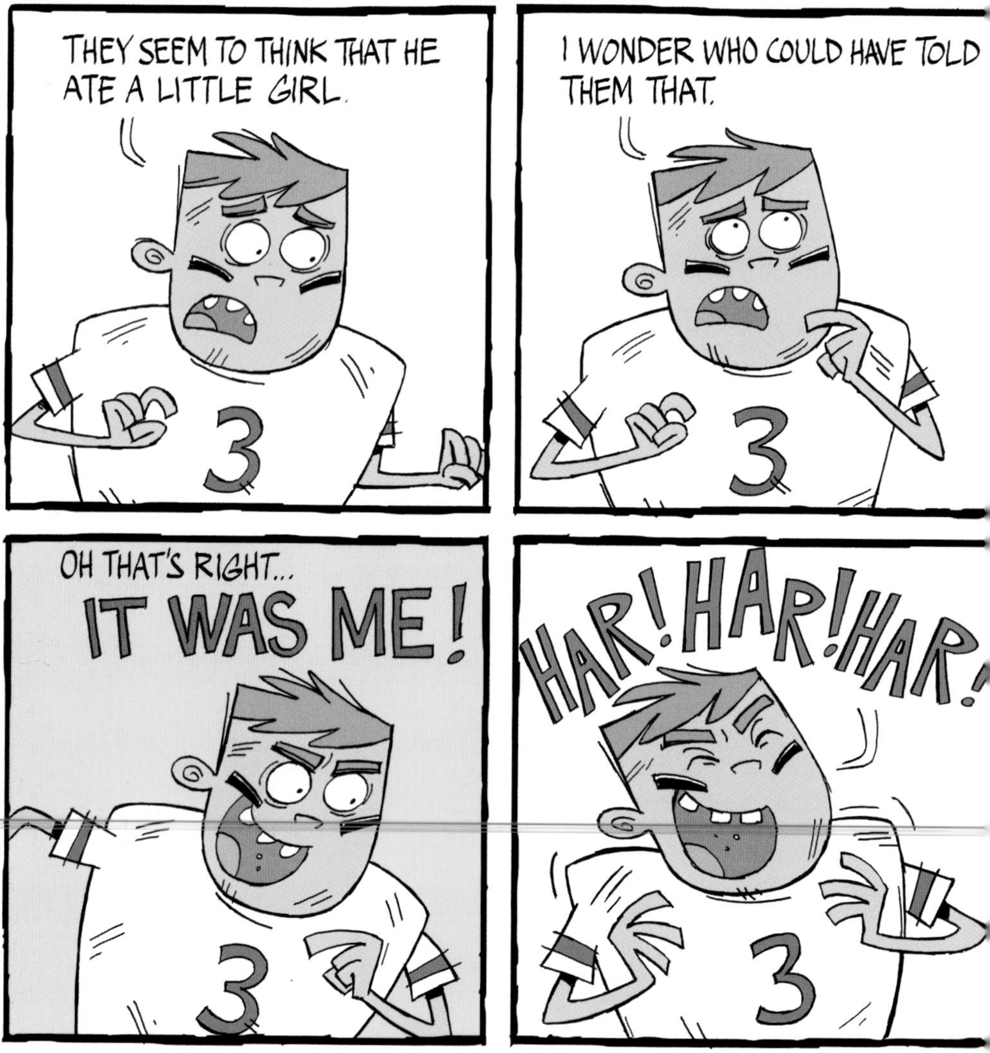
THEY SEEM TO THINK THAT HE ATE A LITTLE GIRL.
I WONDER WHO COULD HAVE TOLD THEM THAT.
OH THAT'S RIGHT...
IT WAS ME!
HAR! HAR! HAR!

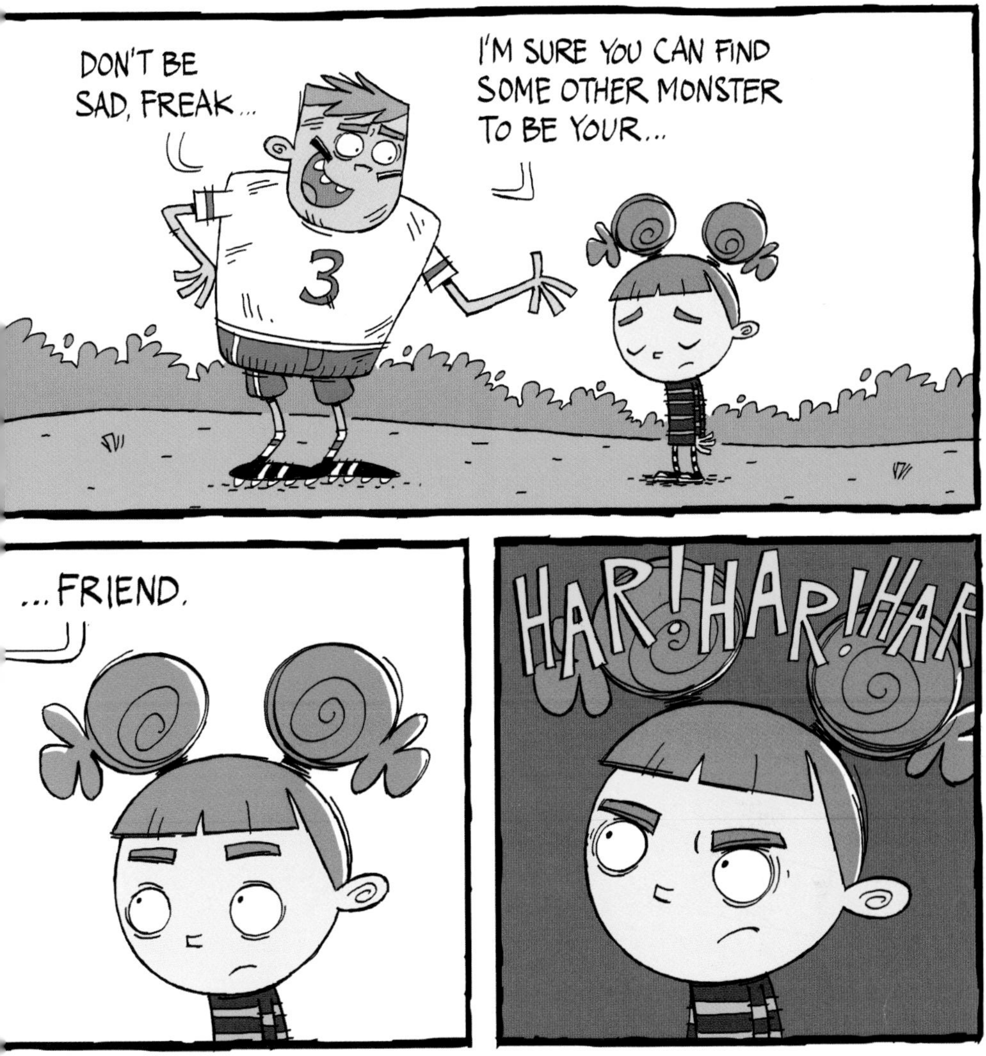
DON'T BE SAD, FREAK...
I'M SURE YOU CAN FIND SOME OTHER MONSTER TO BE YOUR...
...FRIEND.
HAR! HAR! HAR

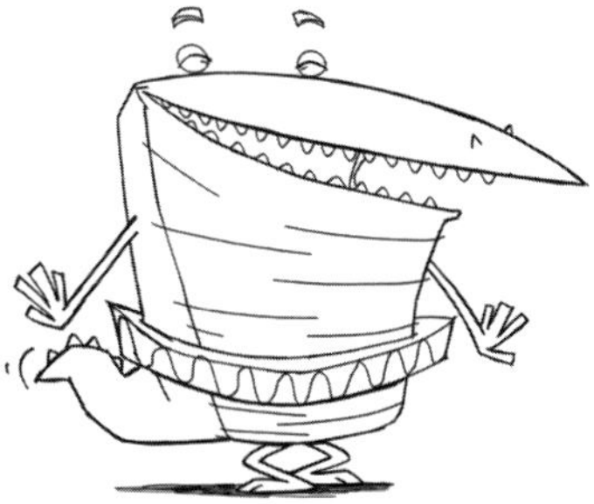

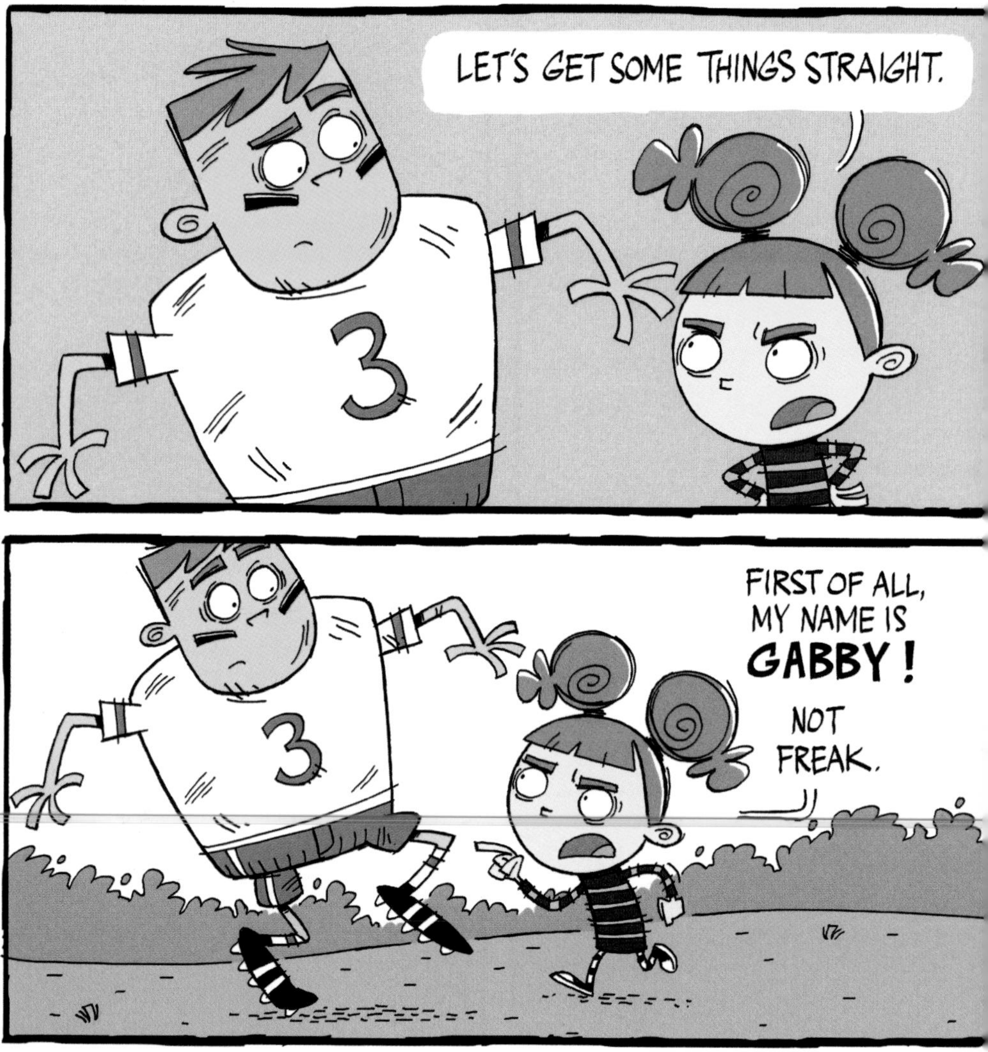
LET'S GET SOME THINGS STRAIGHT.
FIRST OF ALL, MY NAME IS GABBY!
NOT FREAK.

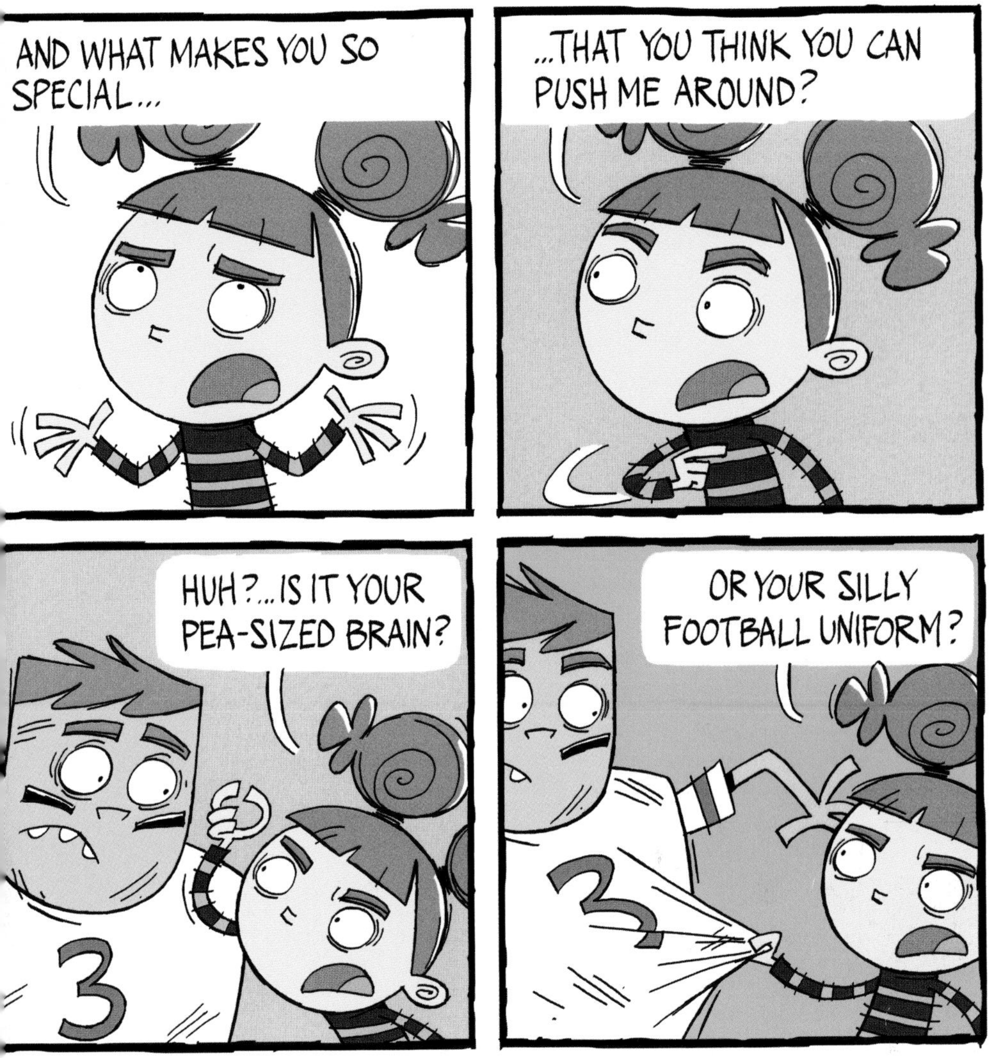
AND WHAT MAKES YOU SO SPECIAL...
...THAT YOU THINK YOU CAN PUSH ME AROUND?
HUH?...IS IT YOUR PEA-SIZED BRAIN?
OR YOUR SILLY FOOTBALL UNIFORM?

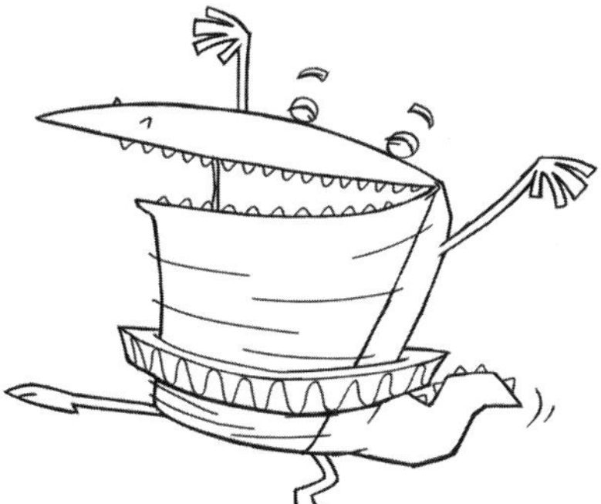

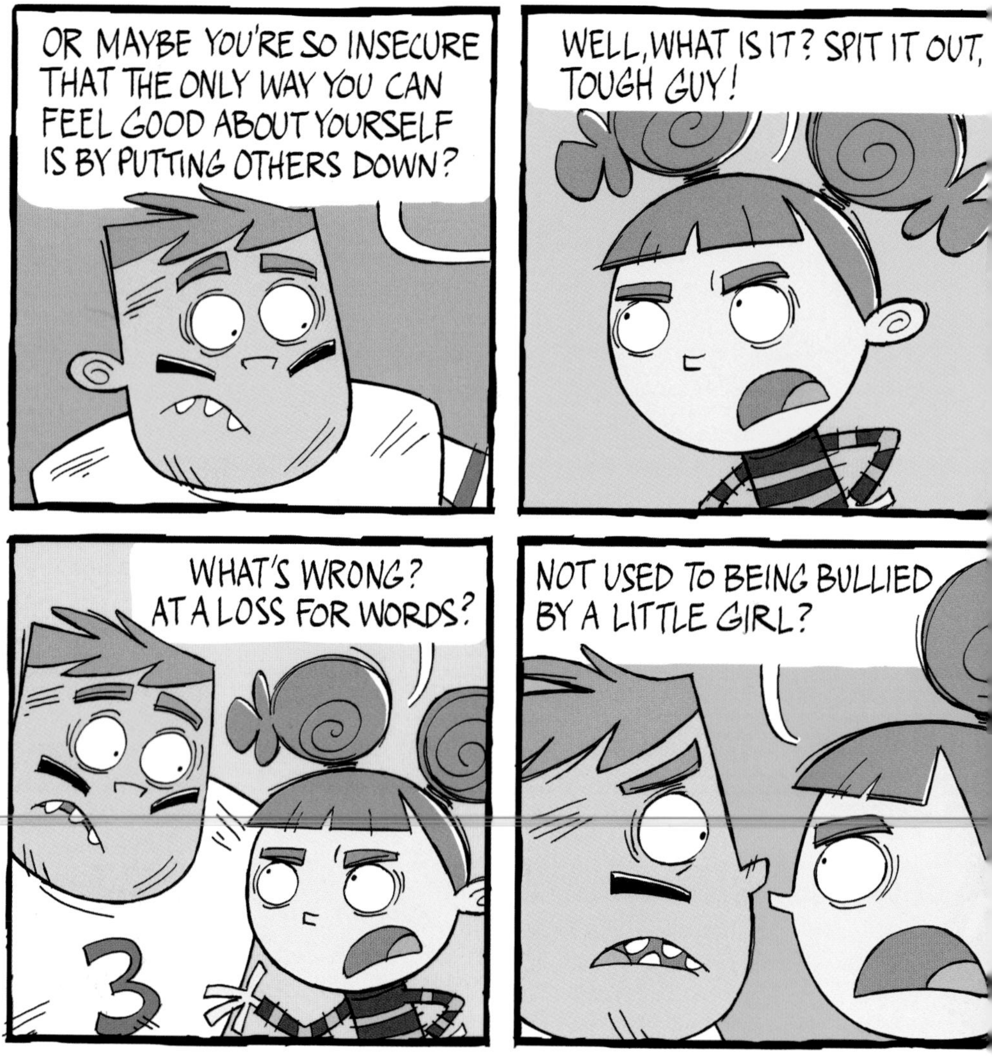
OR MAYBE YOU'RE SO INSECURE THAT THE ONLY WAY YOU CAN FEEL GOOD ABOUT YOURSELF IS BY PUTTING OTHERS DOWN?
WELL, WHAT IS IT? SPIT IT OUT, TOUGH GUY!
WHAT'S WRONG? AT A LOSS FOR WORDS?
3
NOT USED TO BEING BULLIED BY A LITTLE GIRL?

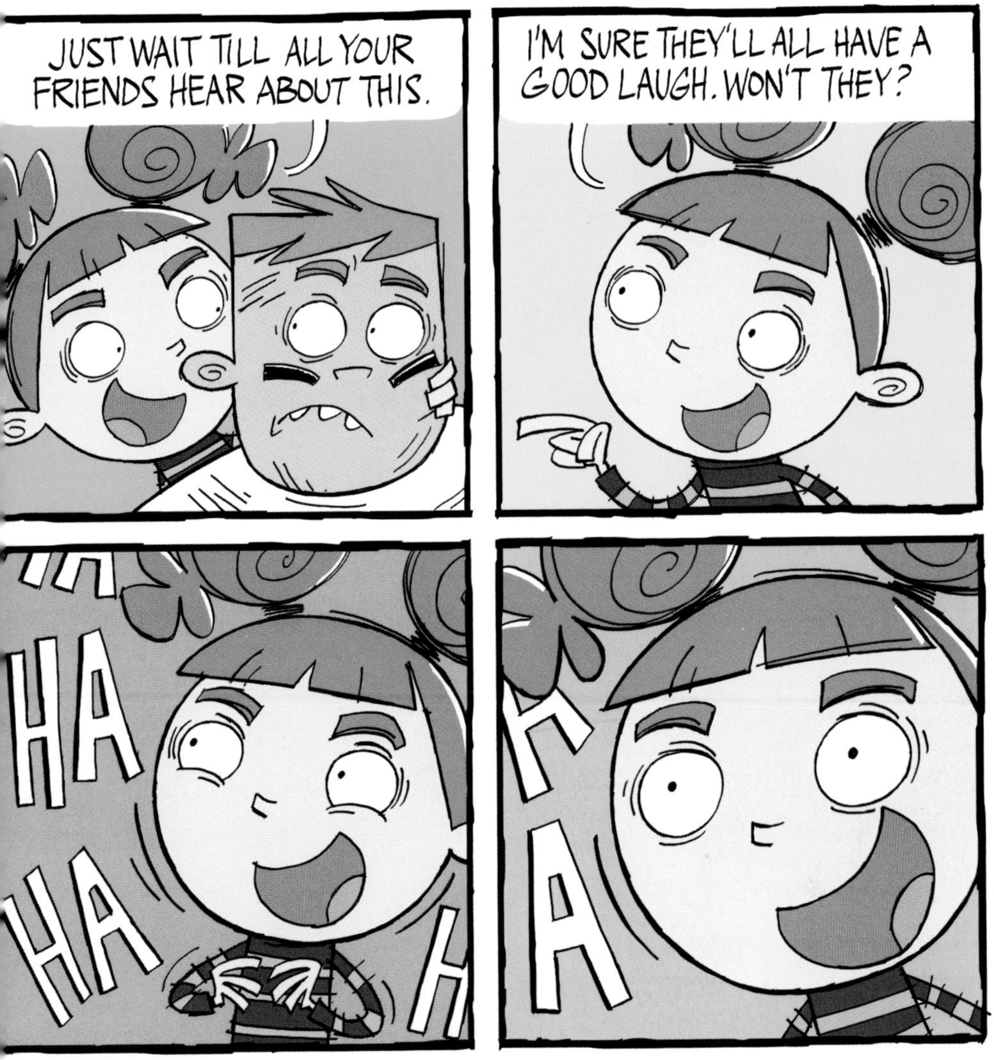
JUST WAIT TILL ALL YOUR FRIENDS HEAR ABOUT THIS.
I'M SURE THEY'LL ALL HAVE A GOOD LAUGH. WON'T THEY?
HA
HA
HA
H
A

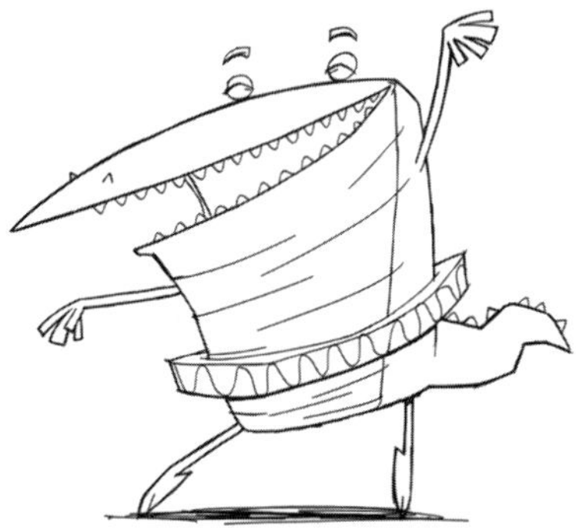

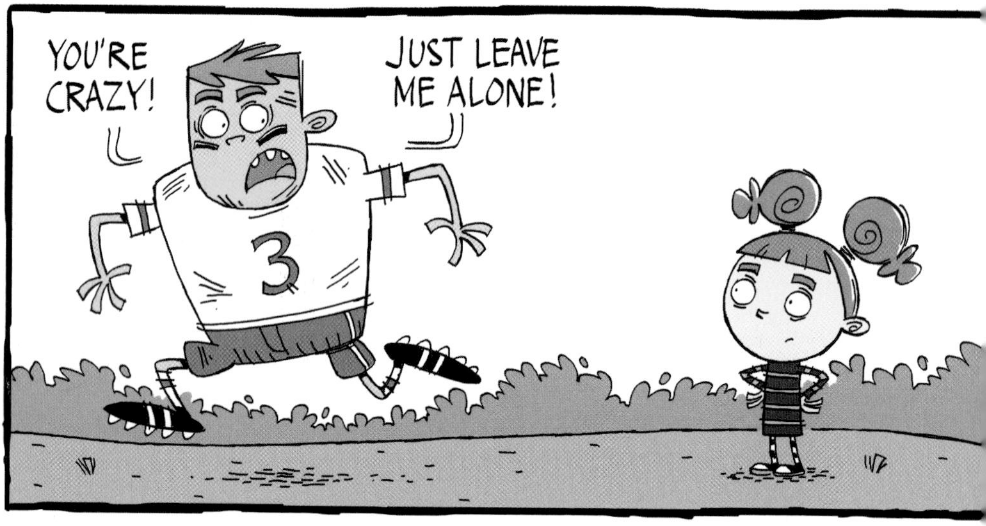
YOU'RE CRAZY!
JUST LEAVE ME ALONE!

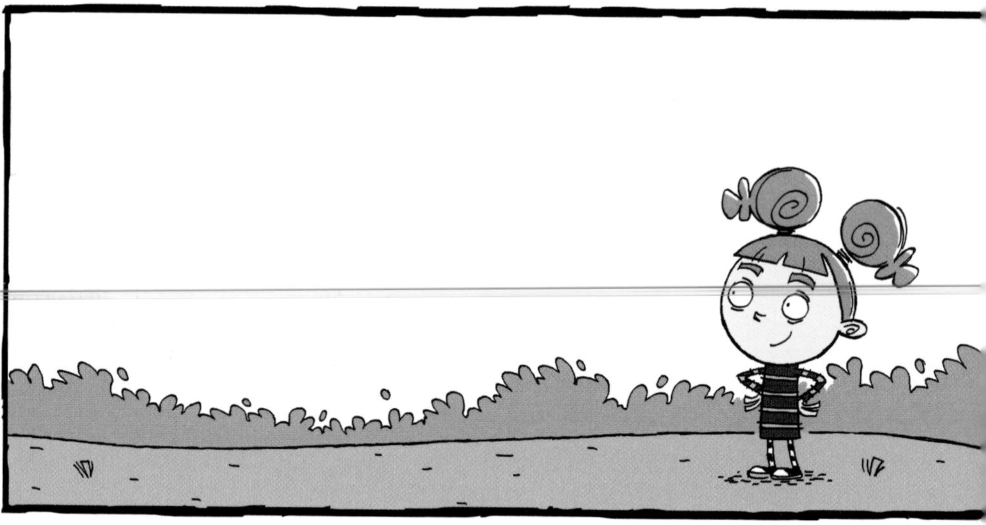

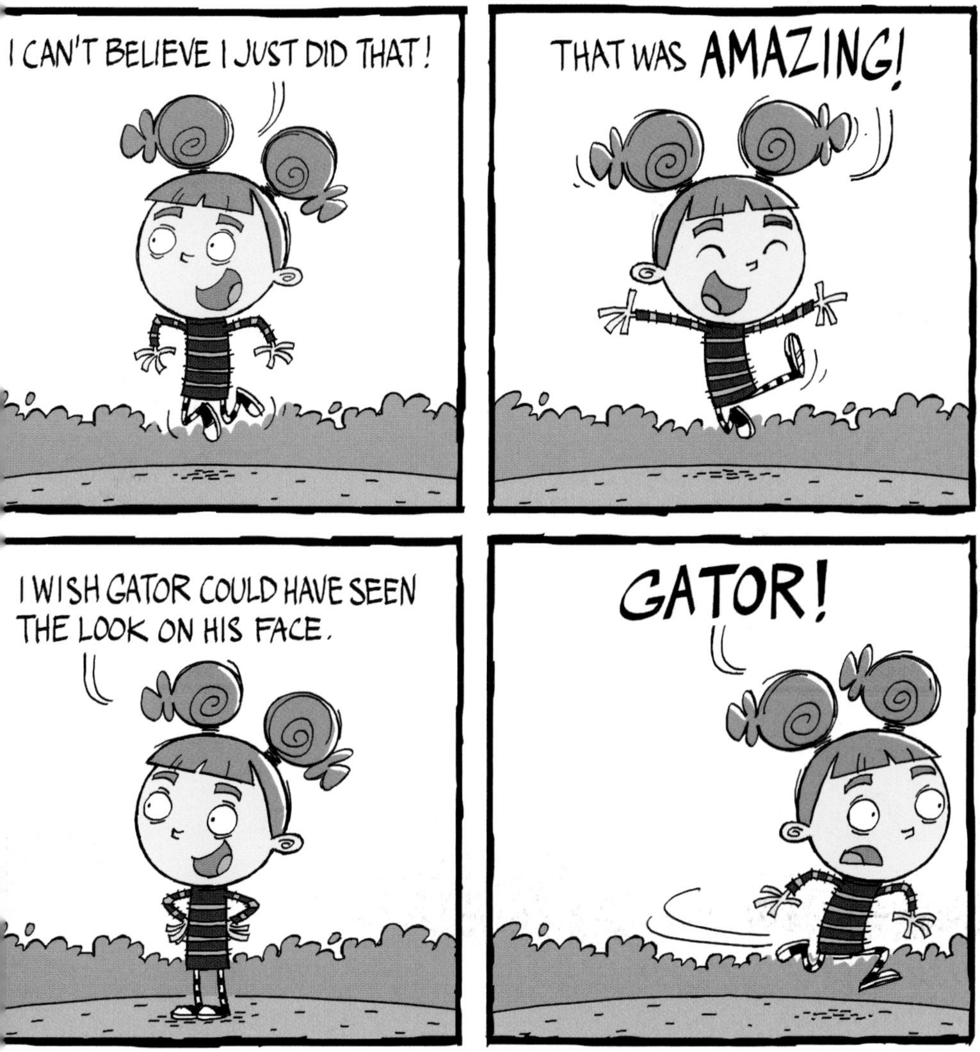
I CAN'T BELIEVE I JUST DID THAT!
THAT WAS AMAZING!
I WISH GATOR COULD HAVE SEEN THE LOOK ON HIS FACE.
GATOR!

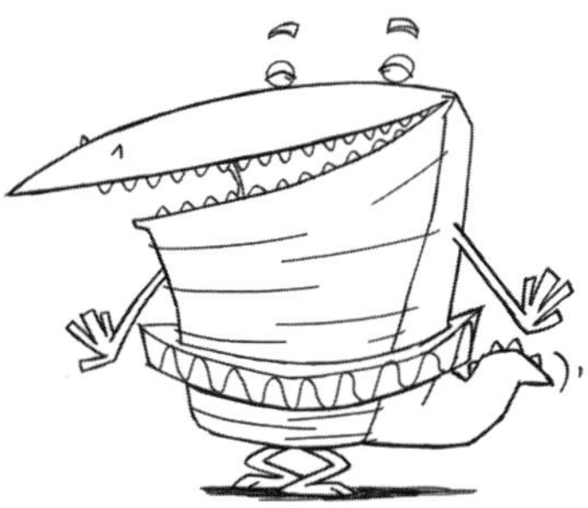

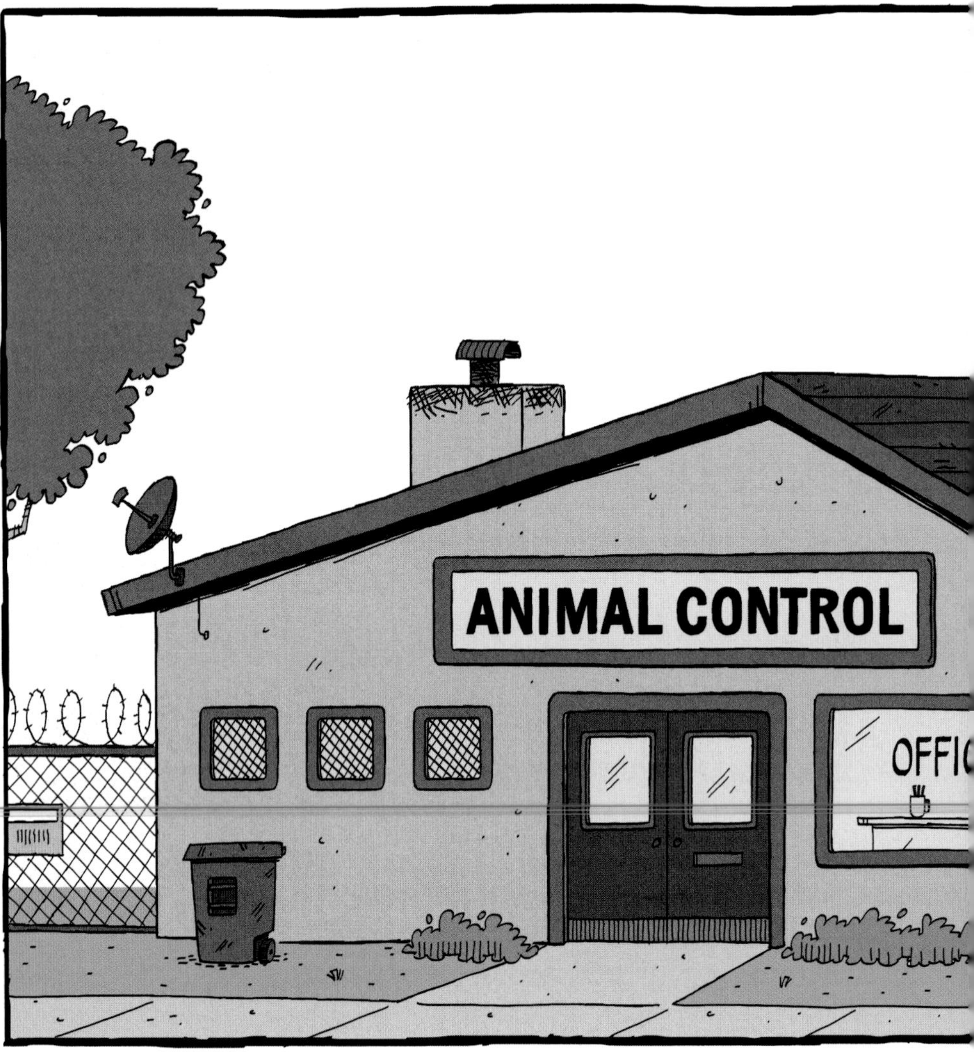
ANIMAL CONTROL
OFFIC

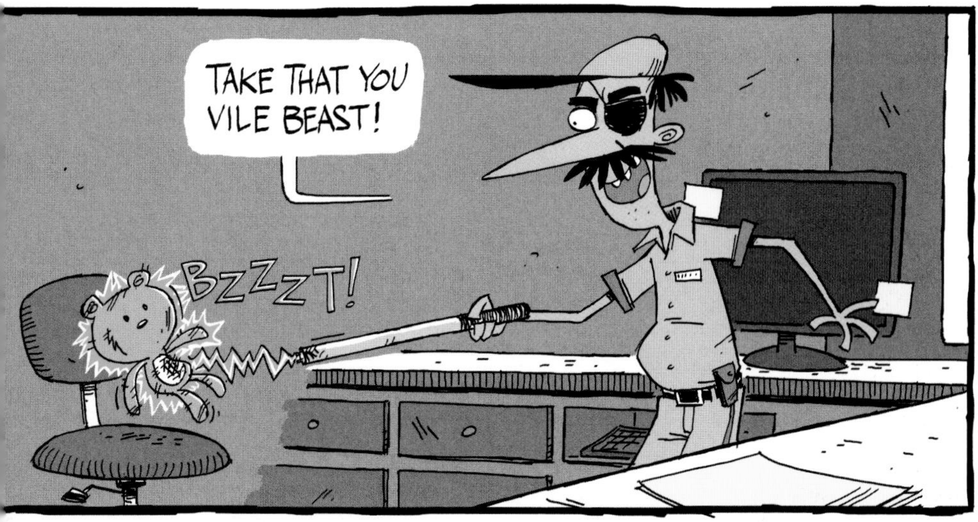
TAKE THAT YOU VILE BEAST!
BZZZZT!

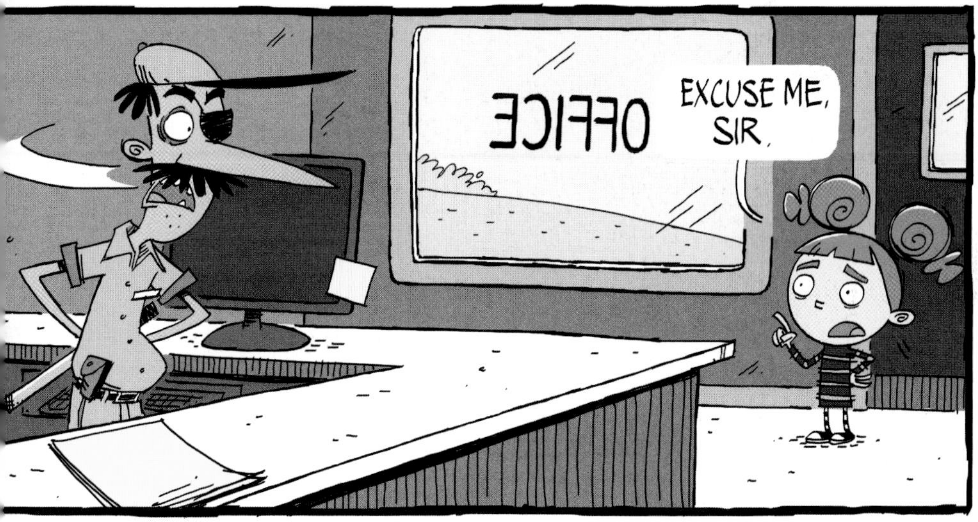
OFFICE
EXCUSE ME, SIR.

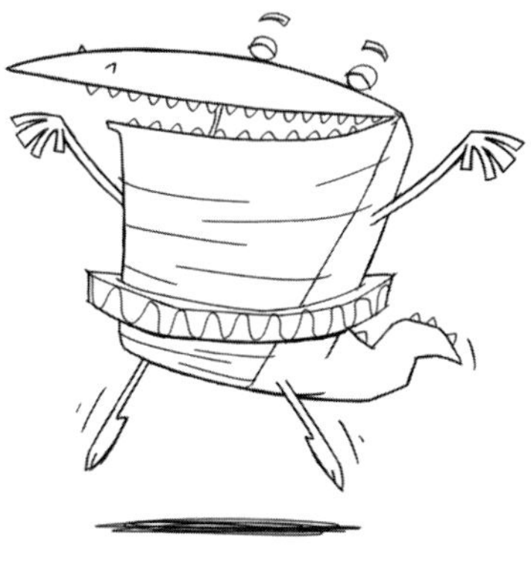

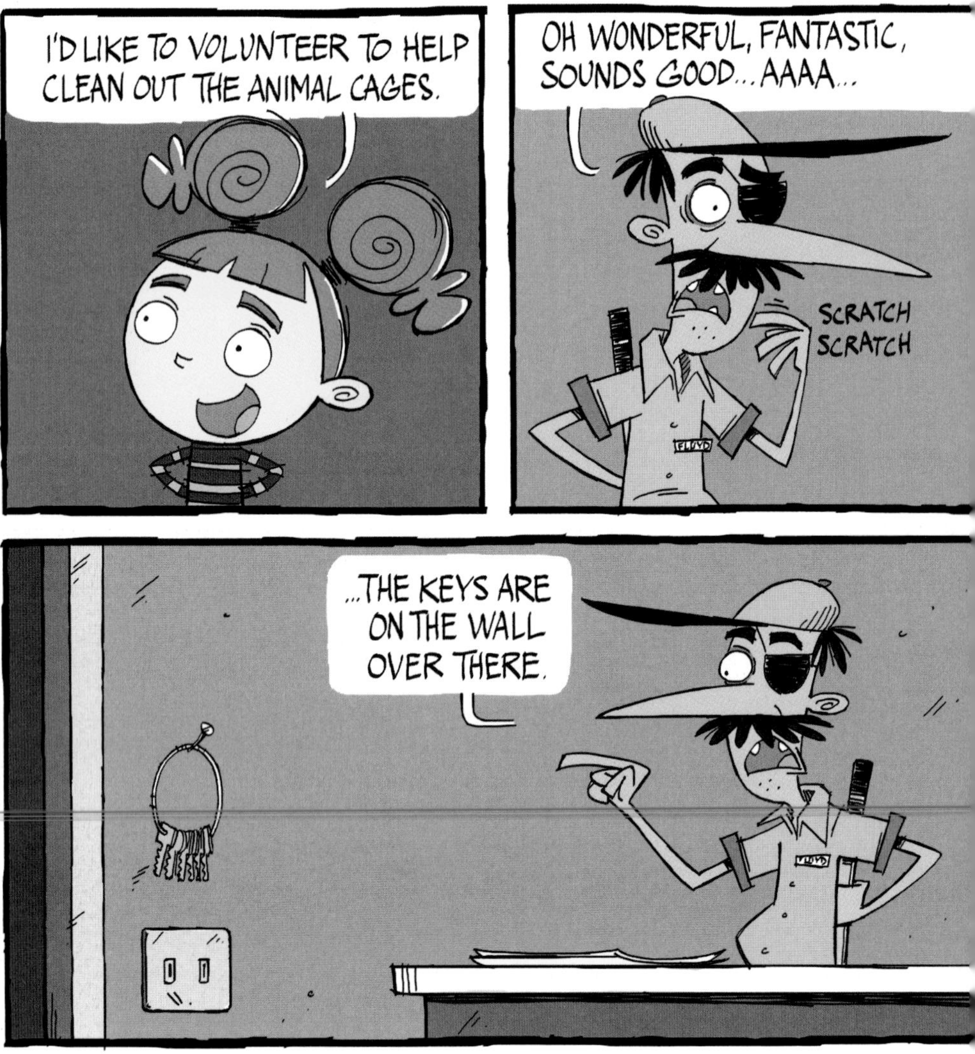
I'D LIKE TO VOLUNTEER TO HELP CLEAN OUT THE ANIMAL CAGES.
OH WONDERFUL, FANTASTIC, SOUNDS GOOD... AAAA...
SCRATCH SCRATCH
FLOYD
...THE KEYS ARE ON THE WALL OVER THERE.
FLOYD

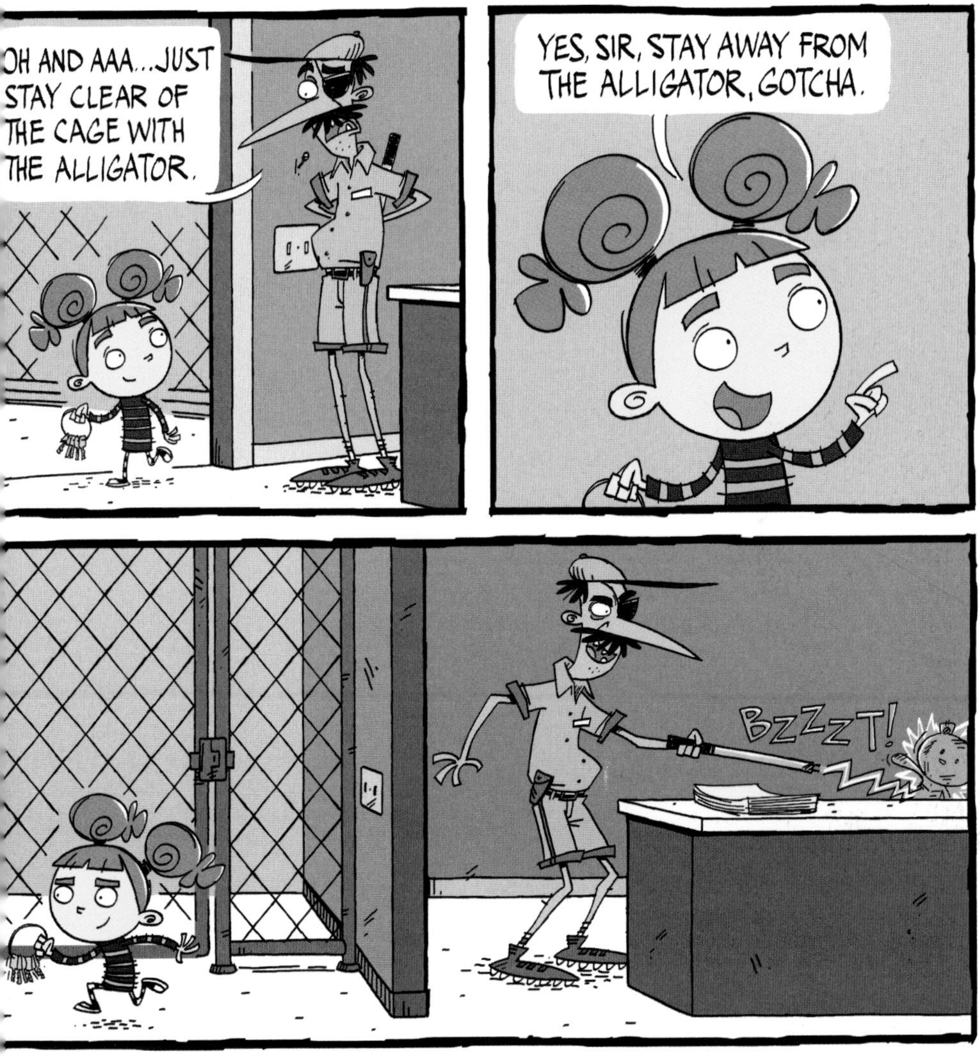
OH AND AAA...JUST STAY CLEAR OF THE CAGE WITH THE ALLIGATOR.
YES, SIR, STAY AWAY FROM THE ALLIGATOR, GOTCHA.
BZZZT!

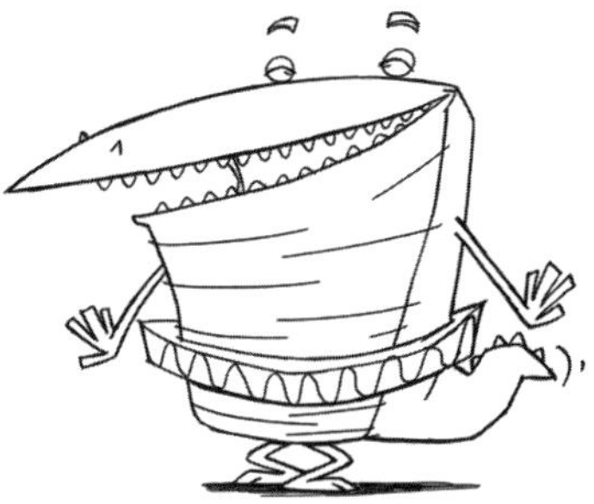

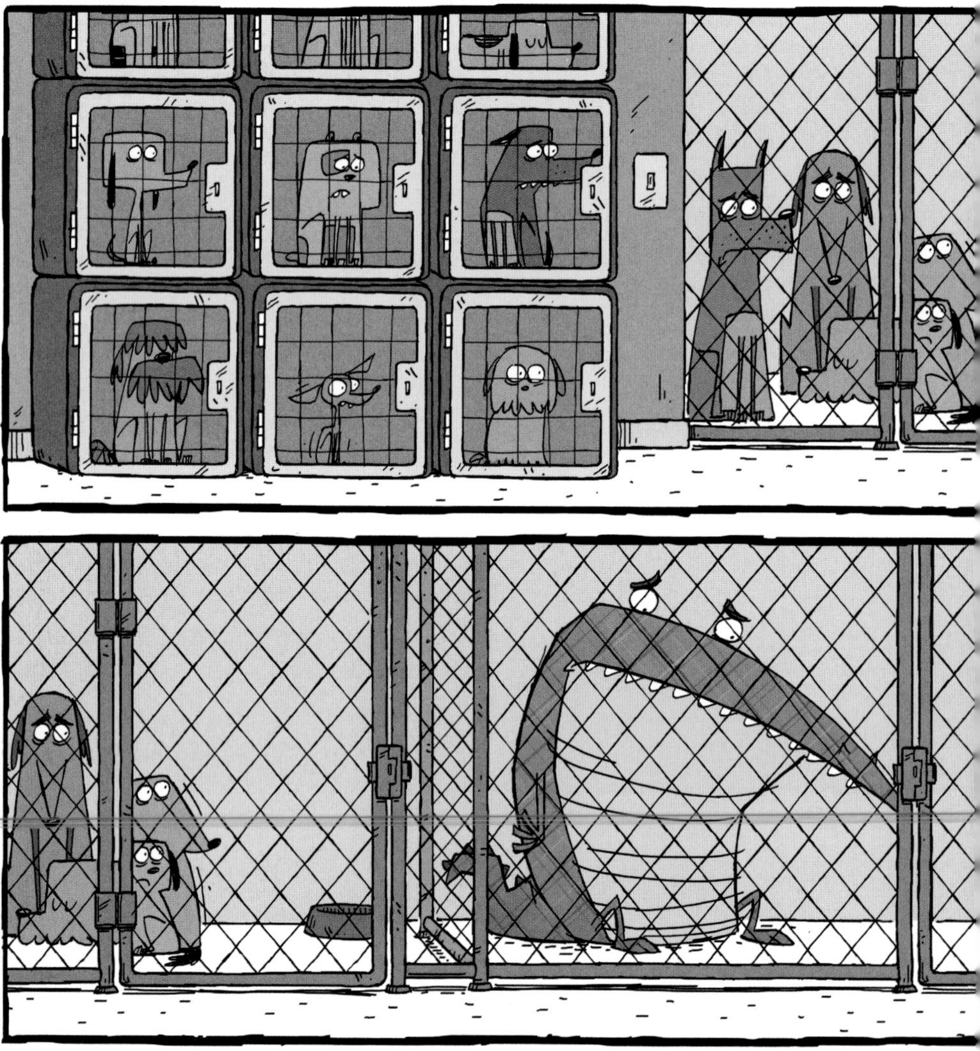

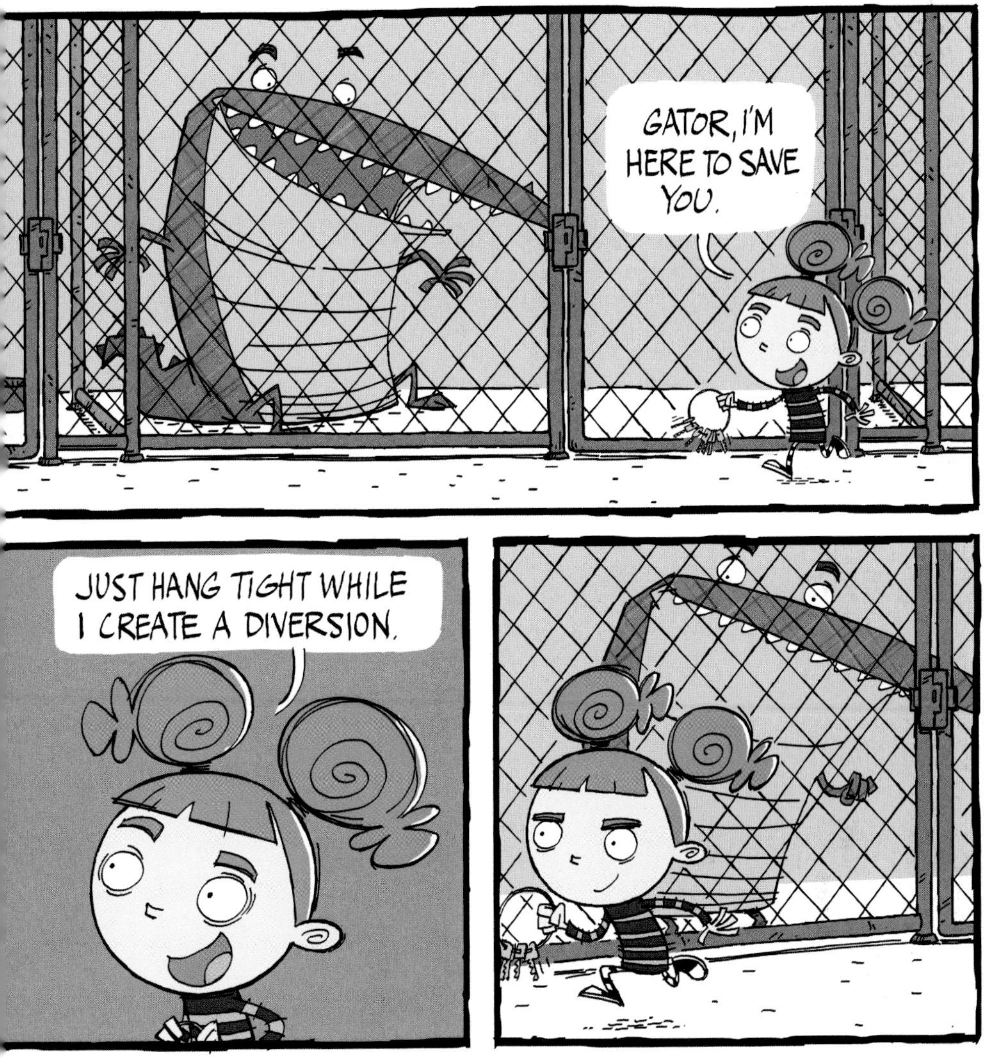
GATOR, I'M HERE TO SAVE YOU.
JUST HANG TIGHT WHILE I CREATE A DIVERSION.

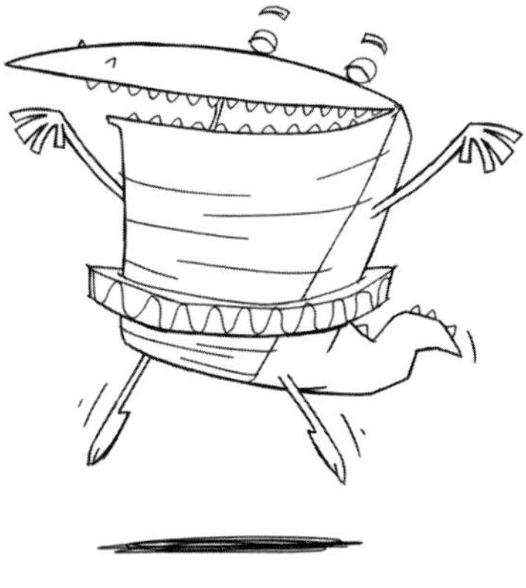

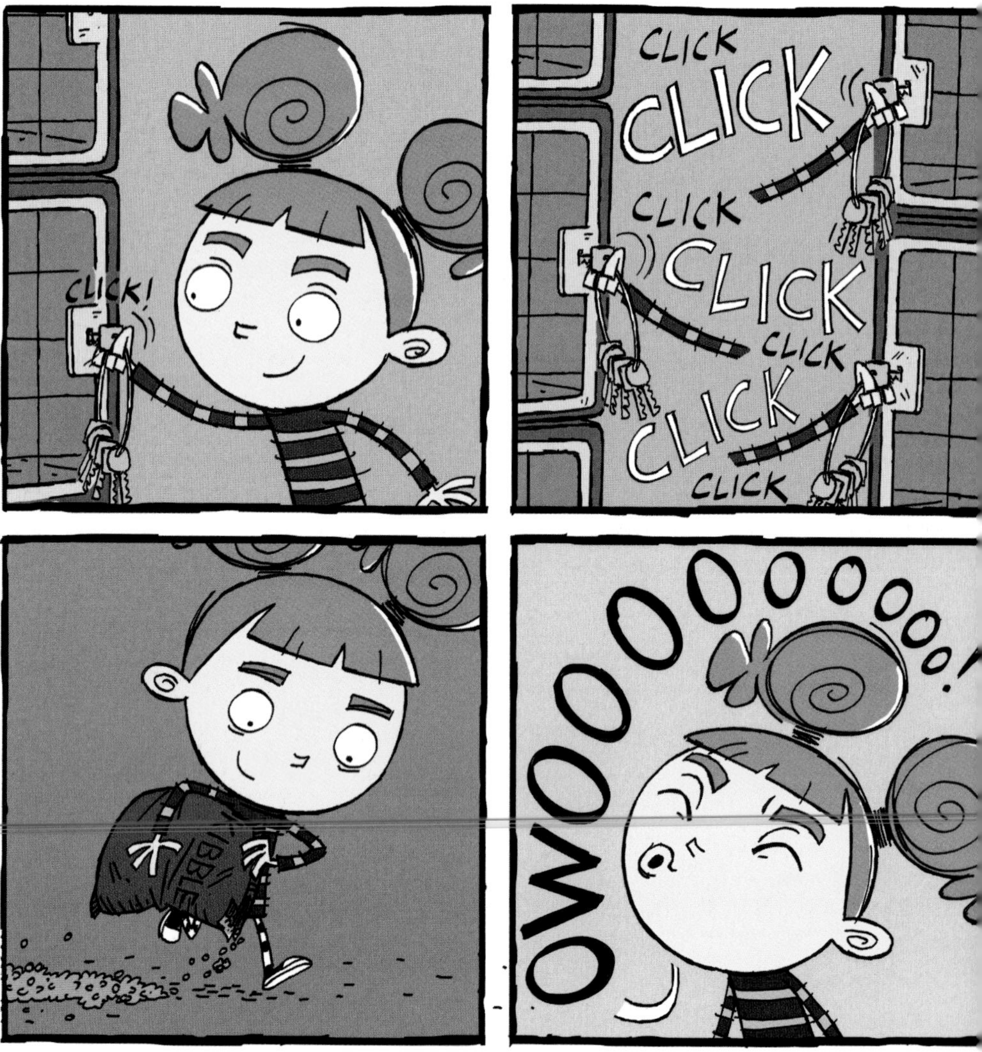
CLICK!
CLICK
CLICK
CLICK
CLICK
CLICK
CLICK
CLICK
OWOOOOOOOoo!

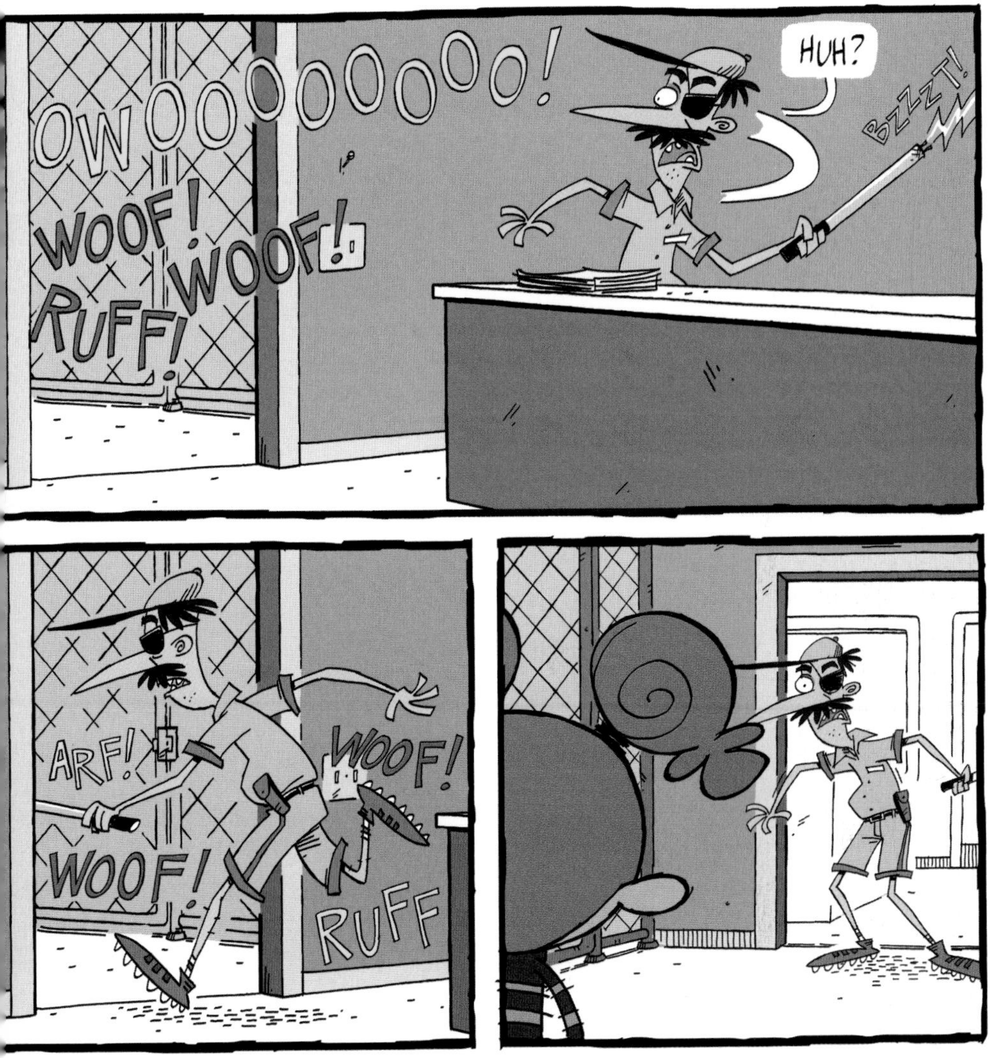
OWOOOOOOOOO!
WOOF!
WOOF!
RUFF!
HUH?
BZZZT!
ARF!
WOOF!
WOOF!
RUFF

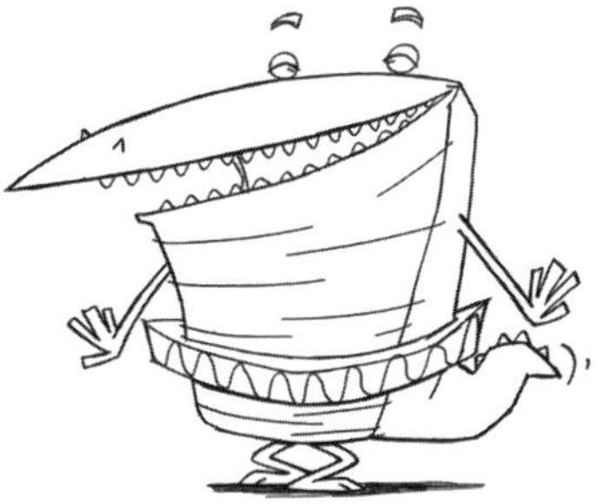

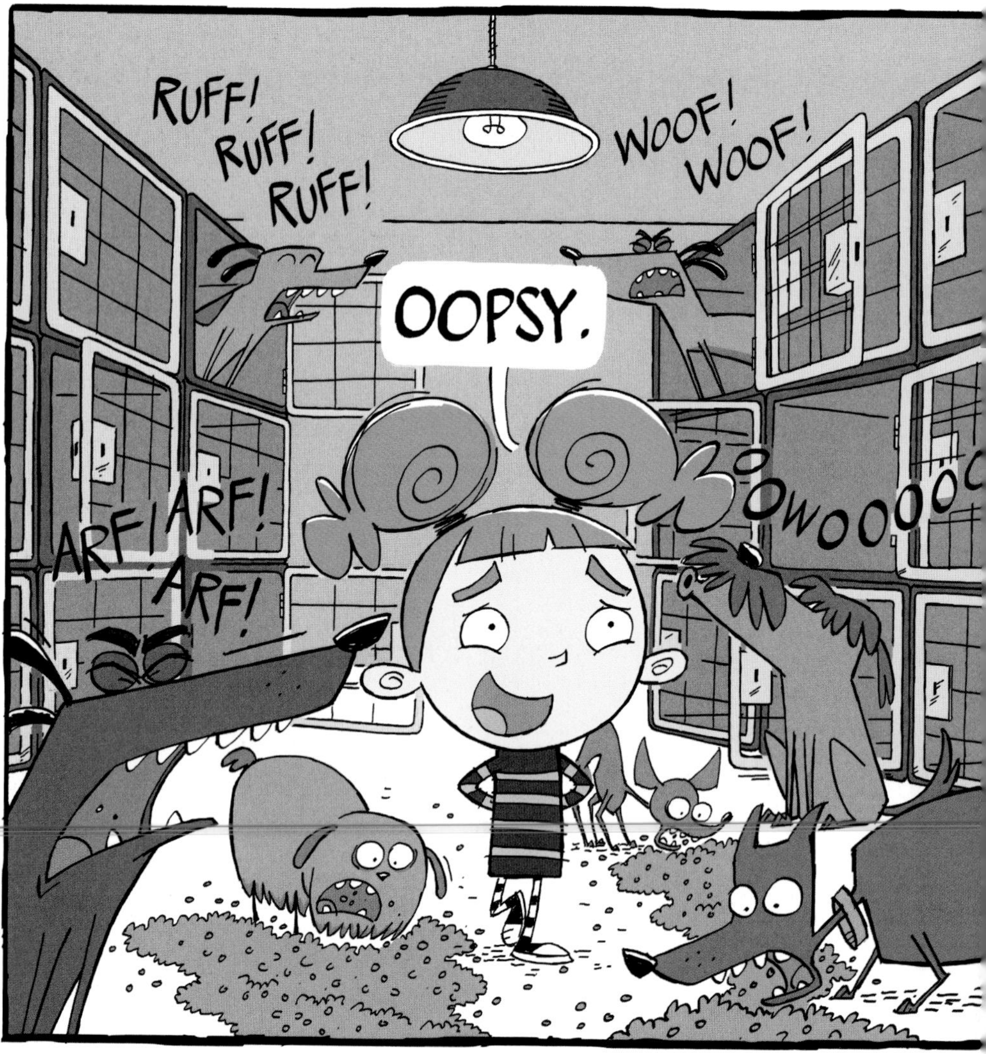
RUFF! RUFF! RUFF!
WOOF! WOOF!
OOPSY.
ARF! ARF! ARF!
OOWOOOOO

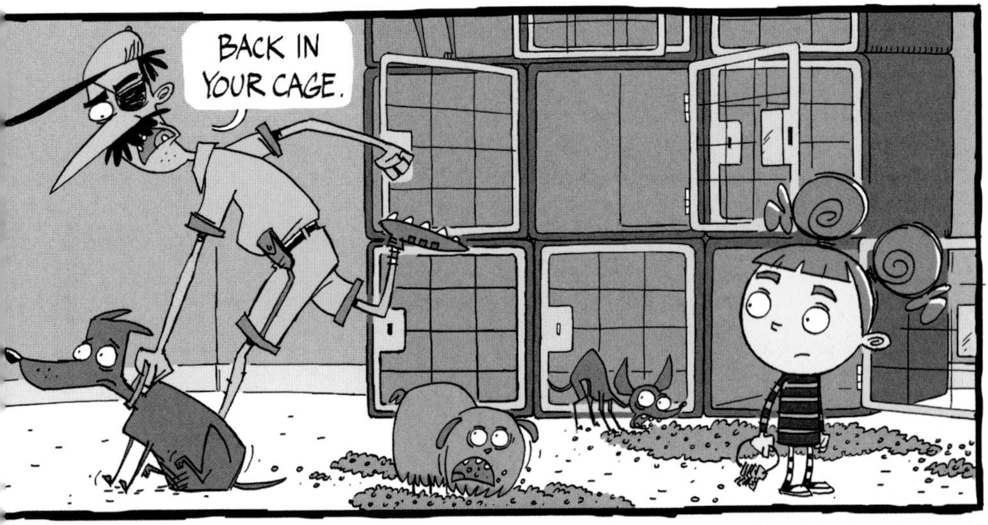
BACK IN YOUR CAGE.

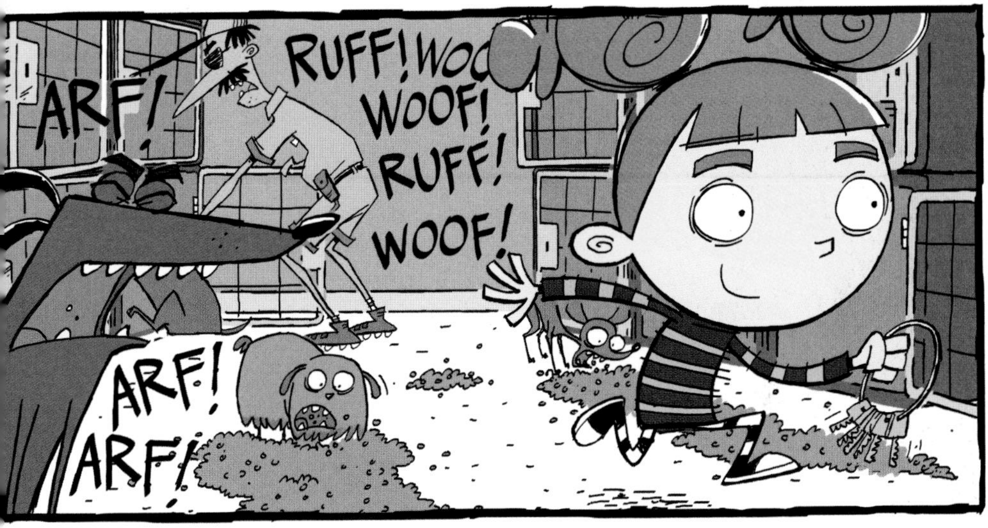
ARF!
RUFF! WOO
WOOF!
RUFF!
WOOF!
ARF!
ARF!

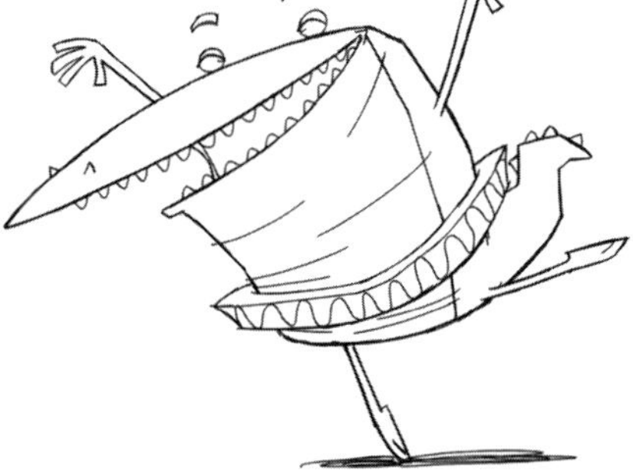

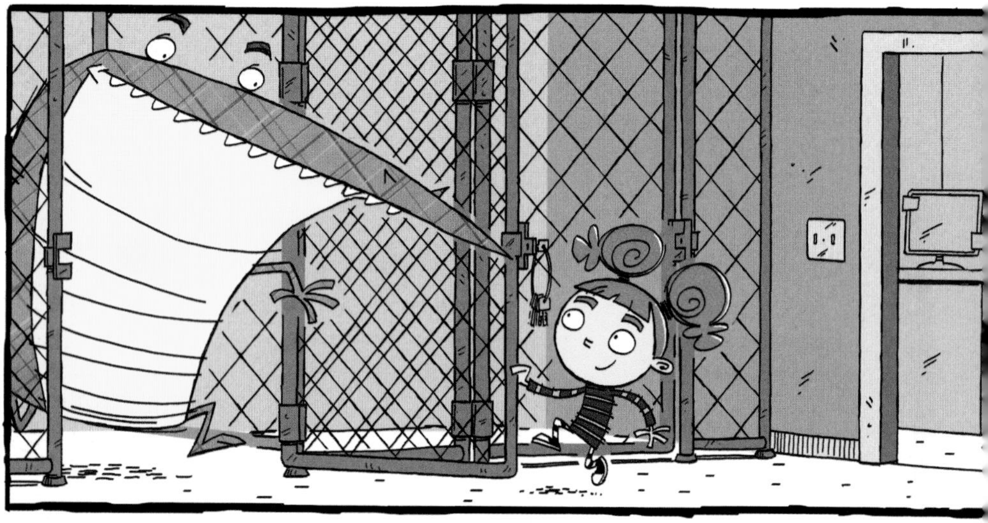

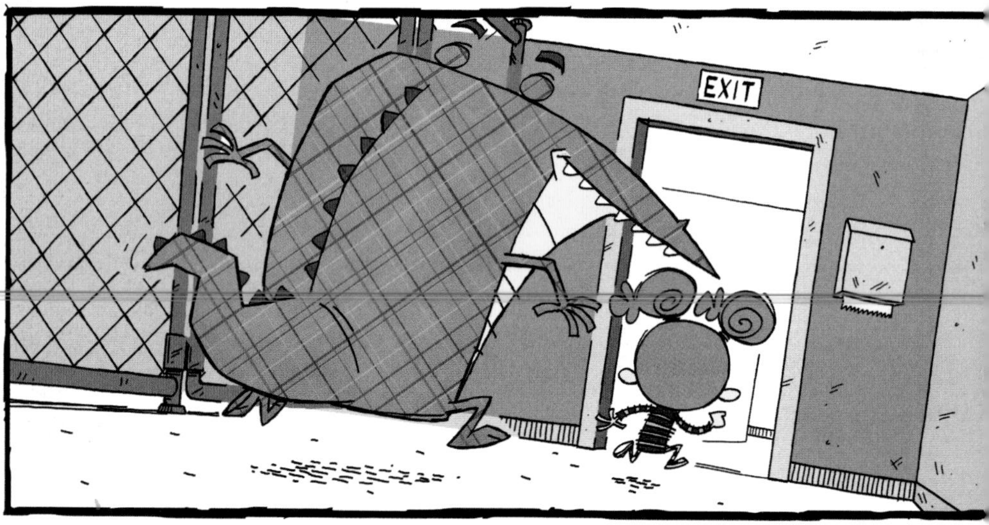
EXIT

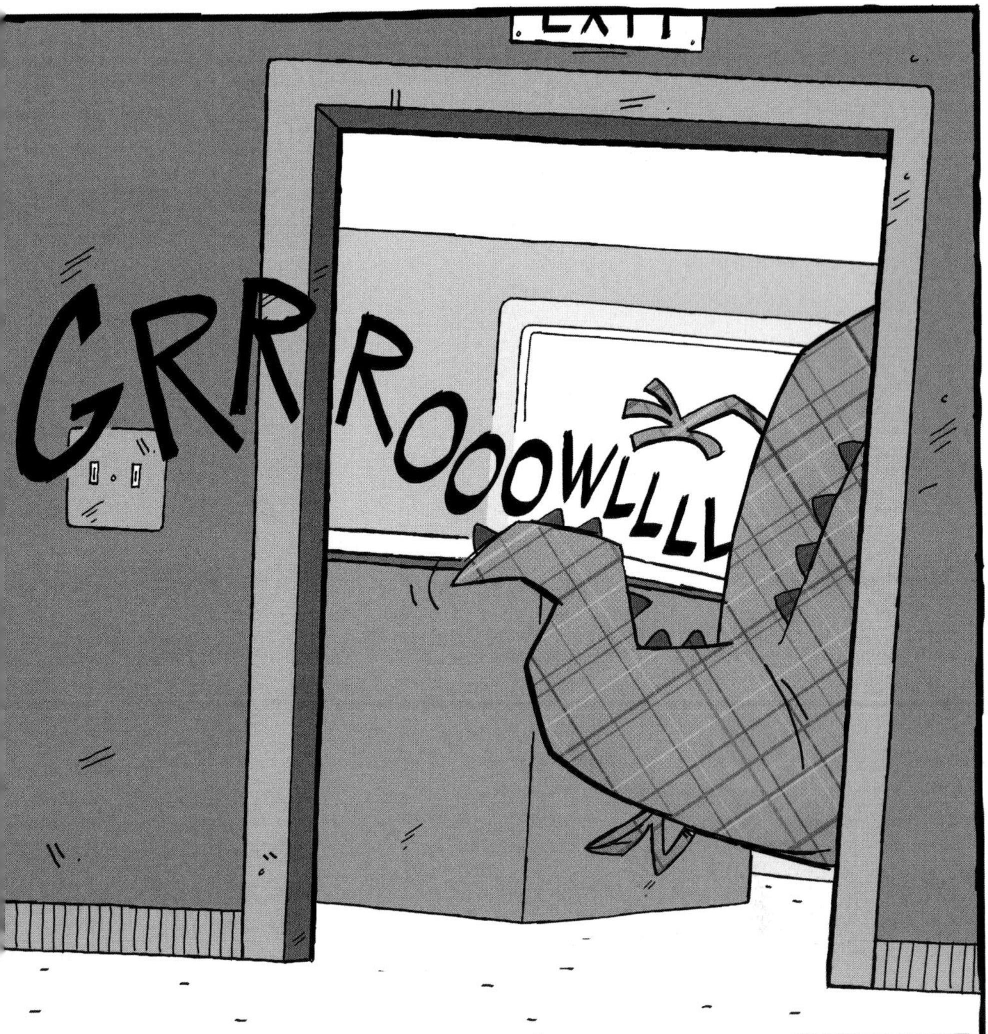
GRRROOOWLLLL

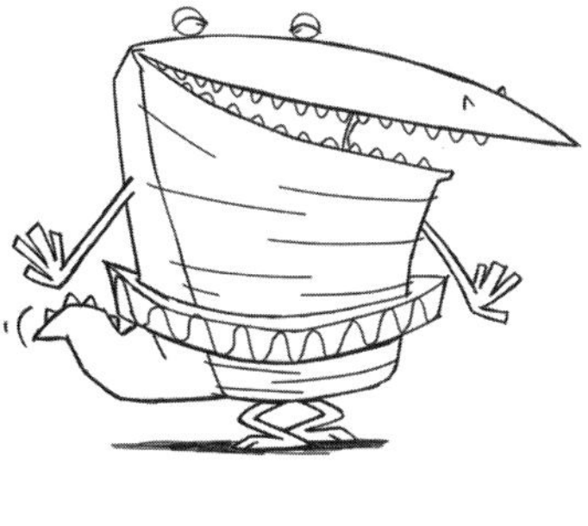

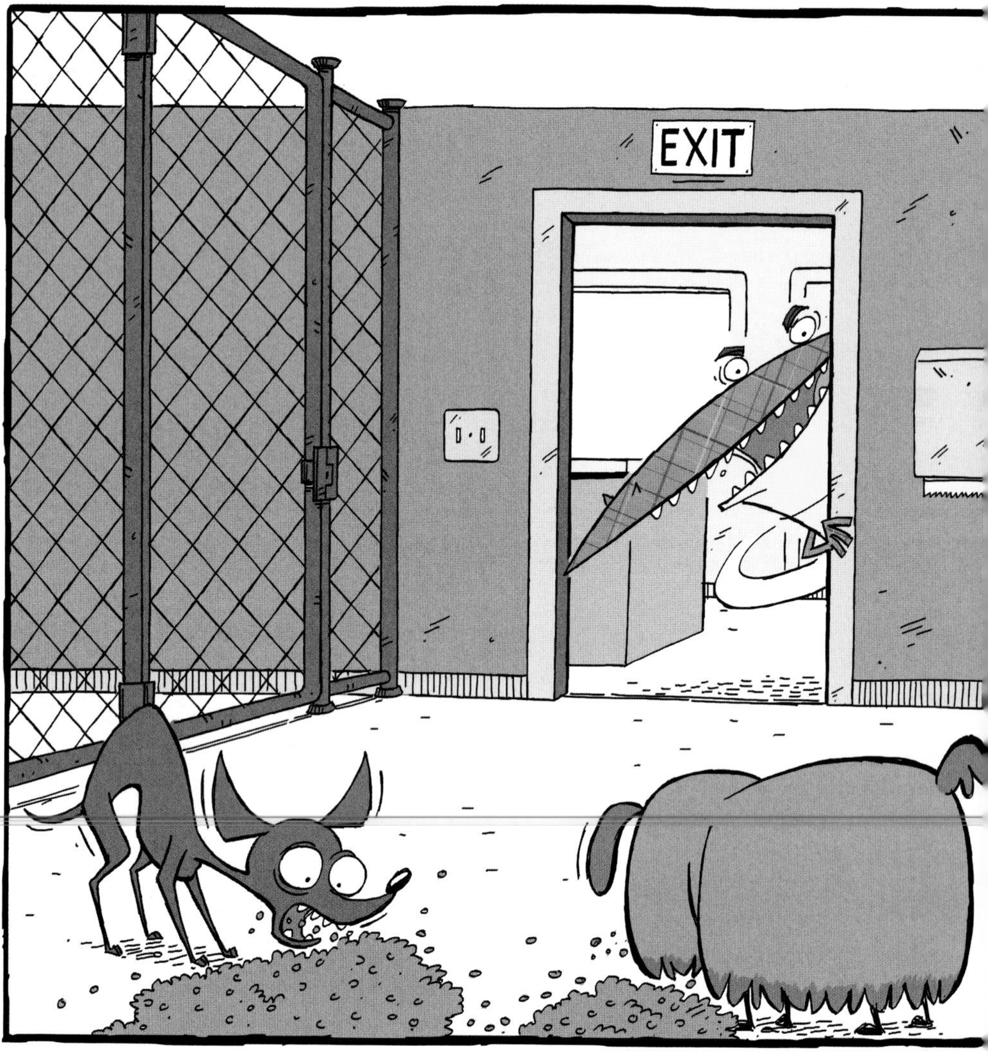
EXIT

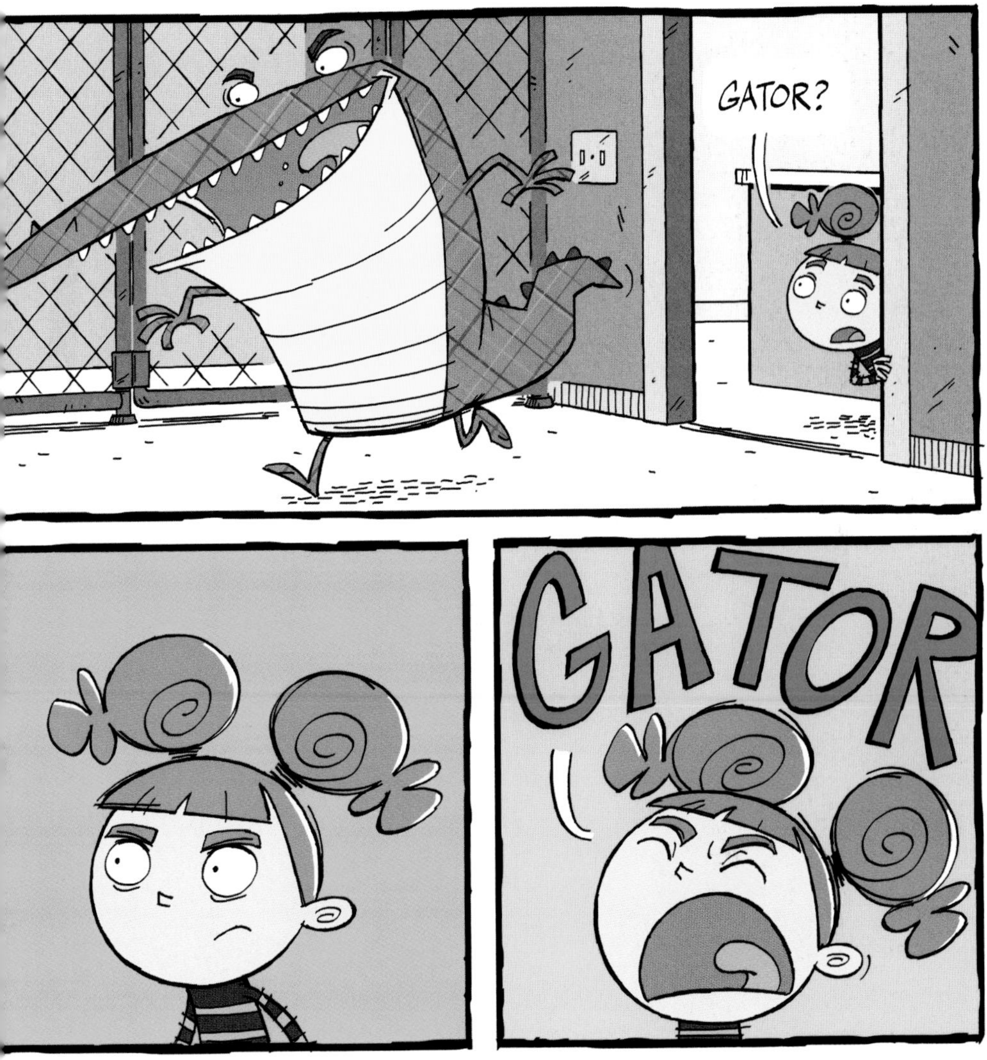
GATOR?
GATOR

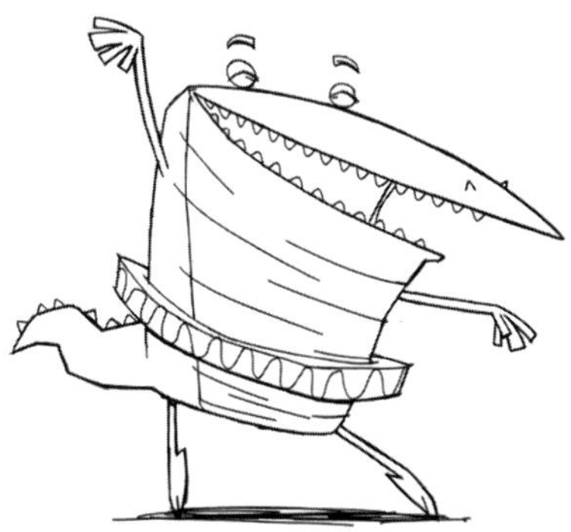

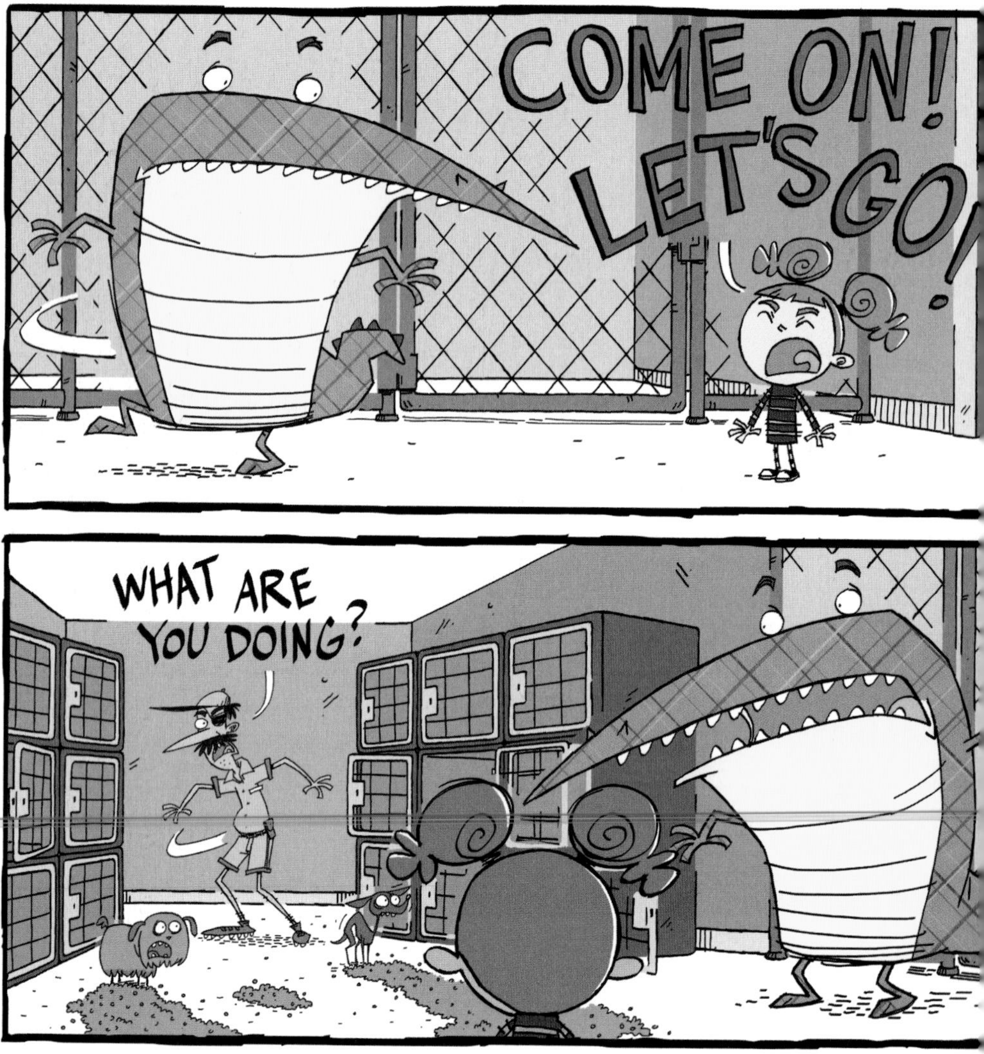
COME ON! LET'S GO!
WHAT ARE YOU DOING?

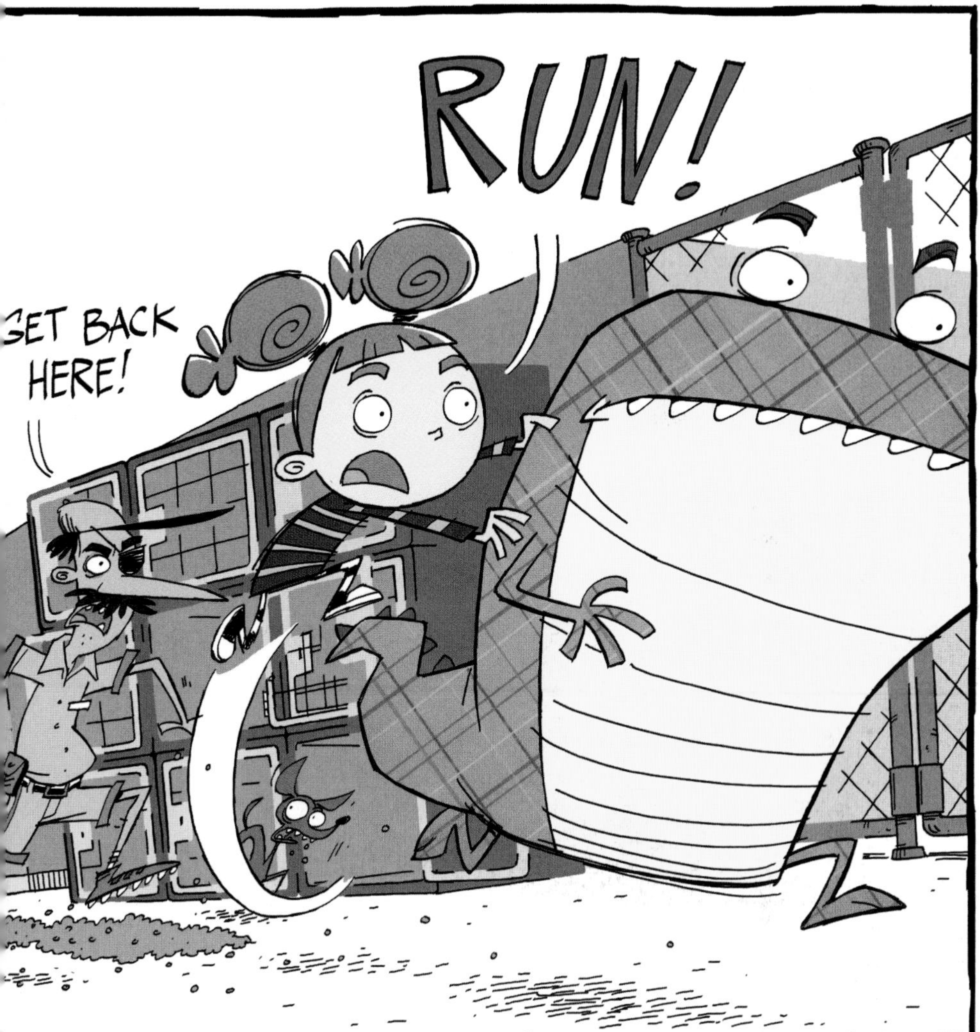
RUN!
GET BACK HERE!

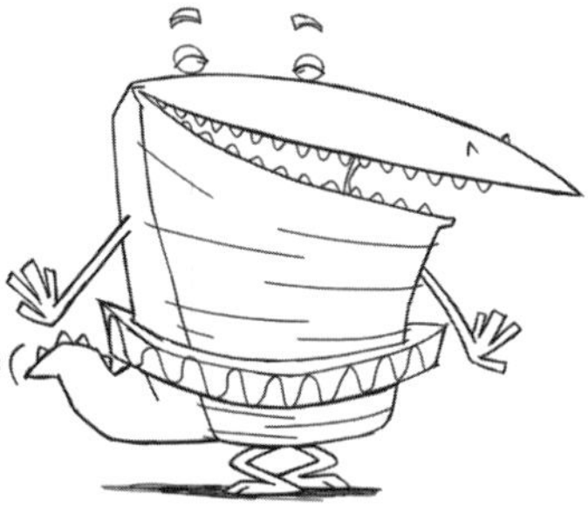

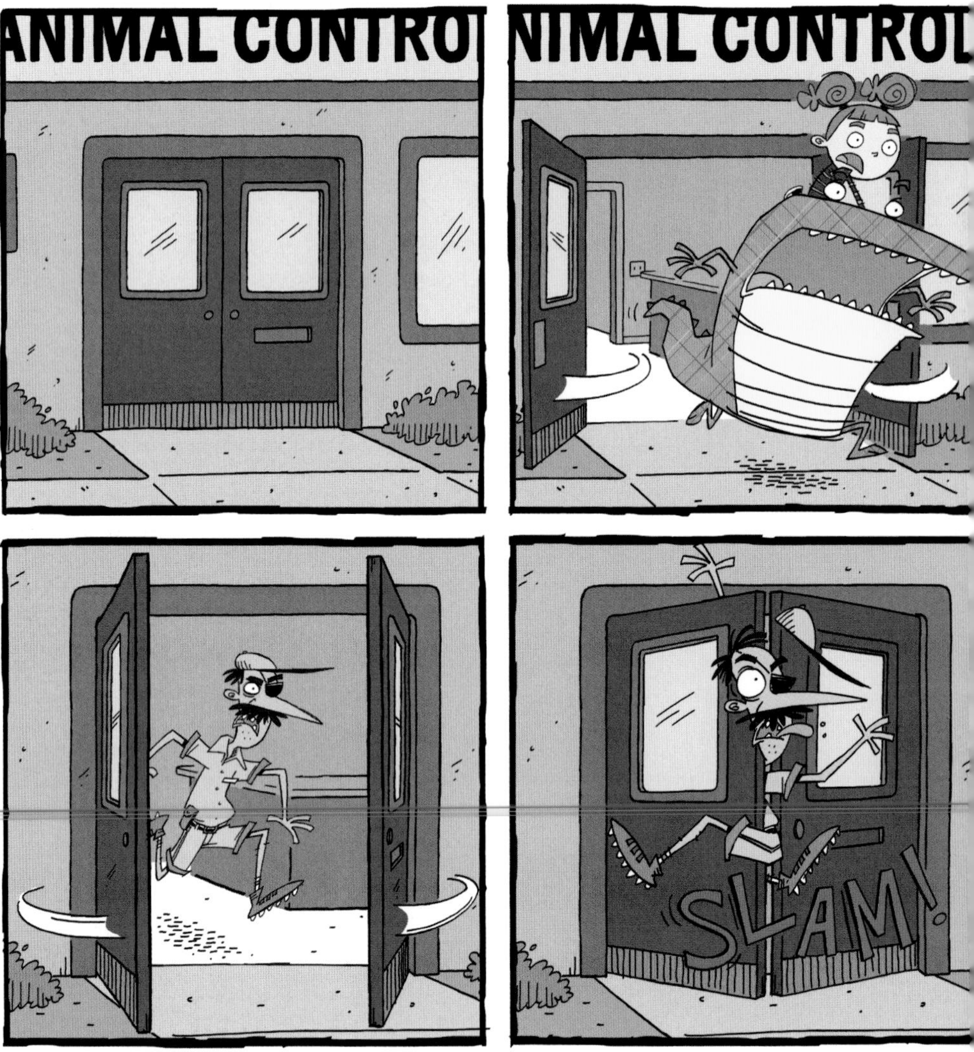
ANIMAL CONTROL
NIMAL CONTROL
SLAM!

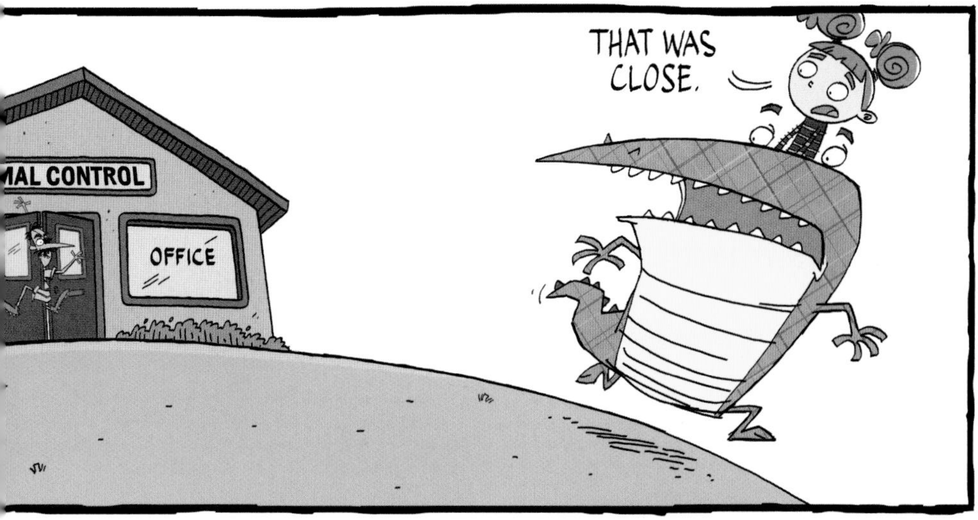
THAT WAS CLOSE.
MAL CONTROL
OFFICE

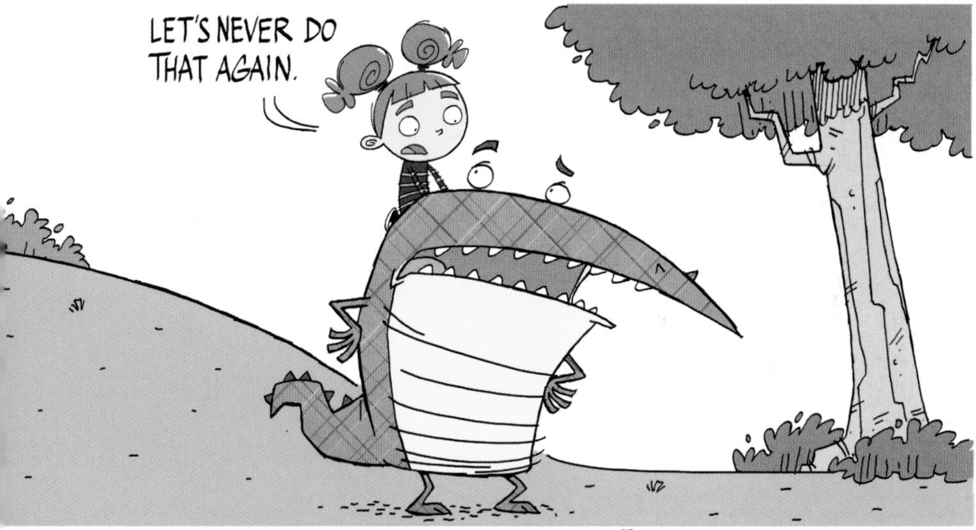
LET'S NEVER DO THAT AGAIN.

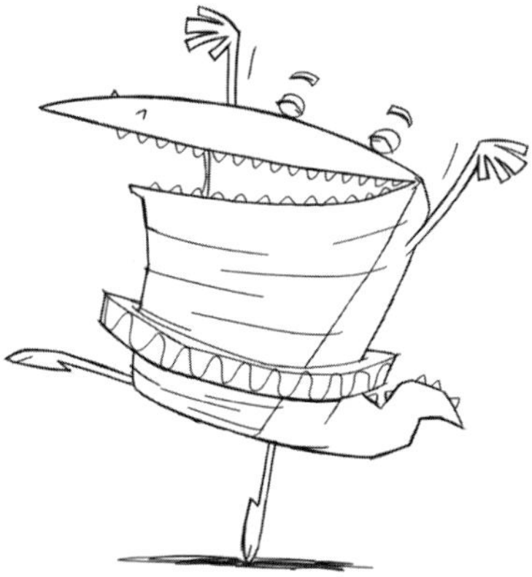

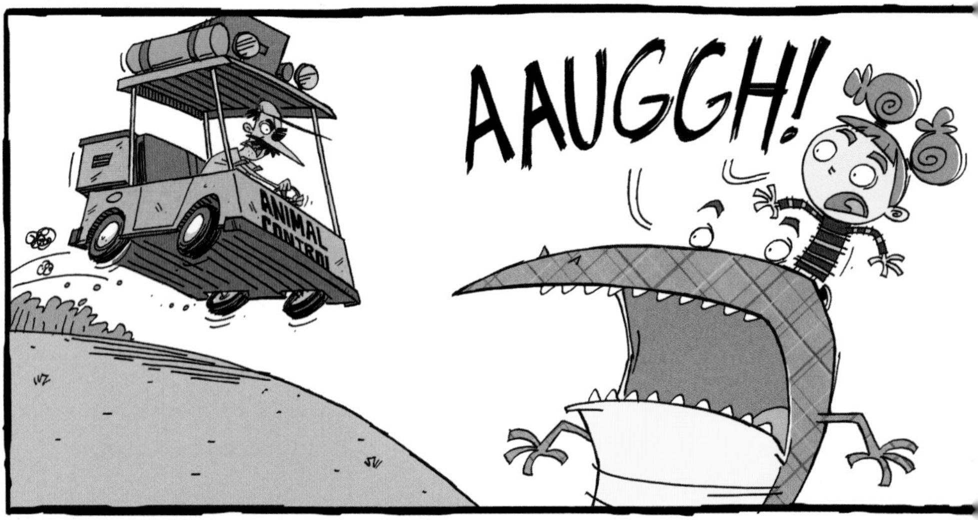
ANIMAL CONTROL
AAUGGH!

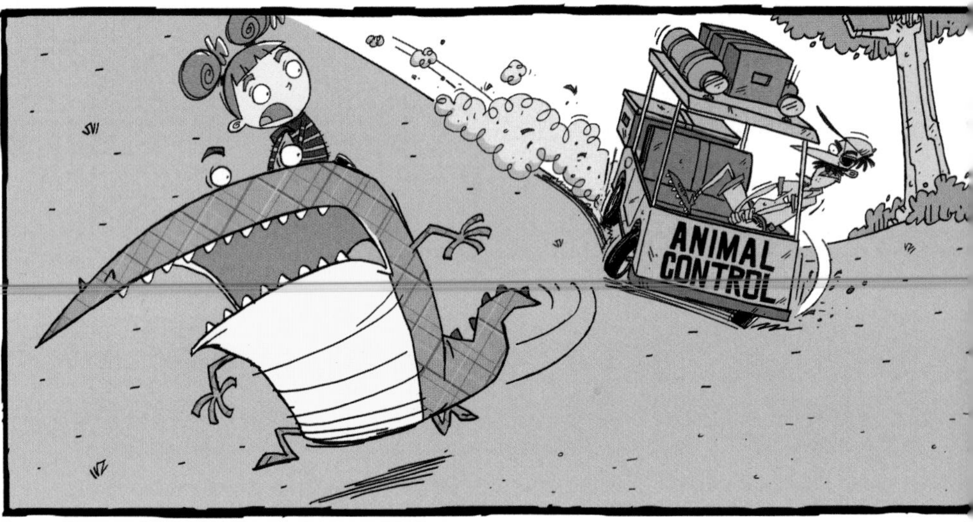
ANIMAL CONTROL

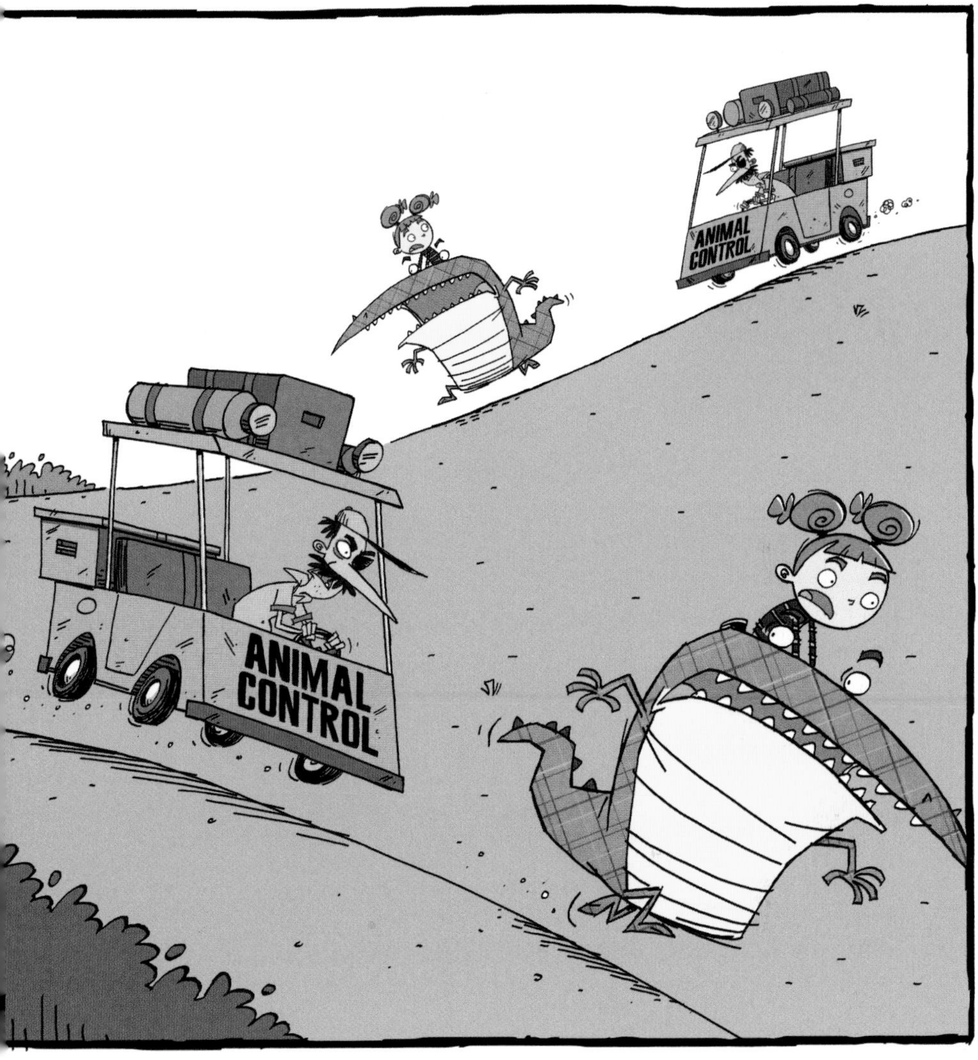
ANIMAL CONTROL
ANIMAL CONTROL

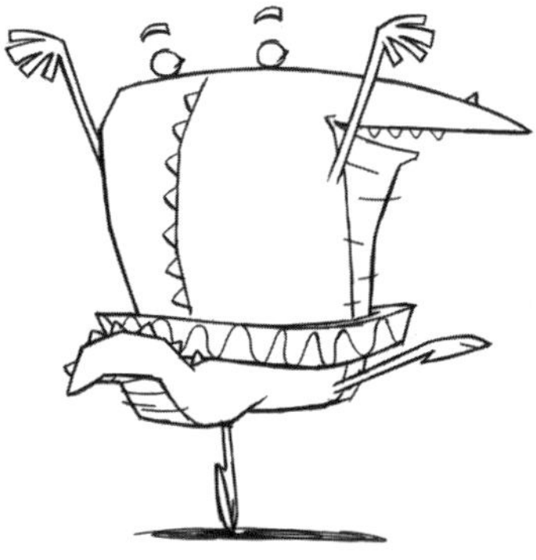

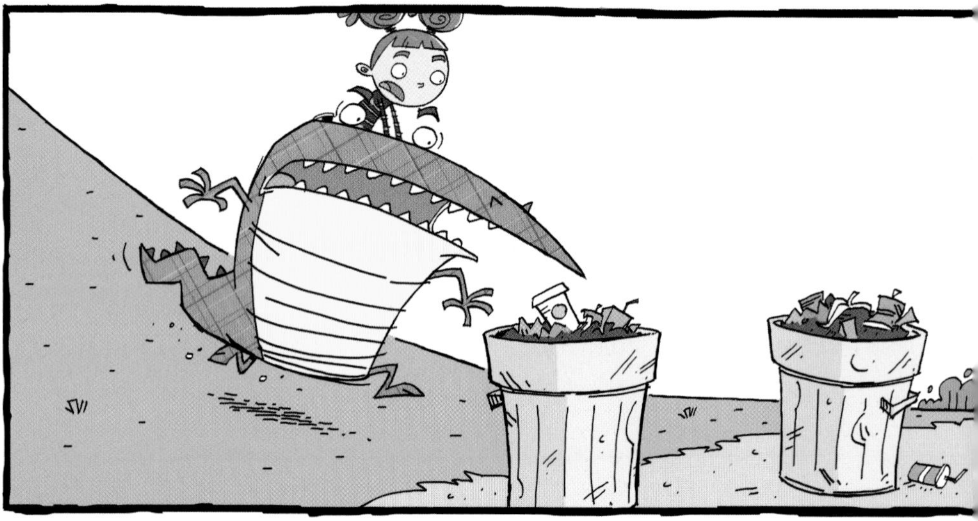

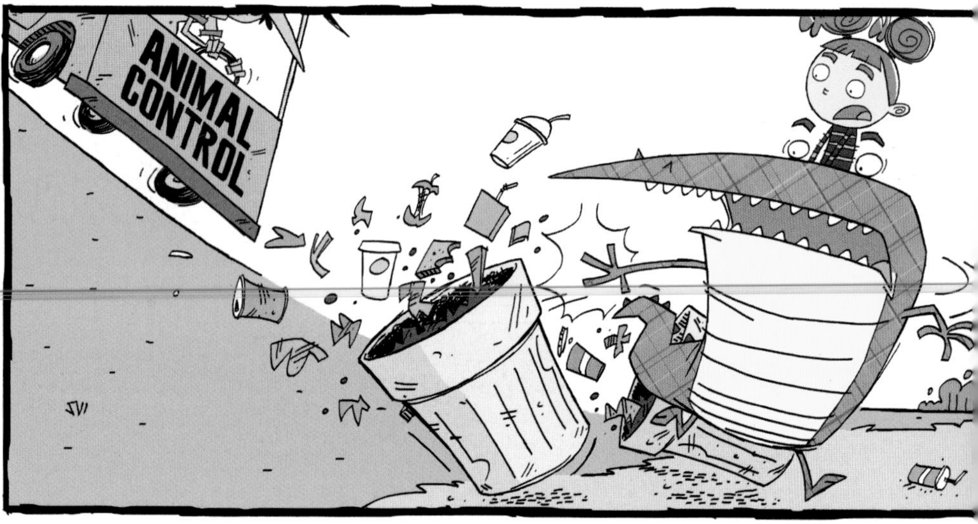
ANIMAL
CONTROL

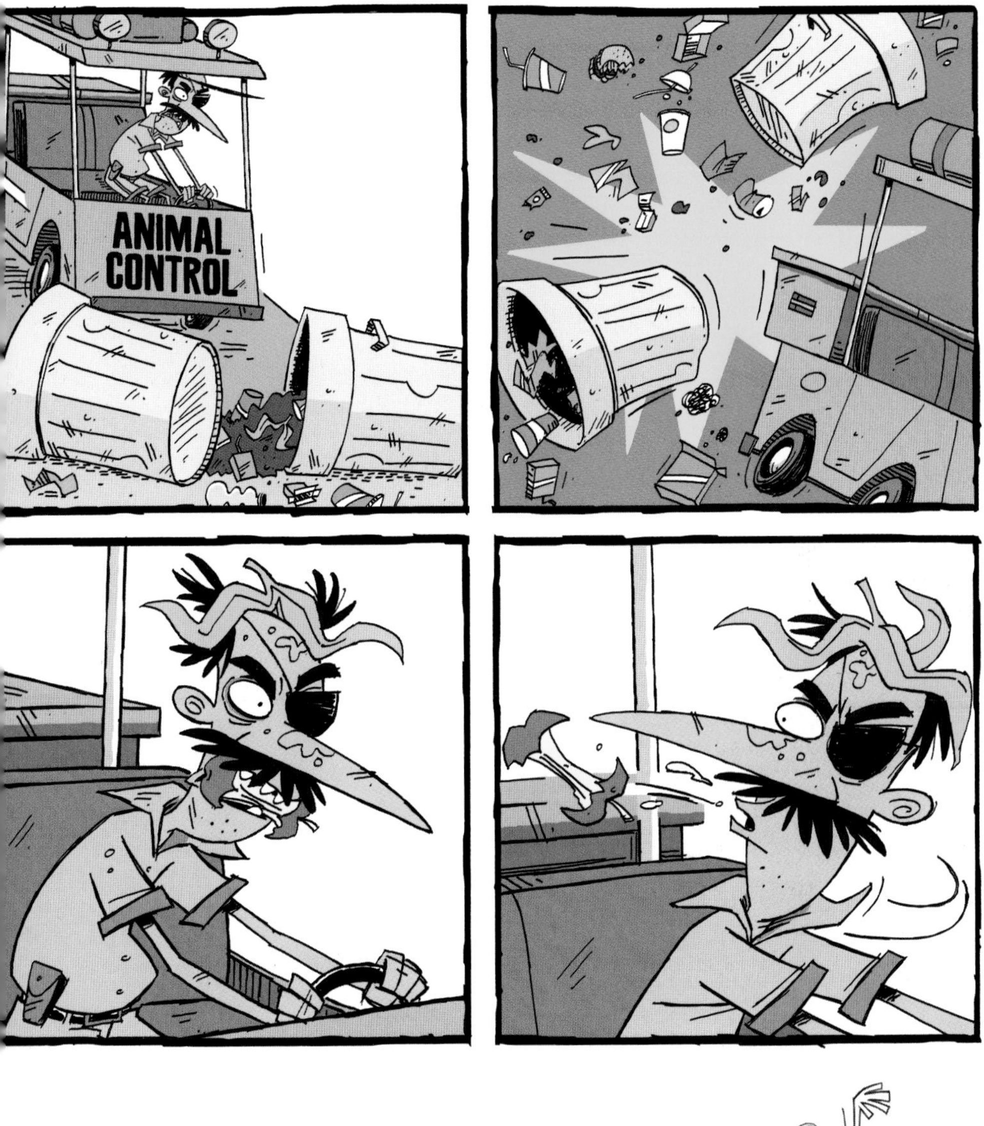
ANIMAL
CONTROL

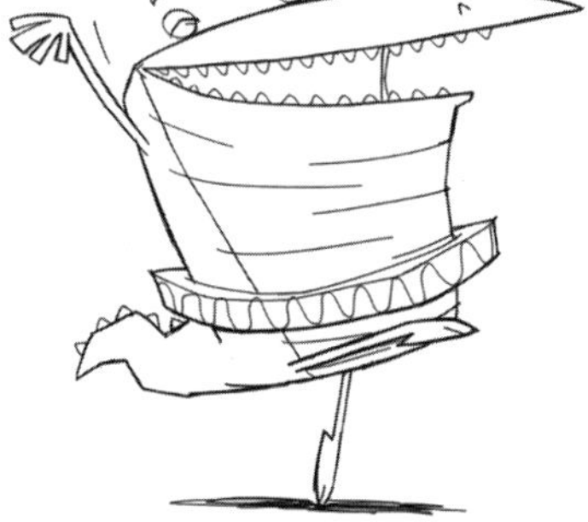

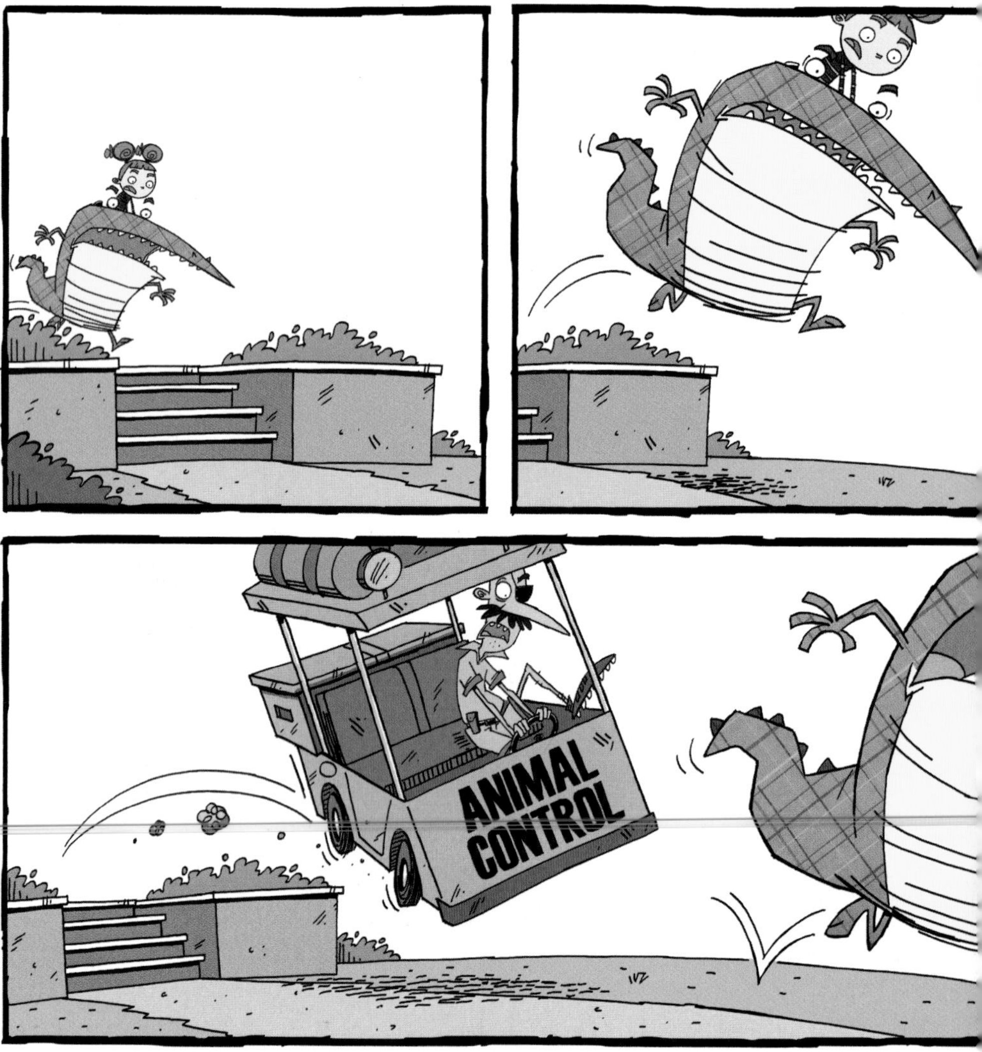
ANIMAL CONTROL

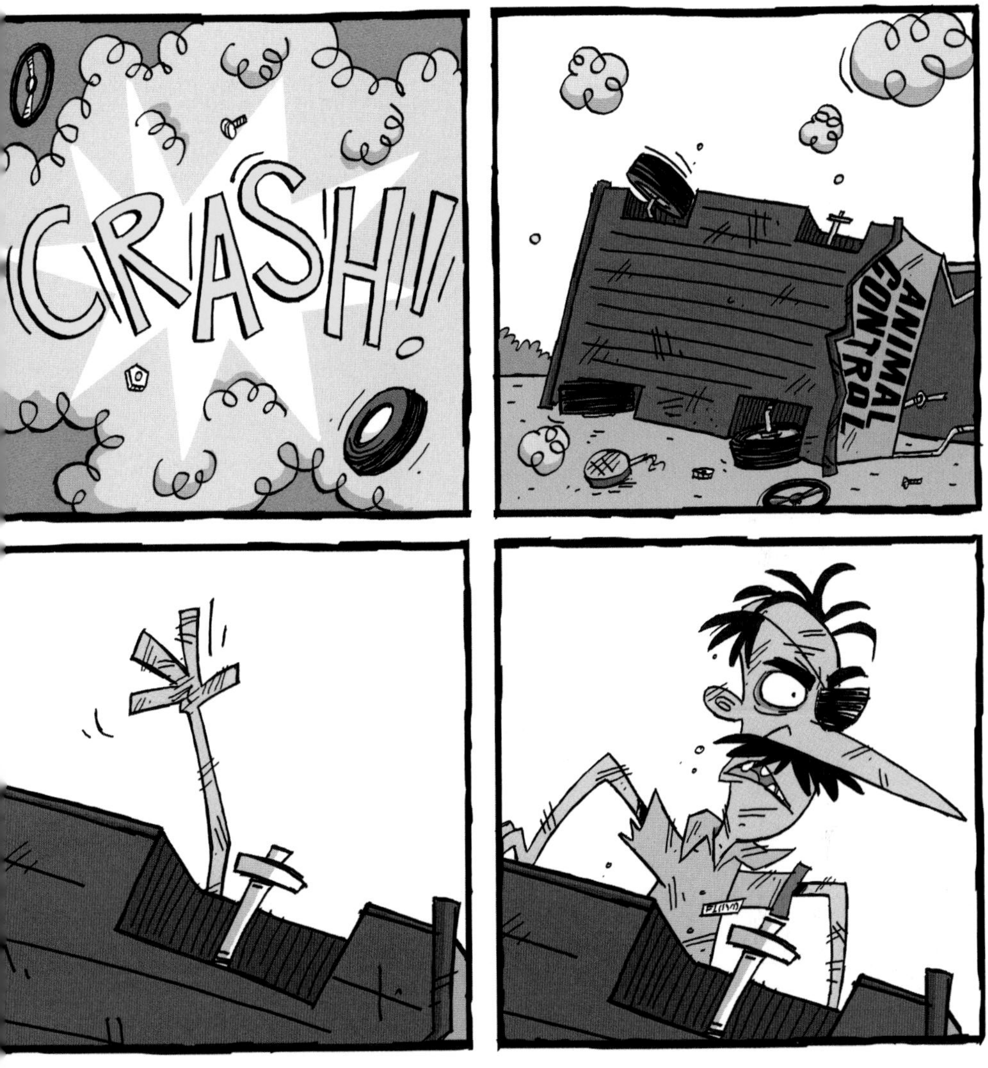
CRASH!!
ANIMAL CONTROL

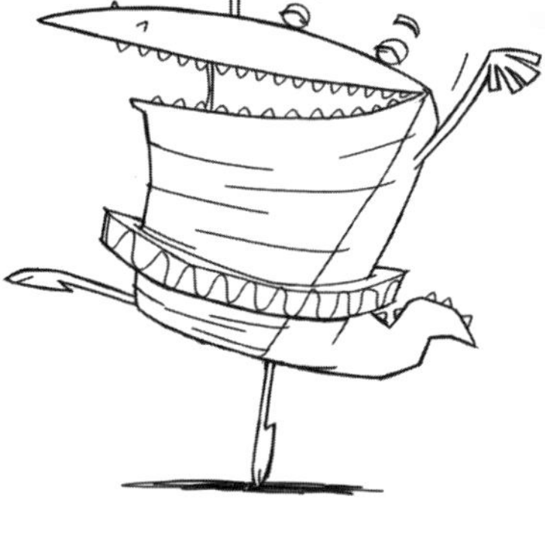

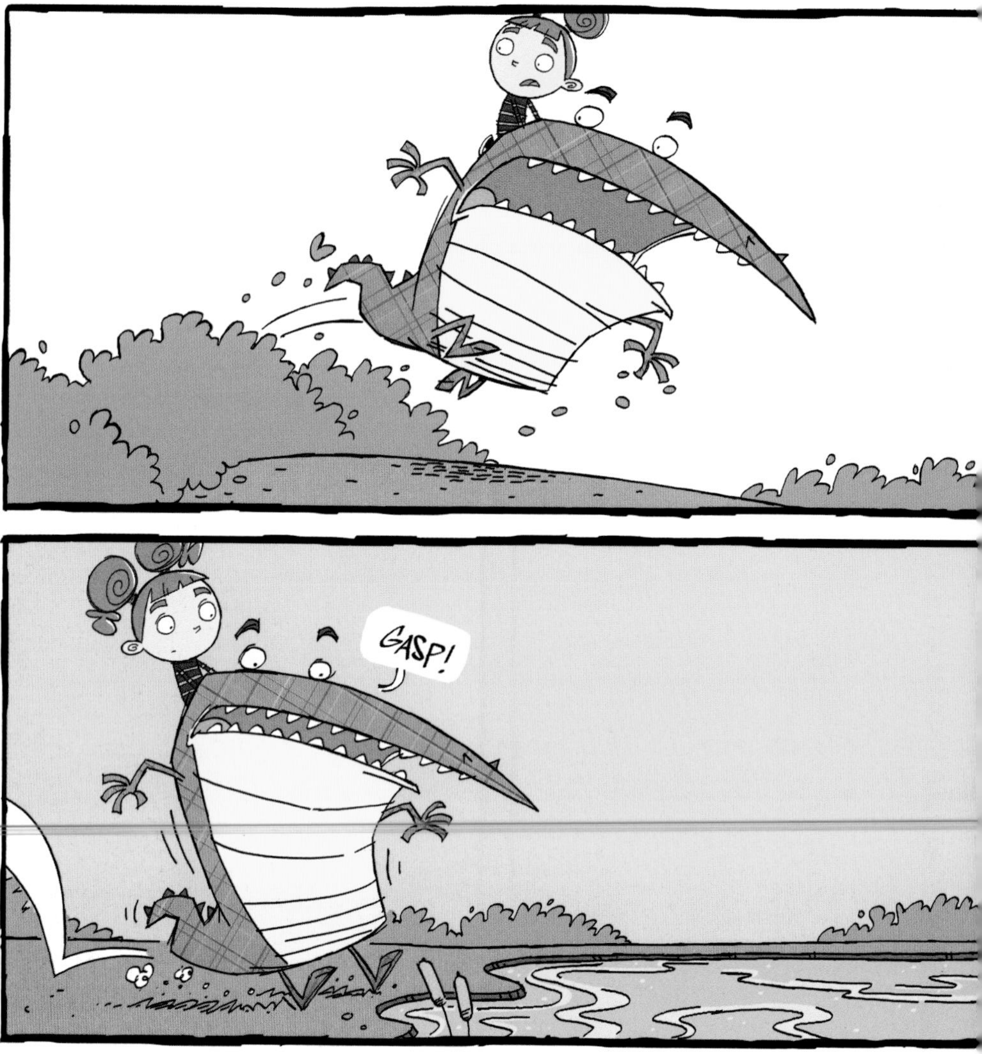
GASP!

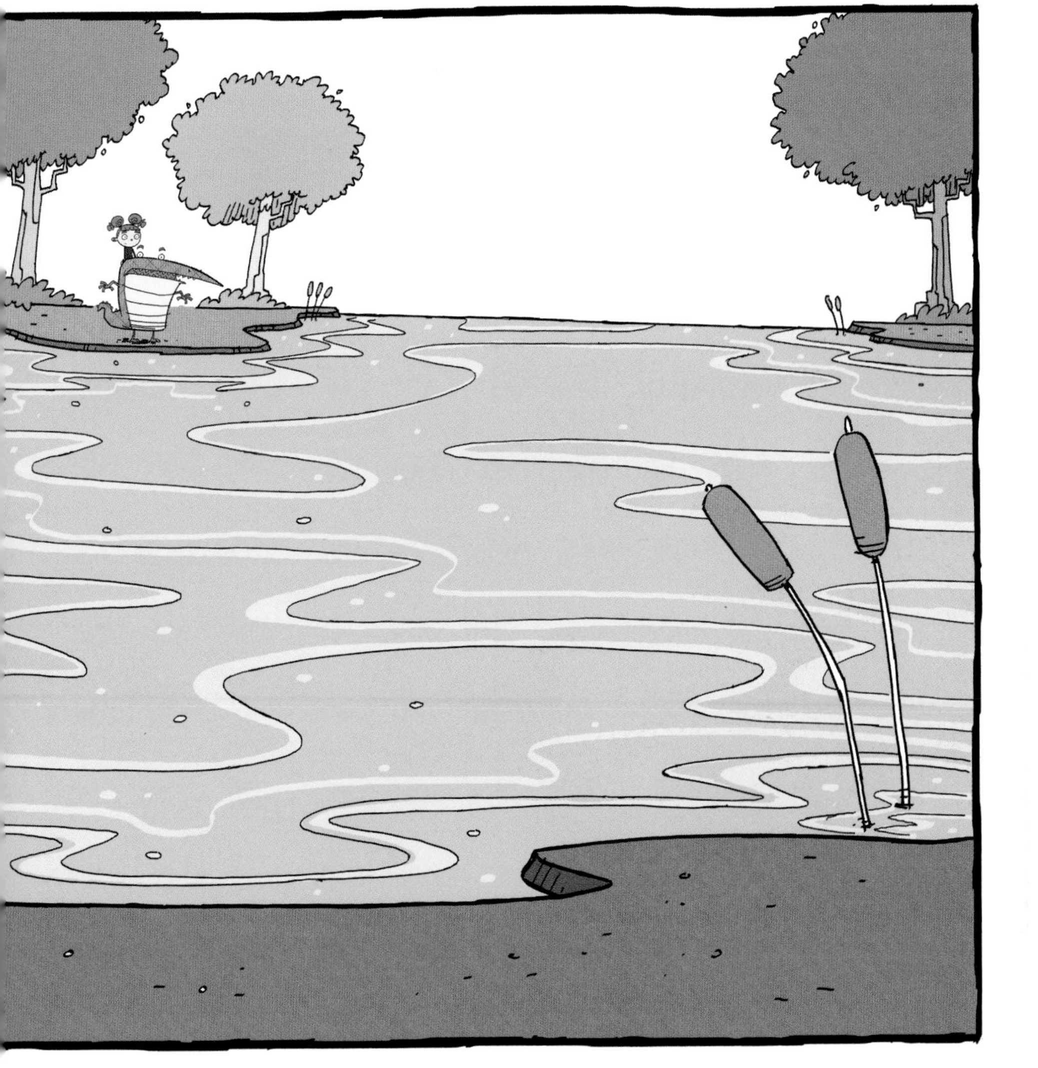

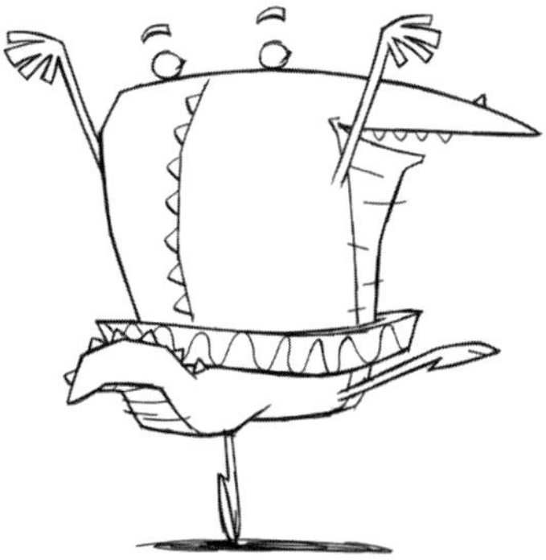

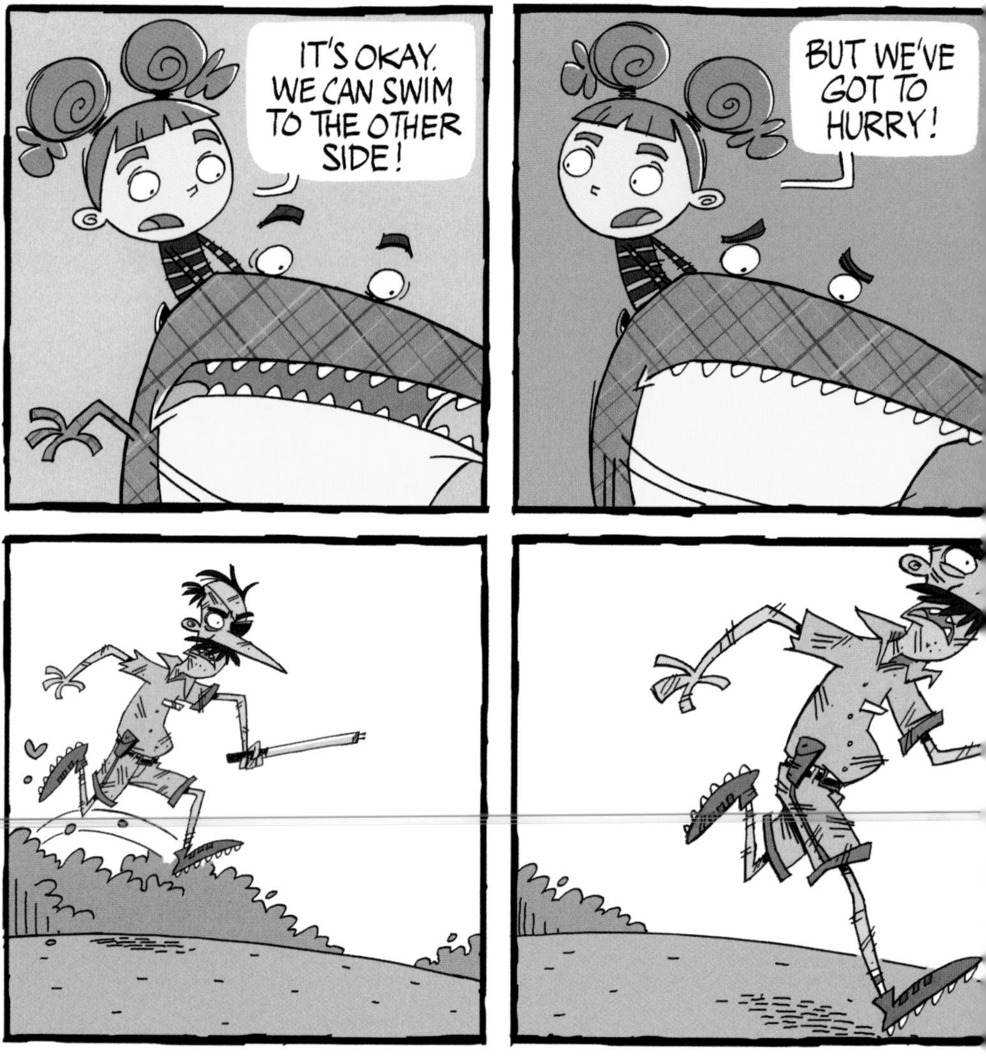
IT'S OKAY. WE CAN SWIM TO THE OTHER SIDE!
BUT WE'VE GOT TO HURRY!

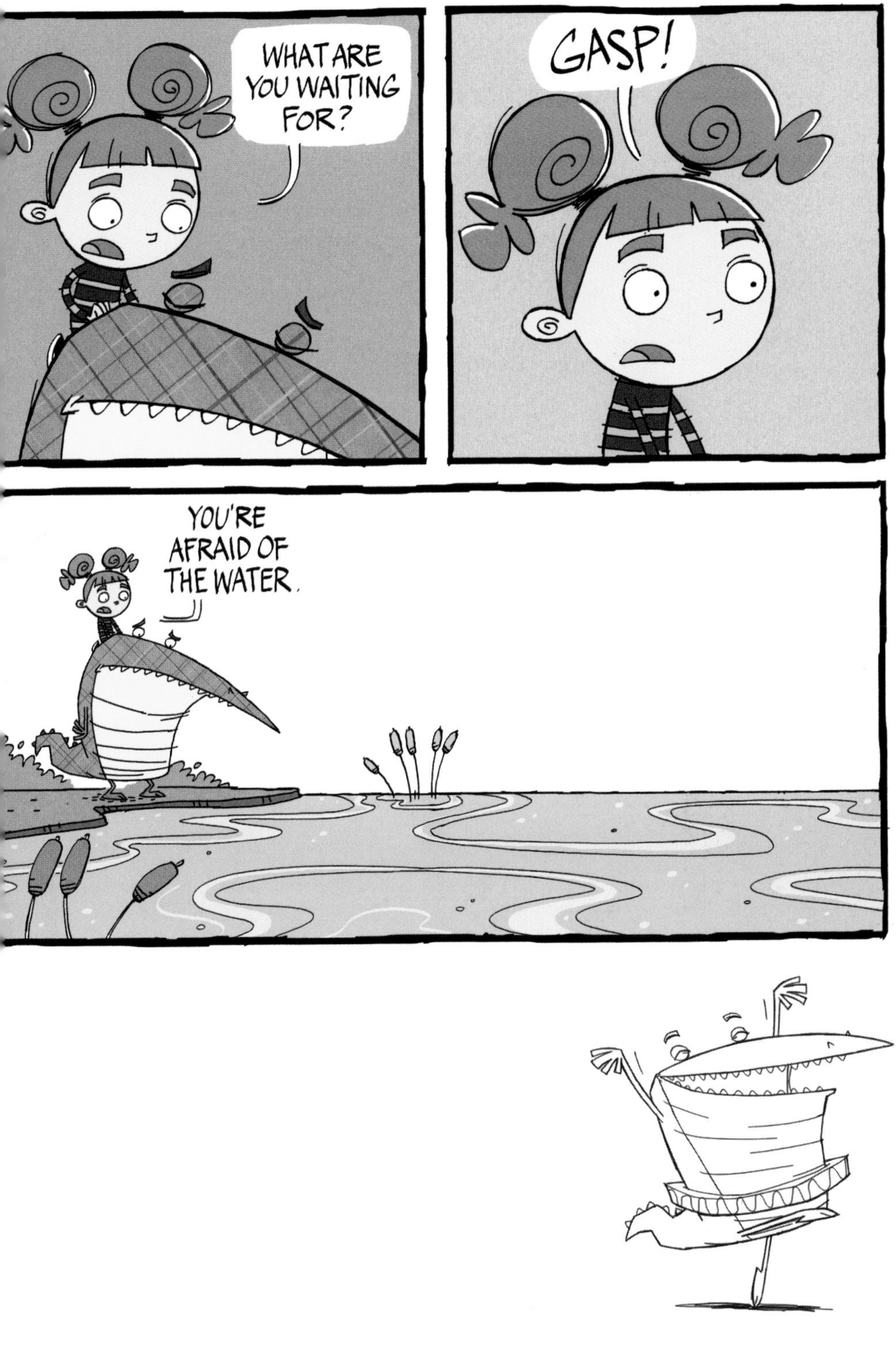
WHAT ARE YOU WAITING FOR?
GASP!
YOU'RE AFRAID OF THE WATER.

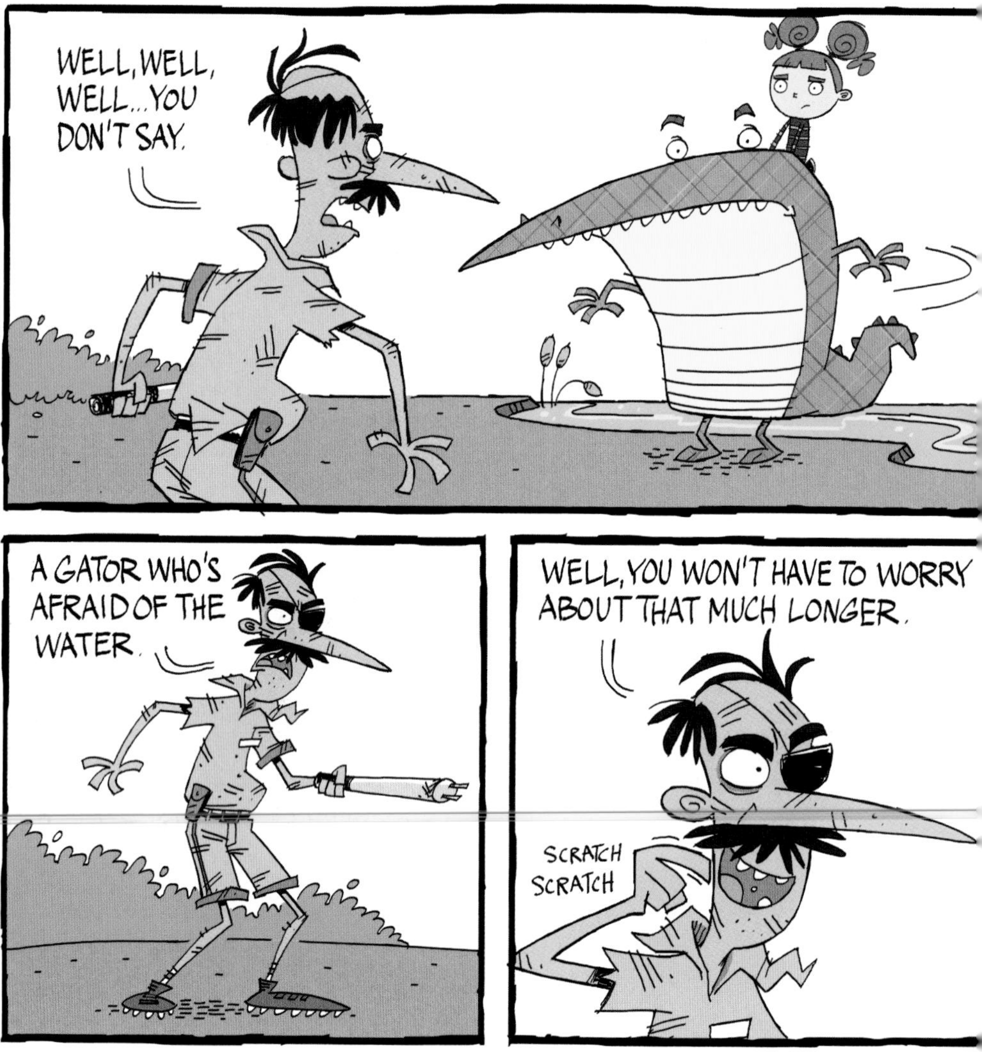
WELL, WELL, WELL... YOU DON'T SAY.
A GATOR WHO'S AFRAID OF THE WATER.
WELL, YOU WON'T HAVE TO WORRY ABOUT THAT MUCH LONGER.
SCRATCH SCRATCH

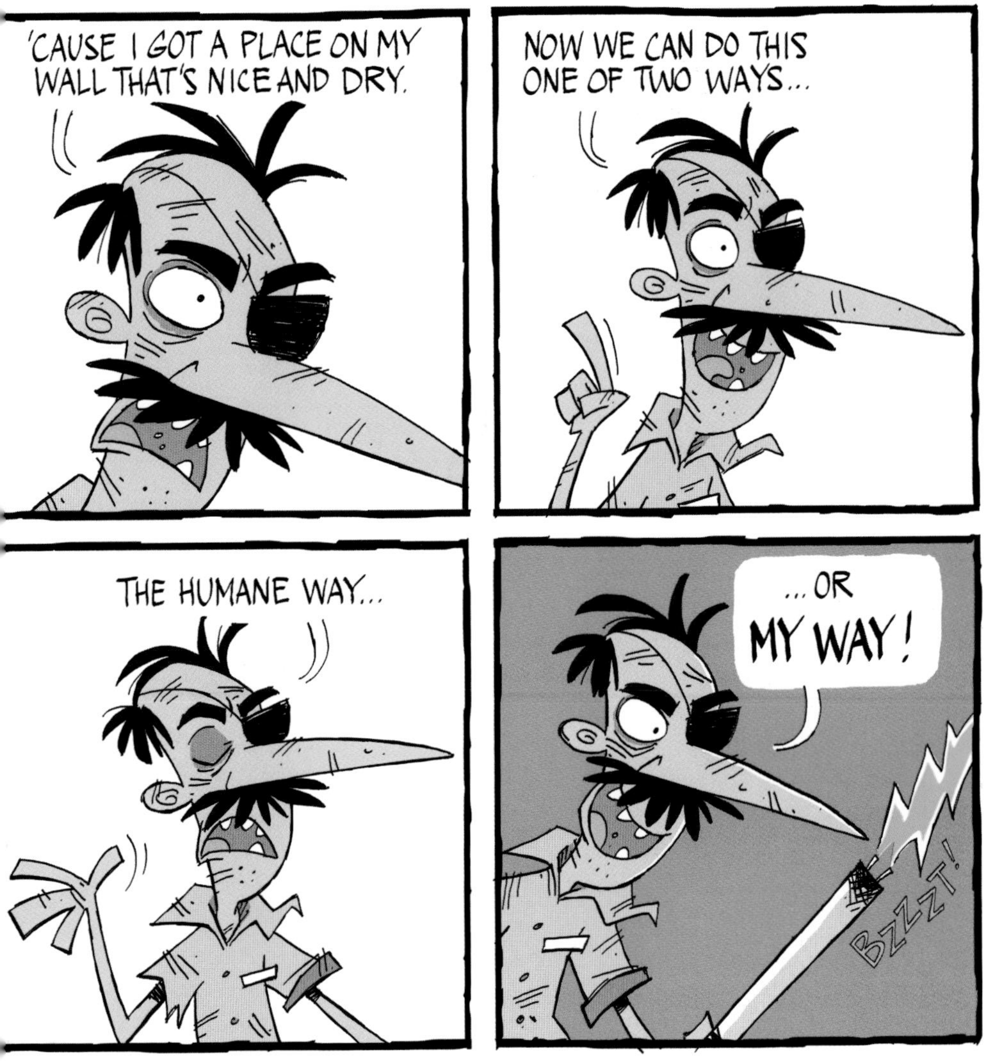
'CAUSE I GOT A PLACE ON MY WALL THAT'S NICE AND DRY.
NOW WE CAN DO THIS ONE OF TWO WAYS...
THE HUMANE WAY...
...OR MY WAY!
BZZZT!

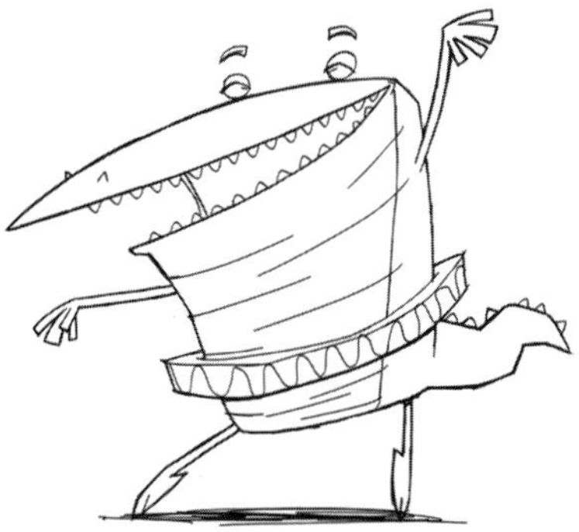

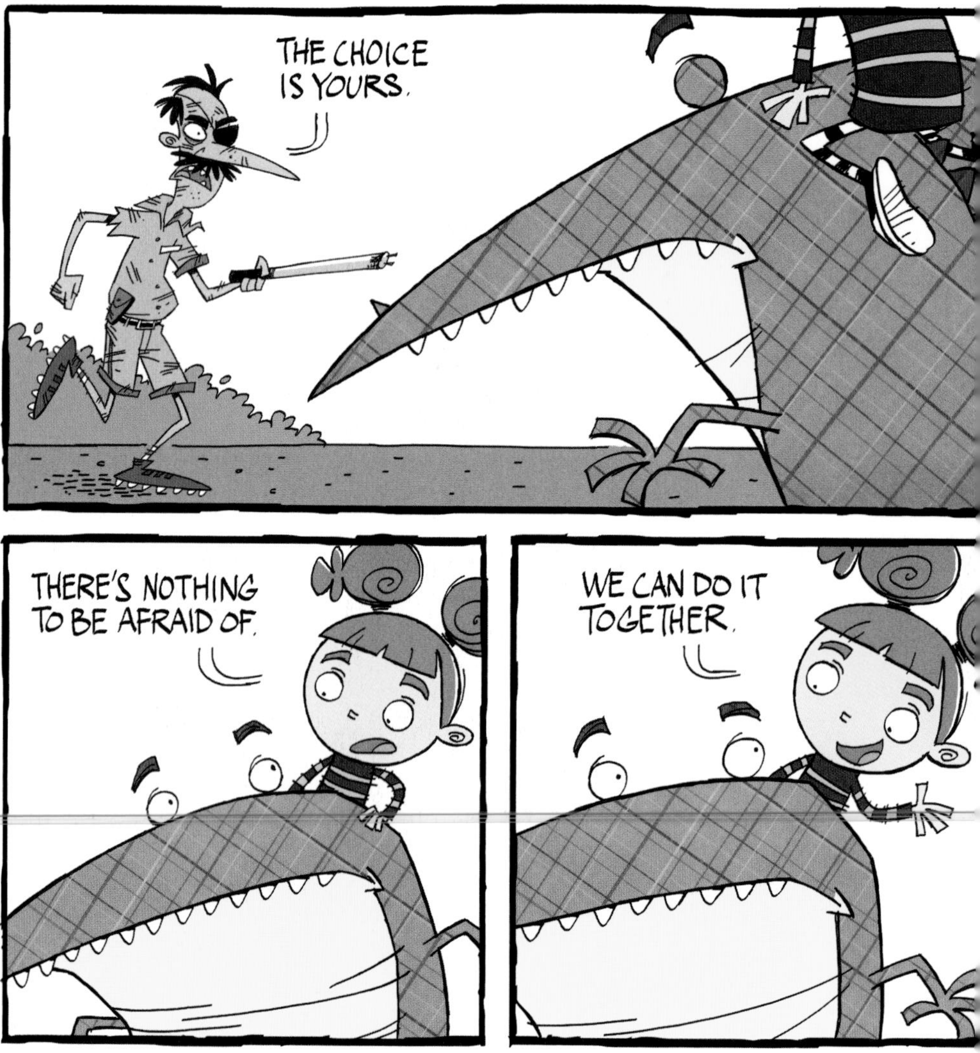
THE CHOICE IS YOURS.
THERE'S NOTHING TO BE AFRAID OF.
WE CAN DO IT TOGETHER.

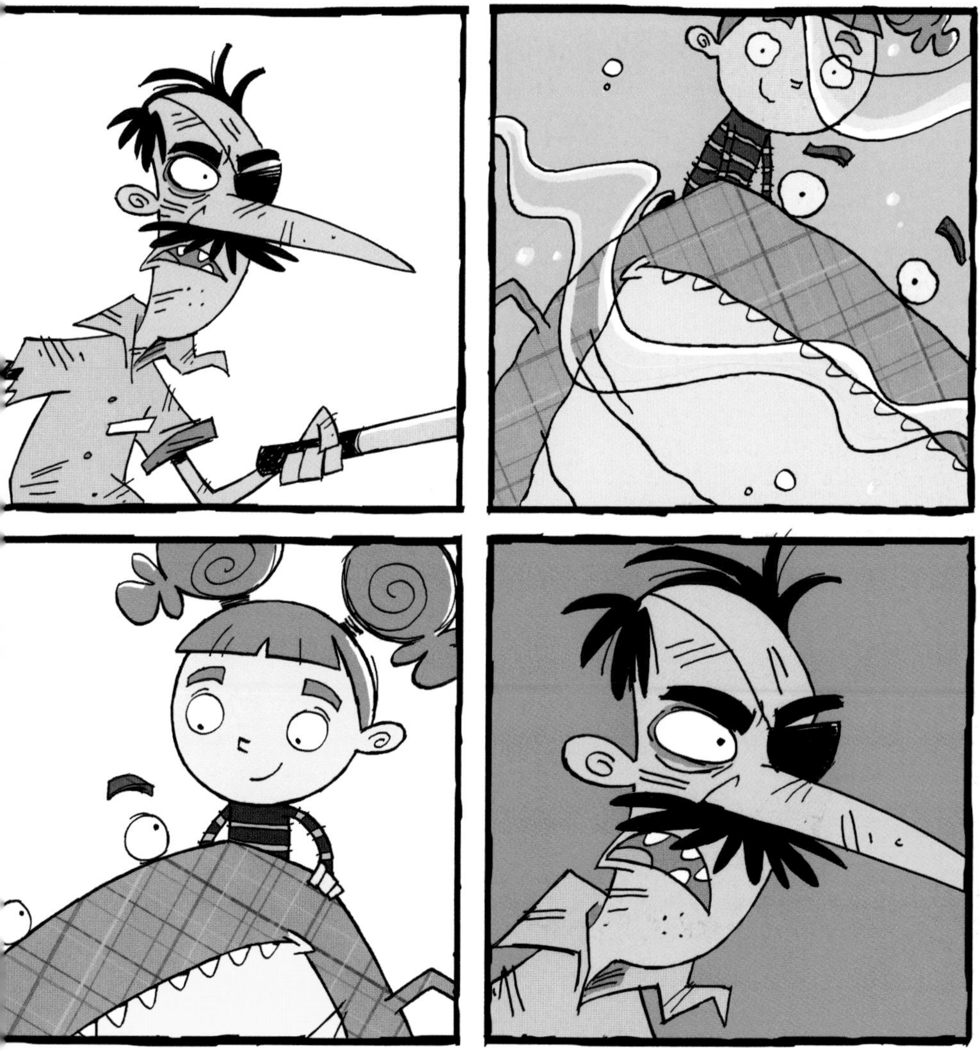

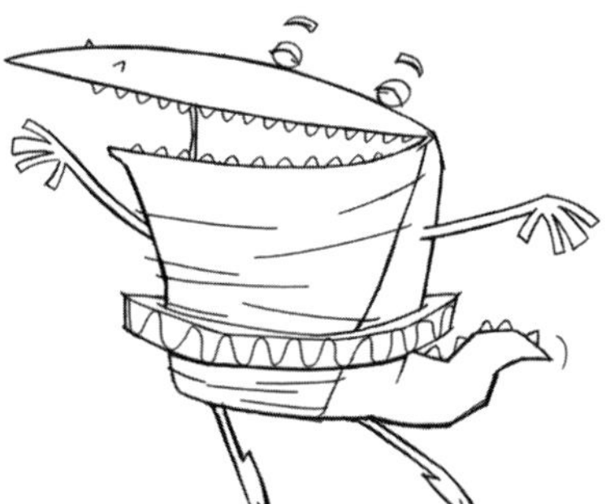

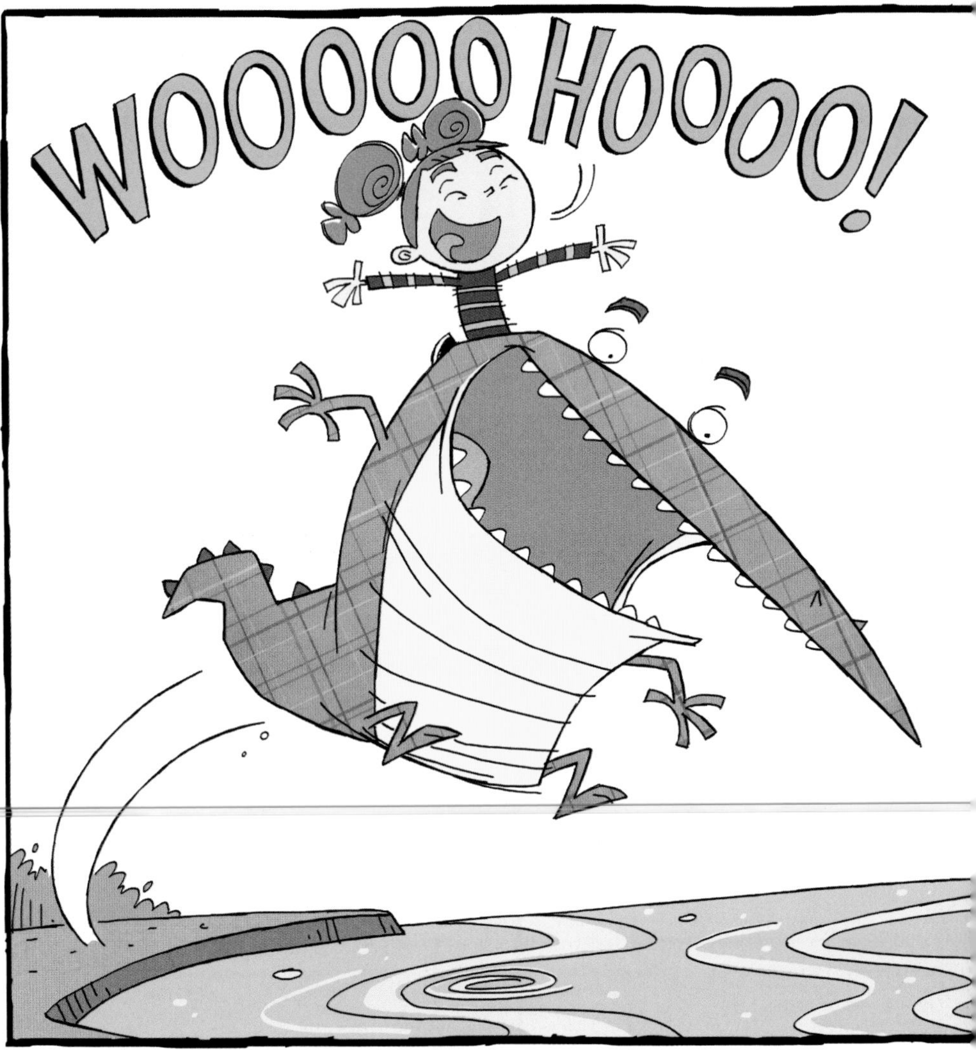
WOOOOO HOOOOO!

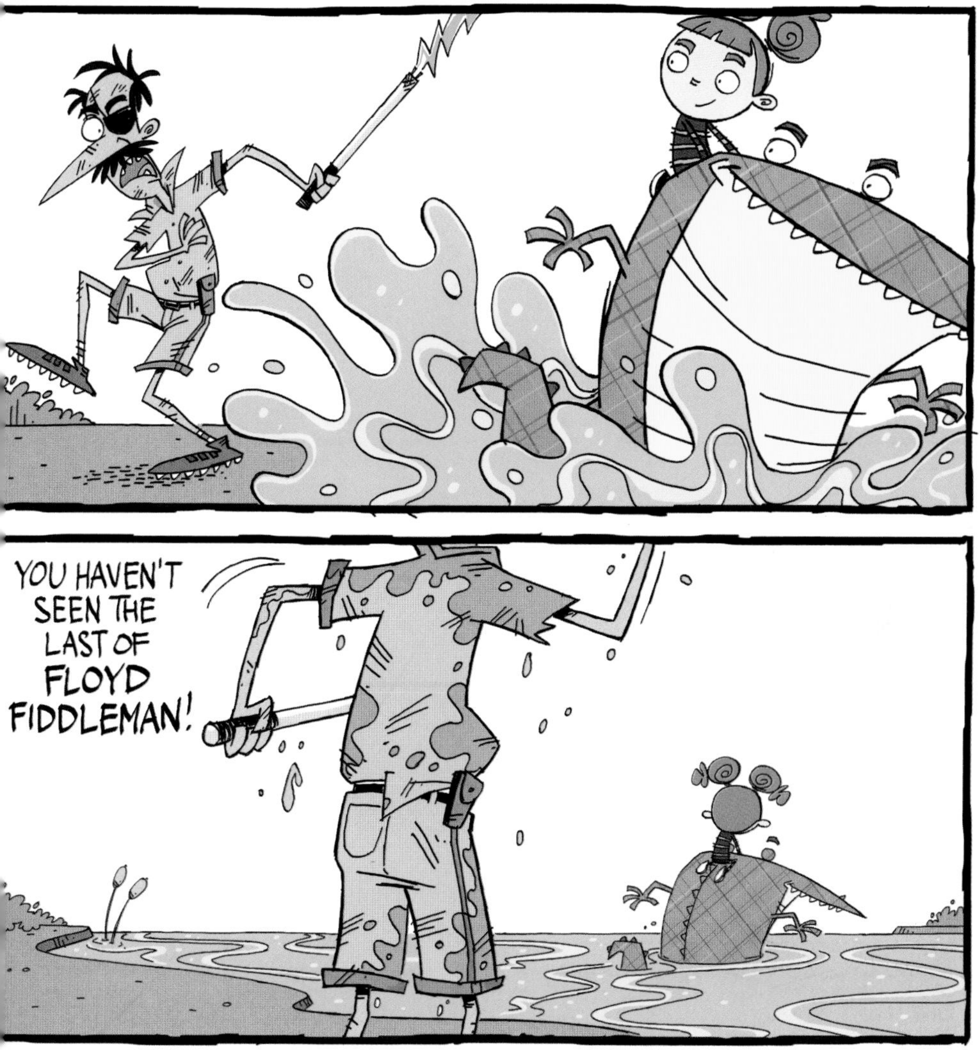
YOU HAVEN'T SEEN THE LAST OF FLOYD FIDDLEMAN!

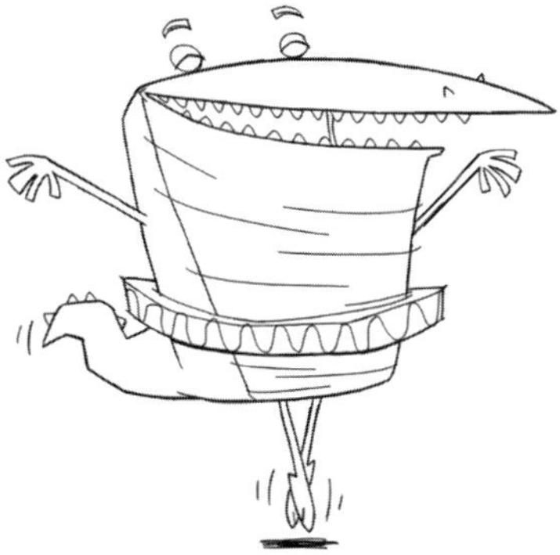

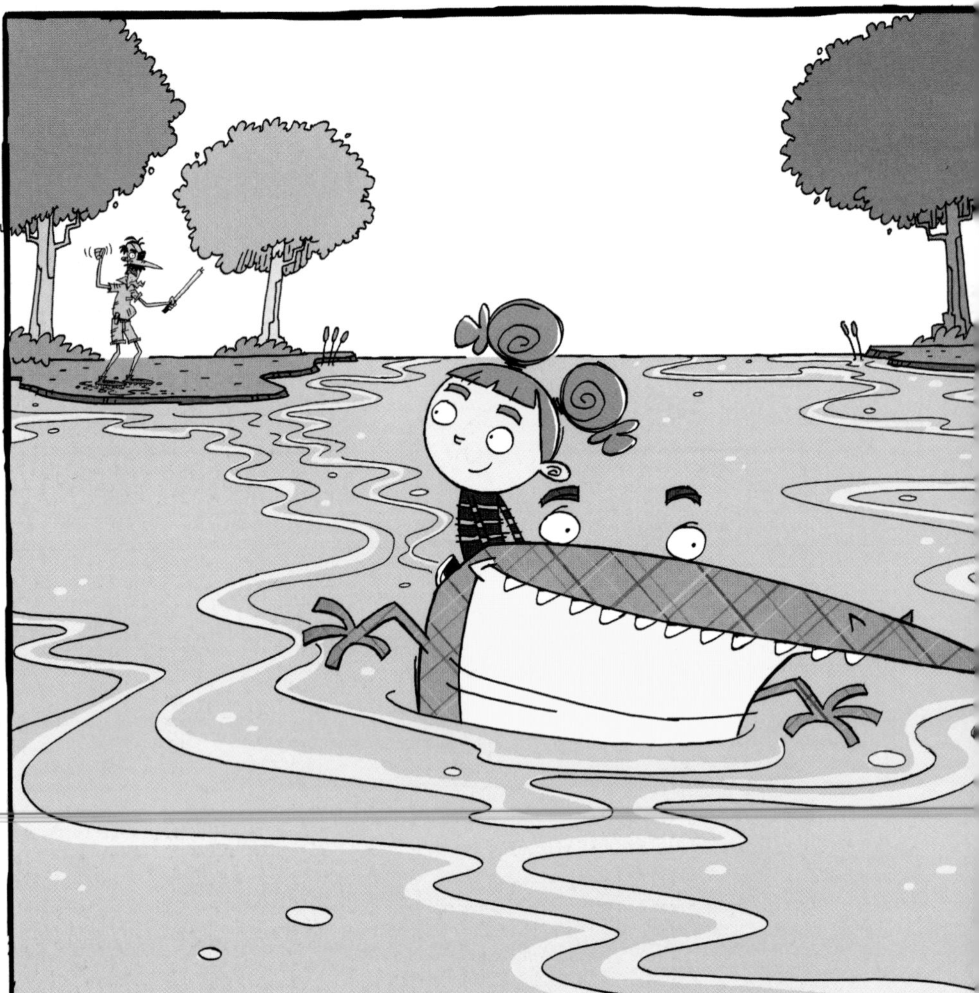

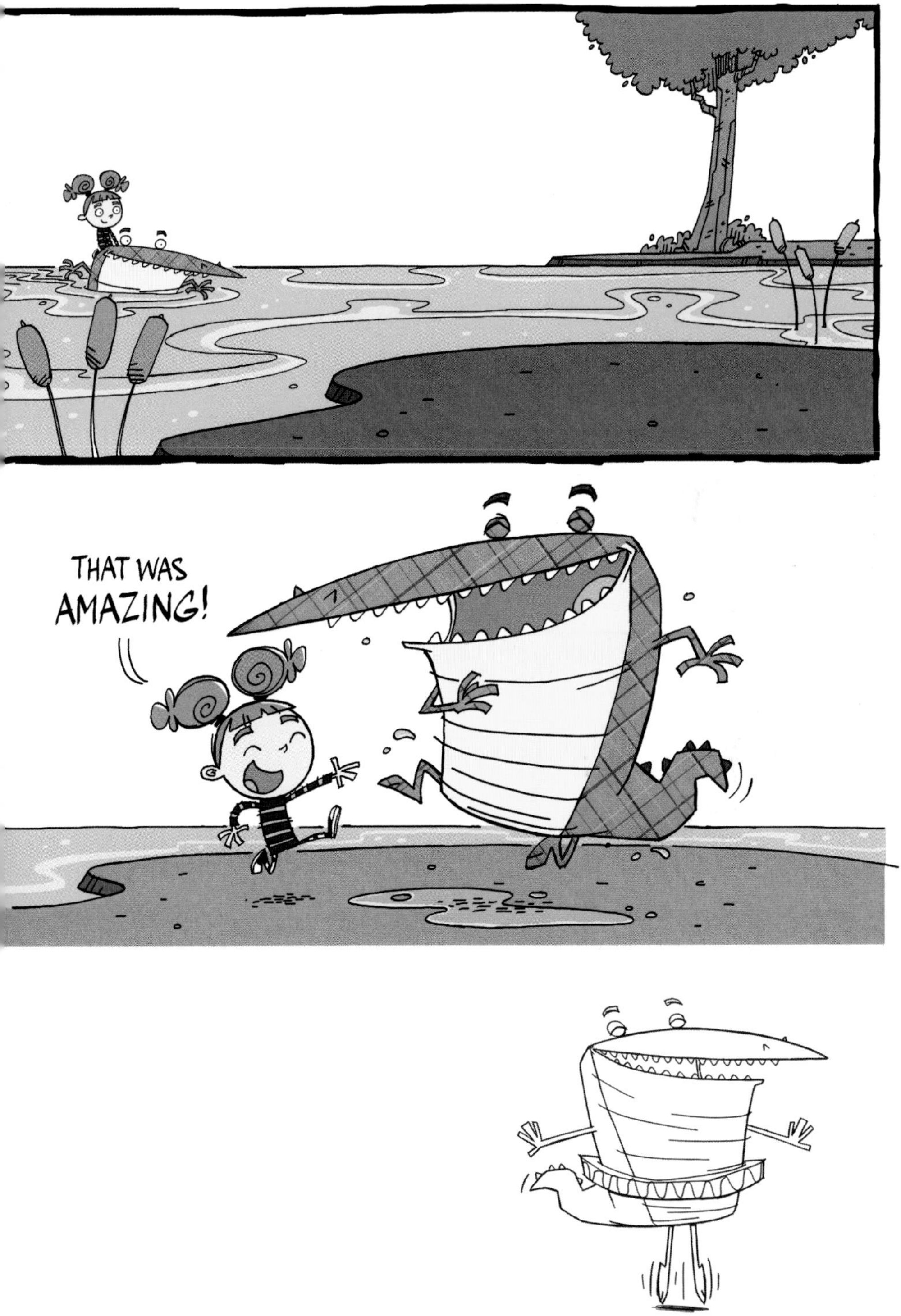
THAT WAS AMAZING!

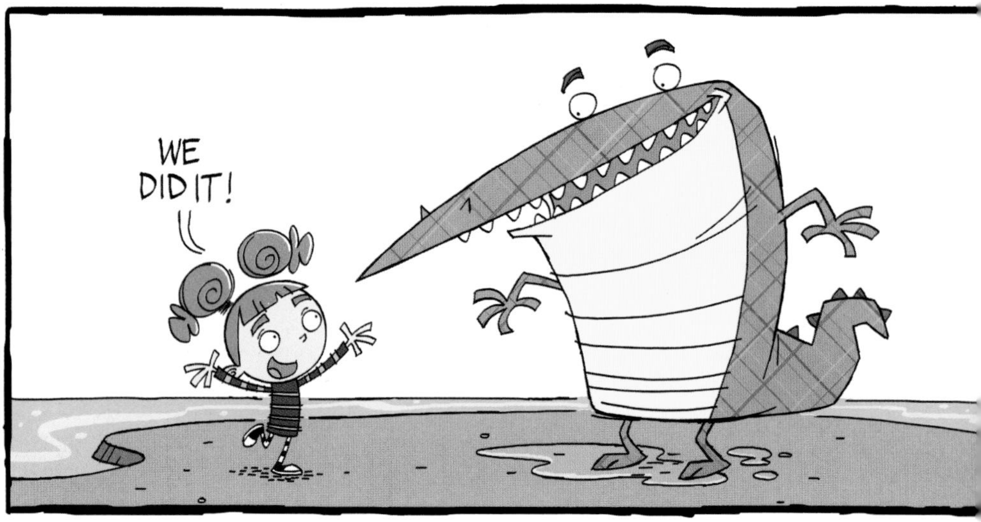
WE DID IT!

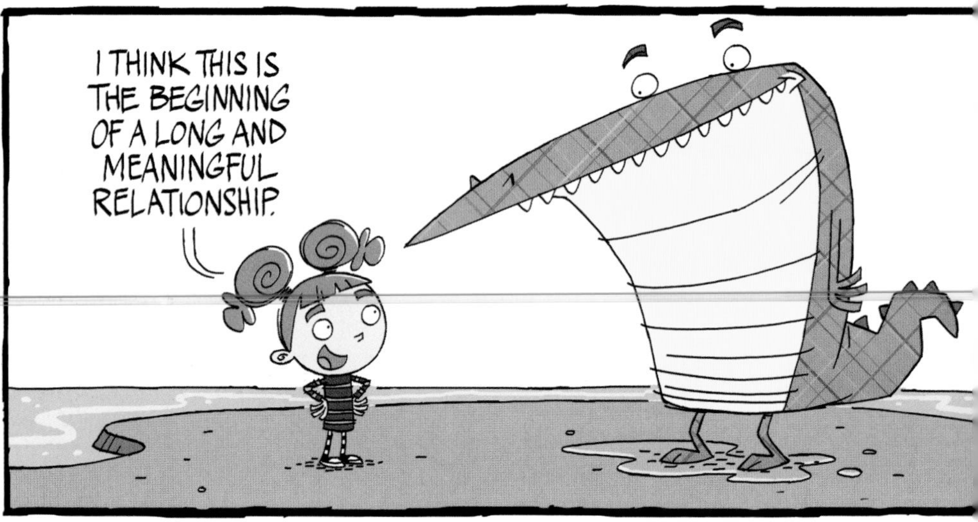
I THINK THIS IS THE BEGINNING OF A LONG AND MEANINGFUL RELATIONSHIP.

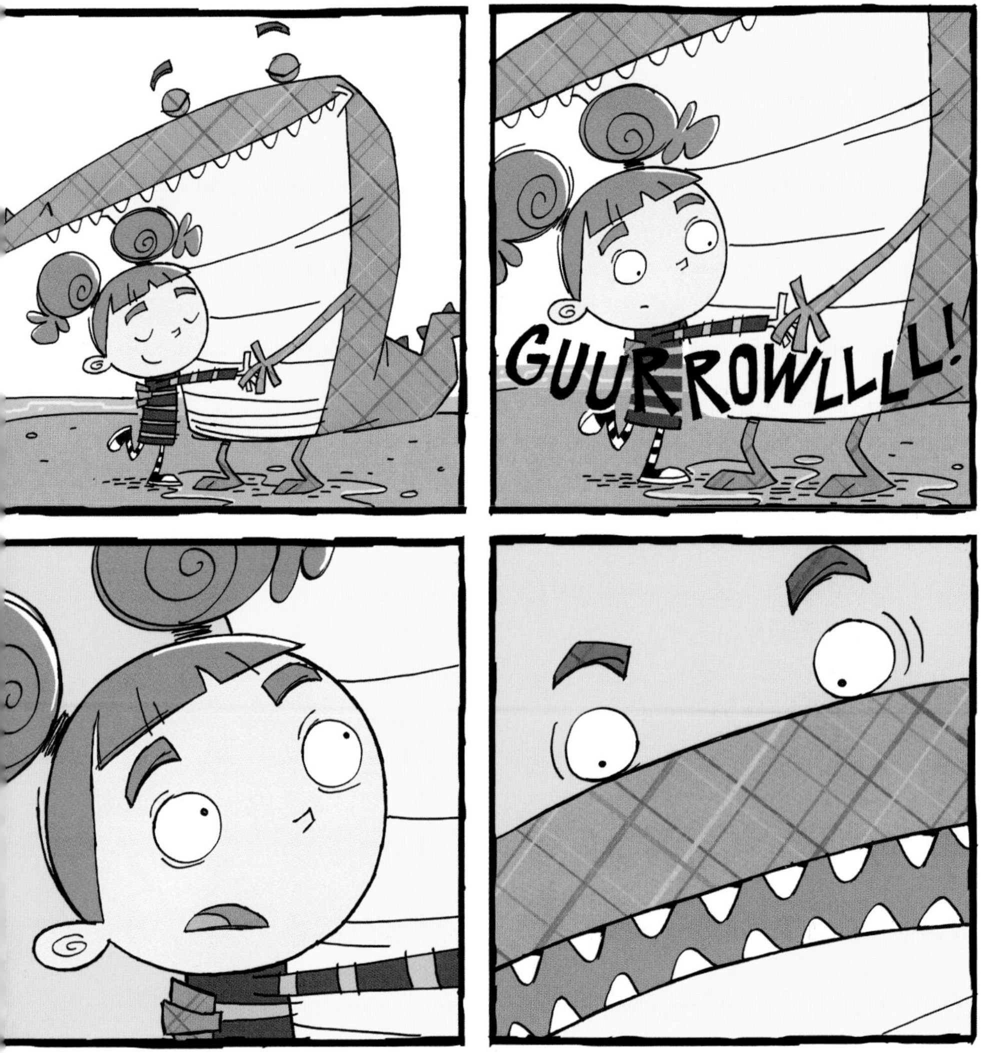
GUURROWLLLL!

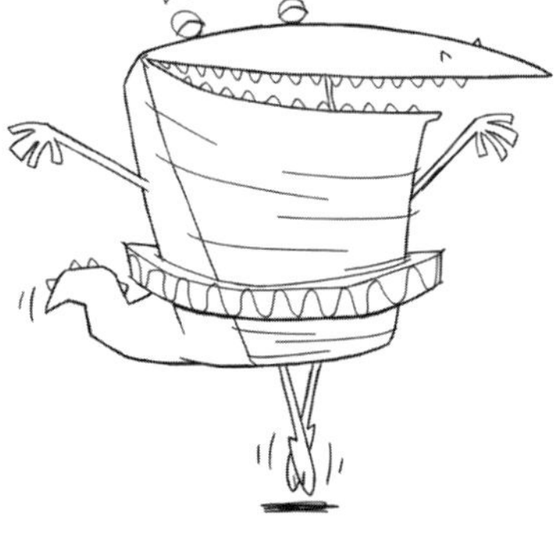

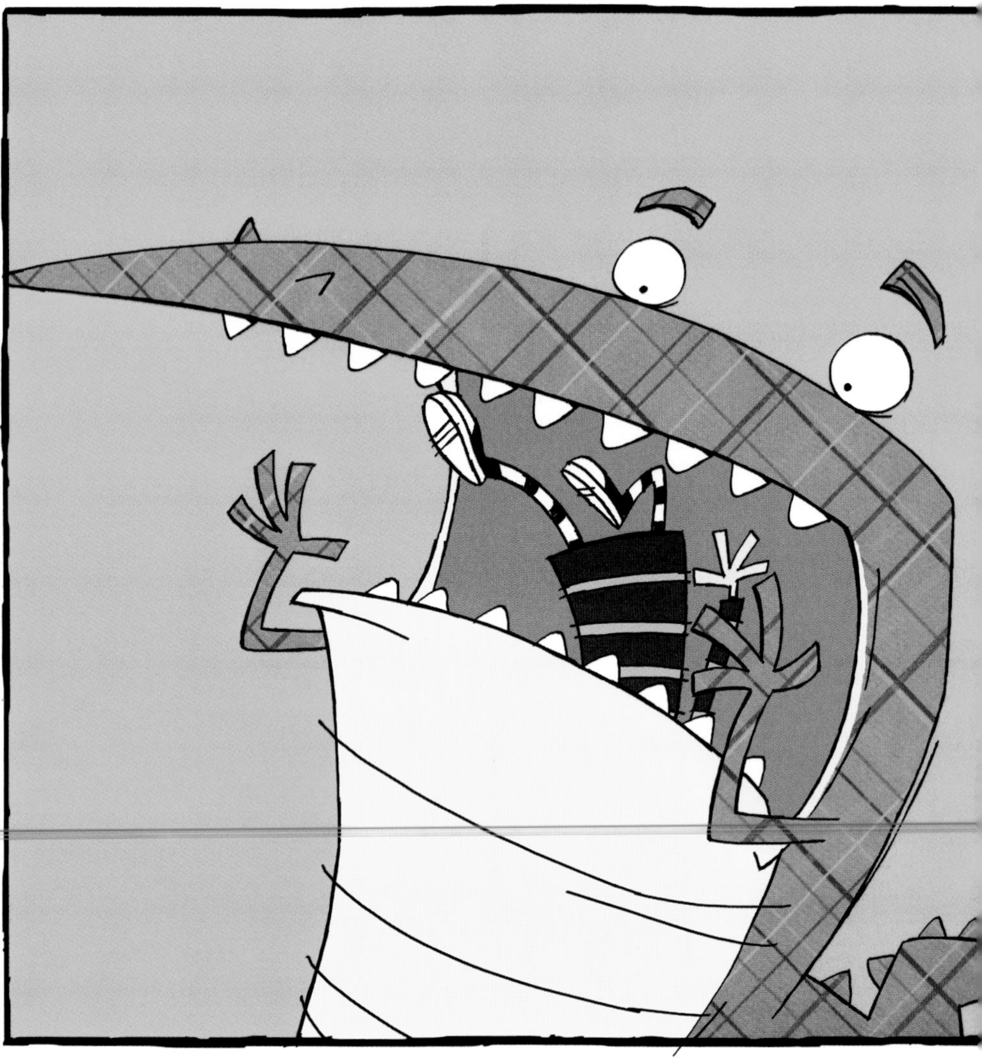

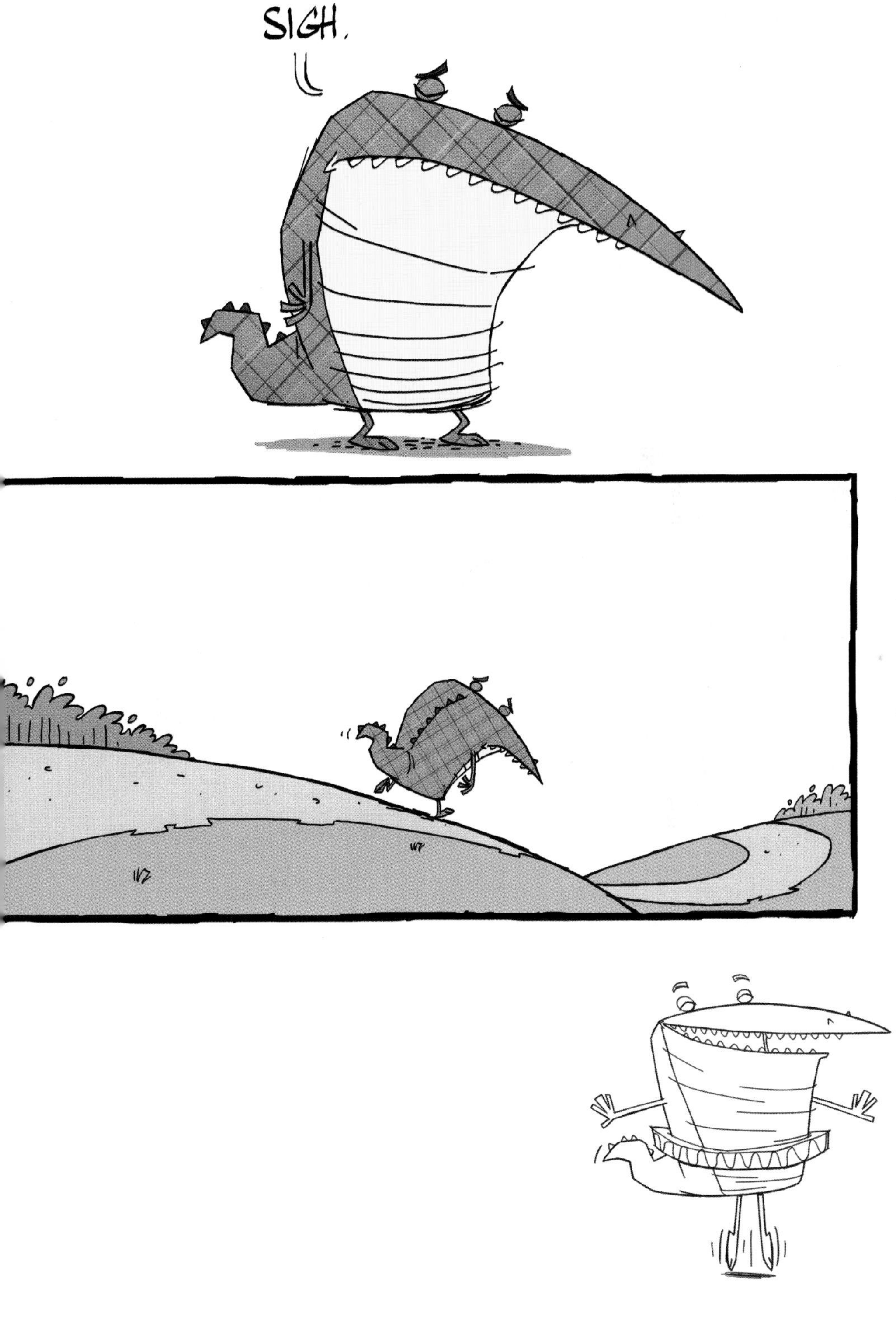
SIGH.

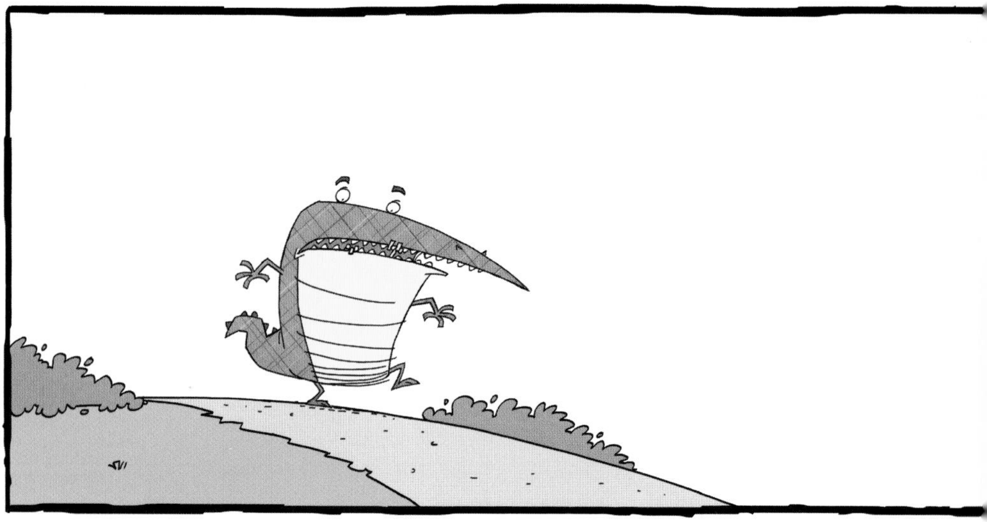

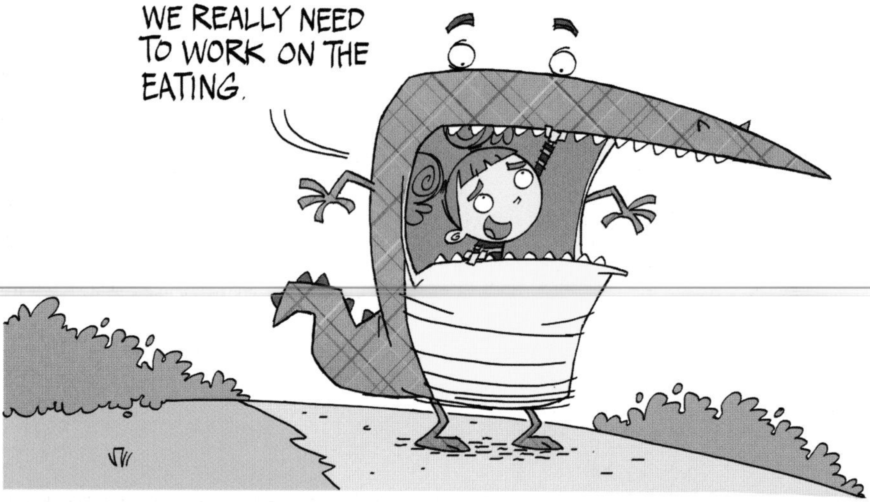
WE REALLY NEED TO WORK ON THE EATING.

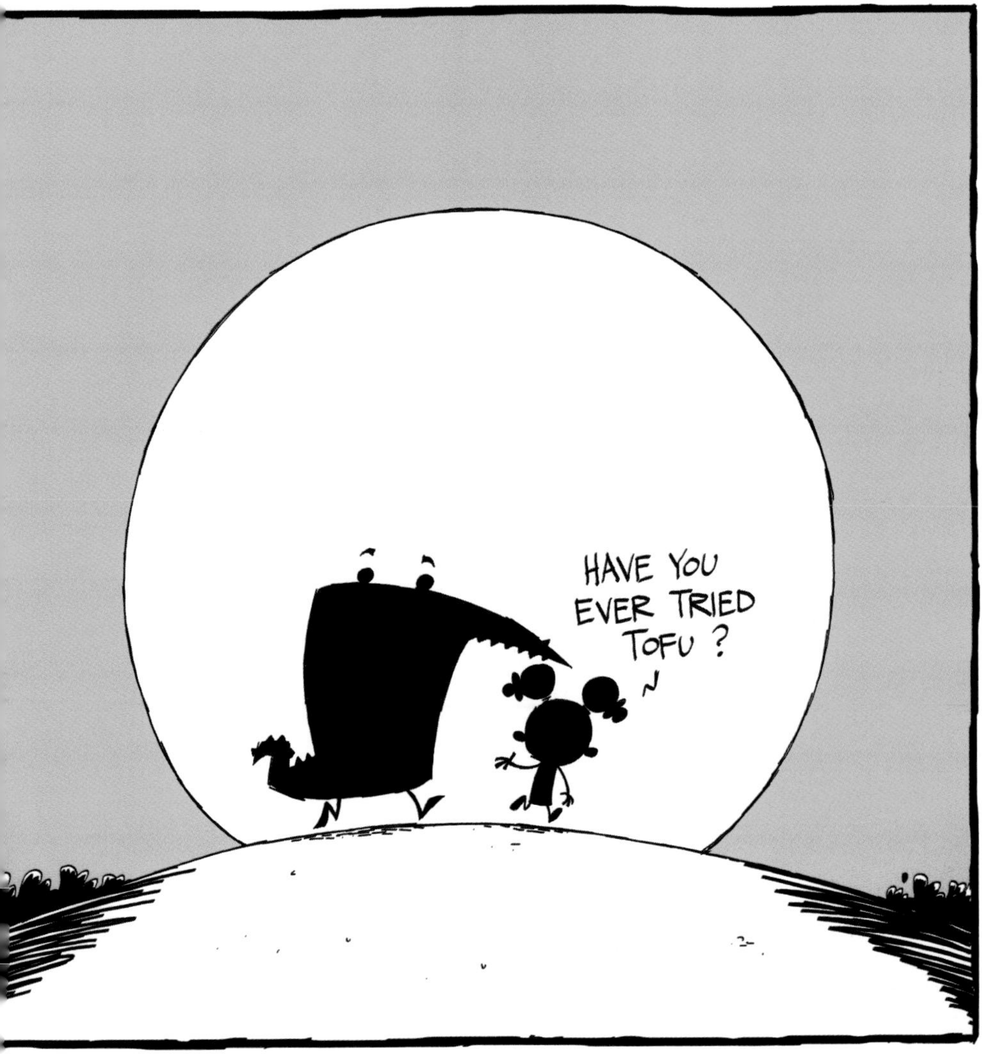
HAVE YOU EVER TRIED TOFU ?

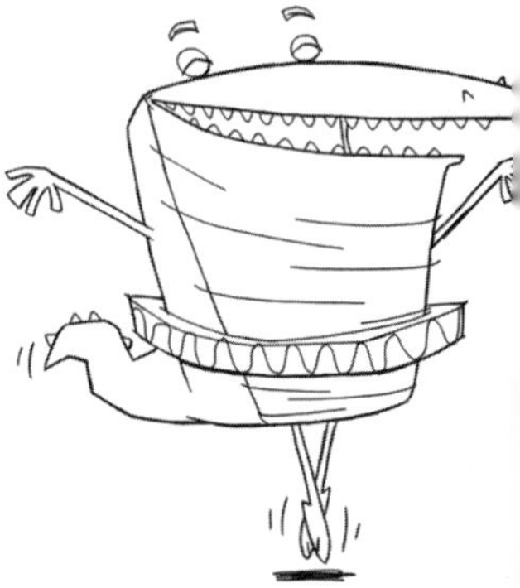

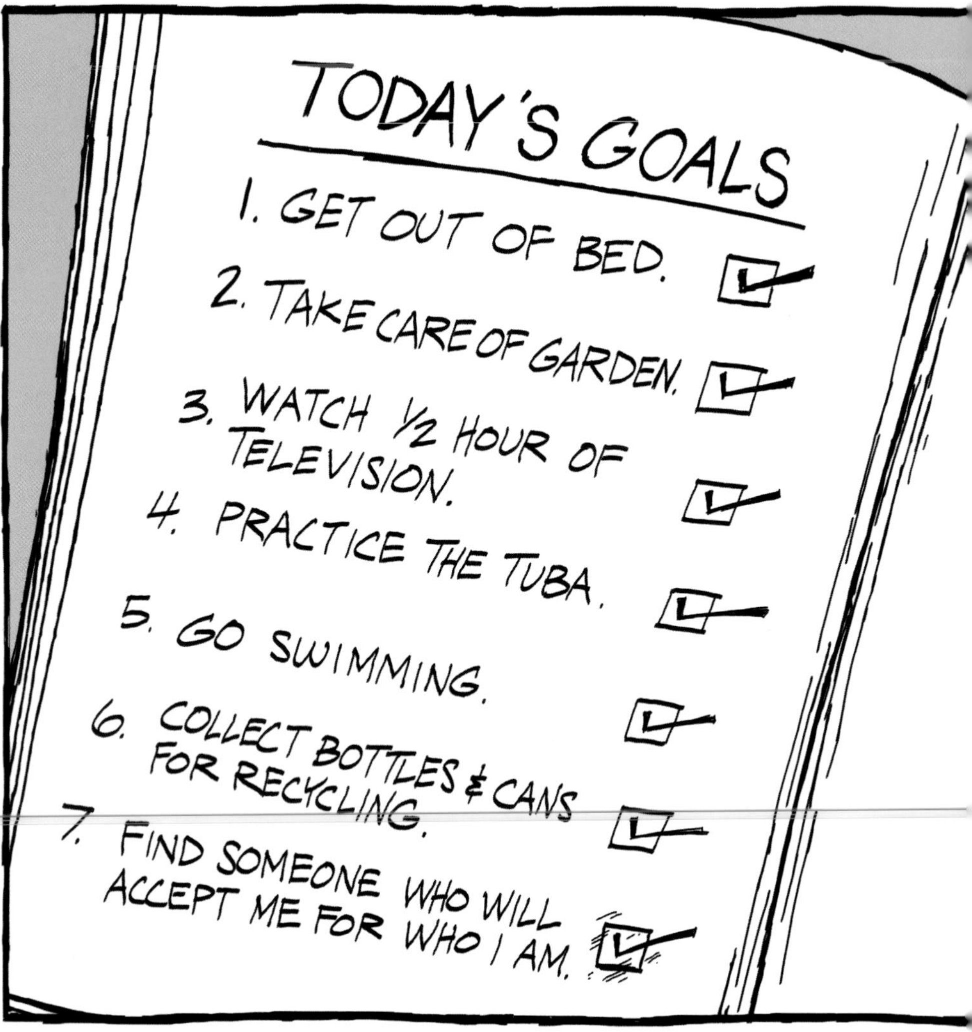
TODAY'S GOALS
1. GET OUT OF BED.
2. TAKE CARE OF GARDEN.
3. WATCH ½ HOUR OF TELEVISION.
4. PRACTICE THE TUBA.
5. GO SWIMMING.
6. COLLECT BOTTLES & CANS FOR RECYCLING.
7. FIND SOMEONE WHO WILL ACCEPT ME FOR WHO I AM.